Mick Herron's first Jackson Lamb thriller, *Slow Horses*, was shortlisted for the CWA Ian Fleming Steel Dagger and picked as one of the best twenty spy novels of all time by the *Daily Telegraph*. The second, *Dead Lions*, won the CWA Goldsboro Gold Dagger. The third, *Real Tigers*, was shortlisted for the Theakston Old Peculier Crime Novel of the Year and both the CWA Goldsboro Gold Dagger and the CWA Ian Fleming Steel Dagger. The fourth, *Spook Street*, has been shortlisted for both the Gold and Steel Daggers. Mick Herron was born in Newcastle upon Tyne, and now lives in Oxford.

Praise for Mick Herron's Jackson Lamb thrillers

'Mick Herron is shaping up to be the great spy novelist of our age'

Daily Telegraph *****

'Close to the class of Graham Greene'

Daily Mail

'Surely among the finest British spy fiction of the past 20 years . . . a narrative of breath-taking ingenuity. Brilliant'

Metro

'The new king of the spy thriller'

Mail on Sunday

'The new spy master'

Evening Standard

Praise for
SLOW HORSES

**Shortlisted for the CWA Ian Fleming
Steel Dagger Award**

'The most enjoyable spy novel in years'
Mail on Sunday

'A funny, stylish, satirical, gripping story'
Guardian

'Stylish and engaging'
Washington Post

Praise for
DEAD LIONS

**Winner of the CWA Gold Dagger Award
A BBC *Front Row* best crime
novel of the year
A *Times* crime and thriller
book of the year**

**'Herron may be the most literate, and
slyest, thriller writer in English today'**
Publishers Weekly

Also by Mick Herron

Jackson Lamb thrillers

SLOW HORSES
DEAD LIONS
REAL TIGERS

Zoë Boehm thrillers

DOWN CEMETERY ROAD
THE LAST VOICE YOU HEAR
WHY WE DIE
SMOKE AND WHISPERS

RECONSTRUCTION
NOBODY WALKS

SPOOK STREET

MICK
HERRON

JOHN MURRAY

First published in Great Britain in 2017 by John Murray (Publishers)
An Hachette UK Company

First published in paperback in 2017

9

A CIP catalogue record for this title is available from the British Library

ISBN 978-1-47362-129-9
Ebook ISBN 978-1-47362-128-2

Typeset in Bembo by Palimpsest Book Production Limited,
Falkirk, Stirlingshire

Printed and bound by Clays Ltd, Elcograf S.p.A.

John Murray policy is to use papers that are natural, renewable and recyclable
products and made from wood grown in sustainable forests. The logging
and manufacturing processes are expected to conform to the environmental
regulations of the country of origin.

John Murray (Publishers)
Carmelite House
50 Victoria Embankment
London EC4Y 0DZ

www.johnmurray.co.uk

To Juliet and Paul
(in lieu of a wedding present)

I

S O THIS WAS WHAT springtime in London was like: the
women in knee-length dresses of blue-and-white hoops;
the men with dark jackets over sweaters in pastel shades. Both
sexes carried shoulder bags with more flaps and fastenings
than necessary, the females' either red or black, the males' a
healthy, masculine buff colour, and caps made an occasional
appearance too, alongside headbands – let's not forget the
headbands. Headbands, in rainbow stripes, lent the women an
overeager look, as if they grasped too keenly at a fashion of
their youth, though the genuinely youthful sported the same
accessory with apparent unconcern. Feet wore sandals or flip-
flops, faces wore wide-eyed content, and body language was
at once mute and expressive, capturing a single moment of
well-being and beaming it everywhere. They were both uplit
and downlit, these plastic springtime celebrants, and a piano
tinkled melodious background nonsense for their pleasure,
and a miniature waterfall drummed an unwavering beat, and
Samit Chatterjee watched all of it through narrowed eyes, his
thin features alert and suspicious.

Outside, the first working day of the year ground miserably
on, heaving its bloated, hungover weight towards mid-afternoon, but inside Westacres – a cavernous retail pleasure dome
on London's western fringe – the theme was of the spring

to come, though by the time it arrived the window displays would be redolent of lazy summer outings instead. In its almanac of images, on a page already turned, the New Year had been represented by sledges and scarves and friendly robins, but reality made few compromises, and life this side of the windows bore little resemblance to that enjoyed by the mannequins. Here, jaded shoppers trudged from one outlet to the next, their passage made hazardous by the slick wet floor; here, the exhausted paused to rest on the concrete ledge surrounding the water feature, in which a styrofoam cup bobbed, froth scumming its rim. This fountain was the centre-piece of a hub at which corridors from each point of the compass met, and sooner or later everyone using Westacres passed by it. So naturally it was here Samit mostly lingered, the better to scrutinise the punters.

For whom he had little fondness. If Westacres was a temple, as he'd heard it described, its worshippers were lax in their observations. None of the truly faithful would dump takeaway litter in their cathedral's font, and no one who genuinely sought to uphold their religion's tenets consumed a six-pack of Strongbow by 9.30 a.m., then upchucked on their church's floor. As a devout Muslim, Samit abhorred the practices he daily bore witness to, but as one of Westacres' dedicated team of Community Regulation Officers – or Security Guards, as they called themselves – he forbore from calling down divine retribution on the ungodly, and contented himself with issuing stern warnings to litterbugs and escorting the inebriated from the premises. The rest of the time he offered directions, helped locate wandering infants, and once – he still thought about this, often – chased and apprehended a shoplifter.

There was no such excitement this afternoon. The air was damp and miserable, a tickle at the back of Samit's throat suggested an oncoming cold, and he was wondering where he might cadge a cup of tea when they appeared: three youths approaching along the eastern corridor, one carrying a large black holdall. Samit forgot his throat. It was one of the great paradoxes of the shopping centre experience that it was imperative for profit and prosperity to get the youngsters in, but for the sake of harmony and a peaceful life, you really didn't want them hanging around. Ideally, they should turn up, hand over their money, and bugger off. So when youth turned up in threes, carrying a black holdall, it was wise to suspect foul motives. Or at the very least, be prepared for high jinks.

So Samit did a 360-degree scan, to discover two more groups coming down the northern avenue, one of young women who appeared to find the world a source of unending hilarity; the other a mixed bunch, all saggy-crotched jeans and unlaced trainers, broadcasting the usual Jamaican patois of the London-born teenager. And towards the west was the same story, oncoming teens, any number of them, and suddenly the groups didn't appear to be separate but a mass gathering, governed by a single intelligence. And yes, it was still the holidays, and you had to expect a high youth turnout, but . . . In case of doubt, call it in, Samit had been told. And this was a case of doubt: not just the kids, the sheer number of kids – more appearing all the time – but the way they were heading towards him; as if Samit Chatterjee were about to witness the first flowering of a new movement; the overthrow, perhaps, of this colossal temple he was here to guard.

Colleagues were arriving now, dragged along by the undertow. Samit waved urgently, and unclipped his radio just as the original trio came to a halt mid-arena and placed their holdall on the floor. While he was pressing his transmit button they were unzipping the bag and revealing its contents. And as he spoke, it started – at the same precise moment the whole crowd, dozens upon dozens of kids, milling by the fountain, blocking the entrances to shops, climbing onto the water feature's surround; every single one of them, it seemed, stripped off their jackets and coats to reveal bright happy shirts beneath, all lurid primaries and swirls of colour, and that was when the boys hit buttons on the retro ghetto-blaster they'd unpacked, and the whole shopping centre was swamped by loud loud noise, a deep bass beat.

Living for the sunshine, woah-oh

And they were dancing, all of them, arms thrown over heads, and legs kicking high, hips swaying, feet going every which way – nobody had taken dance lessons, that was for sure, but these kids knew how to have fun, and fun was what they were having.

I'm living for the summer

And didn't it feel good? A flash mob, Samit realised. A major craze eight or ten years ago, rediscovered by a new generation. Samit had seen one before, at Liverpool Street: he'd been on the outskirts, longing to join in, but something – something? Teenage embarrassment – had held him back, and he could only watch as a crowd unfurled in joyous, planned spontaneity. This one, of course, was happening on his watch, so ought to be stopped, but for the moment there was nothing he could do – only dogs and megaphones could break this up now. And even adults were letting their hair down, tapping away to a summertime beat; one of them, right in the middle, unbuttoning his overcoat. And for one blind moment Samit too was washed away in the swelling joy of being alive, despite the cold, despite the damp, and he found his lips twitching – whether to smile or sing along with the chorus, *living for the sunshine woah-oh*, even Samit himself wasn't sure, and he had to raise a hand to his mouth to disguise his reaction. This gesture helped shield his teeth, by which he was later identified.

For the blast, when it came, left little intact. It shattered bone and pulverised mortality, and reduced all nearby life to charred stubble. Windows became shrapnel and the fountain hissed as flaming chunks of masonry, brick, plastic and flesh rained into it. An angry fireball swallowed the music and the dancers both, and sent a wave of heat and air pulsing down all four avenues, while the springtime dummies in their pristine clothing were blown away behind a memory of glass. It lasted seconds, but never stopped, and those it left behind – parents and families, lovers and friends – would ever after mark the date as one of unanswered phone calls and uncollected cars; a day when something like the sun bloomed in all the wrong places, searing its indelible image into the lives of those it found there.

Part One

Something Like the Sun

2

H EAT RISES, AS IS commonly known, but not always without effort. In Slough House, its ascent is marked by a series of bangs and gurgles, an audible diary of a forced and painful passage through cranky piping, and if you could magic the plumbing out of the structure and view it as a free-standing exoskeleton, it would be all leaks and dribbles: an arthritic dinosaur, its joints angled awkwardly where fractures have messily healed; its limbs a mismatched muddle; its extremities stained and rusting, and weakly pumping out warmth. And the boiler, the heart of this beast, wouldn't so much beat as flutter in a trip-hop rhythm, its occasional bursts of enthusiasm producing explosions of heat in unlikely places; its irregular palpitations a result of pockets of air straining for escape. From doors away you can hear its knocking, this antiquated heating system, and it sounds like a monkey-wrench tapping on an iron railing; like a coded message transmitted from one locked cell to another.

It's a wasteful, unworkable mess, but then this shabby set of offices – hard by Barbican underground station, on Aldersgate Street, in the borough of Finsbury – isn't exactly noted for its efficiency, of equipment or personnel. Indeed, its inhabitants might as well be banging on pipes with spanners themselves for all their communication skills are worth, though on this cold January morning, two days after an appalling act at Westacres shopping centre claimed upwards of forty lives, other noises can be heard in Slough House. Not in Jackson Lamb's room, for once: of all the building's occupants, he may be the one most obviously in tune with its rackety plumbing, being no stranger to internal gurglings and sudden warm belches himself, but for the moment his office is empty, and his radiator its sole source of clamour. In the room opposite, though – until a few months back, Catherine Standish's; now Moira Tregorian's – there is at least some conversation taking place, though of a necessarily one-sided nature, Moira Tregorian currently being the room's sole occupant: her monologue consists of single, emphatic syllables – a *tchah* here, a *duh* there – interspersed with the odd unfractured phrase – *never thought I'd see the day* and *what on earth's this when it's at home?* A younger listener might assume Moira to be delivering these fragments down a telephone, but in fact they are directed at the papers on her desk, papers which have accumulated in the absence of Catherine Standish, and have done so in a manner uncontaminated by organisational principle, whether chronological, alphabetical or commonsensical, since they were deposited there by Lamb, whose mania for order has some way to go before it might be classed as neurotic, or even observable. There are many sheets of paper, and each of them has to be somewhere, and discovering which of the many possible somewheres that might be is Moira's job today, as it was yesterday, and will be tomorrow. Had he done so deliberately, Lamb could hardly have come up with a more apt introduction to life under his command, here in this administrative oubliette of the Intelligence Service, but the truth is, Lamb hasn't so much consigned the documents to Moira's care as banished them from his own, out of sight/out of mind being his solution to unwanted paperwork. Moira, whose second day in Slough House this is, and who has yet to meet Jackson Lamb, has already decided she'll be having a few sharp words with him when that event comes to pass. And while she is nodding vigorously at this thought the radiator growls like a demented cat, startling her so she drops the papers she is holding, and has to scramble to retrieve them before they disarrange themselves again.

Meanwhile, from the landing below, other noise floats up: a murmur from the kitchen, where a kettle has lately boiled, and a recently opened fridge is humming. In the kitchen are River Cartwright and Louisa Guy, both with warm mugs in their hands, and Louisa is maintaining a nearly unbroken commentary on the trials and tribulations accompanying the purchase of her new flat. This is quite some distance away, as London flats tend to be if they're affordable, but the picture she paints of its size, its comfort, its uncluttered surfaces, is evidence of a new contentment that River would be genuinely glad to witness, were he not brooding about something else. And all the while, behind him, the door to his office creaks on a squeaky hinge, not because anyone is currently using it, but in general protest at the draughts that haunt Slough House, and in a more particular complaint directed at the commotion arising from the next floor down.

But while his door remains unused, River's office is not empty, for his new colleague – a slow horse for some two months now – sits within, slumped in his chair, the hood of his hoodie pulled over his head. Apart from his fingers he is still, but these move unceasingly, his keyboard pushed aside the better to accommodate this, and while an observer would see nothing more than an advanced case of the fidgets, what J. K. Coe is describing on the scuffed surface of his desk is a silent replica of what's coursing through his head via his iPod: Keith Jarrett's improvised piano recital from Osaka, 8 November

1976, one of the Sun Bear concerts; Coe's fingers miming the melodies Jarrett discovered on the night, all those miles and all those years away. It's a soundless echo of another man's genius, and it serves a dual purpose: of tamping down Coe's thoughts, which are dismal, and of drowning out the noises his mind would otherwise entertain: the sound of wet meat dropping to the floor, for instance, or the buzz of an electric carving knife wielded by a naked intruder. But all this he keeps to himself, and as far as River and the other denizens of Slough House are concerned, J. K. Coe is a riddle wrapped in a mystery inside an enigma, the whole package then refashioned in the shape of a surly, uncommunicative twat.

Though even if he were yodelling, he'd not be heard over the commotion from the floor below. Not that this racket is emanating from Roderick Ho's room, or no more of it than usual (the humming of computers; the tinnitus-rattle of Ho's own iPod, loaded with more aggressive music than Coe's; his nasal whistling, of which he is unaware; the rubbery squeak his swivel-chair emits when he shifts his buttocks); no, what's surprising about the atmosphere in Ho's room – or what would surprise anyone who chose to hang out there, which no one does, because it's Ho's room – is that it's upbeat. Cheerful, even. As if something other than his own sense of superiority is warming Roddy Ho's cockles these days, which would be handy, given the inability of his radiator to warm anything much, cockles or otherwise: it coughs now, and spits fizzily from its valve, spurting water onto the carpet. Ho doesn't notice, and nor does he register the following gurgle from deep within the system's pipes – a noise that would disturb any number of serious beasts: horses, lions, tigers – but this is not so much because Ho is a preternaturally cool character, whatever his own views on that subject, and more because he simply can't hear it. And the reason for this is that the lapping and gurgling of the radiator's innards, the banging and clicking of pipes, the splashy rattling of the system's exoskeleton, are all drowned out by the noise from next door, where Marcus Longridge is waterboarding Shirley Dander.

'Blurgh—bleurgh—off—coff—blargh!'
 'Yeah, I didn't follow any of that.'
 'Blearrrgh!'
 'Sorry, does that mean—'
 'BLARGH!'
 '—uncle?'
The chair to which Shirley was tied with belts and scarves was angled against her desk, and nearly crashed to the floor when she arched her back. A loud crack suggested structural damage, at the same moment as the flannel that had covered her face slapped the carpet like a dead sea creature hitting a rock. Shirley herself made similar noises for a while; if you were asked to guess, you might hazard that someone was trying to turn themselves inside out, without using tools.

Marcus, whistling softly, replaced the jug on a filing cabinet. Some water had splashed his sweater, a pale-blue merino V-neck, and he tried to brush it away, with as much success as that usually has. Then he sat and stared at his monitor, which had long defaulted to its screensaver: a black background around which an orange ball careened, bumping against its borders, never getting anywhere. Yeah: Marcus knew how *that* felt.

After a few minutes Shirley stopped coughing.

After a few minutes more, she said, 'It wasn't as bad as you said.'

'You lasted less than seven seconds.'

'Bollocks. That was about half an hour, and—'

'Seven seconds, first drops to whatever it was you said.

Blurgh? Blargh?' He banged his hand on his keyboard, and the screensaver vanished. 'Not our agreed safety word, by the way.'

'But you stopped anyway.'

'What can I tell you? Getting soft.'

A spreadsheet opened into view. Marcus couldn't immediately recall what it represented. Not a lot of work had happened in this office lately.

Shirley freed herself from scarves and belts. 'You didn't time it properly.'

'I timed it immaculately,' he said, drawing the word out: *im-mac-u-late-ly*. 'It's like I said, no one can cope with that shit. That's why it's so popular with the vampires.'

The vampires being those whose job it was to draw blood from stones.

Shirley lobbed the wet flannel at him. Without taking his eyes from the screen he caught it one-handed, and scowled as water scattered everywhere: '*Thank* you.'

'You're welcome.' She towelled her head dry: a five-second pummel. 'Gonna let me do you now?'

'In. Your. Dreams.'

She stuck her tongue out. Then said, 'So. You'd be prepared to do that?'

'Just did, didn't I?'

'For real, I mean. And keep doing it.'

Marcus looked up. 'If it'd stop another Westacres, hell, yes. I'd keep doing it until the bastard told me everything. And drown him doing it, wouldn't bother me none.'

'It would be murder.'

'Blowing up forty-two kids in a shopping centre is murder. Waterboarding a suspected terrorist to death, that's house-keeping.'

'The philosophy of Marcus Longridge, volume one.'

'Pretty much sums it up. Someone's got to do this shit. Or

would you rather let the terrorist walk, for fear of violating his human rights?'

'He was only a suspect a moment ago.'

'And we both know what being a suspect means.'

'He's still got rights.'

'Like those kids had? Tell their parents.'

He was getting loud now, which they'd both got into the habit of not worrying about, Lamb not having been around lately. This didn't mean he couldn't show up any moment, of course – his large frame creepily silent on the stairs, so the first you knew of his presence was his nicotine breath and sour outlook: *Having fun, are we?* – but until that happened, Shirley's view was, they might as well keep on skiving.

She said, 'Maybe. I just don't think it's that simple.'

'Yeah, things get simple real quick at the sharp end. I thought you'd have worked that out by now. Anyway,' and he indicated the chair she'd been sitting on, 'better shift that into Ho's office.'

'Why?'

'It broke.'

'Oh. Yeah. Think he'll snitch?'

'Not if he values that bum-fluff he calls a beard,' said Marcus, briefly stroking his own. 'He rats us out to Lamb, I'll rip it from his chin.'

Probably a figure of speech, thought Shirley, but possibly a treat in store.

Marcus being Marcus, it could go either way.

Had he been aware that he was the subject of his colleagues' violent fantasies, Roderick Ho would have put it down to jealousy.

Fact was, he looked *fantastic*.

Don't just take his word for it, either.

He'd arrived, as usual, in a terrific mood: swanned in wearing a brand-new jacket (waist-length black leather – when you've got it, flaunt it!) and popped the tab on a Red Bull which he chug-a-lugged while his kit warmed up. Seriously, seriously, this was starting to harsh his mellow: his gear at the Rod-pad ran to higher specs than the Service provided, but what are you gonna do – explain to Jackson Lamb that some heavy-duty cap-ex was required if Slough House was to come crawling out of the nineties? . . . He paused for a moment, allowing that scenario to take shape: 'Jackson, Jackson, trust me – the suits, man, they've got to get this sorted. Asking me to work with that crap is like, well, put it this way. Would you ask Paul Pogba to kick a tin can around?' And Lamb chuckling, throwing his hands up in mock-surrender: 'You win, you win. I'll get the pointy-heads at the Park to loosen the purse-strings . . .'

That struck the right note, he decided.

If Lamb ever showed up, definitely the way to play it.

Meanwhile, he cracked his knuckles, clicked on Amazon, wrote a one-star review of a random book, then checked his beard in the mirror he'd fixed to the anglepoise. Devilishly stylish. The odd red strand among the black, but nothing a little tweezer-work couldn't handle, and if it wasn't entirely symmetrical, five minutes with the old kitchen scissors soon had things on track. Looking this good took effort. Not rocket science, but it managed to evade some of the lamebrains round here – naming no River Cartwrights, of course.

Heh heh heh.

Cartwright was upstairs in the kitchen, chatting to Louisa. There'd been a time, not long back, when Roddy had had to play it cool with Louisa. It had been clear she'd taken a shine to him: embarrassing, but there it was – it wasn't like she was a total dog; in the right light, she cast a nice shadow, but she was *old*, mid-thirties, and when women got to that age, a taint of desperation clung to them. Weaken for a moment, and they'd be picking out curtains and suggesting quiet nights in. Which was not how Roderick Ho played the game: so sayonara, babes. Being a tactful kind of guy, he'd managed to convey to her without having to put it into actual words that the Rod was off-limits – that Rod's rod was not in her future – and give her her due, she'd managed to accept that without too much fuss, the odd wistful, what-might-have-been glance excepted. In other circumstances, he thought, there'd have been no harm in it – throwing a single woman the occasional boner was an act of charity – but a regular ram-Rodding was not on the agenda, and it would have been cruel to get her hopes up.

Besides, if the chick caught him providing consolation to another woman, he'd be in serious trouble.

Dig that singular.

Chick, not 'chicks'.

Roddy Ho has got himself a girlfriend.

Still humming, still in a terrific mood, and still looking fantastic, Ho returned to his screen, metaphorically rolled his sleeves up, and splash-dived into the Dark Web, deaf to the continual gurgling of his radiator, and the sloshing in the pipes connecting his room to everyone else's.

What *was* that blessed noise?

Only she didn't need telling what it was, thank you very much, because it was the radiator again, sounding like a sick cat doing its business. Putting the most recently sorted stack of papers down – not that 'sorted' was the right word, their category being 'documents without a date' – Moira Tregorian paused in her efforts and surveyed her new domain.

Her office was on the top floor; it was the one vacated by her predecessor, and nearest Mr Lamb's. The personal possessions Catherine Standish had left behind (her departure had been abrupt) were in a cardboard box, sealed with packing tape: her non-official-issue pens, a glass paperweight; a full bottle of whisky, wrapped in tissue paper – the woman had had a drink problem, but then, that was Slough House. Everyone here had problems, or what you now had to call 'issues'. Moira supposed that was why she'd been assigned here, to provide overdue backbone.

Dust everywhere, of course. The whole building felt neglected; seemed to revel in the condition, as if the appearance of a duster might cause structural conniptions. And condensation fogged the windows, and had pooled in puddles on the frame, where it was blossoming into mould, and much more of this and the whole place would be falling around your ears . . . Well. Someone needed to take a firm hand. This had clearly been beyond poor Catherine Standish, but once you let the bottle be your friend, you were letting yourself in for sorry times indeed.

It had not escaped her that among the forms awaiting attention were Standish's discharge papers, needing only Jackson Lamb's signature.

And it had long been Moira Tregorian's credo that paperwork was what kept battleships afloat: you could have all your admirals out on deck in their fancy get-up, but without the right paperwork, you'd never get out of the harbour. She had always been a force for order, and didn't care who knew it. In Regent's Park, she'd kept the Queens of the Database in trim, ensuring that their timekeeping was precise and their equipment regularly serviced; that the plants they insisted on were disposed of once they died; that the stationery they got through at a rate of knots was replenished weekly, and a log kept of who was taking what, because Moira Tregorian wasn't born blind and she wasn't born stupid. Post-it notes might be made of paper, but they didn't grow on trees. And every so often, just to show there wasn't much she couldn't turn her hand to, she'd taken a shift as duty officer: fielding emergency calls and whatnot. None of it terribly complicated, if you asked her – but then, she was an office manager, and proud of it. Things needed managing. You only had to cast an eye around to get an inkling of what happened otherwise. And chaos was a breeding ground for evil.

Another thump from downstairs suggested that chaos was winning the battle for Slough House. In the absence of any other champion, Moira gave a long-suffering sigh, and headed down to investigate.

'How old would you say she was?'

'Fifties, mid,' Louisa said. 'So . . .'

''Bout the same as Catherine,' River said.

'Uh-huh.'

'Almost like a replacement,' River said. 'You know. One in, one out.'

'. . . You been talking to Shirley?'

'Why? What did she say?'

'Doesn't matter,' Louisa said. She shook her head, not in self-contradiction but to remove her hair from her eyes; it was longer now, and she had to pin it back when actually doing anything: reading, working, driving. She'd let the highlights grow out and it had reverted to its natural brown, a little darker during these winter months. It would fade up once the spring arrived, if the spring brought sunshine; and if it didn't, hell, she could always cheat, and squeeze a little sunlight from a bottle.

Right now, spring felt a long way distant.

River said, 'Ought to get some work done, I suppose,' but sounded like he had things on his mind, tiptoeing around a different conversation entirely.

Louisa wondered if he was going to ask her for a date, and what she'd say if he did.

Almost certainly no. She'd got to know him this past half-year, and his virtues stacked up well against the other locals: he wasn't married like Marcus, a creep like Ho, or a possible psychopath like his new room-mate. On the other hand, he wasn't Min Harper, either. Min had been dead now for longer than they'd been a couple, and there was no sense in which she was seeking a replacement for him, but still: date a colleague, and comparisons would be made. That could only get ugly. So the occasional drink after work was fine, but anything more serious was out of bounds.

That was almost certainly what she thought, she thought. But she also thought it might be best to head him off if it looked like he was going to say anything.

'Doing anything later?' he asked.

'Yeah, no, what? Later?'

''Cause there's something I want to talk to you about, only here's maybe not the best place.'

Oh fuck, she thought. Here we go.

'I'm sorry, is this a private conversation?'

And here was Moira Tregorian, a name Louisa had spent much of yesterday trying to get her head round. Tregorian kept splitting into separate syllables, and rearranging itself: what was it, Cornish? She didn't want to ask in case the answer bored her rigid. People could get funny about their ancestry.

'No, we were just talking,' River said.

'Hmmm,' said Moira Tregorian, and the younger pair exchanged a glance. Neither had spoken much to Moira yet, and *Hmmm* wasn't a promising start.

She was in her fifties, sure, but that was where her resemblance to Catherine Standish ended. Catherine had had something of the spectral about her, and a resilience too, an inner strength that had allowed her to conquer her alcoholism, or at any rate, enabled her to continue the daily struggle. Neither River nor Louisa could remember her complaining about anything, which, given her daily exposure to Jackson Lamb, indicated Mandela-like patience. Moira Tregorian might turn out to be many things, but spectral wasn't going to be one of them, and patient didn't look promising. Her lips were pursed, and her jowls trembled slightly with pent-up something or other. All that aside, she was five-three or so, with dusty-coloured hair arranged like a mop, and wore a red cardigan Lamb would have something to say about, if he ever showed up. Lamb wasn't a fan of bright colours, and claimed they made him nauseous, and also violent.

'Because it seems to me,' Moira said, 'that two days after a major terrorist incident on British soil, there might be more useful things you could be doing. This is still an arm of the Intelligence Service, isn't it?'

Well, it was and it wasn't.

Slough House was a branch of the Service, certainly, but 'arm' was pitching it strong. As was 'finger', come to that; fingers could be on the button or on the pulse. Fingernails, now: those, you clipped, discarded, and never wanted to see again. So Slough House was a fingernail of the Service: a fair step from Regent's Park geographically, and on another planet in most other ways. Slough House was where you ended up when all the bright avenues were closed to you. It was where they sent you when they wanted you to go away, but didn't want to sack you in case you got litigious about it.

And while it was true that national security had been stepped up to the highest notch, things hadn't yet reached the pass where anyone was screaming down a telephone: 'Get me the slow horses!'

Louisa said, 'If there was something we could do, we'd be doing it. But we don't have the resources or the information to do anything useful here in the office. And in case you haven't noticed yet, they don't put us out on the streets.'

'No, well. That's as may be.'

'Which is why Marcus and Shirley are blowing off steam. I can't speak for Coe, but my guess is he's zoning out at his desk. And Ho'll be grooming his beard. I think that's all of us accounted for.'

'Is Mr Lamb not expected?' Moira asked.

'Lamb?'

'Mr Lamb, yes.'

River and Louisa exchanged a glance. 'He's not been around much lately,' Louisa said.

'Hence,' said River, and waved a vague hand. Hence people talking in kitchens and torturing each other in offices. When the cat was away, Lamb had been known to remark, the mice started farting about with notions of democratic freedom. Then the cat returned in a tank.

('Remind me,' River had once asked him, 'back in the Cold War – whose side were you on?')

'Only he's invited me to lunch.'

In the silence that followed, the radiator on the landing belched in an oddly familiar way, as if it were working up an impression.

'I think I may have just had a small stroke,' Louisa said at last. 'You can't possibly have said what I thought I just heard.'

River said, 'Have you met Jackson?'

'He sent me an email.'

'Is that a no?'

'We haven't met in person.'

'Have you heard about him?'

Moira Tregorian said, 'I'm told he's a bit of a character.'

'Did nobody tell you which bit?'

'There's no need for—'

Louisa said, 'Seriously, you haven't met him, but he sent you an email asking you to lunch? When?'

'He just said "soon".'

'Which might mean today.'

'Well . . . Yes, I thought it might.'

'Action stations,' murmured River.

They escaped, but before they disappeared into their separate rooms River said, 'So, you okay for later?'

'Yeah, no, what? Later?'

'Quick drink,' said River. 'Thing is . . .'

Here it comes, thought Louisa.

'. . . I'm worried about my grandfather.'

Though the rain had stopped, it still shook from the trees when the wind blew, spattering the windows, and still dripped from the guttering over the porch, which was thick with leaves. A lagoon had appeared in the lane, drowning the grassy verge, and in the village a burst main had closed the road for a day and a half, water pumping through the tarmac in its familiar, implacable way. Fire you could fight, and even halfway tame; water went where it chose, taking a hundred years to wear away a rock, or a minute and a half to pick the same rock up and carry it two miles distant. It altered the landscape too, so that when he looked from his window at first light he might have been transported elsewhere in his sleep; the whole house shipped off to a realm where trees groped upwards from the depths, and a tracery of hedgework scraped the surfaces of lakes. Bewildered by difference, you could lose your bearings. Which was the last thing you wanted to happen to you, because one day it would be the last thing that did.

It was important to keep track of where you were.

Knowing when you were was equally critical.

A good job, thought David Cartwright – River's grand-father; the O.B. – that he had a head for dates.

4 January. The year, as ever, the current one.

His house was in Kent; old house, big garden, not that he did as much of that since Rose had died. Winter provided an alibi: *Can't wait to be back out there, my boy. Life's better with a trowel in your hand.* Gardening, come to that, was what he'd been doing the first time he'd laid eyes on River. Funny way to meet your grandson, already seven years old. River's mother's fault, he'd thought then, but such straightforward judgements seemed less clear now. He was tying his tie as he had these thoughts; watching his hands in the mirror as they made complicated movements beyond the reach of his conscious brain. Some things were best done without thinking. Raising a daughter, it had turned out, not one of them.

Tie seemed straight enough, though. Important to maintain standards. You read about these old chaps in their pee-stained corduroys, with their vests on backwards, and dribble on their chins.

'That ever happens to me,' he'd instructed River more than once, 'shoot me like a horse.'

'Exactly like a horse,' River would reply drily.

Dammit, that was the name they gave them, there at Slough House. The slow horses. Treading on a young man's toes, that was; reminding him of the balls-up he'd made of things.

Not that his own copybook was free of blot. If they'd had a Slough House in his day, who knew? He might have whiled his own career away in terminal frustration; forced to sit it out on the bench, watching others carried shoulder-high round the boundary. Laps of honour and whatnot. That was what the boy thought, of course; that it was all about guts and glory – truth was, it was all about flesh and blood. Medals weren't won in the sunshine. Backs were stabbed in the dark. It was a messy business, and maybe the boy was better off out of it, though there was no telling him that, of course. Wouldn't be a Cartwright otherwise. Just like his mother, whom David Cartwright had missed acutely for years, without admitting it to anyone, even Rose.

. . . All these thoughts and he was still here in the hallway. What was it he'd been going to do? A blank moment came and went so smoothly it left barely a ripple. He was going to walk to the village. He needed to stock up on bread and bacon and whatever. His grandson might call round later, and he wanted to have some food in.

His grandson was called River.

Before he left, though, he needed to check his tie was straight.

In the same way a tongue keeps probing a sore tooth, the conversation in Marcus and Shirley's office kept returning to Roderick Ho – specifically, the wholly improbable, end-of-days-indicating, suggestion that he no longer flew solo.

'You think he's really found a woman?'

'He might have. It's surprising what some people leave lying around.'

'Because it could easily turn out to be a chick with a dick or whatever. And he'd be the last to know.'

'Even Ho—'

Shirley said, 'Seriously, trust me. Last to know.'

'Yeah, okay,' Marcus said. 'But he seems convinced.' He directed a sour look towards the doorway, and Ho's office beyond. 'Says he's a one-woman man now.'

'He probably meant cumulatively.'

Marcus, who hadn't been laid since his wife's car was repo'ed, grunted.

Louisa had peered round the door three minutes back to give them a heads-up on a possible Lamb appearance: as a result, the pair were staring at their screens; a reasonable facsimile of work, except that Shirley was still wet. Marcus's monitor throbbed in front of him. Even after all this time in Slough House he found it hard to adjust to its routines; switch mind and body off, become an automaton, processing random information sets. Burnt-out vehicles, that was his spreadsheet: burnt-out cars and vans – hardly an unusual sight in British cities. He'd seen one himself last week, in a supermarket car park; a black husk squatting in a pool of sooty residue. It would have been joy-ridden there then set alight, as the simplest way of eradicating evidence – the kids who'd taken it convinced that the forces of law and order were itching to go CSI on their gangsta asses; ready to swab DNA from seats, prints from the steering wheel. Safer just to torch that baby, and watch it crack and buckle in the heat.

But what if it wasn't as simple as that, Lamb wanted to know? (Important corollary: Lamb didn't want to know – Lamb couldn't care less. Lamb had just hit on another way of wasting a slow horse's time.) What if these torch-happy kids weren't just lighting up their stolen rides; what if they were experimenting with ways of blowing cars up – calculating blast radiuses; measuring the potential damage varying payloads could deliver? So here was Marcus, whose role in life had been kicking down doors, retooling himself as an analyst; staring at a screen which broke down five years' worth of vehicular arson by make, location, accelerant used, and a dozen other variables . . . There was always the possibility Lamb had a point – anyone who found the notion too high-concept just had to turn the TV on and watch footage of the onesie-clad forensics crew picking through Westacres' ashes. But either way, this wasn't the part of the process Marcus should have been involved in. He should be the one they called when they had a suspect holed up in a tower block with hostages. The one they decked out in Kevlar and dropped down a chimney: *Merry Christmas, assholes*.

Control, alt, delete.

The radiator gurgled noisily, interrupting his chain of thought, but at least it meant heat was moving around the building, which meant someone was paying bills. Marcus wasn't. Marcus was accumulating a drawerful of red letters: final demands for electricity and gas. Cassie was talking about taking the kids, going to her mother's 'for a bit', and that was even without knowing about the unpaid bills – her repossessed car had been the final straw.

'You said you'd got it under control.'

His gambling, she meant.

'You said you'd drawn a line, walked away. No more money down the drain. You *promised*, Marcus.'

And he'd meant it, too, but how did you stop money disappearing once it had decided to go? It was even less responsive to persuasion than Cassie.

He thought: I've turned into one of those men worth more dead than alive. More of us than you'd think. It's not just the Jihadi Johns out there in the scrublands, living off camel meat and sleeping in holes but with a million-dollar price tag on their heads: it's the rest of us too. Us poor working saps in debt to our eyeballs, a never-ending mortgage, and bills papering the walls; barely enough spare cash for a cup of coffee, but shouldering game-changing amounts of life insurance. I could keel over right here right now, and the death-in-service payout would solve all my problems. The house would be free and clear; money left over to see the kids through university.

Best thing all round, except for being dead. But that's going to happen sooner or later, so why not here at my desk? . . . He should raise that as a joke with Cassie, except she might not laugh. And no amount of Kevlar offered protection from a woman's disappointment.

The slamming of a keyboard roused him from his reverie. Shirley was having hardware issues, and resolving them in her traditional manner.

'. . . You got an AFM later?' he asked.

'Who needs to know?' she snarled.

'Nobody at all,' said Marcus, and tapped at his own keyboard randomly for a moment, as if by altering the rows of figures on his screen, he might also change the facts he was confronted with: not simply the half-a-decade's worth of destroyed cars, but his own dwindling net worth; the sums snapping at his heels growing ever larger, ever more vicious, and his ability to outpace them weakening by the day.

If he was going to walk to the village he'd need his wellingtons. Yesterday, he'd had to return home before he'd got fifty yards – a soft-shoe shuffle back down the drive; slippers jettisoned into the bin, soaked and useless. Well, a moment of absent-mindedness, and there'd been no witnesses. This was one of the advantages of living in semi-isolation, though you could never be certain there were no stoats watching.

'Know what I mean by stoats?'

River rarely forgot anything. David Cartwright had taught him well.

'You see a stoat, you pretend you haven't,' River said.

'Except you never see a stoat.'

'You never see them,' River agreed. 'But you know they're there.'

Because the signs they left were legion. The bent grasses

28

where they'd knelt; the lopped-off branch that had obscured their view. Cigarette ends in a tidy heap. *Don't have the boy picking up old fag ends*, Rose had scolded. But it was best the boy was taught to be on his guard, because once the stoats had you in their sights it was the devil's own job shaking them off.

A good morning for training, then. Besides, all boys like splashing in puddles so – one welly on; the other angled for entry – he bellowed for River to come join him for a walk. But even as his words went crashing through the empty house, he noticed their falsity: that was not the voice he'd had when River had been a boy. And River's boyhood was over; the days of teaching him about stoats and bogeymen, the myths and legends of Spook Street, had been gone longer than Rose . . .

David Cartwright shook his head. An old man's fancy – a memory rising to the surface, like a bubble from a frog. He lowered his foot into the second welly, chuckling. The boy ever learned he had these moments of inattention, he'd never hear the end of it. Besides, stoats weren't what they used to be. These days they used drones and satellite imagery; they planted tiny cameras in your house. Your every movement charted.

Wellington on, he stood up straight. Little bit of exercise, that was the ticket. It was true, there'd been times lately when he'd worried he'd come adrift. He'd doze off of an afternoon, forgivable lapse in an old codger, and come to in a panic: the fire seething in the grate, lamplight softly glowing; everything as it ought to be, but still that knocking in his chest: what had happened while he'd slept? Walls had been known to fall. Things had emerged from under bridges. It was a relief when the world he woke to was the same as the one he'd left.

But that wasn't always the case, was it? Sometimes the world did shift on its axis. Just two days ago, there'd been a suicide bomber in a British shopping centre — what did they call it? A flash mob . . . The blackest of black jokes; a flash mob ignited, and all those young lives destroyed. For a moment, standing by his own front door, David Cartwright felt it as a personal loss, something he could have prevented. And then that loss shifted shape, and Rose was telling him to be sure to wear his Barbour, not that dreadful old raincoat. And to carry his umbrella, just in case.

Keys in pocket. Wellingtons on feet. What was it he'd been thinking about, some dreadful thing or other? It slid past him like smoke, nothing he could get a grip on. Tucking himself into his raincoat — the Barbour made him feel he was pretending to be country folk — and leaving his umbrella hanging like a bat on its hook, he let himself out the door.

In the office above Marcus and Shirley's heads, other fingers tapped away: their movements fluid, the keyboard imaginary, the notes they followed apparently random but always searching for the melody beneath; a tune that would echo, build and repeat itself for thirty minutes or so, its themes at first withheld, sometimes stumbling, but ultimately laid bare. And while this happened, nothing else did. That was its lure for Jason Kevin Coe; the clean white page it opened in his mind, temporarily erasing the nightmares scribbled there.

We feel that you're not . . . happy in your work.

He could not remember how he had answered this question, which, anyway, was not a question. He had the feeling he'd simply sat, fingers twitching in his lap. Reaching for a tune that swirled around his head.

Coe wasn't sure when this had begun. It hadn't been a conscious decision, to mime his way through a series of improvised piano recitals; it was simply something he'd discovered himself doing, or rather, had discovered somebody else discovering him doing – he'd been on a bus, moving in fits and starts along a crowded Regent Street, when he noticed that the young woman next to him was edging away, casting worried glances at him, at his fingers, which were thrumming a non-existent keyboard. He hadn't until that moment connected the music in his head with the movement of his hands. At the time, he hadn't even been wearing his iPod. The music was simply inside him, something he relied on in moments of anxiety, which now included, he was barely surprised to learn, travelling in fits and starts in a crowded bus on Regent Street.

We were wondering if a transfer might not be in your best interests.

Always that *we*, underlining the plurality of the forces lined against him. Not that it was the Service's HR department that gave him sleepless nights.

Today, beneath his grey hoodie, J. K. Coe wore a T-shirt and jeans ripped at the knee. It had been a while since he'd worn anything else. He was three-days unshaven, and while unarguably clean – he showered twice daily; more often when time allowed – there always followed him a whiff of something that seemed to float at the outer edge of his ability to smell it. Sometimes, he worried it was the smell of shit. But really he knew it was fear; the odour of his own worst memory, when he'd been tied naked to a chair while another man, also naked, threatened him with an electric carving knife. In his dreams, in his insomniac nightmares, he relived what might have happened; the ripping of steel through his flesh; the wet slap of his innards as they hit the plastic sheets spread on the floor. When his fingers weren't searching for music they crept to his stomach, interlocked across his belly, struggled to hold inside what might have been carved out.

All of this had taken place at home, in his fifth-floor flat. He'd bought when he'd been earning well in banking, before he'd sickened of that career, shortly before everybody else had sickened of it too, and people began to look on bankers like there ought to be bags to collect them in. A narrow escape, he'd thought at the time, having fallen back on his degree subject and taken a post with the Service's Psych Eval section, where he hoped to prove useful. A modest ambition, and no longer a career target.

Slough House might be a better fit, we think. Fewer . . . alarms.

In the weeks and months following his ordeal, Coe had tired of most things. Food lost flavour, and alcohol served to make him throw up long before he'd achieved any kind of anaesthetised state. If he'd had ready access to weed or stronger he'd have given it a shot, but acquiring illegal substances demanded social interaction; interaction with people he could imagine providing . . . 'alarms'. He couldn't read for long without becoming furious. Music was all that was left. Coe had never played the piano in his life, and it was a toss-up as to whether his fingers were going in the right direction when the notes in his head climbed the scale; nevertheless, here he was, exiled to Slough House with the other catastrophes of the intelligence world; sentenced to plough away at a series of unpromising projects with no end in sight, instead of which he was making unheard music on an unplayable instrument, and finding in the process, if not peace, then at least a certain amount of white space.

From across the room, River Cartwright watched him dispassionately. If he'd learned anything as a slow horse, it was that there was no helping some people – sometimes, you had to let them drown. Which was what it looked like J.K. Coe was doing: not waving but drowning, scrabbling for purchase on a desk that was never going to keep him afloat. Whichever shore he was poling for, he'd either make it or he wouldn't. Until that happened, River planned on leaving him be.

Besides, he had troubles of his own.

At the junction where the driveway met the lane lay the Great Lake, an annual event caused by poor drainage. David Cartwright skirted it unsteadily, one careful footstep after another along what remained of the kerb: little more than a series of narrow stepping-stones. The hedgerow shivered at his passage, and tipped a pint of water straight into his boot, blast it! But now he was over, and back on firm ground. He waved a greeting at his neighbours' house, though its windows were dark, and squelched past the bus shelter, where a newspaper lay plastered to the floor. Torn images of parental grief screamed up. A streetlamp flickered uncertainly, unsure whether it should be on or off.

The lane led to the village in meandering fashion, literally going round the houses, but the footpath through the wood was direct. A wooden kissing-gate, semi-obscured by hedge, offered entrance. *You watch your step now*, Rose admonished. The way was carpeted with leaves, thickly sludged with them in places, but he'd always been mindful of treacherous ground, something he'd learned when plotting a course through history. You lived your life day by day, the O.B. thought, but days were mere splinters of time, no useful measure. The sudden events that blind us with their light had roots in the slowly turning decades. Even now, he could make out shapes from the past behind the headlines, like predators glimpsed through murky waters. Twenty years retired, and he still knew when there were stoats on his trail. His neighbours' house shouldn't be empty at this hour: the cleaning woman should be there, unlikely to be vacuuming in the dark. And that flickering streetlamp: no doubt its innards had been tampered with, the better to insert some surveillance device.

He waited. Of all the sounds in the wood, all the damp rustlings and furtive scratchings, none paused, to allow him to focus on their absence. Everything continued as it had been. But then, he would expect no different. These were not amateurs.

'But if you know it's a trap,' the boy said, 'shouldn't you avoid it?'

'No. You want them to think you're oblivious to their presence. And then, first time they blink – *pouf !* You're gone.'

He blinked – *pouf!* – and River was gone too.

The trees grumbled rustily. Someone whistled in imitation of a bird, and someone whistled back. The O.B. waited, but that was it for the time being. Carefully, eyes alert for snares among the leaves, he headed towards the village.

'Think he's an issue or a fuck-up?'

'Who are we talking about now?'

'Mr Air Piano.'

Marcus pretended to consider the matter. Sometimes it was easiest to go with Shirley's flow. When Lamb wasn't around she grew restless, as if his absence required celebration; and since Shirley's definition of celebration was wide, anything that didn't involve controlled substances was, on the whole, to be encouraged.

'You want to offer a little context?' he asked.

'Well, you and me, we're issues. You've got your gambling addiction—'

'It's not an addiction—'

'And me, apparently I'm "irritable".'

'You broke a dude's nose, Shirl.'

'He was asking for it.'

'He was asking for a couple of quid.'

'Same thing.'

34

'For Children in Need.'

'He was dressed as a fucking rabbit. I assumed he was dangerous.'

'That's probably the only reason you're not in prison,' Marcus conceded.

'Yeah, well. They wouldn't have got me at all if it wasn't for those pesky kids.'

Who had caught it on camera, and stuck it on YouTube. The whole dressed-as-a-rabbit thing was mitigation, of course, and the arresting officer had been charity-mugged herself three times that morning, and in the end the assault charges had been sidestepped on condition Shirley sign up for AFM.

Anger Fucking Management. Twice a week, in Shoreditch.

('Don't set off any new trends,' Marcus warned her when he found out. 'I took an idiot round Shoreditch once. That's how hipsters started.')

'And I'm assuming River and Louisa are fuck-ups,' he said now.

'Well, *duh.*'

'Catherine was an issue. Min was a fuck-up.'

'And Ho's a dickhead, but you always get outliers. So what's Jasper Konrad, that's what I want to know. And what is it with the air piano?' She mimicked his action, trilling up and down a non-existent instrument. 'Who's he think he is, Elton John?'

'You want to know what he's hearing in his head, go ask him. But don't blame me if the voices tell him to carve you up.'

'Yeah, 'cause he looks like he could be dangerous. Probably takes two of him to scramble an egg.' She stopped pretending to play the piano. 'Tell you what, though,' she said. 'If I was River, I'd be worried.'

'How so?'

'Youngish white guy, fucked up and seething. We've already got one of those. It's like River's being replaced.'

Marcus said, 'You have a weird way of looking at things.'

'You wait and see. Then tell me I'm wrong.'

She started banging at her keyboard again, her actual one, and Marcus couldn't tell if she was working out aggression, or writing an email.

Suppressing a sigh, he returned to work.

When he emerged from the footpath a car was heading down the lane, and it slowed at the sight of him, seemed about to halt, then sped up. He resolutely did not turn to watch it – they wanted him to react. Best keep his powder dry. And he was not quite defenceless, as they would discover to their cost.

No, he would make straight for the shop; in/out, back to camp. It might not be a simple exfiltration – the woman behind the counter was a chatty one; you could barely prise yourself loose with a crowbar – but lately, it occurred to him, she had been chatting less, listening more; coaxing out details it might have been wiser to preserve. He'd been explaining to her how history was never a closed book. Look at Russia: complete basket case. That hadn't been the plan, but that was the thing about history: push it down in one place, it springs up in another, like ill-laid lino.

He'd said, 'And there's always a price to pay. You make decisions, and people die, and that's what you live with, day and night, ever after. But I wouldn't have done things any differently.'

She'd said, 'David, you worked at the Ministry of Transport. I'm sure people were inconvenienced, but I don't suppose many of them died.'

Of course he had. The Ministry of Transport was his cover story; the alibi that papered over forty-something years of working life. So in the village, that's what he'd been: a pen-pusher with a brief for trains or roads or airports – you couldn't expect him to remember. It was hard enough keeping track of what he'd actually done, without recalling everything he'd merely pretended to do.

So he'd laughed it off, 'Figure of speech, dear lady,' but she'd have been on the phone as soon as he'd left, letting them know his cover was springing leaks. These were the lengths to which they were going. They were replacing members of his community, so that those he'd lived among for years were no longer to be trusted.

('The best of us are thieves and scoundrels,' he'd told River more than once. 'As for the worst . . .'

'Slough House,' River would say. 'Jackson Lamb. Remember?')

And River was his most obvious asset, his most trusted fellow human. What if they replaced him too? He could open the door to his only grandson and find a viper slithering inside.

If that happened, measures would have to be taken. Because he was not quite defenceless, as they would discover to their cost.

He crossed the lane, glad of his wellingtons, and entered the shop, setting the bell above the door jangling. What was it he'd wanted? Basic supplies: bread and bacon, milk and teabags. But already there was the sense of entering enemy territory, of having wandered into the path of stoats, because the lady of the shop was staring at him in something like horror, something like pity; was coming round the counter with one hand washing the other, her mouth stretching ever wider.

'Oh, David,' she said. 'David, your trousers . . .'

And when the O.B. looked down it took him a moment to understand what she was getting at, because he was certainly wearing trousers, tucked into his wellingtons, and the lady of the shop had reached him and taken his hand before it dawned on him that what he was looking at was not the thick dark tweed of everyday use, but the dark-red paisley-patterned cotton of his pyjamas.

And morning gives way to afternoon, and evening falls, as it usually does. In Kent, daylight slinks away across the fields as streetlights wink on one by one, each casting a tight umbrella over its own little stage, while in the heart of London darkness loiters in corners, and peeps from behind curtains. In Slough House, the heating has died with as much effort as it took to come to life, the death rattle of its pipes sounding a knell over the afternoon's activities, such as they were. In the end, Lamb has shown neither his face nor any other part of his anatomy, but the expectation of a dismal event can be as draining as its occurrence, and the atmosphere retains an edge of disquiet, despite the horses' departure. First to go was Roderick Ho, followed closely by Marcus Longridge and Shirley Dander. J. K. Coe may have been next – he was simply there one moment and then not, like the shine on an apple – but what's certain is that Louisa Guy and River Cartwright left together, their destination the nearest pub in which they might expect to encounter no one they know. Moira Tregorian is last to leave, but before doing so yields to the temptation of entering Lamb's office, which has overcome its top-floor location to assert a natural inclination towards cellardom. Dankness is its signature odour, with notes of stale flatulence and mouldy bread. A suspicious mind might even conjecture that smoking has taken place here. The blinds, as ever, are drawn, and the overhead bulbs have blown, so for illumination Moira is forced to rely on the lamp atop a pile of telephone directories to one side of the desk. The light this casts is yellow and sickly, and mostly serves to rearrange shadows. On Lamb's desk, the piles of paper have an unread look and are curling at the edges; on his shelves, the clutter is a challenge to the tidy-minded intruder. Tidy-minded Moira Tregorian certainly is, but simple-minded she isn't, quite, and she overcomes the urge to begin instilling order. Instead, she hovers a moment, wondering about this man into whose orbit she has been cast, whom she has yet to encounter, and who seems to collect empty bottles. It is clear that her predecessor has let things slide to the extent that bringing Mr Lamb to heel might prove a wearisome business. Moira Tregorian sighs to punctuate this thought, then turns the lamp off and makes her way down the stairs and into the damp and gloomy air of Aldersgate Street.

Behind her Slough House creaks and bangs, and surrenders to the chill.

3

THERE WAS A PUB near the church where they'd filmed *Shakespeare in Love*, and Louisa bagged a table under a diamond-patterned window while River fetched drinks. It still seemed odd, this – even a casual drink after work felt like two-timing Min's memory. But nothing stayed still. It was like moving from one room to another: you'd been there, and now you were here. Sooner or later, you closed the door between.

Three months back, Louisa had shifted the fridge in her studio flat and chiselled a lump of plaster from the wall. Nestled there was the uncut diamond, a fingernail-sized chunk of light, she'd acquired when the heist at the Needle came unstuck, shortly after Min's death. In a pub near Hatton Garden, she approached a man she'd been staking out for weeks: an appraiser at one of the smaller local jewellers, someone she knew would pay cash for an unprovenanced stone; not a fortune – daylight robbery, even – but that was an irony she could appreciate, and he could presumably guess at. Lumped together with her scraps of savings, it was enough for a deposit on an apartment some way out of town. 'Apartment' was an estate agent's word, making the property sound bigger than it was, but she was no longer sleeping in her kitchen, and her living-room window had a view of a park, and she was paying a mortgage, not rent. Sometimes at night she'd sit with the curtains open, a glass of wine in her hand, looking down on trees waving in the wind; not thinking about Min exactly, or about anything much, but being glad she was there and no longer in her poky studio with its constant cooking odours, and heavy bass noises thrumming from passing cars. Glad, too, she was no longer on bar stools every other evening, hooking up with strangers. She wasn't drinking so much, and was sleeping better. She woke early, but was mostly untroubled by dreams.

And this, having a drink with River, this was okay too. When you'd been through a war together – even a small one – it lent you a connection you weren't going to find in a hook-up. They'd both shot people. This didn't get aired much, but it was always there on the table.

He returned with the drinks: a vodka–lime for her for old times' sake, and a pint of bitter for him for £4.80. Prices in London were getting out of hand.

Because she wasn't yet ready for conversation, she hit the burning question of the day before he was seated:

'Why'd you think Lamb's invited the Moira to lunch?'

'The Moira' was what they'd taken to calling her; one of those unplanned habits that foster relationships.

River said, 'He might have been pulling her leg.'

'Cruel, even for Lamb.'

'I dunno. Actually taking her to lunch would be crueller. Besides, *taking* her – paying for it? How likely is that?'

Lamb had a distinctly *droit de seigneur* approach to mealtimes.

Louisa sipped her vodka and felt it hit the right buttons: suddenly the bar's edges were less harsh, and the noise from the other patrons subsided to a background murmur, waves collapsing on a beach. River looked better in this light too: the light of the evening's first drink. He was fair-haired, pale-skinned, grey-eyed, and while these things were always true, they were usually run–of–the–mill details, swamped by the particularities

41

of the moment: that he looked knackered, hungover, or pissed off, all of which were routine for a slow horse. His nose was a little sharp, true, and the mole on his upper lip grew larger when you noticed it, but basically he was fit enough, which was a good reason to go slow on the vodka-limes. Been there, done that. Her next phase of life involved domestic tranquillity, and avoiding unwise shagging choices.

So: conversation.

'Moira, anyway,' she said. 'That's an oldies' name. Your aunt's called Moira.'

'I don't have any aunts.'

'You know what I mean, though.'

'Unless I do,' River continued. 'I might have, come to think of it.'

'Yeah, 'cause who's got time to go around remembering whether they've got aunts?'

He said, 'Well, I never knew my father.'

'Oh.'

'Or if he had sisters. Or what they were called.'

'Oh, right, yeah, did I know that? I think I knew that. Sorry.'

'It's what happened,' said River. 'That's all.'

'Your mother never told you who he was? No hints, no clues?'

'She's a stubborn woman, my mother. She decided before I was born that he wasn't part of her life any more. And that's one path she's never deviated from.'

This being an unusual circumstance, Louisa surmised.

Sundry details of their lives had been exchanged, but had frequently fallen into that abyss where facts of no relevance or interest were stored. This was because for most of that time, they'd been locked in separate miseries, exile to Slough House being a shared condition only in the way that long-term imprisonment was – you might knock about together in the yard, but when the cell doors slammed shut, you were alone. Sharing had been killing time, that was all. Later, with Min, her interest in other people had been dimmed for the inverse reason: the natural selfishness happiness carries with it. So Louisa might have absorbed any amount of information about River's life, but basically what she knew about him was he'd stood next to her once while bullets flew. She supposed most office relationships progressed along similar lines. Well, except for the bit about bullets.

So it was with the sense that she was covering territory she might have been expected to be familiar with that she said, 'She's not a big part of your life, then.'

'Not a big presence, anyway. My grandparents brought me up.'

'David Cartwright.'

'The one and only. Rose, my nan – she died a while ago.'

'And now you're worried about him.'

'Yes,' River said. 'I'm worried about him.'

'Getting forgetful?'

'Uh-huh.'

'Is that so bad? I mean, yeah, okay, it's bad, but . . . How old is he, anyway?'

'Eighties,' River said. 'Eighty . . . four? Yeah, four.'

Louisa said, 'Not so very old. Not these days.'

'Kind of is, though,' River said.

She didn't reply, because he was right. Eighty-four kind of was old.

Her glass was nearly empty, but because River was still working on his pint she didn't make a move towards a fresh round. Besides, it wasn't the moment to break off talking. River had the absorbed air of one getting something off his chest, but with a way to go before he'd mined down to the real stuff.

She said, 'How forgetful are we talking? Days of the week or his own name?'

'Somewhere in between, I guess.'

'Is he on meds?'

'Statins. Nothing else I know of. And I would, because . . .'

'Because you've been through his bathroom cabinet. Have you talked to him about it?'

He gave her a look.

'Okay, not easy. But is there anyone you can talk to? Neighbours, anyone?'

'His neighbours think he's a retired civil servant.'

'Well, he sort of is.'

'But not the kind they think. And the last thing I want is to discover he's been sharing his life story with the postman.'

'Is that likely?'

'I don't know, Louisa. Every time I see him, a bit more of him has slipped away. It's like the light gets dimmer. He's always been the anchor in my life. Now, I sometimes catch a look in his eye like he doesn't know where he is, and it frightens me. I don't know what to do about it.'

She let her hand lie on his for a moment. He nodded at the contact, then broke it to pick up his beer glass, which he drained. Then he said, 'Fancy another?'

'Yes. But it's my round.'

At the bar, she briefly locked looks with a man down the far end. Six months ago, that would have been enough to trigger an evening's descent into carnal oblivion; six months from now, who knew, it might be enough to kickstart conversation. For the moment, there were other priorities. She looked away, paid for her drinks, and carried them back to the table thinking about the O.B., a term she'd heard River use – Old Bastard: a term of affection in this case. There were all sorts of legends in the Service – she worked for one of them, for God's sake

44

– but David Cartwright's was the kind that withstood scrutiny. Never actually First Desk, but the power behind several incumbents of that throne. Of all the secrets he'd been privy to, a good number could still be radioactive. If he began to leak, there'd be concerned faces at Regent's Park and elsewhere.

Seated again, she said, 'Would they – I mean, the Park. Do they get involved, situations like this?'

'No. I doubt it, anyway. Well, I wouldn't have put much past Ingrid Tearney, and Diana Taverner probably has men killed just to keep in practice, but Tearney's out the door, and from what I hear, Lady Di's using both hands to keep a grip on her desk. She's probably not authorising clandestine wet work on the old brigade, just to make sure they don't talk out of turn.'

Louisa said, 'Yeah, I wasn't actually suggesting they'd have him murdered, though I can see you've put some thought into that. I was more wondering about a home or something. A home for distressed former spooks. Didn't there used to be something like that?'

'Sorry. Must be getting paranoid.'

'Goes with the territory.'

He said, 'There was a place, but it was closed down a few years ago. Austerity measure.'

'Christ.'

'Yeah. Anyway, it's not a fate he'd take to lightly. You'd need a crash squad to prise him from his house if he thought you were trying that on.'

'So he's aware of what's happening?'

'No. I don't know. I just meant generally . . . It's not like he's forgotten who he is. It's more like he's forgotten that that's not who he is any more. Some days, I think he's still fighting the Cold War.'

'A lot of old people live in the past.'

'But not many of them have his past to live in. He keeps

45

a gun in the house, Louisa. He's supposed to keep it in a gun safe — I mean, technically, he's not supposed to have it at all, but given that he does, he's supposed to keep it in a safe. But last week I found it on the kitchen table. He said something about keeping the stoats away.'

'Stoats?'

'What they used to call watchers. When you were under surveillance.' River paused to take a drink, then said, 'God, I don't know. After the last few days, the bomb at Westacres, maybe the fate of one old man isn't something to get worked up about.'

'He's your grandfather. Of course you're upset.'

'Yeah.' He looked at his watch. 'And I ought to make a move.'

'You're going to see him now?'

'Yep. Thanks, Louisa. For, you know. Listening.'

'Well. We should stick together.' And then, in case he thought she meant the pair of them, added, 'Slough House, I mean. Nobody else is looking out for us.' She paused. 'I miss Catherine.'

'So do I.'

'Do you think Lamb does?'

'. . . Seriously?'

'He's not been much in evidence since she quit.'

River said, 'He misses having an alcoholic around. He got a lot of mileage out of that.' He finished his beer and stood. 'I have to go. I'll just make the next train.'

'I hope he's okay.'

'Thanks. But I don't think this is something he's likely to get better from.'

'Maybe not. But, you know. He's not necessarily going to start reciting his memoirs on the village green.'

'That's not what really worries me.'

'What does?'

River said, 'That someone'll come to the door and he'll shoot them.'

From the train window River looked out on London's dark edges and thought about his mother.

He didn't do this often. They spoke on the phone occasionally, usually while she was abroad – this gave her licence to broadcast how much she missed him, how he should 'pop on a plane' to Antibes, Cap Ferrat, Santa Monica, Gstaad, where they could hunker down for some mother–son time. All safe in the knowledge it wasn't going to happen. When she was in-country, on the other hand, River found out about it afterwards, or not at all. *I was so busy, darling, not a minute to myself. You know I was* desperate *to see you.* But this had long ceased to distress him. When they were together, it felt more like an audience, as if he were a cub reporter summoned to the presence of a fading movie star. The pictures had got small. He was simply there to bear witness to that fact.

And the Isobel Dunstable commanding such attention was a long cry from the young woman who'd dumped him on his grandparents' doorstep when he was seven, and taken off for two years with a man whose name he couldn't remember. He wasn't confident she could, either. But her mercurial twenties were way behind her, and in her respectable widowhood, while she might admit to the occasional youthful indiscretion, she was hardly going to put her hand up to a period of anarchy. Which didn't mean she'd re-established friendly terms with her father. In some ancient era – before River's appearance in the world – they'd had what Rose had called 'a falling out'. She was big on understatement, his grandmother, but not one for betraying confidences. The details weren't hers to provide, she'd told him. And neither combatant was offering clues.

The last time he'd seen them together had been at Rose's funeral, where they hadn't exchanged a word that he'd observed – and he had observed. River Cartwright, junior spook. He had missed the original Cold War by some years. This one would do until the next came along.

He wondered if his mother should know what state the Old Bastard was in, and which of them he'd be betraying most by divulging it.

The carriage was heavy with wet overcoat smells, and every time a train passed in the opposite direction the windows slapped open. Meanwhile, the man opposite River was explaining to his mobile phone, at some volume, how quickly he had assimilated the implications of the recent changes to Stamp Duty. That everyone hadn't yet banded together and hanged him by his braces was testament to the forbearance of the British commuter.

His grandfather thought about her often, he knew. He would ask River, carefully offhand, 'whether he'd heard from his mother' – never using 'Isobel', as if this would presume on a deeper acquaintance than they shared. And when River answered that she was fine, as far as he knew, 'That's good, then,' David would say, or something like. 'That's good, isn't it?'

But the Old Bastard himself was not fine. What River had told Louisa was only a small part of the truth, the worst of which was that on a recent visit, the old man hadn't known him. So carefully had he carried this off that it wasn't until he'd been there half an hour that River realised. His grand-father was covering his lapse like a pro: echoing statements River had made; offering bland follow-ups that concealed his ignorance. The O.B. had never been a joe. But he had lived his life among them, and knew how to adapt.

River often stayed over mid-week, but he'd headed back to London on that occasion. The thought of his grandfather lying awake all night, terrified of the stranger in the spare room, was more than he could bear.

The financial guru opposite was growing more pleased with himself by the minute. He was more or less River's age but about a thousand times his net worth, going by shirt and shoes. Still, money wasn't everything: River leaned across, tapped him on the knee, and said, 'Would you mind finishing your call now?' His tone was polite, but his eyes weren't.

The man blinked, then said, 'What did you say?'

River repeated his request, but this time it wasn't a request.

The man stared at him for four seconds, weighing alternatives. Then said, 'Look, I'll call you back,' and put his phone away.

'Thank you,' said River.

A sidewind buffeted the train, and two windows slammed open again.

Louisa had said: *Yeah, I wasn't actually suggesting they'd have him murdered, though I can see you've put some thought into that.*

But how could he, his grandfather's son, not have done?

And what really worries me, River had wanted to tell her, is that he's always loved telling stories. Even now, visits meant sitting in the O.B.'s study, sharing a drink and hearing secrets. That these had grown confused, frequently petering out down lanes that led nowhere, didn't mean they were no longer secret, and the thought of the O.B. on his daily pilgrimage round the village – butcher, baker, post office lady – weaving for all the same webs he'd spun River, had kept him awake two nights on the trot. The locals thought his grandfather had been a big wheel in the Ministry of Transport, one of the wheels which kept all the others turning, and they'd think his tales of a covert past the fantasies of a failing mind. But that didn't mean they wouldn't attract attention. David Cartwright was not a forgotten man round Regent's Park: he had seen the Service through choppy waters; never his own hand on the tiller, but a light grip on the elbow of whoever was steering. It was he who'd picked the stars by which the Service read its maps. And now he was old, and old spies grew forgetful, and among the things they forgot was remembering what not to say. More covers were blown by the need for a friendly ear than were ever dismantled by opposition hoods. So elderly spies had an eye kept on them, in case they came unbuttoned, and maybe there were times – how could he not have thought about this? – when the Service reached out a gloved hand and eased an old spook's passage from this life.

Better that, the thinking would go, than have a legend like David Cartwright unspool his memories in public, for the world and his or her civil partner to hear, and sell to the Sunday papers.

They'd send stoats first, to check the lie of the land.

And the O.B. kept a gun in his house which he no longer stored in a gun safe.

The train trundled on towards his destination. Different scenarios played out in his head – there were only so many ways a story could end.

It could happen very quickly, and there needn't be anyone else involved. Help the old man into a bath. A quick tug on his ankles and it would be over.

Jesus Christ, would you listen to yourself?

But: *That ever happens to me* he'd instructed River more than once, *shoot me like a horse.* He'd meant getting older than nature intended; losing his mind, losing his marbles. And he hadn't been making a jest. Nothing more frightening, to someone who'd lived by his wits, than to be slowly losing them.

And there was a dilemma for you, River thought drily. Could you do what he wanted, even though it would destroy you? Or will your scruples, your love for him, your cowardice, keep you from doing the only real favour he's ever asked, and condemn him to a living hell?

Maybe he should seek his mother's advice.

Through the window, he could see trees splashing about in the wind. He had a ten-minute walk from the station, and was going to get wet. But it suited his mood.

The man opposite caught his eye, and looked away hurriedly. River stared back for a while, at the man's reflection in the glass, but his thoughts were elsewhere: out among those cold swaying trees, in the unforgiving weather, in the dark.

When the doorbell rang the jangly noise went on longer than necessary, exploring the house, checking upstairs and down for occupants. David Cartwright was in his study, his usual chair, books stacked next to him. Topmost was *Bleak House*, through which he had been leafing lately; skating over the surface, because he no longer had the patience to submerge himself in detail. The more he did so, the more the characters came apart; their cover stories exposed as threadbare fictions.

The bell rang again.

River had a key, but rarely used it, which was his way of acknowledging his grandfather's sovereignty. The O.B. had a fear of becoming a charity case; someone the neighbours checked on; popping a head round the door 'to make sure you're all right', meaning not dead yet. He wasn't dead yet. He rose and went into the hallway. Through the front door's pebbled glass he could make out a shape backlit by the nearby streetlight, which was no longer flickering. This seemed significant, though he couldn't think why.

Without approaching further, he said, 'Who's there?'

'It's me.'

He waited.

'. . . Grandad? It's me, River.'

It didn't sound like River. Then again, it had been a long day and he was tired; distraught, too, by the memory of his trip to the village in his pyjama trousers. The lady from the shop, she claimed her name was Alice, had driven him home, chattering all the while as if this were normal. She had waited while he'd changed, and when he came down she'd boiled the kettle: 'nice cup of tea', the universal panacea. They had sat at the kitchen table eating a slice of cake, and he had asked her several trick questions, and she had fielded them all nicely. Even now he couldn't be absolutely certain she was an imposter any more than he could prove he'd been slipped some memory-twisting drug. They wanted him askew from reality, that was their plan; wanted him declared harmless and senile, the better to squeeze him dry when the time came. And to that end they would make use of those who loved him, because that was how things worked on Spook Street. Your friends and neighbours were not to be trusted, but it was your family you had to fear.

'Grandad? Are you all right in there?'

The shape shifted; became hooded and intense. Whoever it was had raised a flattened palm to their brow and was peering through the mottled glass.

'What was your grandmother's name?'

'. . . What?'

'Simple question.'

River, if that's who it was, fell silent.

'Because if you can't even—'

'Her name was Rose, Grandad. Your wife's name was Rose. And your daughter, my mother, she's Isobel.'

Which proved nothing. Any fool could do research.

The man banged on the door again. 'Grandad? Are you okay?'

Let the enemy in. Pretend your guard is down. He wasn't defenceless, as this imposter might yet discover to his cost.

He turned the latch and opened the door to the stranger on his doorstep. It was a creditable likeness. They had done their job well. If he was as fuddled as they thought, this man would pass as River Cartwright.

And this man was pushing on the door now, making David step back. He closed it behind him. 'Cold out.'

'Where've you come from?'

'You know where I've come from.' He glanced down. 'You need to put some slippers on.'

The O.B. looked down at his feet: socks only, on the cold tiles.

'Where are your slippers?'

He had thrown his slippers away, but didn't want to admit this, because it would lead to more questions – why had he thrown them away; how had they got wet; why was he wandering in the rain with only slippers on his feet? To admit to confusion was to play into their hands. So he simply glared at the young man in a way that made it plain he would be questioned no more on this topic.

In return, he received a quizzical look; a head tilted to one side in a way that River himself had. 'Did something happen today?'

'No.'

'Are you sure? You seem . . . confused.'

'I'm fine,' he snapped.

Once, he had sat in the Prime Minister's office while First Desk briefed her on unexpected troop movements on the East German border, a brief later agreed to have had a calming effect on the PM in particular, on policy in general, during Westminster's jumpiest week since October sixty-two. And which, very much to the point, had been written by Cartwright himself – he, David Cartwright, had taken a planing tool to history; had smoothed away a rough edge, and ensured that the lives of hundreds of thousands of people continued on their serene course instead of being capsized by the possibility of war. And that was just one day in his life. One day in a long life, crammed with incident: what made today so special? No lives had been ruptured, no navies sunk. He'd walked to the shops in his pyjama trousers, that was all. It could have happened to anyone.

'It's cold in here.'

'I'm all right.'

'You should have the heating on.'

Heat dulls the senses, keeps you unwary.

The young man who was calling himself River walked into the kitchen, acting like he owned the place. He cast a professional eye over the surfaces, checking for signs of neglect – unwashed crockery, crops of mould. He'd be a long time looking. Rose Cartwright had run a tight ship, and her widowed husband did the same.

'Have you eaten, Grandfather?'

'Yes.'

He'd eaten cake. A cup of tea and a slice of cake, as prepared by the Alice woman. This man would know that already, of course. He'd have been fully briefed.

'Would you like me to run you a bath?'

'When have I ever needed you to do that?'

'Grandad, you look cold to the bone. And there's no fire lit. How long have you been sitting without the heating on? I'll run you a bath so you can warm yourself up, and then I'll light a fire.'

'River never . . .'

He lost his thread.

'I'm River.'

'Have you spoken to your mother lately?'

'She's fine. She sends her love.'

She never does that, the O.B. thought.

'Why does your voice sound strange?'

'Slight cold, nothing to worry about. I'm not contagious. Now let's get upstairs.'

And this was not his grandson. Not the River he had first met in the garden; a scruffy-haired boy, T-shirted and unhappy. Isobel was already motoring down the lane with her latest unsuitable beau: that was the last they'd see of her for two years.

He'd been on his knees, with a trowel. He could remember their conversation as if it had been yesterday:

We all make mistakes, River. Made a couple myself, and some have hurt other people. They're the ones you shouldn't get over. The ones you're meant to learn from.

He had always treated River as an equal, never condescended to him.

Am I going to live here now?

Yes. Can't think what else to do with you.

It turned out it was as easy as that to allow someone into your life.

River Cartwright had been bone of his bone, the warm glow of his heart, since the boy was seven. And would they dare send an imposter to his home if the real River was at liberty, or even alive?

'Grandfather?'

'. . . What?'

'Shall I run you a bath?'

'Yes,' he said. 'Yes, why not do that.'

'Good. I think that would be best.'

'You go on up,' David Cartwright told this stranger. 'I just need to fetch something from the study.'

Because he was not as defenceless as they seemed to think.

4

A MOBILE PHONE VIBRATING on a hard surface sounds like a fart. That this was not an unusual sound in Jackson Lamb's bedroom, or indeed his vicinity, might have been why it failed to rouse him immediately: his surfacing was a slow, painful experience, like that of a whale being tugged to shore. When at last he emerged, tarred and feathered by sleep, the phone escaped his grasp like a sliver of soap, forcing him to lean over the side of the bed and fumble about on the floor.

Mission accomplished, he answered with a single word: 'Fuck?'

Twenty seconds later he said, 'Fuck,' and disconnected.

For a while after that he lay in the dark, which stank like a wrestling ring. The room's torpor suggested he'd turned the heating on at some point, and forgotten to turn it off at another. He wore boxers, one sock and a tie, which was inexorably knotted at the point it became impossible to loop over his head, and well short of that at which he'd be able to wriggle the rest of his body through it. Still, at least he'd made some attempt to get undressed: life was on an upward curve. Or had been, until the phone call.

He said 'Fuck' again, and hauled himself out of bed.

Breakfast was two pints of tapwater and four Nurofen. Shaving was out of the question, but he released himself from yesterday's tie with the kitchen scissors and found a fresh suit, which meant one that had been in his actual wardrobe, if not on a hanger. Locating his shoes was another ten minutes' work. In the end, the missing one turned up outside his front door, though when he tried to wedge his foot inside, it seemed to have shrunk overnight. Closer examination revealed a sock still in occupation. Scrunching this into a ball, he crammed it into a pocket; then, shod at last, though in unlaced shoes, clomped out to his car, wiped the mouse droppings from the driver's seat, and set off for Kent.

The streets weren't exactly deserted – it was a little after two – but were threadbare enough that he could drive on auto-pilot. On the fringes of the capital streetlights became more sporadic, then gave way to darkened roads whose rises and dips were sketched in by oncoming traffic. Lamb smoked as he drove, and each time he reached the filter he wound the window down and flicked the butt into the night, where it spat orange sparks into cold damp air.

Bright glittering beads at rabbit level observed his passage. Just once the car rucked, and wheels mashed fur and bone into ten yards of tarmac. The expression on Lamb's face didn't change, even as his cigarette shed a worm of ash into his lap.

He parked on a verge, where his tyres would leave treadmarks in the grass, and sat for a while without moving. The car's heater had rendered the air thick and rubberised, but this had more established odours to compete with, like cigarette smoke, and the half-portion of chow mein which had slipped under the passenger seat an aeon ago, and would now require a high-powered vacuum cleaner or a certified zoologist to remove. Lamb himself wasn't odour-free, come to that. He plugged another cigarette into his mouth without lighting it. Rubbing the corners of his eyes with his thumb and ring finger instead, he revived the images of other cars' headlights, which looped briefly across the inside of his eyelids before spinning away into nothing.

It was a starless night, thick black cloud wrapping the sky, and the streetlamps were wreathed in mist, the hedgerows heavy with collected rain. The houses here were large and detached, each walled or fenced off from its neighbour; islanded by lawn and flowerbed, and anchored to the earth by the weight of a century or so. Their gateposts were chipped or crumbling, their driveways as rutted as farmyards, and their hallways would be stuffed with Labradors and welling-tons, with overcoats handed down from father to son – a tightness masquerading as tradition, unless it was the other way round – because it was old money, in all its shabby glory, that owned villages like this. There'd be poorer elements, their function to mow lawns and repair boilers, but the foxes here would be red and bushy, the squirrels fat and cheeky, unlike their nicotine-addicted counterparts in London parks and alleys, while the human inhabitants would be bluff, smug, and brimming with the confidence born of inherited wealth. Lamb took care to slam the door when he hauled himself out into the cold. There was little point in discretion. He could already see upstairs curtains twitching in the nearest house.

A police car was parked by David Cartwright's gate. Two other unmarked vehicles were nearby, one with a goon behind the wheel; the other empty, its hazards flashing. He felt its warmth as he passed. Cartwright's front door was ajar, light puddling onto the driveway. A uniformed policeman stood there, observing Lamb's approach with the wary contempt a street copper feels for the Funny Brigade. 'Help you, sir,' he said: three bare words, neither question nor statement. Lamb might as well have pulled a string on his back.

In place of an answer, Lamb produced the belch that had been brewing for the past five minutes.

'Very convincing, sir. But I'm going to need to see something laminated.'

Lamb sighed, and reached for his Service ID.

In the hallway a technician was dusting the banister for fingerprints, looking every inch an extra in a TV show. Star power was provided by the blonde in the black suit talking on her mobile. Her hair was bound in a severe back-knot, but if that was an attempt to dim her wattage, it failed; she could have painted a beard on and still sucked up all the local attention. When she saw Lamb she finished her conversation and slotted her phone into her jacket pocket. She was wearing a white blouse under the suit: her eyes were blue, her manner all business. But she didn't offer her hand.

'You're Lamb,' she told him.

'Thanks,' he said. 'This time of night, I'm plagued by doubts.'

'We've not met. I'm Emma Flyte.'

'I guessed.'

Emma Flyte was the new Head Dog, in charge of the Service's internal police squad. The Dogs sniffed out all manner of heresies, from the sale of secrets to injudicious sexual encounters: the honeytrap was older than chess, but stupidity was even older. So the Dogs were used to a long leash, roaming whatever corridors they chose, but were currently in the doghouse themselves: Dame Ingrid Tearney, erstwhile head of the Service, had used their offices to further her own interests, and while initiative was frequently applauded, getting caught exercising it was not. Emma Flyte, an ex-police officer, was the new administration's clean-sheet appointment, though as more than one commentator had noted, if Regent's Park was looking to the Met for an injection of integrity, it was in serious danger of an irony meltdown.

She said, 'You know Mr Cartwright?'

'Which one?'

'Either. Both.'

'The younger one works for me. His grandfather gave me a job once. You want to show me the damage?'

She handed him a pair of paper boots. 'Treat it as a crime scene.'

Lamb left a lot of crime scenes in his wake. Arriving at one after the event was something of a novelty.

So was putting on a pair of paper boots, or so Flyte seemed to think. She watched with fascination as he attempted to slip the first one over his left shoe without bending over.

'It might help if you did your laces up.'

'I don't suppose . . .'

She didn't grace that with so much as a smile.

Sighing, he got down to floor level and tied his laces. That done, the paper boots went on easily. When he regained his feet, his face was red and he was breathing heavily.

'I'd say you're out of shape,' she told him. 'But I'm not sure what shape you're aiming for.'

He leered. 'Offering to take me in hand?'

'Not even with these on.' She wore latex gloves. 'It's in the bathroom. That's upstairs,' she added, as if his general know-ledge wasn't necessarily reliable in such matters.

Lamb led the way. The staircase was narrow for the size of the house, the pattern on its carpet a faded blurry mix of blue and gold. On the wall was a series of prints, pencil sketches of hands and faces, as if the artist was working up to something big but hadn't got there yet. On the topmost one, an outstretched palm, the glass was smeared with blood. Lamb paused, then glanced down at the technician below. 'Missed a bit.'

The landing was lined with books, shelved around a windowseat looking onto the front garden. The nearest open door was a bedroom, Lamb assumed the old man's; lining a corridor were three other doors, one closed, with, at the far end, another set of stairs: attics and boxrooms, one-time servants' quarters. On the wall opposite one of the open doors was another bloody handprint. You didn't have to be a detective. He took the cigarette from his mouth, wedged it behind his ear, and jammed his hands into his pockets.

Behind him, she said, 'Lamb?'

He paused.

'It's bad in there.'

'I've seen bad before,' he told her, and entered the bathroom.

The body lay on the floor, which was where bodies usually ended up, in Lamb's experience. He'd seen them hung in trees too, and washed up on shorelines, and a few snagged on barbed wire, dangling like broken puppets. But by and large, when you had a body, the floor was where it was going to finish. A little of this one had washed over the bathtub, too: its face was a pulped absence, a reminder that flesh and bone were temporary at best, and prone to rearrangement. He was probably imagining the smell of cordite in the air. Blood and shit were more prominent: besides, the trigger had been pulled on this scene easily a couple of hours ago.

'He was carrying this.' Flyte handed him a laminated card, much like the one he'd shown the policeman, but fresher, newer. When he held it at the right angle, its hologram configured into something like River Cartwright's face.

'Uh-huh.'

He crouched down for a closer look, without any of the creaking or visible effort he'd made when tying his laces. The body wore jeans, black boots, a black V-neck over a white sweatshirt. It had had teeth once, and a nose, eyes, all the usual stuff, but none of that was currently available for identification purposes. The hair was carrying a lot of evidential weight, then: this was fairish, leaning towards brown, though substantially bloodied up at the moment. Cut short, but not excessively so, which fitted Lamb's memory of his last sighting of River Cartwright. There were no rings on the fingers, no jewellery of any kind. That, too, was a match.

'Did he have any identifying marks?' Flyte asked.

'He used to have a face,' Lamb said. 'That any help?'

'Tattoos? Scars? Piercings?'

'How the fuck should I know? I make them wear clothes round the office.'

'We'll do blood work. But the faster we can do this, the better.'

'A mole,' Lamb said. 'He had a mole on his upper lip.' He glanced at the bathtub. 'You're gonna need a pair of tweezers and a sieve.'

'So this is him.'

'What do you think?'

'I'd appreciate a response.'

Lamb passed a hand across his face, but when he took it away his expression hadn't altered. 'It's him,' he said.

'You're sure?'

'It's River Cartwright,' Lamb said, and rose easily and left the room.

She caught up with him in the garden. He was smoking a cigarette, though the one behind his ear was still in place. Way overhead, a tear in the clouds allowed moonlight through: this cast a silvery tint on damp grass and wet hedges. A set of cast-iron furniture was arranged on the crazy-paved patio.

One of its matching chairs had toppled over: it lay in a mad position, legs in the air, like a stranded tortoise.

'You okay?' she asked.

'Bit of a head,' said Lamb. 'I'm not normally a drinker, but I had a sherry before dinner.'

'I'll skip the pastoral stuff, then. He was shot twice. Both times in the face.'

'Seems excessive. Though he could be annoying, I'll give you that.'

'You don't seem too concerned.'

The look Lamb gave her was blandly unexpressive. 'I've lost joes before.'

'You were an Active.'

'While you were still in mittens. The neighbours hear anything?'

'Not until we turned up.'

'So who called it in?'

'He had a panic button.'

'Police?'

'No. Us.'

'So what was the response time?'

She said, 'We don't come out of this well. He pressed it at 21:03. First responder got here at 21:49.'

'Forty-six minutes,' said Lamb. 'Good job it wasn't an emergency.'

'It was his third call in three weeks. The two previous occasions, he'd forgotten what the button was for. He'd pressed it to find out.'

Lamb tapped his temple with a finger.

She rolled her eyes. 'His last medical checked out okay. He'd admitted occasional memory lapses, but nothing significant. He could remember the date, his phone number. Who the PM was.'

'Impressive,' Lamb agreed. 'Could he remember what he looks like?'

'All I'm saying, there was no reason to think he was anything other than a bit scatty. And certainly none to expect this.'

'And here's me thinking the panic button was for the unexpected.' Lamb squashed his cigarette end on the table. 'If we were first responders, why are there woodentops here?'

'SOP when there's a body.'

He whistled. 'I knew we'd gone corporate. I didn't know we'd been spayed.'

'You're maybe out of the loop. These days, we try to operate within the law. Which means drink-driving's a definite no-no, by the way. Did you not get that memo?'

'Couldn't read it. My decoder ring's broken. So where is he, anyway?'

'Where's who?'

'David Cartwright, who do you think?'

'Well, that's the thing,' said Emma Flyte after a pause. 'We have no idea.'

'I thought you said he had a button. Did nobody mention they're traceable?'

'Thanks, I'll make a note. But I've already traced his particular button to the kitchen table.'

'Did you look underneath it?'

'He's not in the house, he's not out here in the garden. Not with the nearest neighbours. We could do a canvass, but until we get word on how to play this, we don't want to be flying too many flags.'

'What about the gun?'

She shook her head.

'So, to sum up,' said Lamb. 'A former senior spook – I mean, seriously, this guy knows more secrets than the Queen's had chicken dinners – blows his grandson's face clean off then disappears into the night, armed. Oh yeah, and he's lost his marbles.' He shook his head. 'This is not gonna play well on Twitter.'

'At least we picked the right week to bury bad news.'

'What, Westacres? You're joking. Any bomb that goes off in London is an Intelligence Service fuck-up, which ironically enough describes young Cartwright too. Trust me, there'll be keyboard warriors joining the dots as soon as this hits the Web.'

'We'll wrap it up before it comes to that.'

'The next sound you hear will be me, expressing confidence.' He farted, and reached for the cigarette behind his ear.

Something rustled down the far end of the garden, but it was just the great outdoors, not a former senior spook. Lamb lit his cigarette, still staring in that direction. The clouds overhead healed themselves, and what little moonlight there'd been shimmered out of view.

'So you're the boss of the famous Slough House,' Flyte said. 'Isn't that where they keep the rejects?'

'They don't like to be called that.'

'So what do you call them?'

'Rejects,' said Lamb. He broke off his study of the darkness and turned to face her. 'And you're the new broom. For some reason, I was expecting someone less . . . female.'

'Do I detect a trace of sexism?'

'Christ, not you too. Sexism, sexism, blah blah blah. It's like you're all constantly on the rag.' He exhaled a blue cloud. 'How long have you been a Dog?'

'Two months.'

'And before that?'

'I spent eleven years in the Met.'

'Uniform?'

'Why do you ask?'

'Just painting a mental picture.'

'I spent some years in uniform, naturally.'

'Have you still got it?'

She rolled her eyes.

'Don't be shy,' he said. 'A figure like yours, and a uniform handy. That's gonna make some man very happy.'

'Maybe I'm gay.'

'Well, picturing that's gonna make a *lot* of men very happy.'

'This isn't an appropriate conversation, Lamb. Apart from anything else, one of your team just died.'

'I'm working through my grief. I might need a little leeway.'

'I think what you need is to go. Thanks for your input. We'll confirm your identification once the blood work's through.'

'No hurry. I'd hate it to clash with my denial phase.' He dropped his cigarette and trod on it. 'The last Top Dog had a run-in with an iron bar, did they tell you that? He's upright again, but I heard they've pinned feeding instructions to his shirt.'

'The grapevine says it was young Cartwright wielding the bar.'

'Grapevines say a lot of things. But it's mostly the wine talking. The guy before him, he was altogether classier.'

'Bad Sam Chapman.'

'That was just a name. He wasn't that bad.'

'Except for the bit about losing a quarter of a billion pounds.'

'I said he wasn't bad. I didn't say he was perfect.' Lamb put his hands in his pockets. 'Good luck with finding the old bastard. That's what the boy used to call him.'

'Affectionately, I hope.'

'River thought so. But he was a bastard all right. I guarantee that.'

As he brushed past, she wrinkled her nose and said, 'Have you showered lately?'

'Tempting offer,' he said. 'But I don't think that's appropriate right now. Apart from anything else, one of my team just died.'

He walked through the open French windows and into the house.

'No, really,' Emma Flyte murmured to his back. 'You had me at "fuck".'

In London, dawn broke along the familiar fault lines, grey light seeping through cracks, drawing round the edges of the tallest buildings. The forecast was for more dull weather, a promise kept by the rain rolling in to dampen the capital's streets: taxis were already on the prowl as the first wave of commuters came crashing out of the Tube stations, wondering where its umbrellas were. Where once there'd have been newspaper vendors on corners, now there were kagoul-clad youngsters, mostly Asian, handing out the free-sheets to passers-by, many of whom were using them as makeshift rain protection. The warning lights at pedestrian crossings counted down to zero, buses came lumbering out of the gloom, and another day dragged itself from sleep, inviting miserable winter to do its worst, again.

A COBRA meeting had been called for 7.30, the early start a traditional method of indicating the serious intentions of all concerned. We may not be getting anywhere, the subtext read, but at least we've had very little sleep. Pre-meeting meetings were thus taking place from 6.00 onwards, as various head desks herded their ducks into a row, and some of the faces round the tables were new: over the past months, significant changes had been rung in the personnel called forth by crisis. Life in Whitehall's corridors was sometimes compared to a game of musical chairs, an image conjuring genteel notions of women in bonnets, men in stiff collars, and a well-rehearsed string quartet pausing mid-note. No pushing, no shoving, no tears before bedtime: a gentle ruffle of applause awaiting the victor. But the reality was more like a mosh pit, with thrash metal accompaniment. Most of those playing were too deafened by reverb to notice when the music stopped, and losers wore the imprints of winners' boots on their faces. Still and all, it sometimes happened that the most skilful players of the game found themselves outmanoeuvred. Peter Judd, for example, erstwhile Home Secretary and Prime Minister manqué, had retired into what passed for him as private life, his business interests – the official story going – having become incompatible with a political career. Dame Ingrid Tearney, former head of the Intelligence Service, had likewise surrendered the reins of office, in her case to take up a role at one of the heritage charities dedicated to preserving Britain's traditional verities: not so different in aim, perhaps, from her former life, but involving, it was to be hoped, less carnage. And there'd been other retirements too, from Westminster; none of them – it can't be repeated often enough – remotely connected with ongoing police investigations into the sexual abuse of children: on the contrary, all were dictated by loftier concerns – to allow fresh blood into the body politic; to make way for younger guns; to give elbow room to the distaff side, as one outgoing notable put it, his vocabulary indicating how firmly his finger was held to the pulse of contemporary life. So the music had stopped, the music had started again, and bruised and bloodied players were licking wounds and picking sides.

And as a result of all this change, of course, most things remained the same.

In a room some storeys below the breaking dawn, the lately appointed First Desk of Regent's Park was speaking.

'First, the big picture. This is new. Something we've never seen before. Crowds as targets, yes, that's always been the fear, whether it's football stadiums or market squares, but this takes terrorism to a whole new level. These kids were invited.'

Claude Whelan was a short man with a high forehead and a pinched way of speaking: words issued from him as if in perforated sheets; his full stops almost audible. But his manner was generally pleasant, and informality the key to his character. While suit and tie remained de rigueur among the Park's male aristocracy, Whelan turned up on his first day wearing a polo shirt under his jacket, 'and it was like,' one of the Queens of the Database breathlessly uttered, 'a fresh breeze had blown through the whole building.'

'We've always known we're defenceless against the individual extremist. Groups, yes, because groups have to communicate, but the lone wolf, who puts something together in his garage and sets it off in his local supermarket – when they're completely under the radar, we can't stop them. We all know that, deep down – everybody knows. But the advantage we've always had is that lone-wolf types tend to stick out. They tend to be odd, to arouse suspicion, and they tend – Hollywood notwithstanding – to be functionally moronic, so more of them plaster themselves over those same garages than ever make it as far as the shops.'

He was fifties, childless, but with a wife whose photograph adorned his desk, and whose image he was prone to introduce to visitors: 'Claire,' he'd say. 'Lost without her.' And sometimes with the words would come a furrowing of the brow, as if the phrase weren't a simple mechanical tribute but a glimpse into an alternative state of being, where the landscape was a wasteland across which he'd wander mapless, his footprints circling nowhere.

'This one appears to have been different. This one planned

his attack carefully, down to the hijacking of the Twitter feed on which the event was first mentioned. That feed belongs to one Richard Wyatt, twenty-one, a student at the LSE, who has a large number of followers owing to his role on the college's entertainments committee. The tweet appeared at 8.47 a.m. on Monday the 1st, the day before the event. It read, "Mob needed for dance duty", followed by three exclamation marks and a hashtag, "flashthemall". We are satisfied that Mr Wyatt was not responsible for its appearance.'

As for Whelan's office: that was more fodder for the gossips. His predecessor, Dame Ingrid Tearney – a sweet old lady who drank fresh blood for breakfast – had occupied a room in the grand, and grandly visible, section of Regent's Park whose windows overlooked the park itself, and whose walls were dappled in summer by the shadows of waving branches. But Whelan had decided that his place was among his staff, most of whom laboured away hidden from sunlight, if you didn't count the spring-effect bulbs. And so he'd taken one of the smaller offices on the hub, an open-hearted gesture which immediately endeared him to the junior spooks, but put everyone else's back up.

'By mid-afternoon, the flash-mob announcement had been re-tweeted over four hundred times and a page had appeared on Facebook. This was the work of one Craig Harrison, twenty-two, unemployed, of Bristol. We're almost certain he's innocent of anything more than an enthusiasm for public mischief, but the fact that he didn't actually attend the gathering sounded alarm bells. His story is that he couldn't afford the train fare to London, but nevertheless wanted to be part of what he describes as a "messin' bang". Once the penny had dropped that a bang is precisely what ensued, Mr Harrison was quick to add that this is a slang term for a party, and he was not admitting prior knowledge of the attack. Investigation has borne out his claim to poverty, but as we speak, Mr Harrison's interrogation has yet to be concluded.'

But a few ruffled feathers aside, things had gone smoothly so far. Claude Whelan's breezy entrance may have made papers rustle, even blown one or two from unregarded shelves and cast them fluttering to the floor, but it hadn't caused locks to fall apart, or twisted handles on doors best left shut. 'That chap Whelan,' a voice Down the Corridor had remarked, 'underneath it all, he's One of Us.'

Sometimes, that's all it takes.

'So what about the event itself? Our bomber can be reasonably assured of a crowd turning up, because his target audience will respond to the call of Twitter. That would have been enough for some of his ilk, but no, he wants an actual party to happen, because he knows that that will magnify the horror of the event a hundredfold. A thousand. Now, I'm not going to apologise for showing you the footage again, though God knows we've seen it often enough already, but the definition here's higher than we've managed so far. Here's what we have.' He raised a hand and clicked his fingers. 'There. Now we're looking at the CCTV film. The shopping mall, the kids arriving, the trio with the music machine.' He waved an imaginary baton at a point in the air behind him. 'And *stop*.'

He paused, as if allowing his invisible audience to soak in the invisible scene he'd freeze-framed.

'These three boys. We know from the radio chatter that at least one of Westacres' security guards, one Samit Chatterjee, guessed something was up when they appeared. Good for him, though sadly he was among the victims. The boys are Jacob Lee, Lucas Fairweather and Sanjay Singh. All sixteen, all at the same local school, inseparable friends according to reports. None with any known involvement with any extremist groups, none with any kind of police record . . . except for Fairweather.'

With a gesture, he aimed his imaginary baton at Fairweather, around whose non-existent image a black circle was no doubt appearing.

'Fairweather was cautioned last June after being arrested at a party that got out of hand. The party was in a house belonging to the parents of another schoolfriend. They were away, and their son's planned party ended up being tweeted about – initially by Fairweather – so the expected hundred-or-so guests morphed into a mob about two thousand strong. It made the national press, and brought the unfortunate parents storming back from holiday eager to press charges on ring-leaders. Fairweather, like I say, was one of them, and while charges weren't actually brought, he enjoyed fifteen minutes' notoriety. And that, we think, is what attracted the attention of our bomber.'

Another pause. Perhaps the film moved forward a few jerky frames. Perhaps it remained frozen on the image of three youths, one of them carrying a large black holdall; all of them – boys, bag, futures – now blasted into nothingness.

'On the same morning the first tweet went out, Lucas Fairweather received a text message from a pay-as-you-go mobile. It read, "Lucas, want some laughs?" He replied "Who U?" "Friend", the stranger replied. And so it went on. The full transcript is in your folders. By the thirty-eighth exchange, Lucas Fairweather and the stranger, who was calling himself Dwight Passenger, were the best of friends. And Passenger had persuaded Lucas to provide the music for the flash mob. Excuse me.'

Claude Whelan took a sip of water from the glass on the table in front of him. Then said:

'Another little taste of notoriety for Lucas Fairweather.

Presumably he enjoyed the attention. But it's clear he had no idea what he and his friends were stepping into.'

A wave of the hand to indicate that the film should roll again.

'So. The music starts, and everyone strips off their coats and starts dancing. In the corner of the frame, you can see our security guard, Mr Chatterjee, who, ah, stood down, as it were, once it seemed that nothing worse than an impromptu dance was in the offing. And for the next two and a half minutes, that's all it was. A flash mob. They were briefly popular in the mid-noughties, bit of a nuisance if you were caught in one, but just youthful high spirits really. If only this one was – well. We all know it wasn't. Because meanwhile, *this* man appears, at 3.04 p.m., two and a half minutes after the music starts. And while everyone around him is dancing, he unbuttons his overcoat and—'

A phone rang.

'Christ. Sorry, Claude. *Sorry sorry sorry*. Really better take this.'

'That's okay, Diana.'

'Really sorry. I'll just be a mo.'

And Diana Taverner slipped out of the meeting room, mobile in hand, leaving Claude Whelan on his own, mentally rehearsing the remainder of the talk he'd be delivering to the PM's COBRA session in just over an hour's time.

It was a mostly one-sided conversation that took place in the corridor: Taverner – Lady Di, though not to her face – listening, nodding, asking questions. There were no windows here, but a set of glass doors offered a reflection, and she adjusted the fit of her jacket as she listened, brushed lint from her lapel. Her hair was chestnut brown, naturally curly, shorter than ever. The odd grey stranger had been making an appearance, and she found them easier to weed out of a neater crop. Just one of life's many battles.

The grey hairs, she assumed, were not unconnected to the career-frightening developments of last year, when the internal power struggles common to any high-stakes operation had accidentally triggered a small war in one of the Service's off-post facilities west of the city. A lot of the shooting had taken place underground, and the area itself was notable mainly for the number of residents who jumped under trains leaving Paddington, but still: you can only let so many bodies fall before someone notices the thumps. It was the excuse several of the big chins on the Limitations Committee had been waiting for; revenge for having seen one of their own ground into mince, after being caught with his hand in the till. Criminal, yes; treasonous even, if you wanted to split hairs, but the chap was stripped of his *knighthood* for pity's sake. Could hardly show his face in his club once he'd served his three months, less time off for having been at Harrow.

So the bloodbath out near Hayes was mirrored by a more serious one in Regent's Park, and while Diana Taverner had survived the cull, it had been a close-run thing. Favours had been called in, and blackmail threats made good on. It was a rocky road to tread – she knew where a lot of bodies were buried, but, having put a number of them in the ground herself, it wasn't wise to draw attention to the fact – and her long-held ambition of settling behind First Desk was one of the bargaining chips she'd had to surrender, or at least pretend to. So now she was back where it was starting to feel like she'd always been: second-desking Ops, and offering ungrudging, whole-hearted support to the interloper who'd stolen her job. This time round, one Claude Whelan, from over the river, where the intelligence weasels lived.

She said, 'Okay, Emma. It's a mess we don't need, but let's

not go to panic stations. If it's not on Twitter, the press'll never know it happened. So get the local Noddies on board. They can beat the bushes or the shrubbery or whatever they have down there until the old man turns up. Meanwhile, have one of our legals put the word to whoever's in charge. Let them know it's a security issue, and that Cartwright's ours when they have him. Stress that it's unrelated to the Westacres event. That'll make them think it is related, and be more likely to cooperate. Update me in an hour. And try not to step on anyone's toes.'

She ended the call.

The weasels from over the river dealt in data rather than human assets: feeding intelligence into gaming programs to assess real-world outcomes; running long-distance psychiatric evaluations of foreign notables; stress-testing domestic security systems for loopholes, all of which meant they spent more time with a mouse in their hands than they did interacting with humans, so it was no surprise they were all fucking weird. Whelan, though, seemed level-headed and socialised, which made him either an outlier or a born politician, and for the time being she was his go-to-guy; the only lifebelt he'd find in the notoriously treacherous waters of Regent's Park.

She stepped back into the room. 'Sorry about that.'

Whelan was gathering his papers into a pile, slipping them inside a cardboard folder. 'Serious?'

'Not Westacres. A former agent – David Cartwright?'

'Of course. I never met him, but I know who you mean.'

'Yes, well, there's been an incident at his home. It looks like the old boy shot an intruder and disappeared.'

'Good lord!'

'It gets worse. The "intruder" was his grandson, who's a current member of the Service. Bit of a mess all round. But Emma Flyte's on the scene. She'll lock it down.'

'The grandson. Is he – dead?'

'Very. Do you want to run through the rest of your debrief?'

Her switchblade turn took him aback. 'Not sure we have time. Any feedback so far?'

Taverner said, 'You're going to have to speed it up, especially at the beginning. Everybody knows it was a damn tragedy, and the PM gets his rhetoric from his scriptwriters. All he wants from you is fresh info he can drip-feed the media, plus something he can withhold for later dissemination when it all dries up. Which it will. This is going to be long, hard and cold. You want to get that across too, though nobody will listen. They'll still expect answers tomorrow.'

'Okay. Anything else?'

'They'll want to know why nobody at Westacres was prepared for the flash mob. It wasn't the world's best-kept secret.'

'No, but Westacres' security staff aren't GCHQ. They look for shoplifters, they're not scanning the internet for potential threat. As for our own surveillance, if it crossed our radar, or Cheltenham's, it wouldn't have held their attention more than a minute. Why would it? It's a student prank, not an IS plot.'

'Fine, but put that up front. Make it part of the narrative, not an excuse we've come up with afterwards. And don't worry about Cheltenham, either. If GCHQ fuck up, that's their problem.'

'This is our united front?'

'This is zero-sum politics. If GCHQ gain influence, we lose it. That simple. You've got the fact sheet on Robert Winters?'

Robert Winters was the 3.04 man. The man who'd turned up at the Westacres flash mob and blown the children to Kingdom Come.

'Everything we know about him, yes.'

'Don't stray beyond that for now. Speculation isn't going to help.'

Whelan tucked the folder under his arm and said, 'Thank you, Diana. I appreciate your input.'

'Your first week. Not what you'd call a gentle introduction.'

'No, well. I wasn't expecting an easy ride.' He hesitated. 'I know you had, ah, ambitions of your own.'

She was shaking her head before he'd finished. 'Wasn't going to happen, Claude. I was too closely associated with Dame Ingrid and, well, once it turned out she was toxic . . .'

'The penalties of loyalty.'

'That's a kind way of putting it.'

Five minutes' prep would have taught him that she and Ingrid Tearney had been sworn enemies, and whatever else you might say about the weasels, they always did their prep.

As casually as he could manage, he said, 'Anything else, Diana, before I go see the headmaster? Anything you're not sharing?'

'Anything I find out, you'll know one minute later.'

'A minute's a long time in intelligence work.'

'Figure of speech, Claude. I won't hold anything back.'

'Good. Because like you said, it's a zero-sum game. Anyone not for me is against me. I hope we're clear on that.'

'As glass, Claude,' she said. 'Oh, one thing. Your autograph.' She'd left papers, neatly stapled, on the table, and she collected them now. 'Times three, I'm afraid. Everything in triplicate.'

'Some things never change. Do I need to read all this?'

'I ought to insist. You'll discover more about where we source our office supplies than you ever dreamed possible.'

'One of the things I love about this job. Its refreshingly traditional attitude towards red tape.' He skimmed the top set, signed all three on their final page, then left the room at a trot.

Lady Di watched him go, hugging the papers to her chest, then reached for her mobile and redialled Emma Flyte.

'Change of plan,' she said. 'I need to see you.'

5

THE COBRA MEETING WAS well underway when Slough House came to life, if the heavy scraping of its back door counted as life: Roderick Ho, his red puffa jacket shiny new, its cuffs and pocket edgings trimmed with hi-viz silver. His earbuds were mainlining chainsaw guitars to his brain when his phone vibrated with an incoming text. That'll be the ball and chain, he thought fondly. Checking I've not copped off with a City-bound babe on the Central line – women who worked in banking looked like they shopped at Victoria's Secret. No wonder the girlfriends of alpha-types like Roddy Ho got nervous around rush hour. His head still pounding to a jack-hammer beat he clicked to his messages, expecting to read 'Kim', but it was from Lamb. He read the text halfway up the first flight of stairs and said, 'Jesus.' And then he said 'Jesus' again, and then he stomped the rest of the way up to his office.

When Moira Tregorian arrived, he was on his back in River's room, fiddling around with cables. She tried to go past but the sight of a pair of legs protruding from beneath a desk defeated her, and she was back fifteen seconds later, coat still on.

'Is everything all right?'

He didn't reply.

'Is the network down?'

Because if the Secret Service's network was down, things were potentially serious. Maybe she ought to hide under a desk too.

But he still didn't reply, and it only then occurred to her she was looking at Roderick Ho's legs, not River Cartwright's – Cartwright a lot less likely to be wearing jeans with purple embroidery on the thighs – so chances were their owner's head was plugged into a Walkman, or whatever they were called. There was a strong argument that such devices should not be countenanced in the office, but it gave her the excuse to do what she did next, which was kick Ho on the soles of his feet.

Which didn't hurt, but at least made him bang his head on the desk.

'Ow! Christ!'

'Yes, well, there's no need for that.'

Ho pushed himself out and scowled up at her. 'What you do that for?' he shouted.

She tugged at her earlobe.

Ho pulled his buds out and said, 'What you do that for?' with equal petulance but less volume.

'Because you weren't responding to me.'

'Yeah, well, I didn't hear you.'

'Precisely.'

Ho rubbed his head. Talking to women frequently left him bruised. It would be easy to start thinking they were all mad and violent.

'So – what are you doing?'

'Swapping PCs. This one's better than the spare in my room.'

'But isn't it Cartwright's?'

'Oh, yeah, you haven't heard. He's dead.'

'He's *what*?'

'Lamb texted me. I'm kind of his right-hand,' Ho said. 'The

others, well. Not exactly your high-fliers. Let's face it, Shirley's a nutjob, and—'

'He's *dead*?'

Ho said, 'Lamb just identified his body.'

'Dear dear me,' Moira said faintly.

There was movement behind her as Louisa arrived. 'What's going on?'

'I'm just swapping—'

'Young Cartwright's dead,' Moira told her.

'No.'

'Mr Lamb just texted—'

'No.'

'I'm sorry, but—'

'No.'

Louisa left the room and entered her own office, closing the door behind her as softly as a breeze.

'Oh dear. I didn't handle that very well.'

'Handle what?' said Ho.

J. K. Coe arrived, half invisible in his hoodie. If he registered the presence of intruders, he didn't say; just slumped at his desk and booted up. Already his fingers were tapping away, caressing invisible keys.

'Did you hear?' Moira Tregorian said.

She had as much luck with him as she'd had with Ho.

'Is everyone deaf?'

Something about her body language, the warning vibes, got through to Coe. He pulled his earbuds out and looked her way from the safety of his hood.

'It's Cartwright. River. Lamb's texted to say he's . . .'

It occurred to her she wasn't making the best job of breaking the news, but on the other hand, there were only so many ways of finishing this particular sentence.

'. . . dead.'

Coe stared for a moment or two, then looked at Ho, who had temporarily abandoned his plan of cannibalising River's kit.

'It was me Lamb texted,' he said, to underline who was whose right hand.

Coe stared a bit longer, then said, 'Uh-huh.'

This was the longest speech either had heard him deliver.

More noise from downstairs: Shirley and Marcus, arriving together. And noise from the hallway too, as Louisa re-emerged from her office and came back into River's room, her eyes the colour of burnt matches. 'What the *hell* are you talking about?'

Ho said, 'I was just swapping—'

'Not you, dickhead. *Her.*'

'Who's a dickhead? Oh, him,' Shirley said from the doorway.

'Not a fucking word. Anyone.' This included everyone in Louisa's orbit: Marcus too, on the landing with Shirley. 'Except you.' This to Moira. 'What. The *fuck*. Are you talking about?'

'I really don't appreciate—'

'You have to understand this. You really have to understand this. I am *this close* to wringing your fucking—'

'Louisa.'

It was Marcus, his hand on her elbow.

'Louisa, you need to cool it. Just sit down, yeah?'

And she wanted to scream that she'd sit down when she was good and ready and what the hell did he know about it, anyway? Because he hadn't been there when this bitch had said what she'd said, that River was dead – how could he be dead? But she didn't say any of that because she was shaking too hard. It was as if she'd fallen from a tree into cold, cold water, and would never be warm again.

A chair was being scraped across a floor, and that was Shirley. Two arms were lowering her into it, and that was Marcus.

Who said, 'And now I really need to know what the hell is going down.'

There are only so many ways of ringing a doorbell: the brief dash delivered by the confident; the short dot of those who don't want to disturb you; and the gonna-lean-on-this-thing-till-it-opens approach favoured by bailiffs, ex-husbands and anyone else unused to a friendly welcome.

'Jackson,' Catherine Standish said. 'What a surprise.'

This without a flicker of emotion.

Catherine lived in an art deco block in St John's Wood; a building with rounded corners and metal-framed windows, vaguely futuristic once, and charmingly retro thereafter. In the lobby the tiles were polished to an ice rink sheen, and the lift had an actual dial over it, indicating which floor it was on. She sometimes imagined a Hollywood musical breaking out there: some business with a bellhop; a haughty matron with fur coat and lorgnette; and Fred twirling Ginger in and out of the lift while its doors slid open and shut: yes/no, yes/no ... Not prone to whimsy, Catherine occasionally indulged herself when it came to where she lived. There'd been a time when a future in a series of shop doorways had not seemed implausible. A one-bedder in St John's Wood was a safe haven in anybody's book.

Though not enough so to keep Jackson Lamb at bay.

'Nice welcome,' he said. 'You might have put some feeling into it.'

'I did. Just not the kind you were hoping for.'

'Going to invite me in?'

'No.'

'Mind if I come in anyway?'

She stepped aside.

The last time Lamb had been here, it had been the middle of the night, and the slow horses were being rounded up.

Today it was morning, and she was dressed . . . All things considered, his appearance wasn't much of a shock. Some fates you escape. Others keep turning up regardless.

While most guests would hover in the hallway, awaiting further invitation, Lamb barrelled through to her sitting room. 'How about a drink?'

'At this hour?'

'I meant tea,' he said, with an air of shocked innocence.

'Of course you did. Why are you here?'

'Can't drop in on an old friend?'

'Possibly. But why are you here?'

'I've just come from identifying River Cartwright's body,' he said. 'And I wanted you to be the first to know.'

'River . . .'

'His body.'

'How . . .?'

'Two bullets to the head. Face, actually. Doesn't leave much, you'll not be surprised to learn.'

Catherine turned away to look out of the window onto the street below. There was little happening there. A man walking a dog, a cockapoo or labradoodle or something, one of those breeds that didn't exist one day and was everywhere the next: all bright eyes and floppy tongues. She watched him wait for it to do its business by the side of the road, then scoop its mess into a plastic bag. If he leaves it hanging off the hedge, she thought, I'll open the window and throw something – the iron, the coffee table. But he didn't. He walked on, bag swinging by his side. Sometimes people behaved like they were supposed to. Quite a lot of the time, probably. But it was easy to start believing otherwise, the line of work she'd been in.

She thought: River Cartwright, and tried to imagine how she must be feeling now, having just been told he'd been killed, two bullets to the face. But she couldn't reach whatever feelings this information might be supposed to deliver. She could only watch the man and his dog continue up the quiet road, until they were lost to sight.

'You're not going to respond?'

'This is me, responding,' she said. 'Where did it happen?'

'In a bathroom. Just like old times, eh?'

Because she'd found her former boss, Charles Partner, dead in his bathroom, gun in his hand.

Bullet in his head.

Just the one. Few suicides took two.

'Have you told the others?'

'Sent Ho a text. I expect he'll have spread it round by now.'

Despite herself, despite all she knew of him, this time she was actually shocked. 'You sent a *text*?'

'You thought I'd tweet it? Jesus, Standish. A man died.'

'You know what that'll do to Louisa?'

'That's why I sent it to Ho. You think you invented tact?'

He was holding a cigarette now. It had appeared in his hand just like that: no sign of a packet.

She shook her head; at the cigarette, at him, at the way he broke news, which was the way he broke everything else: with a certain grim joy at watching it shatter.

He said, 'You didn't ask whose bathroom.'

'Whose bathroom?'

He wagged a finger. 'Sorry. Need to know.'

'You're enjoying this.'

'I'd enjoy it more with a cup of tea. I've been up since sparrowfart.'

'For God's sake—'

'Are you alone? I should have asked.'

She said, 'Do I look like I have company?'

'Had to ask. Hard to shake off a reputation, isn't it?'

'You'd know. Everyone you've ever met has you pegged as

84

an utter bastard. Now was there anything else? Because you're free to leave any time.'

'His grandfather's.'

'. . . What?'

'It was his grandfather's bathroom. The O.B.?'

'That's what River called him,' Catherine agreed. 'I'm not sure you have the right.'

Lamb said, 'Ah, don't you hate it when people have private jokes? It's like everyone's a fucking spy.' He tucked the cigarette behind his ear. 'You haven't asked who yet.'

'Haven't asked who what?'

'Who shot River,' Lamb said. 'Are you just out of bed? You're not exactly firing on all cylinders.'

'I'm still reeling from your presence,' she told him. 'I'd feel a lot happier if you weren't here.'

'Then I'll go.'

'Thank you.'

'Just as soon as I've had that cup of tea,' he said, and bared yellow teeth.

A barge was puttering down the Thames, rubbish piled high in its middle, and there were seagulls all over it, a great boiling mass of them, arguing and scrapping for riches. Earth has not anything to show more fair. For Diana Taverner, it looked like politics as usual. She was waiting by a railing near the Globe, on a stretch of pavement which fell neatly into a CCTV blind spot, so highly prized by those aware of the fact. It was before ten, and while once pedestrian traffic would have been at a lull, all decent citizens at their jobs, now there were streams of people passing, a good proportion of them plugged into smartphone and tablet, working on the move. From a distance, there'd be little to choose between the upbeat rat-a-tat of their mobile conferencing and the screaming of the gulls, which was heading downriver now, and might make it as far as the sea. She checked her watch: two minutes to the hour. And then Emma Flyte was there, one gloved hand on the railing, an immaculate profile taking in the view: the City, draped in the beauty of the morning.

A garment unsuitable for the season, today being wet and cold.

'News?' asked Diana.

Flyte said, 'He's still missing.'

'Wonderful. How old is he, ninety?'

'Not quite.' She paused. 'Someone's reported a stolen car. About a mile away.'

'You think he could walk a mile?'

'I'm told he's an old bastard,' said Flyte. 'They tend to be tough.'

'Who said that?'

'Jackson Lamb.'

'Ah.' For some reason, whenever Lamb came up in conversation Diana felt a reflexive need to smoke. 'The thing about Jackson is, he gives lessons to corkscrews. If he tells you the right time, it's because he's just stolen your watch.'

'I've heard similar said of you,' said Flyte in a level tone.

Taverner regarded her. Emma Flyte shouldn't be in the Service, she should be on a catwalk – that was the kind of judgement the Park's dinosaurs were prone to passing when a perfect ten hoved into view. But seriously: Christ. Watching her hail a taxi must be like seeing the flag drop on a chariot race. Which didn't earn her any latitude with Lady Di, but it was interesting to note she had spirit to go with her looks. 'Yes, but when it's said of me it's a compliment,' she said.

'I know.'

Okay, that was better.

She conquered the nicotine twitch, because it never did to

show weakness early in the game, and while Diana Taverner had been playing for a while now, the game always started anew when fresh blood joined. She had yet to work out whether Flyte was a team player, let alone whose team she was on. In part, that was what this meeting was for. And team player or not, Flyte had worked that much out for herself, because now she said, 'You didn't bring me here just for a heads-up on the Cartwright mess.'

'No.'

'So what is it you wanted?'

Which wasn't quite the tone Diana had been hoping for, but was at least a start. A pawn shifted out there, front and centre. She'd never learned the notation, but she knew what the object was: to hang, draw and quarter the opposition's king.

She said, 'Giti Rahman.'

'She's one of your girls.'

'On the hub, that's right.'

One of the brightest and the best, in fact; an appraisal she had confirmed a little less than three hours previously. Currently she was taking some crash-time in one of the Park's sleeping pods, or Diana hoped she was. Where she wanted Giti Rahman to be right now was dreamland, because the information she'd uncovered was such that the Park itself might come crashing round their ears if she was awake and broadcasting it.

Flyte said, 'What about her?'

'I need her taken care of.'

The barge, some hundred yards downriver now, let out a whistle; a curiously jaunty note for what was basically a waterborne dustbin. The gulls ballooned away, scrambled for purchase in the air, then renewed their cackling onslaught.

'I'm going to have to ask you to be a little more specific.'

'Good grief, what on earth do you think I'm asking?'

'I'm not about to speculate, Ms Taverner. I simply want to be sure that whatever it is, you have the authority to ask me to do it, and I'm going to be comfortable carrying it out.'

'How very extraordinary,' Diana said smoothly, though it was in fact useful to have the parameters clarified. 'I wasn't aware that I had to meet your standards when issuing instructions. I'd better check your terms and conditions. Better check my own, in fact. No, what I had in mind was a C&C.'

Collect and comfort, in the jargon. Meaning scoop up and isolate, and cause no harm doing so.

'If that doesn't offend your code of ethics, obviously,' she added.

Flyte wouldn't be drawn on that. 'Where?'

'The Dogs have their own safe house, I believe.'

'Several,' said Flyte. 'Where is she now?'

'In a sleeping pod. Wake her up, dust her down, and get her off the premises before you put the mufflers on. I don't want anyone knowing she's in your hands.'

'How long for?'

'Until I say otherwise.'

'I'll need overtime authorised.'

'The budget will stretch. One of the advantages of being on red alert.'

'Is this to do with Westacres?'

'I'm pretty sure I can issue orders without needing to explain my reasons,' Diana said. 'Unless you're about to tell me that's not so?'

'I'll have to check my terms and conditions,' Flyte said, without the faintest suggestion of a smile. 'But just out of curiosity, why are we here? And not in your office?'

'Not everything we do should be behind closed doors,' Diana said. 'All part of the new openness.'

'And nothing to do with keeping this particular order secret?'

'If you have something to say, Emma, why not say it? We'll both feel much better, I'm sure.'

'The Dogs aren't a private army,' Flyte said. 'Forgetting that brought Mr Whelan's predecessor grief.'

'Dame Ingrid retired with honours.'

'Only because the Tower's just for tourists these days.'

'Yes, well. I'm not saying there weren't those who felt she deserved a bullet in the head more than a whip-round when she left, but you can't read too much into that. She didn't have my gift for getting on with people.' This didn't produce a smile either. Diana sighed. 'All right, if it makes you feel more comfortable.' She produced the warrant she'd had Claude Whelan sign; the third sheet of a supposed triplicate. 'Good enough?'

Emma Flyte read it before responding. 'More than,' she said, and made to tuck it into her jacket pocket, but Diana extended a hand.

'This stays under wraps. You report only to me, and I report to Claude in confidence. That's the chain of command. Are we clear?'

'We are.'

'I do hope we're going to get along, Emma. You came to us with impeccable credentials.'

Flyte relinquished her grip on the warrant, and Diana made it disappear.

'Thank you.'

'I'll get onto it now,' Flyte said.

Diana Taverner watched her walk away, noticing the number of men, women too, who glanced her way as she passed. Not the greatest asset for a member of the Service, but it cut both ways. Who was going to believe that's what she was?

The seagulls' cries were ever more distant. You moved the rubbish somewhere else, and the racket followed it. It all seemed so simple, put like that. Complications only set in once you moved away from the metaphorical.

Free from observation she awarded herself a cigarette, willing her mind into a blank: no plots, no plans, no corkscrew machinations. Around her, the world carried on: business as usual on a January morning, and London recovering from the seismic shock of violence. In front of her, only the river: grey, and endlessly travelling elsewhere.

The kettle boiled and a switch flipped up to turn it off. When she was a child, electric kettles hadn't been invented, or not in her house – kettles back then had sat on the stove top, and when they boiled they whistled, so you'd come and turn the gas off. Nothing about the process had been automatic. Catherine was thinking these thoughts largely to stop herself thinking any others: it was dangerous having thoughts with Jackson Lamb standing behind you. He might not be able to read the contents of your head, but he could make you think he could. Sometimes, that was enough.

'If you want to grieve, go right ahead,' he told her. 'I'm here for you.'

'I can't begin to describe how that makes me feel.'

'You're welcome.'

She threw a teabag into a mug, and poured boiling water on top of it.

'Not having one yourself?'

'I've things to do, Jackson. When you've drunk that, you might want to leave.'

She left it on the counter and leaned against the wall, arms folded. Lamb studied the mug as if he'd never encountered one in quite this state before, and sniffed suspiciously. 'Got a spoon?'

Catherine slammed a drawer open and shut again, and all but threw one at him.

He said, 'It was his grandfather shot him.'

'I'm sure it was an accident.'

'You should be a lawyer. I'm halfway convinced already.' He mushed the teabag against the side of the mug with the spoon, then fished it out and dumped it on the counter. 'Milk in the fridge?'

'You don't take milk.'

'Maybe I've changed.'

'Chance would be a fine thing.' She tore a sheet of kitchen roll from a holder on the wall, and used it to scoop up the teabag. 'His grandfather wouldn't have shot him on purpose.'

'Twice?'

'Whatever.'

'You just lost the jury, Standish. Once could be an accident, I'll grant you. The second shot, right in the face? That takes carelessness to a whole new level.'

'He's an old man.' She dumped her little parcel in the bin. 'Confused, frightened. He probably thought River was an intruder.'

'That why he lured him up to the bathroom?'

'Why are you asking me?'

'Just walking you through the stages. You seem to have put denial behind you quite swiftly.'

'Well, you have a way of hustling people straight on to anger. Are you going to drink that?'

'It's still hot. Don't want to scald myself. Any biscuits?'

'No.'

He said, 'It's almost like you don't want me here. But what kind of boss would I be if I abandoned you when you've just had a shock? Anything might happen.'

'You're no kind of boss. I quit, remember? Or tried to. I've sent the same letter to HR three times.'

'I know. They keep forwarding it to me. Something about ratifying the paperwork?'

'For God's sake, Lamb, what's your problem? You spent years goading me, and I finally did what you wanted. Just sign the damn papers and let me get on with my life.'

'Just making sure you know your own mind. Think how I'd feel if you wound up full of regret and had a relapse. Wouldn't want that on my conscience, you getting all weepy and hitting the bottle.' He sipped his tea delicately. 'They say drunks are just looking for an excuse. I'm not blaming you. It's a disease.'

'Jackson—'

'Did you hear that?'

'What? No. Nothing.'

'Funny. Could've sworn I heard something.'

'There are people downstairs. It's a flat, remember? Jackson, you shouldn't be here, you should be at Slough House. You don't leave your crew on their own when one of them just died. Didn't you tell me that once?'

'It doesn't sound like the sort of thing I'd say.' He put the mug back on the counter, unfinished. 'That is quite possibly the worst cup of tea I've had anywhere. And I'm including France in that.'

'I'll be sure to pass your complaint to the management. Are you ready to go now?'

'Oh, I think my work here is done.' He looked round the kitchen for the first time, and in anyone else, that might have been the prelude to a compliment: it was a small, compact space radiating efficiency and homely comfort, everything where it ought to be. Even the calendar looked thoughtful: an Alma Tadema beauty, leaning on a block of marble. The little white squares underneath it, one for each day of the month, were all blank. 'And I can see you're busy.'

In the hallway, she opened her front door for him.

'No messages for the others?' Lamb said, pulling his gloves on. 'Words of condolence?'

'Tell them I'll be in touch.'

'Grand. And what about the Old Bastard?'

'. . . What about him?'

'You planning on keeping him in your bedroom forever, or do you want me to arrange for someone to come fetch him?'

After a moment or two Catherine closed the door, and Lamb peeled his gloves off again.

In Slough House all were still gathered in River Cartwright's office, which was presumably now J. K. Coe's office, though he'd made no attempt to stamp his authority upon it. Instead he was slumped in his habitual position, his hood obscuring his face. For once, though – perhaps as a mark of respect – his hands were at rest. His fingers twitched at intervals, but no improvised silences were being wrung from the woodwork.

Moira, somewhat hesitantly, had laid out what was known, which wasn't much. And then they had grown quiet, while on the street outside traffic swished past on a wet road, and the day, which should have been growing lighter, seemed to have stalled at a glum grey question mark.

'I feel bad now,' Shirley said at last.

'It's barely ten,' Marcus pointed out. 'You always feel bad before ten.'

'About what I said the other day, I mean. About him being replaced.'

'Yeah, well,' he said philosophically. 'Fuck it.'

'Was he married?' Moira asked.

Ho snorted.

'He had family,' said Louisa. 'His grandfather. He was going to see him last night. How can anyone get killed going to see their grandfather?'

'You can die swallowing a peanut,' Ho said.

Louisa stared at him.

'Not an allergy, I mean. Just, when it goes down wrong.'

Marcus said, 'Might be best if you don't speak again today.'

'Where's Lamb, anyway?' Louisa asked.

'Not here.'

'Well he fucking ought to be. One of his joes just got killed.'

'Are we sure he's dead?'

'Lamb identified the body,' Ho said.

'That doesn't fill me with confidence. Does it fill you with confidence?'

After a pause, Shirley said, 'Well, I wouldn't want him identifying mine.'

'Louisa,' Marcus began.

'No. This is not fucking happening. Not again.'

'Again?' Moira asked.

'This is not the time,' Marcus said.

'We are not sitting here remembering another dead colleague while that little bastard loots his computer.'

'Move away from the computer,' Marcus told Ho.

'It's not actually Cartwright's—'

'Like, now.'

Ho rolled his eyes – this was *exactly* the kind of thing he was always telling Kim, his girlfriend, about – but moved away from River's PC.

J. K. Coe said, 'What did Lamb write?'

The room fell silent.

'He speaks?' Shirley said. 'Nobody told me he speaks.'

'What do you mean?' Louisa said. 'Write what?'

'I think he means Lamb's text,' said Marcus. 'You mean Lamb's text?'

Coe nodded.

'He means Lamb's text,' Marcus confirmed.

'He sent it to me,' said Ho. 'What makes it your business?'

'I swear to God,' said Marcus, 'this is like being trapped in a special school. Ho? Read him the fucking text.'

Ho sighed theatrically and produced his smartphone. He'd just finished tapping the code in when Shirley snatched it from his hands.

'Hey, you can't—'

'Just did.'

Ho reached for her, but had a wise moment and refrained. She might be shorter than him but they both knew – everybody knew – she could rip him up like confetti if she wanted, and scatter him like rice.

She found his messages, and read the one from Lamb. 'Will be late in. Up all night identifying Cartwright's body.'

'Will be late?' Moira repeated. 'Well. That's a little . . .'

'You haven't met him yet, have you?'

Louisa said, '"Cartwright's"? He said "Cartwright's"?'

'Louisa—'

'He doesn't say the body's River's.'

'Who else could he mean?'

'River's grandfather. Maybe he means the O.B.'s body.'

'Why would Lamb be identifying the O.B.'s—'

'Because this is *not* fucking happening!'

'Louisa,' Marcus said gently. 'If he didn't mean River, then where is River? He'd be here by now if—'

'He was alive,' Moira blurted.

'Yeah, thanks,' Shirley muttered.

But J. K. Coe said, 'I think he probably is.'

6

L EAFLESS TREES ON THE skyline resembled plumes of smoke, and the sky itself was a grey dome, holding the world in place. Every so often dark flecks scarred its surface, which he thought were probably geese: maybe swans, but probably geese. It was doubtful that it mattered, but he'd slipped his moorings now, and even the most Lilliputian detail might help anchor him to solid ground.

River Cartwright, unobserved – he hoped – took the passport from his jacket pocket, and examined it again by the light from the train window.

'I knew he wasn't you,' his grandfather had said.

This would have seemed a small triumph, most days: that the O.B. knew who was and who wasn't his grandson. But the photo in the passport would have fooled a casual acquaintance, and given pause to some who knew him well. It wasn't just the physical similarity; it was the light in the eye, the tilt of the jaw. *You look at a camera like you don't trust it*, a girlfriend had told him once. *As if you're not saying 'Cheese' but 'Fancy your chances?'* This character had that same attitude.

Of course, the light in his eye was well and truly out now. Adam Lockhead.

A name that meant nothing to River.

Who had gone through Adam Lockhead's pockets, there

in the bathroom. The passport; a wallet holding a hundred or so euros; the return half of a Eurostar ticket. Some loose change, a pocket-sized packet of tissues, a chocolate bar wrapper and a crumpled café receipt. Nothing to indicate what he'd been after; nothing to explain why he had planned to kill David Cartwright, if that's what he'd intended.

To think otherwise was to allow the possibility that an innocent visitor had turned up to be shot in the head for his pains.

I'm worried someone'll come to the door and he'll shoot them.

In the city, when you heard something that sounded like a gunshot, you waited to hear it a second time, and when you didn't, you put it down to a backfiring car. River wasn't sure the same held true of the country. At any moment the quiet of the evening might be sawn in two by approaching sirens, and once that happened, they'd be sucked into the maw of Regent's Park: a security blanket dropped over them like a cover on a parrot's cage. No more talking, or not to each other.

'You're sure you've not seen him before?' he asked.

'I knew he wasn't you,' his grandfather repeated.

On the kitchen table lay the panic button the O.B. had been issued with, back when he could be trusted with such things. Lately, he'd activated it at least once that River was aware of. 'False alarm, false alarm,' he'd asserted, though River suspected he'd simply forgotten what it was for. Pressing it was a way of finding out. And since pressing it in these circumstances was pretty much exactly what it was designed for, River, crouching over the body of Adam Lockhead, had wondered whether it wasn't better to go with the flow . . . The Dogs would soon arrive. This kind of mess was what they were for: they cleaned, they disinfected, they made the bad stuff go away. But other words from earlier in the evening were haunting him: the possibility, the breath of an ancient rumour, that Regent's Park might have a habit of lowering a curtain over its former glories.

'Yeah, I wasn't actually suggesting they'd have him murdered,' Louisa had said. 'Though I can see you've put some thought into that.'

He put some more into it now.

A stranger, upstairs in his grandfather's house.

A stranger who looked enough like River to at least get through the door.

A stranger apparently running a bath.

A quick tug on an old man's heels . . .

'We have to go.'

'River?'

'Grandfather, it's not safe here.'

'Stoats?' his grandfather said, perking up.

'That's right. Stoats.'

'I'll need my wellingtons.'

He would, too, because they'd be leaving on foot. There was a car in the garage, a museum-quality Morris Minor, but River couldn't remember when it had last been on the road, and besides, it was best not to make your escape in the first vehicle they'd look for. This was one of the stupid roundabout thoughts he allowed to occupy his mind, throwing dust in the way of what needed to be done, while his grandfather clumped downstairs and rooted about for his boots . . . Don't think about it. Just do it.

He fired his grandfather's gun into what was left of Adam Lockhead's face.

Then he left his ID and phone in Lockhead's pocket, taking the passport, the wallet, the ticket, the litter.

Sitting on the train now, his heartbeat echoing the clatter of its wheels, he knew that that had been the moment when it happened – not sneaking away from the house; not leaving his grandfather in the empty bus shelter while he scouted the road for a stealable car; not the journey into London along dark roads, with every approaching headlight a threat, and one stomach-flipping episode when a police car had screamed up behind him, lights ablaze, only to go pelting past; not abandoning the car behind a West End supermarket and hopping on a night bus; not turning up at Catherine's door, because it was the only safe place he could think of – all of these had been stages on the journey, but putting the bullet into Adam Lockhead's corpse was when he had crossed the threshold. The point at which he'd stepped outside.

Spook Street was the phrase his grandfather used. When you lived on Spook Street you wrapped up tight: watched every word, guarded every secret. But there were other territories. Beyond Spook Street it was all joe country – even here, with the friendly French landscape pelting past at a hundred miles an hour, he was in joe country, and there was no telling what came next.

He had only the vaguest idea of where he was going; simply that he was walking back the cat, retracing a dead man's journey. But he knew this much: he wasn't sitting in Slough House, his energies being sucked away with every tick of the clock. He was alive, and alert to the game . . . The leafless trees on the skyline were plumes of smoke, and the sky itself a grey dome, holding the world in place. This was what joe country looked like. He tucked the passport out of sight and closed his eyes, but didn't sleep.

The old man was asleep, or looked it, only his head visible. His body might have been a fold in the duvet. Lamb regarded him from the doorway, his face expressionless. The fluttery noise was David Cartwright's breathing: regular, but not deep. The curtains were drawn but thin grey January light seeped in, painting everything it touched the same lonely colour: the fitted wardrobes each side of the bed, in which Catherine's many similar outfits doubtless hung, all those long-sleeved, high-necked, mid-calf dresses she favoured, like a governess's Sunday best; the dressing table on which a few tubs were arranged, moisturising creams and the like, and from a corner of whose mirror a pair of necklaces hung, one of black beads Lamb had never seen before, and the other a slim gold chain she often wore, and probably had sentimental associations; even the pair of scarves draped over a chair, both in dark colours, but one threaded with gold: they were all grey-toned in this light, washed of vitality, though nothing more so than the O.B.'s face, which might have been a deathmask, were it not for that fluttery breathing.

'Happy now?'

Lamb said, 'You know me. When am I not full of joie de fucking vivre?'

'So maybe you could leave my bedroom now?'

'Hey!' he shouted suddenly.

'Jackson—!'

The old man's eyes opened, and any doubt that he'd been genuinely asleep vanished with the frightened yelp he made.

'Out! Now!' Her voice was taut with fury.

Lamb watched a moment longer as David Cartwright tried to raise his head from the pillow, his eyes soaking up the frightening unfamiliarity of his surroundings. Fingers crept out from the covers and took what grip they could. He looked like an illustration from a hundred-year-old ghost story.

And then Catherine Standish was pushing him out of the room, closing the door behind him; remaining inside with the old man. He could hear soothing noises, interrupted by an odd sort of squawking, as if she had a chicken with hiccups in there, rather than a former Service legend.

Lamb went into her sitting room. When she joined him, he was picking through the postcards on her mantelpiece, checking each for messages, though most were museum-bought.

'Was that necessary?'

'I do apologise,' said Lamb. 'I was forgetting he was a vulnerable old man.'

'Yes, well—'

'I was thinking more of him being a nasty old spook with more blood on his hands than you've had gin for breakfast. When did they get here?'

'"They"?'

'This is me you're talking to. River brought him, right?'

'I thought you'd identified River's body.'

'Wishful thinking,' said Lamb. 'Though to be fair, he looked like River might, if you put two bullets in his head. Which could yet happen, the aggravation he's causing.'

'They got here about four.'

'He's had more sleep than I've had, then.' Without warning, Lamb collapsed onto the two-seater sofa, which was stronger than it looked and didn't buckle. 'What was their story?'

'They didn't really have one.'

'And you took them in?'

'River wouldn't have come if he'd had anywhere else to go.'

'The last refuge of the desperate,' said Lamb. 'Yeah, I can see how you fill that role.' He was holding a cigarette, of course: it had appeared in his hand by magic. He slotted it into his mouth and sucked it thoughtfully. 'And now he's off on a marvellous adventure.'

'What's going on, Jackson?'

'He didn't tell you?'

'He arrived in the middle of the night, asked me to look after his grandfather, and left.'

'Always mistaking drama for style, that boy. You gonna keep hovering like that? Sit down. Make yourself at home.'

She simmered, but sat anyway: not on the sofa. She said, 'He was in a state. Still is. Confused, not sure what's happening. He called me Rose. Did he really shoot someone in his bathroom? Or was that just you playing games?'

'You have a nasty mind, Standish. It's wasted on this.' He indicated their surroundings: a calm and quiet room, with books on the shelves. 'And yes, he did.'

'Twice?'

'Good question. Know what? I don't think so. Old, confused man, like you said, I think once he's shot someone, first thing he's gonna do is drop the gun. I hate ageism, as you know, but old people are pretty useless.'

'I can't tell you how much I haven't missed your observations.'

'That's good, because I have more.'

He paused, and his eyes shifted focus; he was looking at something that wasn't there. Catherine recognised the signs – as familiar to her as the way he deliberately misheard her comment – and knew he was about to spin a story from whatever fragments he'd so far collected.

'I think someone came to kill the old man,' he said, 'and didn't realise he's a dangerous old fuck. So whoever it is ends up dead in the bathroom, and that's when young Cartwright arrives for one of his cosy at-home evenings with Grandpa. Anyone else, anyone sane, you know what they'd have done at this point? They'd have called it in. Not like the old man's gonna get done for murder, no, what'd happen next is the Dogs arrive, followed by the cleaners, and twenty minutes later it's like it never happened. But that's not what young Cartwright does. Why's that?'

'You're about to tell me.'

'Well, he's a dick, obviously. We have to factor that in. But assuming he's got an actual motive, beyond his tireless desire to play Double-oh Seven, it's probably that he thinks calling the Dogs will make things worse.'

'Seriously?' She was putting it together even as he spoke. 'He thinks it was a Service hit?'

'Well, it was a fuck-up. That's circumstantial evidence right there. And if the old bastard's actually gone loopy, the kid might have a point.'

'What, he was worried the Park has a . . . what have I heard it called, an enhanced retirement package?' she said. 'That never really happened.'

'Are you asking or telling?'

'I'm saying I don't believe it ever did.'

'And I'm the one gets called a wide-eyed idealist. But what you believe's neither here nor there, because it's what River thinks that matters in the circs. And he thinks if he calls the Dogs, they might just finish the job. So he puts another bullet into Mystery Man's face—'

'He *what*?'

'See? I knew you were interested.' Lamb removed the cigarette from his mouth and tucked it behind his ear. Then he fished another from his pocket and plugged it into his mouth. It was possible that he wasn't aware of either of these actions. 'He does that because while Mystery Man might pass for River, he's hardly an identical twin.' He pressed a finger to his upper lip. 'That mole of his, looks like he's been eating crap and missed a bit? Mystery Man doesn't have one, and that's going to be noticed.'

'So he's just muddying the waters.'

'It's what a joe would do,' Lamb said grudgingly.

'It wouldn't buy him more than twenty minutes.'

'He got this far, didn't he? And then further. Where'd he head off to, by the way?'

'He wouldn't tell me.'

Lamb said, 'See, I get told by HR all the time that I never give you lot training, and you know what I always say?'

'You tell them to fuck off.'

'Well, yeah, I tell them to fuck off, but you know what I say after that? I tell them I lead by example. Case in point. If I don't like a question, I answer a different one. Like you did just there.' He gave a complacent smile, and the cigarette dropped from his mouth. He caught it between two fingers. 'I didn't ask whether River told you where he was going, I just asked where he was going.'

'What makes you think I know?'

'Because you're not a great liar. You're good, but you're not great.'

'Excuse me? When did I lie?'

'When you pretended to believe me when I told you he was dead.'

'. . . So?'

'So you know he's somewhere far enough away that I couldn't have got there and back in the time it took me to turn up at your door. Jesus, Standish. It's not rocket science.'

'Not for someone with your twisted thought processes,' she conceded.

They sat in silence and stared at each other, as if this were just another phase of a game they'd both been playing for a long long time.

At last she said, 'He hung his jacket over a chair. I went through his pockets while he was getting his grandfather settled.'

'That must have brought back memories. Didn't you use to roll sailors, back in the day?'

She said, 'He had a passport. British. Alex Lockhead, no, Adam. Adam Lockhead. And a Eurostar ticket, and some euros.'

Lamb groaned. 'Oh, great. The idiot's gone to France.'

'On someone else's passport.' Catherine shook her head. 'I didn't think he'd get past border control.'

'Inside Europe? If the passport's not on a watch list, he could waltz through wearing falsies and a tutu. Though mind you, having a photo that actually resembles him might raise suspicion.' He sniffed. 'Mine makes me look fat.'

'Imagine.'

'So he's over the Channel. But France is a big place. What's he plan to do, stomp up and down the Champs Élysées, waving his arms in the air?'

'There was a café receipt.'

'Of course there was,' said Lamb.

There was a hold-up somewhere: a faulty traffic light, an accident, or – probably – a stretch of road being dug up, with a knock-on effect spreading ever outwards. He'd seen a sign near some roadworks not long ago: two hundred yards of plastic mesh and bollards, not a workman in sight, and a notice reading: WE ARE CURRENTLY EXAMINING THE WATERPIPES IN THIS AREA. AT TIMES, IT WILL LOOK LIKE NO WORK IS BEING DONE. Nothing like getting your alibi in first.

Claude Whelan chuckled, then abruptly stopped. Three days after the Westacres bomb, last thing he needed was a tabloid headline, INTELLIGENCE CHIEF ENJOYING A PRIVATE JOKE. And you never knew when a lens was trained on you, even in the back seat of your smoke-screened official limousine.

He was being driven back from Downing Street. The COBRA session had been long, and last night sleepless; he had ended up in the spare bed, to avoid disturbing Claire. His first COBRA: no wonder he'd been nervous. Nobody had to tell Whelan his elevation had been unexpected. Dame Ingrid Tearney had cast a long shadow, and there were nooks and crannies of the Service still in darkness; after her – as he'd heard it called – *over-managed* tenure, there'd been an expectation that the mantle would pass back to Ops. After all, Charles Partner, the last head of the Service to have hailed from Operations, had overseen a successful, invigorating era that was looked on as a golden age. Had it been more widely known that he'd spent much of his career in the pay of the Soviets, this afterglow might have been tarnished somewhat; as it was, only his apparent suicide cast a retrospective taint of unreliability over his administration, and since this was ascribed by those not in the know to hidden trauma from his days as an Active, it had subsequently been decided that hands-on experience was a drawback, and Partner's successors to date had achieved office mostly by dint of managerial cunning. But following Tearney there'd been rumours of impending 'reform', and while the word had long lost any association with notions of improvement, attaching itself instead to cost-cutting, it had nevertheless been mooted that a new direction might be in the offing, and Ops in the ascendancy once more. Diana Taverner would have been the obvious choice. But Tearney, when she went, had gone with the grace of a scuttled supertanker: it had taken ages, it had been very messy, and it left few onlookers with clean feathers. Reform had thus subsided into the usual face-saving reshuffle, and Whelan, recently gonged after twenty years' service, and very much not associated with the Dame's doings, had been helicoptered in from across the river: a safe pair of hands.

And any secret doubts he harboured about this he'd kept in check this morning. Having laid out the facts rehearsed with Diana Taverner, he'd forged on into the territory that was Robert Winters – the man caught on camera detonating himself in a crowded shopping centre; a made-in-Britain version of all those headlines, which had shrunk over the years to a page-7 sidebar, about events in distant marketplaces. Nothing brought the meaning of 'suicide bomber' home quite so hard as familiar logos glimpsed through the rubble. So there he was – now you see him, now you don't – and they owed his name to the brilliant work of the boys and girls of Regent's Park, who had traced his passage backwards through the streets of London, courtesy of all that CCTV coverage the liberal tendency decried; as if putting a smashed clock together, they had reconstructed the minutes that had ticked down to zero, each stage of the journey rooting Robert Winters more fixedly into the life he had emerged from, and loosening him from the explosive manner in which he had ended it. Here he was in the underground, among crowds of the ignorantly blissful; here he was changing lines at Edgware Road, his blurry features by now more familiar to his watchers than those of their own children. And so it went, step after step, fragments of footage spliced together in reverse order, and if he was still a cipher at this point, assigned a random codename nobody paid attention to, because he was always *he* – *him* – they had known long before they pinned him down that this was the inevitable end of their quest. Nobody so hunted could remain uncaught. *We will have him* was the common refrain, and it became almost irrelevant that *he* was unhavable, that what was left of him could be weighed on a set of kitchen scales; no, *they would have him* – they would bring him back to life through digital magic, interrogate his spirit, undo his evil. And in the end they achieved this much: one final flicker of footage showing him emerging from a backpackers' hostel in Earl's Court, eighty-one minutes before the detonation in Westacres – stepping from a cheap and nasty dive into a grey damp January London; the skies barely distinguishable from the pavements; the pavements wet and littered; the litter pulped and mushy.

Two minutes later a net had dropped over it so thinly meshed an anorexic flea couldn't have slipped through.

The Earl's Court hostel was their crime scene, and it was here, in one of its grubby rooms, that *he* acquired an identity at last, for not only had Robert Winters registered under that name, he had left his passport under his pillow for them to find, alongside the pay-as-you-go he had used to text Lucas Fairweather; and – naturally – as much DNA as the boys and girls could wish for. An amateur error? Pointless to ask: when it comes to suicide bombers, everyone's a first-timer. No, this was a cock being snooked from the other side of death; Robert Winters nailing down his place in history before setting off to create his own sunset. It would be a far far better thing if they buried the passport with his victims and claimed never to have found it. Cheat the bastard of posthumous fame, and in doing so reveal his true nature: that whatever blaze of infamy he'd sought to depart the planet in, *he* had been at heart a nobody, a nothing; not worth the moment it took to learn his name.

Which, philosophically, might have been appealing, but wasn't an acceptable approach to take in a COBRA briefing.

'Robert Winters.'

'Yes, PM.'

(He liked to be addressed as 'PM'. Presumably because he still couldn't believe it himself.)

'A British citizen.'

'That's right, PM.'

'Not a convert . . .?'

Because that would have helped: if the Westacres bomber had been radicalised by conversion. But—

'There's nothing among his possessions to suggest that, no.'

'Pity.'

Claude Whelan couldn't, in good conscience, respond to this.

The PM, though, hadn't finished: 'And no evidence yet of any other extremist affiliation – animals, veggies, climate change?'

'Nothing. But it's early days. We'll have a full working dossier by noon, see what happens when we shake the tree.'

But the PM, for all his faults – and there was an actual list of these in circulation, courtesy of a cadre of his own back-benchers – wasn't always slow on the uptake. 'But if you have to look for it, it's not much of a cause, is it? Terrorists hang their flags out. No point perpetrating a massacre anonymously.'

This had troubled Whelan, too. Leaving a passport in open view was one thing, but he'd have expected a terrorist's bible, a video message, a wonderwall. *Look on my works and tremble* sort of thing. But for the moment, he wanted to emphasise progress.

'The hostel's a staging post. When we have his . . . lair, we'll find motive.'

He regretted *lair* as soon as it was out of his mouth.

Somebody asked, 'What about the bomb? Progress?'

'The HE element, the high explosive, we already knew was Semtex,' Whelan said. 'We've since determined it came from a batch stolen during a raid on a police armoury in Wakefield.'

'The police have Semtex now? When did that start?'

There was a slight ripple of laughter: not as much as if it had been the PM's quip.

Whelan said, 'It was part of a haul seized by HMRC, along with a quantity of firearms, off the Cumbrian coast in ninety-two. Believed at the time to be intended for an IRA splinter group. But there was no proof of that, and no arrests made.'

'Ninety-*two*?' This was the defence minister. 'That's ancient history.'

Whelan suspected he was trying to remember who'd been in government then; whether this was something that could be passed off on the other party. He said, 'The raid on the armoury took place three years later.'

'But it's so *old*.' This from the MoD again. 'It must have been highly unstable . . .'

And then lapsed into silence as it struck everyone present that worries about the explosive's efficacy were misplaced, to say the least.

The meeting had carried on for a further two hours, and had dissolved into rhetoric long before it came to a close. It was as if all those present felt the need to go on the record, even a sealed record, as to their personal disgust at the Westacres event, as if worried that it would otherwise be assumed that they approved. Well, in the internet age, that was probably true. On the other hand, the lengthy discussion of property damage, insurance hikes and likely impact on tourist spending wouldn't have endeared the assembled company to grieving parents, so it was, Whelan supposed, swings and roundabouts.

Meanwhile, he had work to do. By nightfall there'd be a dossier on Robert Winters this thick; they'd have every contact he'd ever made under a microscope, squirming like cancer cells. Walking back the cat, it was called: they'd walk this cat back to Robert Winters' cradle, and scorch the earth it trod on. By nightfall— and his phone rang, interrupting his reverie.

Taverner, the screen read.

The car gave a tumbril-like shudder.

'Diana.'

'Claude,' she said. 'Meeting go well?'

'Fine, yes, I—'

'Good. But we need to talk.'

And something in her tone made Whelan understand that by nightfall he'd have more problems than he had now.

Louisa had made coffee an hour previously, and still it sat, a film developing on its surface. Soon she would pour it away, and maybe refill the cup, and either drink it or not. Life was full of choices.

I think he probably is, J. K. Coe had said; meaning River; meaning alive.

Predictably, Marcus had become cross.

'Just so we're clear. If you've chosen now to speak just so you can mess with our heads, there'll be repercussions. Emphasis on the percussion.'

And Shirley had added: 'And take your bloody hood off. Or I'll do it for you.'

A short acquaintance informed the intelligent that Shirley's threats never stayed empty for long. Slowly, Coe had pulled his hood back, wincing at the light. His face was washed out, his stubble messy; his eyes pale and watery, as if he were staring from the bottom of a pool.

'Jesus. Do you eat? Or exercise? Or anything?'

'Can we stick to the point?' Louisa snapped. 'What did you mean, you don't think River's dead?'

Coe started to speak, but his voice was too thick. He cleared his throat and began again. 'Same as you. Lamb didn't say he is.'

'I just read Lamb's text, fool,' Shirley said. 'Identified his body? Duh?'

'I've met Lamb.'

'So?'

'So he doesn't mince words.'

Louisa said, 'He's right.'

'You want him to be right,' Marcus said. 'There's a difference.'

And maybe that's all it was, she thought now: she wanted Coe to be right because otherwise River was dead, same as Min, and she wasn't sure what she would do in that case – oddly, she found herself thinking of Catherine, wishing Catherine were here. There wouldn't be anything Catherine could do either, but it would make a difference all the same. Right this moment, Louisa was the only woman in Slough House, if you didn't count Shirley and Moira. Company would have been nice.

But Lamb hadn't said River was dead. He'd said he'd identified his body.

And this was exactly the kind of thing Lamb would do, Louisa reflected, just to fuck with them. Let them all think River was dead. Exactly the stupid bastard kind of thing he'd do, though it did leave other questions open, like where River was now, and whose body Lamb had identified.

She stood abruptly, took her cold coffee to the kitchen, poured it down the sink, then went into River's room. J. K. Coe was at his desk, apparently focused on his monitor, though she couldn't see his eyes for his hood. He was stroking the desk in front of him. He didn't look up at her entrance, or when she spoke.

'You were Psych Eval, weren't you?'

He didn't reply.

'Before whatever fuck-up brought you here.'

His fingers continued their caressing motion, and she realised he was plugged into an iPod. Perhaps he genuinely hadn't noticed she was here, she thought, which possibly made what she did next unfair: scooping a stapler from River's desk she lobbed it so it landed on Coe's keyboard. The actual one, not the imaginary one he was playing. The effect startled her as much as the stapler did him. He shot to his feet with a shout of rage, and stuff went flying: his iPod, the chair he'd been sitting on, a mug, its contents.

'*Fuck!*'

'Jesus! I didn't—'

'*Fuck!*'

His hood had fallen back, and he still looked washed-out,

messy and pale, but dangerous too, like a cornered rat. Something glinted in his fist. It disappeared almost immediately into the pocket of his hoodie.

'I shouldn't have done that,' Louisa said.

He seemed about to say something, but changed his mind. Collecting his iPod instead, he righted his chair and slumped back down. The mug remained on the floor, its contents joining the several years' worth of blood, sweat and tears soaked into the carpet. Mostly tears.

'I'm sorry.'

But what was that in your hand, she thought – was that a *knife*?

'What happened?'

This was Marcus, with – inevitably – Shirley in tow, chanting 'Fight! Fight!' under her breath.

'I dropped something,' Louisa said.

'Yeah, right.'

Shirley said, 'Did he talk again? Make him talk again.'

'Shut up, Shirl.' Marcus moved across the room, stooping to collect the fallen mug on his way. This he set in front of Coe before crouching until they were on the same level. 'Are we going to have a problem with you?'

Louisa said, 'It was my fault, Marcus.'

'I'm talking to Little Grey Riding Hood here,' Marcus said, without shifting his gaze. 'I'm wondering if he's planning on starting to act up. You know, loud squawks and flying cups. Shit like that.'

When Coe replied, it was in a near whisper. 'You gonna tie me to a chair and shave my toes off with a carving knife?'

'. . . Don't plan to.'

'Then I'm not scared of you.'

Marcus looked over his shoulder at the women. 'I think I found his boundaries.'

'Leave him alone, Marcus,' Louisa said wearily.

'Yeah, leave him alone, Marcus,' said Lamb.

Christ on a bike, Louisa thought. How did he do that? All he needed was a puff of smoke — and then a more urgent line of enquiry took shape, and she said, 'What happened to River? Is he dead?'

'Fine, thanks. Yourself?'

'Lamb—'

'I realise I may have extended my Christmas break a smidgin, but really, people, has any work gone on here at all?'

His Christmas break had started last September. Louisa could count on her fingers how many times she'd seen him since.

She said, 'Answer the question. River . . .'

'He's not dead.'

Instead of the relief she might have expected, a wave of tiredness came crashing upon her, as if she'd developed an adrenalin leak.

'As far as I know.'

'Then why . . .,' she began, and gave up. The why would emerge in its own good time, or not at all. Pointless to expect better from Jackson Lamb.

Who was surveying his slow horses now, the way a battery farmer might inspect his chickens.

'You.' He pointed at Shirley. 'You look different. Why?'

She patted the top of her head, where her buzz-cut was a softer, downy peach-fuzz. 'I'm letting it grow out.'

'Huh.'

'It makes me look like a young Mia Farrow,' she said. 'If she'd been dark instead of blonde.'

'Yeah,' said Lamb. 'And if she'd eaten Frank Sinatra instead of marrying him.'

Ho, who'd trotted into the room on Lamb's heels, said, 'And I've grown a beard.'

'Really? Where?'

'On my . . .' Ho's voice trailed away.

'This is almost too easy,' Lamb said. Then tilted his head to one side. 'You're different too, though. Not just the chin pubes. How come you look all shiny?'

'He's been showering,' Marcus said.

'Seriously?' Lamb looked at Ho, stunned. 'You've found a *girl*friend?'

'That's not what he—'

'Jesus. And this is an actual relationship? Not an abduction? Well well well.' Lamb dropped the appalled expression, and beamed round at the company. 'See what you can achieve with a little application?' He patted Ho on the shoulder. 'It does me good to see you rise above your disability.'

'I don't have a disability,' Ho said.

'That's the spirit. You should bring her into the office, introduce her.'

'Really?'

'Christ no, not really. It's not a fucking coffee bar. And speaking of the fairer sex, our new lady friend settling in? Where is she, anyway?'

Marcus said, 'Did you just call her a lady?'

'Of course. Always be polite when referring to a woman of a certain age,' Lamb said. 'In case the mad old cow turns vicious.'

Louisa said, 'She's upstairs, I think. In Catherine's office.'

'Now, now. It's not Standish's office any more. Remember?'

'That why you've been sulking?'

He ignored that; focused instead on J. K. Coe, who had clasped his hands on his desktop, as if to make sure they wouldn't betray him. Lamb studied him for a moment or two, then said, 'Does he speak?'

'You'd have to ask him.'

'Do you speak?'

Coe shrugged.

'What was he, raised by hamsters?'

'He was talking earlier,' Shirley said. 'You must've scared him.'

'Are you going to tell us what's going on?' Louisa said.

Now Lamb turned to her. 'What's your problem? You look like Santa shat on your sofa.'

'You let us think River was dead.'

'No, River let you think River was dead. I just didn't spoil the joke.'

'So what's he playing at? Whose body was it? And where?'

'Who am I, Google? I don't know whose body it was, and what Cartwright's playing at, my guess is secret agents. Why change the habit of a lifetime? As for where, it was out in the sticks, at his grandpa's. Why do old people live in the country, do you think? Do they start in the city and just get lost?'

'So somebody's dead, but not River?'

'How many more times?' Lamb rolled his eyes at Ho. 'Women, eh?'

'Yeah, I know what you—'

'Shut up,' Louisa told him.

'So where's River now?' asked Marcus.

'France.'

'Why?'

'That's where the killer came from.'

'We have a killer now?'

'The body in the bathroom,' Lamb said. 'I'm assuming he wasn't a plumber.'

'And he came to kill River?'

'Let's think that through carefully,' said Lamb. 'Using our brain.'

Louisa said, 'He means, whose house was it?'

'But River's often at his grandad's,' Marcus objected. 'If I was gonna hit River, I might follow him and do it there. Out of the city, empty roads, easy getaway.'

'I'm sure we've all spent hours planning the best way of killing River,' Lamb said. 'But our assassin came all the way from France, which sounds more like a job than a hobby. So let's assume he was after Grandpa. Business before pleasure and all that.'

'So who killed the killer?'

'One Cartwright or other. Does it matter?' Lamb slumped heavily into the nearest chair, which was the absent River's. 'What we actually need to know is what the hell's going on. And since young Cartwright's not here to tell us, and old Cartwright's lost the plot, we're going to have to work it out ourselves.'

Louisa said, 'Has he really lost it? The old man?'

'I've had more illuminating conversations with ducks,' Lamb assured her.

'River said he was worried about him.'

'Been confiding in you, has he, young Double-oh Three-and-a-Half?'

'Well, he—'

'But not enough to pick up a phone and let you know he's alive.' He shook his head sadly. 'Kids today, eh? Who'd have 'em?'

Shirley said, 'France is pretty big.'

'Excellent. We have a geographer. Any further insights?'

'All I meant was, River must have had more to go on than just that.'

'Yeah, well, you have a point, oddly enough. River found a train ticket in the dead man's pocket. Plus a café receipt . . . Christ. An actual fucking clue. He must think he's died and gone to heaven.' He looked at Louisa. 'Not literally. Keep your hair on.'

'Where was the café?' she said.

'God knows. Well, him and River.' Lamb pushed his chair back, and with surprising dexterity swung first one then the other foot onto River's desktop. Some unimportant, to Lamb, devastation ensued. 'So. We have what I believe our American chums call a sit-u-a-tion. An assassin with a British passport, but apparently based across the Channel, arrives to take a pop at David Cartwright, but trips over his dick in the process. River's gone haring off like the half-cocked idiot he is, taking the only clue with him, and the old bastard himself doesn't know what time of day it is, let alone why anyone might want to punch his ticket. Leaving us here, now. Any bright ideas? Don't be shy.'

'What do the Dogs say?' Marcus asked.

'The dogs say bow wow,' said Lamb. 'Ask me a harder one.'

'You know what I meant.'

'They're currently scouring Kent for a bewildered pensioner, so I imagine they have their hands full. But any moment now, if they haven't done already, they're going to work out that it's not River who's dead, and alter the course of their investigation. Actually,' he said, 'that might involve asking why I identified the body as River's. So don't be alarmed if we have unexpected company.'

'Why *did* you identify the body as River's?' Louisa said.

'Because, bizarre as it sounds, he's now a joe in the field. And you don't blow a joe's cover.' For a moment, it looked as if Lamb were about to say more, but he clamped his mouth shut instead. And then opened it again to repeat, more softly. 'You don't blow a joe's cover.'

'You could have told *us*.'

'Well, I could. But that would have involved trusting you not to do something dickheaded, like blog about it, or hire a skywriter.' He smiled kindly. 'I know you think of me as a father figure, and want to do well to impress me. But if you weren't all useless fuck-ups, you'd not be here in the first place.'

'You're telling us now,' Shirley pointed out.

'And that's because, like I just said, by now they'll have established that the body isn't River's. So it's become a little moot, see?' He paused. 'I said "a little moot", not a little toot. Don't go getting ideas.'

'Where's David Cartwright now?' Louisa asked.

Lamb hesitated, then said, 'He's safe.'

'There's something you're not telling us.'

He gave her a pitying look. 'If I were to tell you everything I know,' he said, 'you'd grow old and die before I was halfway done.' He shifted his feet suddenly, and a handleless mug that had sat on River's desk, seeing service as a penholder, fell to the floor and completed its useful life. He looked at Ho. 'You're very quiet.'

'What about—'

'No, don't spoil it.'

J. K. Coe spoke. 'We have two fixed points.'

A short silence followed, then Lamb said, 'Did someone fart? Only I heard a squeak, but I'm not smelling anything.'

'What's that mean?' Shirley said. 'Two fixed points?'

'Intended victim. Source of plot.' Coe was snapping his phrases off as soon as they were done, as if they were costing him pain.

Louisa said, 'Triangulation requires three points.'

'Clue's in the name,' Marcus pointed out.

Coe said, 'The old man must have a French connection. He can't tell us but someone will know.' The fingers on his right hand twitched. 'There'll be records.'

'I was wondering about returning him to the shop,' Lamb said. 'But it seems he has a working brain.' He paused. 'He's gonna fit in round here like a monkey at a dog show, but we'll worry about that later. You heard him – find the connection. What ties the old man to France? That'll be our third reference point. Any questions? Good. Off you fuck.'

'Just one,' Shirley said, when safely back in her own office. 'What's all this triangulation shit?'

7

THE BUS SPAT HIM out mid-morning in what would have been called the village square in England, though it wasn't square. More a large junction whose adjoining roads didn't quite meet, leaving this haphazard space of which a low wall carved off one corner, and the stacked tables of a café claimed another. A pair of trees swayed one side of the wall, and there were cars parked underneath, cars the bus was even now missing by inches as it swung away from the bus stop, which was marked as such only by a dog-eared timetable stapled to one of the tree trunks. It was raining softly, else those tables might have been in use, and the air had an edge to it, the unmistakable tang of a recent fire: not leaves or barbecue, something larger. This lent a false idea of warmth to the morning, and River tugged his jacket's zip higher before checking again the café receipt he'd taken from Adam Lockhead's pocket. *Le Ciel Bleu, Angevin.* And there it was, as advertised, behind those stacked tables; lights on, windows misted. Dim shapes moving about inside. The rectangular piece of card on the front door's frosted glass clearly said OPEN, or OUVERT, or would when he got close enough to read it.

But River stayed where he was for the moment, sheltering under the awning of the nearest shop, in whose window a gallimaufry of objects was on display: kitchen gadgets, children's toys, radios, watches, toiletries, brushes, packets of seed, boxes of cat litter, as if the idea was to just chuck a lot of bait around and see what the net dragged in. It reminded him of the market stalls on a street near Slough House, most of which had vanished when the foodies moved in. Random thoughts like this were the product of weariness. He surveyed the goods on offer while he accustomed himself to being here, middle of France, with only half a clue as to what he was doing.

It felt earlier than it was, or perhaps later – the light, anyway, seemed wrong, as if filtered through gauze – but then, his body clock was still set to yesterday. River hadn't had much sleep last night, and didn't have much money. Adam Lockhead's euros had paid for a train ticket from Paris to Poitiers and the bus ticket here from there, but weren't going to get him much further. They didn't have to, though. By lunchtime at the outside, the body at his grandfather's would have been, if not identified as Lockhead, at least unidentified as River Cartwright, which meant using his credit card wouldn't be giving away anything that wasn't already known, other than his location. They'd be looking at his known associates by then, trying to find the old man. With luck, by the time they got to Catherine, he'd have discovered what had brought an assassin from this quiet-seeming town on the River Anglin all the way to his grandfather's house in Kent. Because the last thing he wanted was for the O.B. to be in anyone's custody – not the Park's; not the police's – until he knew where the danger was coming from. Until then it was all joe country, and everyone a potential enemy.

Nobody had left or entered the café while he'd been standing here, and even if they had, what would he have done about it? It was time to take the next step. Collar up against the rain, he left the shelter of the awning, and made for Le Ciel Bleu.

★

She favoured park benches for off-the-books meetings – park benches or shady riverside stretches she was confident were unmonitored, but it was good to mix it up. So she'd told Claude to get out of the car and walk, to wait on the north-east corner of Oxford Circus. There were always crowds there, a good spot to check him for back-up. Maybe she didn't have field savvy – running Ops was a desk job – but you didn't have to know how to strip an engine to drive a car, and Claude Whelan had no clue how near she was until she put a hand on his elbow – almost.

He turned at the last moment. 'Diana.'

'Sorry about the cloak and dagger.'

'No you're not.'

'But some conversations are best kept out of the headlines.'

He was alone. His driver was still in a traffic jam, and tensions had to be running high before First Desk warranted an armed escort.

'What are you up to, Diana?'

'I want to catch a bus. This one will do.'

A bus ride up Oxford Street was a lengthy business at the best of times, and late morning wasn't one of them. She paid cash, so there'd be no Oyster-card record, and they sat upstairs at the back like teenagers, except they weren't texting. Whelan wore an amused expression, to cover whatever forebodings Taverner's phone call had summoned, and she allowed him a minute to get used to where they were, assuming correctly that he hadn't been on a bus in some time.

He'd noticed the flickering monitor on the lower deck. 'You do realise there's CCTV.'

'Which will be wiped tomorrow morning, provided no intervening event requires otherwise.'

'Well, let's try to make sure that doesn't happen. What's going on, Diana?'

'We have a problem, Claude.'

'We do?'

'Well, technically you do. It seems you've supplied misinfor-mation to a COBRA meeting. I don't think that counts as actual treason, but—'

'Misinformation?'

'—it almost certainly amounts to dereliction of duty, and not in a small way, either. How long have you been in office now?'

'How long have I – Diana, what's going on?'

'I'm just wondering if it's a record, that's all. Shortest-serving First Desk.'

He said, 'One of two things is going to happen. Either you start making sense, or I'm getting off this bus. And if it's the latter, then the moment I'm back at the Park, I'll be issuing a suspension notice. Have I made myself clear?'

'Crystal. What did you tell them about Winters?'

'You know what I told them about Winters. That we have his passport, for God's sake. And that we're ninety-nine per cent certain it's the genuine article, which means it's the key to unlocking everything else about him.'

'Yes, you see, that's rather the problem.'

'What is?'

'Robert Winters' passport.'

A bus going in the opposite direction jerked to a halt, and for a moment Whelan was looking past Taverner at another pair, another man and woman, sitting on a different top deck, heading somewhere else. Whoever they were – clandestine lovers, bored professionals – for a second he wished he were part of their conspiracy instead of this one. 'What are you saying?' He hissed the words, his vehemence causing the nearest other passenger, a man four seats in front, to turn.

'Oh, darling, don't be like that,' Diana cooed, and the man

smirked as he looked away. Lovers' spat. Well, sometimes they did.

It occurred to Whelan that one reason she wanted this conversation to take place on a bus was to lessen the possibility he might strangle her.

She said, 'Robert Winters – he's one of ours.'

'He was an *agent*?'

'Not exactly.'

'An asset? Jesus—'

'Not an asset either. He's what they call a cold body. You're familiar with the term?'

'Stop spinning this out. Tell me what you know.'

So she did.

This triangulation shit, the way Marcus explained it, was pretty basic, and had Shirley never attended a standard training session? She probably had a head cold that day, she explained. Since 'head cold' was accepted code for 'cocaine hangover', Marcus acknowledged the likelihood of this. So anyway, this triangulation shit:

'You've got two pieces of information, you can draw a straight line between them, no more. You've got three—'

'Okay, yeah, I get it.'

'You can pinpoint—'

'I said I get it, okay?'

'Now you get it. A minute ago you knew nothing.'

'Yeah, well, I remembered.'

Marcus felt like saying more, but there was no sense poking a stick at Shirley when you didn't need to. Any given day, the odds on her going postal were marginally in favour, and if she'd calmed down lately, that wasn't – Marcus figured – on account of anything in particular getting better, but just things not getting appreciably worse. Everyone drew a line somewhere.

And maybe the AFMs were helping. In fact, now he thought about it, it had been a while since she'd—

'*Christ* on a fucking *pedalo!*'

Okay. Maybe not that long.

He said, 'What now?'

'Password's expired.'

The Service network required a new password every month, for security reasons, though since you could only register a new password by first entering your old one, there were those who questioned the value of this procedure. Shirley was among their number.

'What you looking for?' Marcus asked, as Shirley went through the process of acquiring a new login, which took up some nineteen seconds of her precious bloody time, as she dubbed it under her breath.

'Phone number.'

'Bit early for Chicken Shack.'

'It's never too early for Chicken Shack,' said Shirley. 'Besides, fuck off. This is work.'

Logged in, she accessed the internal phone directory: everyone you might need to contact, at the Park and all other Service outposts – except Slough House. Nobody needed to contact Slough House.

Marcus was curious now, but didn't want to ask. Shirley took pity. 'Molly Doran,' she said.

'The wheelchair wonder?'

'Well, I think of her as the legless legend, but basically, yeah, we're thinking of the same person.'

'Impression I got, she was pretty sick of Slough House. Didn't River try to nick one of her files?'

'News flash. I'm not River.'

'You're a slow horse, though.'

Shirley shrugged. 'She's a walking history book. She'll either know something or not. And tell me or not. Only one way to find out.'

She dialled the number.

The café smelt of coffee and grilled cheese, and the faded pictures on the walls were of girls in rural costumes, with mill-and-cornfield backgrounds. A flyer for a circus had been taped to the door, alongside a coat stand heavy with damp clothing. To River's right was a glass-topped counter whose interior displayed pastries and sandwiches; most of the rest of the floorspace was occupied by chairs and tables, except for immediately in front of the counter, where a child's buggy was parked. Its usual occupant sat in a high chair, slapping the tray with one hand, tugging an ear with the other, and gurgling as his/her — its — mother spooned into it a confection which was luridly green enough to look radioactive, though presumably wasn't. The woman glanced River's way, registered that the buggy was blocking his passage, and turned back to her child. River, offering a Gallic shrug, shifted the buggy enough to get past, then sat at a table against the far wall.

It wasn't quite full. Mother and infant aside, there were only four others; a man in his fifties, with neat beard and pencil-thin eyebrows, reading a paper, and three young men sprawling round an array of cups and crumb-riddled plates and mobile phones. One watched River with open curiosity. The man with the newspaper didn't look his way at all. An amiable woman, a little plump, appeared through a bead-curtained door behind the counter, and plucked a notepad from a shelf as she made her way towards River, pausing en route to cluck over the infant.

'Monsieur?' she said.

River ordered coffee.

He sat with it for half an hour. The three young men left in a noisy dazzle of endearments for the waitress; two girls came in and chattered ceaselessly over toasted sandwiches. River's stomach growled, but he had barely enough cash for the coffee. The newspaper reader was brought another plate: an omelette, with mushrooms folded into it, judging by the smell. The coffee was good, but nowhere near filling. He examined the receipt once more: it was from five days previously, on the old side of the New Year, and Adam Lockhead had enjoyed two bottled beers and a steak-frites. The slip of paper had been crumpled into a ball, a forgotten piece of pocket detritus rather than deliberately retained for expenses; the distinction, in River's mind, meaning that trips to Le Ciel Bleu had been regular, ordinary experiences for Adam Lockhead. Meaning that people here would recognise him; would know where he was staying, who his associates were . . . That, anyway, was what River had been telling himself for twelve hours or more. But it was starting to feel tenuous, here at this end of the argument, and not for the first time in his life he wondered whether his initial instincts might have borne more rigorous inspection.

And would he have got this far, if not for that physical similarity, that coincidence of height and colouring? But then, he told himself, how many different colours did pairs of eyes come in? How many shades of fair did hair possess? Besides, the coincidence wasn't that he looked like Lockhead; it was that Lockhead looked like him. That was the only reason Lockhead had managed to talk himself through the O.B.'s door; was maybe – probably – the reason he'd been chosen for the job in the first place.

The glances the waitress was giving him were gathering force. He'd possibly outstayed a single cup of coffee.

River nodded at her, and she was on him like a flash.

'*Madame*,' he began, then noticed she wore no wedding ring, but it was too late to back down now. '*Je cherche un ami, un gens Anglais?*'

She waited.

'*Il . . .*' His French dried up. Looks like me? Resembles me? He found he was waving an open palm in front of his own face, illustrating a sentence he couldn't create. Bond never had this trouble. Bond, though, would have been talking to a waitress twenty years younger, with inviting cleavage.

She was speaking now, words that included 'man' and 'breakfast' and might have been a response to his half-arsed enquiries, or just a pithy French saw about the most important meal of the day.

When she paused, he said, '*Il habite pres d'ici, je pense.*'

His tense was all wrong, but that didn't matter. Even if his French were perfect, he'd not be getting into Lockhead's extinct status. But either way, the look on the woman's face was one of total incomprehension.

A sudden rattle of syllables to his right interrupted the moment.

It was the bearded man, who had lain his paper down and was speaking to the waitress. There are few things more galling than to have one's efforts at a foreign language require translation into the same, but it seemed to have the desired effect, for the woman simply left a saucer in front of River, on which lay the bill for his coffee, and retreated behind the counter.

'You are looking for a friend, I think,' the man said, in English.

'Yes,' River said, before the possible ambiguity of this approach had sunk in. 'He—'

'He looks like you, yes?'

'You know him?'

'An Englishman?'

'Yes.'

The man shook his head. 'Not English.'

'You're sure?'

'He is a local. Bertrand, I think. Bertrand something.'

'And he comes in here?'

'I have seen him in here.' The man pointed to his eyes, then at River's. 'You share — you have the same expression. Am I saying that correctly?'

'Uh-huh. I mean yes. *Oui*. Do you know where he lives?'

'He is a friend? Or a relative?'

'A cousin,' River said.

'But you do not know his name. Or his nationality. Or where he lives.'

'We're not a close family,' River said.

'Évidemment. I think he was from Les Arbres.'

'Is that another village?'

'A house. A big one. Not so far away.'

'Is it easy to find?'

'Well,' his new friend said. 'Yes and no.'

'I remember you, yes,' Molly Doran told Shirley Dander over the phone.

'That's good.'

'How very confident of you to think so.'

'. . . Sorry?'

'Don't mention it. What is it you're after this time, Ms Dander? Or rather, what is it Jackson's after? I assume you're calling on his behalf.'

'I'm more what you'd call using my initiative.'

'What a nice way of putting it. So exploiting my expertise becomes your achievement, is that how it works?'

Shirley suppressed a sigh. Suppressing sighs was actually quite high on the list of personal goals drawn up at her AFM sessions, so it was like she was ticking a box at the same time. 'How are things with you?' she asked, remembering another target: be aware of other people's issues.

This attempt at heightened awareness met with stupefied silence.

Molly Doran wasn't quite a Service legend, but she was heading that way. Molly ran personnel records at the Park: she trundled round in a bright-red wheelchair on account of having lost her legs way back at the dawn of time, and knew everything, which made her a useful source of information. Every year, she gave a lecture on the Service's research resources to baby spooks: a one-off class which had been known to reduce the intake's hardest customer to a bubbling jelly. Even Lamb was rumoured to be impressed. Shirley, in fact, had heard a myth that Lamb and Molly shared history, which was kind of mind-numbing.

And now, Shirley's polite enquiry comprehensively ignored, it was Molly's turn to speak. 'I gather Mr Coe is now among your number.'

It took Shirley a moment to put the name Coe together with the hooded menace upstairs. 'You know him?'

'I seem to recall sending him Jackson's way once.' She paused. 'If I'd known he was to end up there permanently, I might not have done that.'

A semblance of regret, there, or a passable pretence of the same. Shirley decided to treat this as an opening. 'You know old David Cartwright?' she asked.

The brief silence that greeted this was precisely the amount of time it took to roll a pair of eyes. 'I may have come across the name.'

'Yeah, well, someone tried to whack him last night.'

This next silence was rather more profound.

'Someone . . .'

'Whack him, yeah. Apparently.' She gave Marcus a thumbs-up. This was going well now.

'And that's the reason you're calling.'

'Kind of. See—'

'And might I ask why you insist on conducting your investigation over the phone instead of affording me the basic courtesy of calling round in person?'

'Seriously?'

'I'm accustomed to being taken seriously, yes.'

'Because I don't have clearance to enter the Park,' Shirley said.

'I know.'

She what?

Shirley said: 'Well, if you already know, why—'

'Because I'm trying to make a point, Ms Dander. And my point is, whatever investigation you're conducting, I'm far from convinced you're the one who ought to be conducting it. If you follow my meaning.'

It took Shirley a moment, but yeah, she grasped it.

'Which rather means I'm unlikely to cooperate when you finally get round to drafting your request for information.'

Which was all well and good, it occurred to Shirley, but then why was the cow still hanging on the line, when she could have saved herself several breaths and hung up half a minute ago?

And then came a sudden noise, the like of which she'd never heard before. Terrified, she looked at Marcus, and saw that he, too, had heard it – if he hadn't, she thought afterwards, she'd have happily sworn off narcotics for good; uncomplainingly attended her anger management sessions; might even have gone back to the church, so forever after, she was grateful that Marcus had heard it too, proving that it was really happening, not a hallucinatory nightmare.

Out on the landing, heading down the staircase, was Jackson Lamb. With him was Moira Tregorian.

And the pair of them were laughing happily.

The sound hovered mockingly once they'd gone; it lingered in the stairwell, fluttered about like a moth in search of a bulb. Marcus looked like someone had just swatted him with a shovel. Shirley's own expression was equally graceless. But even as she closed her mouth an idea was forming, and the fact that Molly Doran was still on the line made it glimmer all the brighter.

'Are you still there?' she asked.

A faint sigh supplied the answer.

'Guess what I just heard,' she said.

'I'm certainly not going to do that.'

'You should. You should try. I'll give you three guesses and a major clue.'

'A major clue?'

'Uh-huh.'

Molly Doran said, 'And I imagine the forfeit—'

'I know what that means,' Shirley said.

'Very good. And I imagine the forfeit in the event of my failing to guess correctly is that I have to help you with your enquiries.'

'Yep.'

'Forgive me, but I fail to see what I have to gain from this.'

'Well, if you guess right, I hang up and never bother you again.'

'That does sound tempting,' Molly admitted.

Shirley said, 'The clue is, it was Jackson Lamb made the noise.'

'Well,' Molly said after another pause. 'Given Jackson's limited repertoire, that sounds like the odds are in my favour, doesn't it?'

★

The bus had arrived at a scheduled stop ten minutes previously and had remained there since, engine off, though traffic flowed freely past. None of the passengers made any audible complaint. Either they were regulars and had expected the hiatus, or were new to buses and had lost the will to live. On the top deck, at the back, Diana Taverner was in session with Claude Whelan:

'A cold body,' she said, 'is a ready-made identity. Birth certificate, passport, National Security number, bank account, credit rating, the works. Constructed over the course of years, through official channels. This isn't master forgers at work, this is the wheels of the Civil Service doing what the Civil Service does best. Which is paperwork, Claude. Cradle-to-grave paperwork. That's what a cold body is. All you do is add flesh and blood, and you've got a fully documented life.'

'I thought that was standard practice. Creating false IDs.'

'These aren't false. That's the point. They're real identities awaiting an owner. Don't get me wrong, we can create fakes. And they're good. If we fake a driver's licence, it'll look real to the last detail, but that last detail is the expiry date. Once we reach that, we'll need to make a new one. With a cold body ID, that's not an issue. You simply apply for a renewal. Because the expired one's real, issued by the DVLA.'

Whelan said, 'That must have required full-time maintenance.'

'Of course. Back in the day we had the resources we deserve. But the wardrobe department was closed once the Cold War was declared won, which for all intents and purposes was the day the Wall came down. It was deemed surplus to requirements, but don't get me started on Treasury myopia. No, these days field identities are strictly off the cuff. Even long-term relocation covers are done on the cheap.'

'So what happened to these . . . cold bodies? When wardrobe was discontinued?'

'Mothballed. Or so it was thought.'

'But Robert Winters . . .'

'Was one of them. Yes.'

'How? How in the hell could he be? According to the passport, he's twenty-eight. And you've just told me the project was closed way back—'

'Claude. You're not listening. A cold body was a cradle-to-grave service. Identities created from scratch, in real time. The department had been running since the war, so the IDs it rolled out in the sixties were for twenty-year-olds. And so on. Get the picture?'

'A long-term undertaking,' he said faintly.

'You might say. Which means that when the department ceased to exist, they would have had any number of IDs in different states of preparation. Including one for a two-year-old Robert Winters.'

'If all we're going on is the name—'

'And date and place of birth. Trust me, the Robert Winters who blew himself up in Westacres was a Service creation. There's no other way he could have had that passport.'

'Jesus Christ.'

The bus lumbered into life, shuddering nose to tail.

'How long have you known?' he asked. 'Who brought this to you?'

'One of my kids. A few hours ago.'

'And you didn't think to tell me then?'

'And if I had? What would you have done?'

He struggled to contain his anger. 'What do you think? I'd have included it in my presentation to the PM—'

'And what would have happened then? No, don't bother. I'll tell you. We'd be in lockdown, Claude. The Park, over the river, even bloody Slough House – every department, every agent. We'd have Special Branch, or worse still Six, going through every desk. It would make the Cambridge spies inquiry look like garden party chit-chat.' She paused. 'Which, to be fair, it more or less was.'

'Where's your . . . kid now?'

'With the Dogs.'

'You've used internal security on this? They're supposed to be upholding the law, damn it, not acting as your praetorian guard!'

Taverner shook her head. 'You still don't get it, do you? If even a hint gets out about this, any credibility the Security Services have in this country will be over. Every crackpot conspiracy nut in the world will be calling Westacres a black-flag op, and even normal people will believe it.'

'That's hardly—'

She rolled right over him. 'Do you know how long it took, after the bomb, before rumours of cover-ups were plastered across the internet? Less than two hours. That's the level of trust we're looking at. We are losing this war, Claude, and believe me, it is a war. They said it couldn't be waged on an abstract, and I'll leave that to the philosophers and the pedants, because when you've got broken kids being carried out of a wrecked shopping centre, as far as I'm concerned, that's a war. And we need to be on the front line. *We* do. You and me. Because without our guidance, the Service will be flapping around like a damp sock instead of doing what it was built to do, which is catch these bastards. So let's make sure we're on the same page, here and now, before we get off this bus. And in case you're having difficulty making up your mind, remember this. You signed the C&C.'

'I signed the what?'

'The warrant authorising the Dogs to pick up Giti Rahman – the kid who found this – and hold her.'

'I didn't – *ah.*'

Your signature, please, in triplicate, he recalled.

And: *Do I need to read all this?*

'Which I did,' he said slowly, 'before briefing COBRA.'

Thus proving prior knowledge.

It really was surprising, he thought, how slowly buses moved.

'No need to look like that,' she said after a while. 'I'm on your side.'

'Good to know. But was it really necessary to make sure my balls were in your pocket before declaring your support?'

'It's just politics, Claude. You'll get used to it. And believe me, when the Service is hanging by a thread, the politics get nasty.'

It struck him that Diana Taverner was enjoying this. Or at least looked intensely alert, alive . . . attractive. This was not an observation he wanted to dwell on. Casting it from his mind, he said, 'So what do we do now?'

'We find out how our cold body wound up strapping on a Semtex vest. Which means finding out who had access to these IDs, and plugging them into a light socket until they talk.'

'We don't torture suspects in the UK,' he said automatically.

'Grow up, Claude.'

'And when you say *these* IDs . . .?'

'Yes. Plural. As far as I can tell, there are three cold bodies unaccounted for. Which means there are two more out there still upright. And God only knows what they plan to do next.'

The smell was stronger here, more acrid, and stung River's throat as he walked the narrow road. This was bordered on one side by eight feet of brick with a broken-glass topping, and on the other by a hedgerow beyond which lay fields and then roads, a distant smattering of houses, France. The drizzle persisted, and he was starting to notice that his shoes weren't as waterproof as they might be; that his left foot was chafing against a damp sock. But he'd spent days on the Black Mountains while training; spent nights in ditches evading capture by squaddies. He could survive wet feet. Just so long as he wasn't expected to speak convincing French while doing so.

Thin branches bent over the road, lending shade to what was already grey and toneless. He ran a finger along one, and it came away grey with soot.

Les Arbres: the house. Not so easy to find on account of its not being there any more; on account of it having succumbed to a fire.

Where the main road met a twin-rutted track, the wall bordering Les Arbres' grounds turned right, and became a waist-high, moss-covered mound. Heading down the track, River peered over it into a wooded area: largely leafless but on an upward gradient, so visibility remained limited. There was no sound. He was only a quarter of a mile or so from Angevin, but could have been transported into the heart of a lonelier region. He would barely have been surprised to meet a horse-drawn cart coming up the track to meet him. But he encountered no one, and only once or twice heard a car on the road, heading to or from the village.

'When was the fire?' he had asked his new friend back in the café.

It had been three nights previously.

'Was anyone hurt?'

The house had apparently been empty. At least, no bodies had been found among the wreckage.

'How many people had lived there?'

Nobody had been entirely sure. It had not been a family situation. A commune, rather. If River was familiar with that term.

River was.

'The fire. Was it arson?'

'Deliberate? Yes, it would seem so. There were no vehicles there, yes? Everybody left before the fire started. And the blaze . . . *ha*. Big black clouds, blacker even than the night.'

Meaning petrol had been used, River surmised. Petrol or something; something to burn fast and hard enough that no evidence would remain.

But evidence of what?

He reached a pair of gates; large iron ones with a circular sign attached, PROPRIETE PRIVEE DEFENSE D'ENTRER, in red. They were chained together, but this was as good a place as any to make an entrance. River scrambled over the wall, smearing his hands green in the process, and followed a track the width of a car through the melancholy trees. The smell grew stronger. He was reminded of clearing the grate at his grandfather's house the morning after a late-night session, one in which they'd sat by a dying fire while the O.B. poured out stories, his clarity growing dimmer with the light. But River had always wanted to listen, had always wanted to hear. Never wanted his grandfather's voice silenced. It was unlikely they'd share another such evening, he thought, as he made his way closer to the heart of the now dead fire.

His first sight of the house was unexpected, as he crested a rise he hadn't noticed he was approaching, but in that same first moment it was there, it was gone again too. For the house was no more. What must once have been an impressive structure, three or four storeys high, seven or eight rooms to a floor, was now a ragged outline of walls, with charred lumps of timber piled between. Anything the house had once held had melted to barely recognisable pyramids of scorched and blackened sculpture: window frames and furniture, snakes of cable, lengths of staircase. An enamel sink hovered three feet above the ground, or did at first sight: it was suspended there, in fact, by upright piping. Around it sat the squat lumpy shapes of its former colleagues: a stove, a washing machine, a dishwasher, a fridge. White goods rendered black, half melted. There was a bath, too, embedded in a mess of rubble, the tap-end reaching out of the ruins like the prow of a dying ship.

And though all of this was still wet, it seemed to retain the memory of heat, as if the recent inferno had been too intense an experience to dissipate entirely. The house was gone, but the ghost of what had destroyed it lingered, and all around its ruin the ground was churned up, with heavy tyre tracks moulded in mud, and oily pools in the deeper craters. It must have been deeply violent; not only the fire, but the mission to quell it. The damage done to prevent further harm from spreading – his grandfather would have had a story to illustrate that. But it would have grown confused in the telling, and wound round itself without reaching a conclusion, and River wondered for the first time if he were here investigating the attempt on his grandfather's life, or simply putting distance between himself and the old man, so as not to have to witness his deterioration.

He crouched and laid a palm flat to the ground, but felt no stored warmth: wet flattened grass was all. He wiped his hand on his jeans. This was where Adam Lockhead's journey had started, the one that ended on the O.B.'s bathroom floor. It couldn't be chance that the house had burned so soon before that. But what was the chain that bound the events together?

Something rustled in the woods, but when he scanned the area, nothing caught his eye. The wind, or a small animal. Gossiping trees.

River gazed at the ruined house. If he closed his eyes, he

could see it happening: the flames massively orange against the black sky, and sirens ripping the night apart. It must have been visible for miles; a beacon thrilling the countryside. He didn't know what colour French fire engines were: were they red? They might be yellow. It didn't matter. They had arrived too late, but had doused what was left of the house to prevent the fire spreading. That much had worked. A pair of outhouses two hundred metres or so from the ruins were still standing, and something like a dovecote too, further away, but visible through the trees. And the trees themselves had survived, of course, though they looked thin and bony in the grey afternoon, like a memorial to a holocaust.

Anything that might have been a clue had been reduced to ashes, blown about the fields, and smeared on damp surfaces.

The grey was giving way to something bleaker, something darker. Overhead, the clouds grew heavy, preparing to release more rain, and River's feet had grown no drier, plodding around in mud and filth. He would take shelter back in Angevin, he decided. There would be a local paper, or a local centre of gossip – a church, a bar – where he might discover a name; a piece of thread to tug on. Bertrand Something. That was the name Adam Lockhead had gone under. Or perhaps Adam Lockhead was the name Bertrand Something went under: either way, this ruin shed no light. Another noise emerged from the wood, the cracking of a branch, but again he saw nothing.

A drive led down to the main road. There was another gate there, set between a handsome pair of stone posts, and looking at it was like gazing down a tunnel, the way the trees composed an arch, and he thought that during the summer it must make an impressive sight, the trees in leaf, the drive washed clean of mud. But it wouldn't any longer look like much from the opposite end: the big gates, the trees, the drive, and all of it ending in wrack and ruin. He wondered how long the house had been here, and whether its loss would cut a hole in the village's life the way the bomb in Westacres had in London. And then he turned to make his way back through the wood, and a man stepped out of the trees holding a long single-barrelled gun which he brought to his shoulder in one smooth movement, and then fired, and River's heart stopped.

8

E MMA FLYTE SAID, 'THERE'S nothing to worry about. It's a routine precaution.'

'But I haven't done anything—'

'No one's suggesting that you have.'

They were in what appeared to be an ordinary sitting room: a sofa, chairs, shelving, a TV. But any room you're taken to, rather than enter of your own free will, carries the whiff of the cell. They were not far from Brixton market, a fifteen-minute journey, but that quarter of an hour had rattled Giti Rahman's world.

'In that case, what am I doing here?'

'Awaiting instructions,' Emma said flatly. 'If you need anything, there's an intercom. I'd advise you not to overuse it. Mr Dempsey's patience is not infinite.'

Anyone who knew Mr Dempsey, the Dog assigned to this particular chore, would have agreed that patience was not his forte.

'And the windows are reinforced. I wouldn't recommend you attempt an exit.'

'I'm hardly James Bond.'

'No. If you were, we'd shoot you.' Her reaction made Emma regret that a little. 'A joke, Ms Rahman.'

'It probably sounded funnier in your head.'

Couldn't argue with that.

She locked the door behind her. In the kitchen Dempsey was going through cupboards; had found teabags and a vintage packet of biscuits.

'Call me if she gives trouble.'

Dempsey said, 'Trouble? I'm more worried she'll wet herself.'

Out in the car, Emma sat thinking. Diana Taverner was a slippery lady, and anything with her fingerprints on was likely to be wiped clean before official examination. That the warrant for Giti Rahman's collection had been signed by Claude Whelan could be discounted. Acquiring other people's signatures was no doubt among Lady Di's talents.

Then again, these people were safeguarding national security, and her role was to ease their passage. So Giti Rahman – innocent, guilty, or just in the way – was no longer her concern. David Cartwright, on the other hand, was a task in hand.

She called Devon Welles, whom she'd left in charge at the Cartwright house.

'Anything?'

'. . . Not really.'

'Tell.'

'It was nothing. A car went past, slowed down, as if someone was trying to get a look through the window.'

'Nosy neighbour?'

'Could be. And there's a woodentop on the door, which is always exciting.'

'But you got a plate anyway,' she said.

She liked Welles. He was another ex-copper, with all the right reactions.

'A partial.'

'Run it. Any ID on the body yet?'

'No. Except who it's not.'

'Except . . .?'

'The blood's not a match for Cartwright's grandson.'

'Ah.' She thought a bit. 'Well, that narrows it down by one, I suppose. And means we have two missing persons. Better start with the grandson's associates.'

'He's really called River?'

'So Jackson Lamb assured me. Speaking of whom . . .'

'He misidentified the stiff.'

'The body's a mess,' Emma said. 'No face to speak of. Still, though.'

'An "I don't know" would have done the job,' Welles finished.

'So maybe Lamb's playing his own game. Christ, don't you miss the Met sometimes? At least all the crap was honest crap.'

'Graft, drugs and hookers,' Welles agreed. 'This lot, you just can't trust.'

'So if Lamb wanted us to think young Cartwright's dead, maybe there's other stuff he's keeping quiet. Like where Cartwright actually is. Both of them.'

'Lamb's from that losers' place, right?'

'Slough House.'

'You think the Cartwrights are there?'

'Too obvious. These are spooks, even if they're Vauxhall Conference.' She paused. 'Do they still have a Vauxhall Conference?'

'You're asking a cricket fan,' Welles said. 'So what do you reckon? Check out his colleagues?'

'Also too obvious.' She thought a moment. 'But let's look at Lamb's contacts. Maybe we'll get lucky.'

Call over, she started the car and pulled away with a squeal of rubber. Not the recommended practice when departing a safe house, but sometimes, chatting to a fellow ex-copper, the old instincts took over.

The rabbit looked unscathed, apart from being dead.

River's heart started again.

'Good shot,' he said.

The man raised an eyebrow.

'*Ça, c'était formidable,*' River improvised.

The man held his free hand flat and wiggled it side to side.

Comme ci, comme ça, thought River, and decided that if he were capable of reading French mime, his language skills weren't as tragic as he'd been made to feel.

His new companion wore a waterproof jacket with capacious-looking pockets, from one of which he produced a length of string. Leaning his shotgun against a tree, he tied the rabbit's back legs together, secured the string to his belt, then slung the corpse over his shoulder. Most dead things look smaller, but this remained an impressive piece of meat. With the thought, a hunger pang struck River. The sky growled too, a thundery echo.

'*Anglais?*' the man asked suddenly, his voice higher, lighter, than River might have expected. He was dark, with rook-black hair and angular features, all of which suggested something guttural. Not this soft cadence.

'Yes,' he said.

'You look for someone?'

'The people here.'

'Gone. All gone.' The man snapped his fingers, *pouf*, just like that. They were here and then were gone, in a puff of smoke, except the smoke had been a cloud: a thick black mass of it, pouring upwards through the trees.

And downwards through the trees now came the first fat spats of heavier rain.

The man tugged his collar up, and recovered his shotgun. Then he looked at River's inadequate jacket and shoes.

'You're to be get wet,' he said.

'I am to be that, yes,' River agreed.

'Come.'

And the man led the way through the wood; not along the track River had followed, but set to an invisible course he seemed to know well, avoiding every root that River stumbled over, and every hole in the ground that sought out River's feet.

Patrice pulled into a lay-by, and spread a map against the windscreen. He knew precisely where he was – wouldn't dream of setting foot on hostile land without memorising routes – but it provided an excuse for remaining stationary while he gave thought to what he'd learned.

A police presence round the target's house.

Which was to be expected. Bertrand would have made it look like an old-man accident, but even an old-man accident would require official scrutiny given the old man in question. Except that there had been no confirmation, *parcel delivered*, nor even its obverse, *nobody at home. Will attempt redelivery*.

So. Absence of message plus police presence meant Bertrand's parcel hadn't just not been delivered, it had likely blown up in his face.

This was not out of the question. Patrice loved Bertrand like a brother, but facts were facts: Bertrand had been known to falter at critical moments.

He refolded the map and took out his mobile at the precise moment that a passing bird, a seagull for Christ's sake – he was miles from the sea – shat on his windscreen. There were omens, and then there were your basic illustrations. The phone was answered on its second ring, but he heard only silence. To fill it, he delivered three swift sentences, in French.

More silence.

Then: 'And your parcel?'

'Still undelivered.'

'Try again.'

He ended the call.

Squirting cleanser on the windscreen, he watched as the wipers smeared the seagull's mess into a grey film. Another clean-up job that made things worse. Then he cried, very briefly, for Bertrand, who was probably dead; squirted more cleanser, and ran the wipers again. Then he drove back to London.

The restaurant was near enough to be within Jackson Lamb's compass, new enough for him not to have tried it yet, and canny enough to recognise an awkward customer. Or that was one possible reason for the waiter's nervousness as he showed Lamb and Moira Tregorian to a table he first described as 'nice' before instantly upgrading to 'very good'.

'Do you treat all your new staff to lunch?' Moira asked.

'I treat all my staff the way they deserve,' Lamb said, as the waiter began rattling off that day's specials: something something pulled pork, something medallions, something vinaigrette. Lamb politely let him finish before saying, 'I'll have the beef.'

'Sir, beef's not actually—'

'Rare.'

Moira ordered the Caesar salad.

'And a bottle of the house red,' said Lamb.

'Oh, I don't think I'd better drink anything.'

'Just the bottle of house red then,' said Lamb.

When the waiter had escaped, Lamb scooped up both bread rolls from the basket and split them open with a practised thumb. While he levered the contents of the butter dish into the cavities thus made, he said, his voice at its plummiest, 'So, how are you settling in?'

'It's been a mite discombobulating, I don't mind telling you,' she said, tearing her eyes away from his evisceration of the bread. 'What with everyone thinking Mr Cartwright was dead for some reason.'

'It's a herd mentality,' Lamb said sadly. 'Someone gets hold of the wrong idea, and suddenly everyone believes it. I think that's how the internet works.'

The waiter returned with the wine. He opened it grandly, as if performing a magic trick, poured a splash into Lamb's glass and stood back, the way one might from a lit firework.

'If I cared what it tasted like, I'd have ordered from the bottom of the list,' Lamb said. 'Just fill it up.'

The waiter did as instructed, then fled.

Lamb beamed at Moira suddenly, an expression which would have had the slow horses, with the possible exception of Catherine Standish, covering their heads. 'Tell me,' he said. 'Why do you think you were assigned to Slough House?'

'Well. It's very clear that . . . does everyone call it Slough House?'

'They do.'

'It doesn't have an official name?'

'Trust me, if it did, you wouldn't want to know it.'

'I see,' said Moira, who didn't. 'Well, be that as it may, it's very clear that Slough House needs me, or someone like me.'

'What an original thought.'

'Because everything's such a mess. I don't just mean the offices, though they're bad enough, and as for the lavatories – well. I'll say no more on that subject over lunch. But it's the paperwork, it's the lax standards when it comes to desk management, and as for general behaviour – well. There've been shenanigans. I'll put it no higher than that.'

'Abuse of office equipment?' Lamb suggested.

'Abuse would be a mild term. Very mild.'

Lamb nodded, as if mildness were as much as he could usually bear, and then appeared to notice the glass of wine in front of him. It was a large glass, and currently held about a third of the bottle's contents, so he drained it in two swallows and poured another. 'Sometimes it's self-evident,' he said.

'I . . . what is?'

'The reason why folk end up in Slough House,' Lamb said. He took a bite of the bread roll and chewed hugely for a moment or two. Then said, 'Take young Cartwright. The not so dear departed. He arrived a couple of days after an incident at King's Cross which quite literally made headlines all over the world. Not too difficult to work out what his misdemeanour was.'

'Rather more than a misdemeanour, I'd have thought.'

'There were mitigating circumstances,' Lamb allowed.

'What were they?'

'He was being dicked about,' Lamb said. 'Apologies for the language. Your predecessor was a bad influence.'

'I gather she had . . . issues.'

'Some, yes. And also, she drank like a fish.'

'Oh dear.'

'All behind her now, she claims, but you know what they say.' Lamb reached for his glass. 'Once a lush, always a lush.'

The waiter arrived with their food, and Lamb paused while plates were arranged in front of them, though he didn't take his eyes off Moira Tregorian.

'Enjoy your meal,' the waiter said, with the air of one who wouldn't mind much if Lamb choked to death instead.

Ignoring him, Lamb said to Moira, 'But you know what's interesting about your assignment?'

She paused, her fork hovering over her salad. For the first time, she seemed unsure of her role in this conversation: was she still the new confidante, replacing a sadly inadequate predecessor? Or was Jackson Lamb playing a game of his own, whose rules he hadn't bothered to share?

He said, 'Claude Whelan sent you here. One of his first acts on taking charge. Don't you think that's interesting? Because I do.'

And he smiled in a way that would have had the slow horses – Catherine Standish included – running for shelter, before pouring the rest of the wine into his glass, then waggling the bottle at the waiter.

The O.B. blinked in an owlish way, as if about to turn his head all the way round. 'I used to live here, didn't I?'

'No,' Catherine assured him. 'You've never lived here.'

He'd woken an hour ago and clambered out of bed, and getting dressed had caused him no problems, because he hadn't undressed in the first place. She'd felt bad about this – it had been an act of cruelty, allowing him to crawl under the covers fully clothed, only his shoes discarded – but in the end, not bad enough to attempt to undress him. And they were her covers. And it hadn't been her idea to start with.

'I need somewhere he'll be safe,' River had said. 'With someone I trust.'

Which was a nice touch, but then he'd had an entire journey to rehearse his case; she had about three minutes to put up her defences.

'River – I'm happy you trust me. Really. But you can't just leave him here!'

What does he eat? she wanted to ask. *Do I need to walk him?* Impossible to construct a coherent counter-argument with idiot questions forming in her mind.

'Someone tried to kill him, Catherine.'

'That's supposed to motivate me? What if the killer comes here? River—'

'Don't worry. That won't be happening.'

Something in the way he said this precluded her asking the obvious.

But what was worst about this conversation, what had been really horrible, was the way it was conducted: in furious whispers with the old man in the room, confused fear on his face. She didn't need this. Not today. Not on a bleak January morning with the whole city mired in shocked grief; a beautiful excuse for drowning her own and everyone else's sorrows.

'Please, Catherine.'

'Who wanted him dead?'

'That's what I'm going to find out.'

'Why don't you take him to the Park?'

River didn't answer.

'Oh God,' she said, joining his dots.

So now here she was, and here was the O.B. too, and already the integrity of the safe house was compromised because it had taken Lamb all of five minutes to work out where to find him, and while Lamb was smarter than most people, his wasn't the only brain on Spook Street.

Though not all spook brains worked the way they used to.

'Where's he gone?'

'Where's who gone, David?'

Because she couldn't call him Mr Cartwright: not in these circumstances.

'That boy, that young man.'

'. . . River?'

'What sort of a name is that?'

She'd often wondered . . . 'He's not here. But he'll be back. I promise.' I hope.

'I think he might be up to something,' David Cartwright said.

She had poached him two eggs, and arranged them on toast, and he had eaten hungrily and then drunk three cups of tea, though he'd spilt the third. Now he was in her sitting room, straight-backed on a comfy chair, as if allowing himself to sink into it would compromise his principles. He was still struggling with his grandson: both his name, and the fact of his existence.

'He's not up to anything, David. He's just had to run an errand.'

'Used to know someone called River. About so high.'

The old man placed a palm level with his chest, though as he remained sitting, it was difficult to judge precisely what height he was remembering River to be.

Either way, it was a while ago. 'That's the same River,' Catherine said gently. 'He grew up.'

'Used to know his mother.'

These weren't waters Catherine wanted to swim in. 'Do you have everything you need? Would you like more to eat?'

Listen to yourself, she admonished. She sounded like her own mother: deflecting the threat of emotion with offers of sustenance.

She said, 'His mother, River's mother – that was your daughter. She was called Isobel.' Too late, she realised she'd slipped into the wrong tense. 'That's what she's called, I mean. She's called Isobel.'

A tear was rolling down the old man's cheek. 'I don't have a daughter.'

'You do, you know.'

'No. She told me so. I'm no longer your daughter. She told me that.'

And this was why you offered food, she thought. This was why you deflected emotion: because there was no helping this level of hurt. There was nowhere either of them could go in this conversation.

'Can I get you anything?' she asked again. 'Or are you quite happy?'

A ridiculous question in the circumstances, but it lit something in his eyes. 'Happy,' he said.

'. . . Yes?'

'Grumpy. Sneezy. Doc.'

Oh, for heaven's sake, she thought.

'Dopey. Bashful. Grumpy. And that's all seven.' He tapped his temple. 'Nothing wrong with the old memory banks.'

She didn't point out his error. She didn't do anything. It was like taking a glimpse down a set of cellar stairs, she thought, and becoming suddenly aware of the steep darkness awaiting you. It didn't really matter how careful you were in your descent.

'Where's River?' he asked again.

'He went to France,' she said, invention momentarily beyond her. She was sure that's where he'd gone: she'd found the rail ticket in his pocket.

'France? He can't have gone to France!'

'It's not far. He'll be back soon.'

'No no no.' He'd grown agitated. 'France. Out of the question.'

'It's not dangerous, David. It's only over the Channel.'

But he wasn't convinced. He began to mutter to himself, nothing she could make sense of, and to distance herself from it, she went to the window. Still the same bleak January, under the same grey canopy of sky. A car was pulling up, slipping into the residents' parking area, though it wasn't a familiar vehicle. The woman who emerged was a glacially beautiful blonde in a black suit. It might have been Catherine's Service instincts; might have been her drunk's paranoia. Either way, bells rang loud and clear.

She said, 'Perhaps we should get you out of the way, David.'

River had half expected a hut constructed from fallen branches and moss, but after ten minutes Victor, as his name turned out to be, led him out of the woods and on to a road, and soon after that they were turning down a lane towards a row of modern cottages, with breeze-block walls and aluminium window frames. Rain was pelting down now. While he waited for Victor to unlock the door, River looked down the valley towards Angevin, and its bridge, its church tower, the houses climbing its small collection of streets, all seemed to have huddled closer for shelter. From this perspective it was clear that Les Arbres hadn't been part of the village at all. Not even an outpost, but a walled-off enclave. Whatever had gone on there would have been gossiped about in the bars, but the reality would have been as solid and graspable as the smoke Les Arbres had become.

Victor had had trouble with River's name. 'This is what you are called?'

'I'm afraid so. I mean yes. Yes, River.'

Victor didn't actually say *Bof*, but it was clearly implied.

The house was small, but untidy. A portable television occupied a low table in the centre of the sitting room, and magazines, mostly TV schedules, were scattered about. An overflowing ashtray sat next to an overflowing ashtray, and most other surfaces displayed bruised-looking ornaments: plaster figurines of what were probably saints, though might have been sinners; a number of glass animals. One corner was given over to outdoor equipment: rubber boots, fishing poles, a variety of nets and snares. Victor carefully laid his waterproof over these, sneaking a sly glance River's way as he did so. River thought he could smell a cat, but it was hard to tell. Perhaps Victor had been smoking one. He took his own jacket off, more for politeness than anything else. It didn't feel much less damp in here than outside.

Victor deposited the morning's spoils on the kitchen counter, next to a handy array of knives and cleavers.

'I make tea.'

'Do you have coffee?' said River.

'Tea. You are English.'

'Thank you,' River said. He wasn't much of a tea drinker, but that didn't sound like it would lend itself to straightforward translation.

They drank tea in the small kitchen while rain battered the windows, and the dead rabbit stared reproachfully at River, and Victor smoked a succession of hand-rolled cigarettes, each no fatter than the matches he used to light them.

'You know Les Arbres?' he asked.

'I was looking for someone. Bertrand?'

'A young man, he look like you. I think that was his name, yes.'

'Can you tell me anything about him?'

'Tell you about your friend?'

'I didn't really know him,' River said.

'You are cousins, maybe?'

'We might have been,' River said, thinking this would make things simpler: a man seeking his long-lost cousin.

'Les Arbres, there were people there. Eighteen, twenty? A number like that. All of them men.'

'How long had they been there?'

'Many many years. *Vingt-trois, vingt-quatre.*'

'So . . .' River thought of the dead man on the bathroom floor, whose passport claimed him twenty-eight. 'Were there children?'

'At one time, I think. Then not.' Victor placed a level palm two feet from the floor, then slowly moved it upwards. 'You know?'

Children grew.

The man in the café had spoken of a commune, but Victor thought there had been no women there. Didn't sound like much of a commune to River, who was pretty sure the concept involved sex. An all-male community didn't rule that out, of course, but the presence of children cast a disturbing light.

But what would that have to do with a murder attempt on his grandfather? He said, 'Were they French?'

Victor shrugged. 'French, yes. But Russian too, I think, or Czech. An American. Maybe some English. They did not mix in the village.'

'But went to the café sometimes? Le Ciel Bleu?'

'Sometimes, *bien sur*. There is the *marché*, the market. People stop at the café afterwards. It is natural.'

'Who was their leader, do you know?'

'Leader?'

'Somebody must have been in charge.'

'I do not know about leaders. Probably they were *communiste*. All equal, you know?'

'And what about the fire? Does anyone know how that started?'

'The fire, it was deliberate. They are all gone, and then it burns.'

'At the same time?'

'On the same day, yes. In the afternoon, their cars, they leave towards Poitiers. And soon after, the fire starts. There is much activity, many fire trucks, lots of noise.'

River half wanted to know what colour the fire engines were.

'Maybe the police look for them now,' Victor went on. 'I expect this is so. But your cousin, he did not die in the fire.'

No, he died of a bullet in the face. River didn't reply. He said, 'It's strange, that they lived for so long so near the village, and nobody seems to know anything about them.'

'Maybe we were curious, years ago. But time passes, yes? And you forget to be curious. It is just Les Arbres.'

He rose suddenly, and examined his rabbit. The rain was still beating down, but River thought it was time he made a move. He stood too. 'You've been very kind, Victor,' he said. '*Très gentil. Merci.*'

'*De rien.*' He chose a knife, and gestured with it at the rabbit, then at River. 'You can stay, no? He will taste good.'

'Thank you, but no.'

'It is not all tea. There is wine.'

'It sounds excellent, really. But I'd better head back to Poitiers.'

'As you wish.' With a flash of his wrist Victor buried the blade in the rabbit's corpse, and a moment later seemed to turn the animal inside out, peeling its skin off as if it were a glove. A flake of ash dropped from his roll-up onto the naked meat, and he scraped it away with the knife. 'Maybe there is someone else. Who knows Les Arbres.'

'Really?'

'She is not living at Angevin. Is from next village. I write you address.'

'Who is she?' River asked.

'She is nice lady. Was prostitute, yes? Whore. But nice lady.'

Leaving the knife in the rabbit, Victor found a ballpoint pen and laboriously wrote out, in the margin of an ancient magazine, instructions for River to follow: another road, another few miles, some turnings, a house, Natasha.

'Nice flat.'

'Thank you.'

'Quiet area, too. And you're a reader.' Emma Flyte nodded at Catherine's bookshelves. 'Nothing spoils a good book faster than a lot of background noise.'

'Unless it's unwelcome visitors,' Catherine said.

Emma nodded, as if they'd found common ground. Checking up on Jackson Lamb's known associates had been illuminating only inasmuch as it had revealed how carefully he avoided having any. She'd had to fall back on colleagues, and Catherine Standish had struck her as interesting. For reasons that would no doubt come up soon.

Her scrutiny of the living room over, she said, 'Do you see much of your former colleagues?'

'I don't see much of anyone.'

'And why's that?'

'When you're having sex,' Catherine asked, 'do you prefer to be on top?'

Emma raised an eyebrow.

'Oh, sorry. I assumed it was my turn to ask an impertinent question.'

'There's a reason I'm here.'

'You're not about to produce a religious tract, are you? Because my neighbour Deirdre's a much better bet.'

'If I had a suspicious mind,' Emma said, 'which I do, by the way – I'd be asking myself why you're avoiding answering questions.'

'Oooh, I'm not sure,' said Catherine. 'Something to do with resenting the unwarranted intrusion, perhaps?'

'Unwarranted,' repeated Emma, nodding. 'I see what you did there.'

'I could tell you were sharp.'

'Only you haven't thought that one through. You're still a member of the Service, Ms Standish, which means you're subject to my jurisdiction. Which means I don't need a warrant.'

'Except I resigned some while ago.'

'Mmm, yes, not exactly. You handed in your resignation. The paperwork seems to have stalled, though. Remind me, are you still receiving a salary?'

Which was the point of interest, of course. Ms Standish's peculiarly free-floating status regarding Slough House.

Catherine said, 'Receiving. Not spending.'

'Yes, I think we'll save that one for the inquiry. Meanwhile, you're on the books, you'll answer my questions. All clear so far?'

'It sounds like it will have to be.'

'Good. River Cartwright. When was the last time you had contact?'

'Just before Christmas. He sent me a text.'

'What did it say?'

'"Merry. Christmas,"' Catherine said slowly.

'And nothing since?'

'I was impressed by that much, if you want the honest truth.'

'Are you aware that Jackson Lamb identified his body last night?'

'I am now.'

'You don't seem shocked.'

'Little that Jackson Lamb does shocks me any more.'

'I've just told you that River Cartwright's dead. You don't seem remotely bothered by that.'

'And I've just told you that in four months, I've had a two-word text from him. It's not like he'll leave a huge hole in my life.'

'Or maybe you already know it's not true.'

'You're starting to lose me. Which bit's not true? That he's dead? Or that he sent me a text?'

'Are we going to play games all morning?'

'I wish I could spare the time,' Catherine said. 'But that neighbour I mentioned? I promised I'd drop in on her.'

'Yesterday evening, one of the Cartwrights committed murder,' Emma Flyte said. 'Either River or his grandfather. So you'll understand I'm keen on interviewing both. Have they been here?'

'No.'

'I think you're lying.'

'Why's that?' Catherine asked, sounding genuinely interested.

'Because nothing I've said has come as a remote surprise to you.'

'Perhaps I'm just unflappable.'

'Or well informed. And if it wasn't the Cartwrights, it can only be one man.'

'Lamb,' said Catherine.

'Uh-huh. Mr Lamb. When was he here?'

'First thing.'

'And what did he tell you?'

'Exact words?'

'Please.'

'He said he'd spent the early hours winding up the dyke who's currently boss of the kennel. And that if she turned up here, I was to waste as much of her time as possible.'

Emma stared.

Catherine said, 'I may have skipped the odd f-word. He thinks swearing's big and clever.'

'What's he up to, Ms Standish?'

'He has a joe in the wind, Ms Flyte. He'll be up to whatever he thinks necessary.'

'Having one of your team kill someone isn't the same as having an agent in peril.'

'Well, you've met Lamb. He deals in broad strokes.'

Emma kept staring, and Catherine unflinchingly returned her gaze. On the mantelpiece, a carriage clock struck the hour with a tinkly series of notes.

At length, Emma said, 'When I find the Cartwrights – and I will – I hope it doesn't turn out you knew where they were all along.'

Catherine nodded thoughtfully.

In the hallway, by the open front door, Emma Flyte paused. 'What's that noise?'

'I didn't hear anything,' Catherine said.

'It came from through there. I assume that's your bedroom.'

'I left my radio on.'

'It didn't sound like a radio.'

'I promise you it is.'

'So you left the radio on in your bedroom, behind a closed door.'

'It seems that way, doesn't it?'

'Do you mind if I take a look?'

'Yes.'

'Why?'

'I've had more than enough of your company.'

'That's too bad. Because we already covered the ground rules.'

Closing the front door, Emma stepped across the hallway and into Catherine's bedroom.

It was dark inside – the curtains still drawn – and a muffled noise was emerging from the shape under the duvet. Emma looked back at Catherine.

Catherine shrugged.

Emma reached out and grasped the hem of the duvet; whip-cracked it like a magician removing a tablecloth and let it fall to the floor.

On the bed, Catherine's radio muttered to itself on its throne of pillows.

'You wouldn't think so, but it gets great reception that way,' she said.

Two minutes later, she was watching by the window again as Emma Flyte left the building, climbed into her car and drove away.

A minute after that, she was knocking on her neighbour's door.

'Thanks so much, Deirdre,' she said. 'Such short notice, too.'

'Oh, he was no trouble,' Deirdre assured her. 'Your colleague gone, has she?'

'Just me again,' said Catherine. 'Come on, David. Time to go.'

'I used to live here, didn't I?' said the O.B.

He was limping badly by the time he arrived, his soaking sock chafing his left foot: he was starting to imagine gangrene. The downpour had once more receded to a steady drizzle. Few cars had passed him, and none had stopped to offer a lift. The tea at Victor's was a distant memory, and hunger had become a dull ache.

The scrap of paper on which Victor had scribbled an address was his most treasured possession. He barely dared fish it out to check directions, for fear it would dissolve in the wet air.

But River had a memory for figures, for facts, for details, and didn't need them verified. Eighty minutes after leaving the poacher's cottage he was in the next village, which had arranged itself along the banks of the same river as Angevin, and boasted similar amenities: a narrow bridge, a sombre church, a ruin perched on a mound. The narrow streets probably allowed for little sunlight even when there was any to speak of, and there were alleyways, harbouring flights of stone steps, every dozen yards or so. Seen from above it no doubt made sense; at ground level it was a confusion of ups and downs, of different ways of getting lost. He navigated through it, though. Ignoring the side streets, he followed the main road over the bridge, took the left fork when it divided, and passed a garage on his right. Beyond its forecourt was a row of cottages whose stone façades, darkened by rainfall, were a stern grimace only partly belied by their prettily painted doors: red, white, blue. The blue was Natasha's. River pounded its heavy brass knocker.

He didn't know what he was expecting. A nice lady. A prostitute, yes, a whore, but a nice lady. So what he was doing now, he supposed, was visiting a prostitute, a phrase with a definite subtext. The nice lady opened the door a long fifteen seconds after he'd knocked. Whatever she'd been about to say short-circuited at the sight of him: instead, she said, 'Bertrand? *Mais non . . .*'

'*Non*,' River agreed. '*Excusez, vous êtes Natasha?*'

He did not, he realised, have a surname for her.

After a moment, she said, 'You are not French.'

'*Non*,' he agreed again.

'English?'

To admit this in French would be absurd. 'Yes,' he said.

'What can I do for you?'

She was, he supposed, in her forties; a handsome, strong-featured woman with dark hair falling loosely around her shoulders, and eyes that seemed black to River. She wore jeans, a man's blue shirt, and a thick cardigan with a belt whose ends dangled to her thighs. From her expression, he couldn't tell if she were surprised to see him or simply resigned; as if this were an outcome long in the making.

He said, 'I need to know about Les Arbres.'

'It is burned down. It is no more.'

'I know that. But the people there . . . I need to know about them.'

'Who sent you?'

'A man called Victor.'

A gust of wind pushed at his back; slunk between his legs like an unruly dog.

She said, 'It is bad here. You should come in.'

So River came out of the cold and the wet, and limped into her story.

9

RODERICK HO WAS DRINKING from a bottle that claimed to hold 'smart water', and Shirley couldn't work out which annoyed her more: who he was, or what he was drinking. Smart phones, okay, she could see that. Smart cars. Smart water, though, someone was taking the piss.

But she wasn't going to let him spoil her moment of triumph.

'Old man Cartwright made a number of trips to France in the early nineties,' she announced. 'Before there was a tunnel. Apparently they used something called a ferry? Anyway, he went three or four times, always to the same place. Somewhere near Poitiers, which is about in the middle. Middle of France, I mean.'

Lamb said, 'You know, if I shut my eyes, it's like listening to one of the Reith lectures.'

'Yeah, I don't know what that means.'

'You amaze me.' Lamb paused to belch. Instead of spending the hour or so after lunch formulating department strategy, which he did with his eyes closed and his feet on his desk, he was holding court in Ho's room. The slow horses were there, Moira Tregorian excepted – her, he'd invited to go through the stack of memos that had arrived from the Park since September, and arrange them in order of urgency –

and were relaying the fruits of their research, which, until Shirley piped up, had been non-existent. 'These trips, they were official?'

'Uh-huh.'

'So there's a mission report?'

'There are expenses claims,' Shirley said, 'and a series of status updates on a retired agent, codenamed Henry. But all the updates say is "stable" or "no action necessary".'

Lamb sniffed suspiciously. 'And Molly Doran volunteered this?'

'I dropped your name,' Shirley said.

Probably not worth going into the bet Molly lost.

'So whoever Henry was,' Marcus said, 'he's not as stable as he used to be.'

Ho lowered the bottle, and said, 'Yeah, because it looks like he tried to kill the old man.'

'Such perception,' said Lamb. 'No wonder I think of you as my number two.'

Ho smiled happily.

'What are you smirking at? You do know what a number two is?'

Louisa said, 'But whoever came to kill David Cartwright, it wasn't this mysterious Henry. Not unless he was about three when Cartwright was paying him visits.'

'Why was he doing that?'

As on the previous occasions when J. K. Coe had opened his mouth, this caused a brief silence: not so much people wondering about what he'd said as registering that he'd actually said something.

Ho said, 'I think you missed the bit about the status updates,' and glanced at Lamb for approval.

Who said, 'Listen and learn, grasshopper.'

Coe said, 'He was First Desk in all but name. Why would

he be trotting off to the Continent to check up on a retired spook?'

'Maybe it was the other way round,' said Lamb. 'Maybe checking up on a retired spook was the excuse he needed to go trotting off to the Continent.'

'So this Henry, who we first heard of fifteen seconds ago, might just be a smokescreen?' said Marcus. 'He didn't last long.'

'Are you suggesting Cartwright invented an agent just so he'd get his travel expenses paid?' Louisa said.

'Those ferries weren't cheap,' said Lamb. 'But no. If Henry's an invention, it was to give Cartwright the freedom to go to France in the first place. Like the mad monk said, he was First Desk in all but name. Which didn't mean he couldn't make trips abroad. It just meant he had to have a better reason for making them than "felt like it".'

'So he had some kind of secret mission going on in France in the nineties,' said Louisa. 'And whatever it was, it's come back to bite him.'

'Have I triangulated yet?' said Shirley. 'Because there's more.'

'Did someone start an employee-of-the-month competition?' Lamb asked. 'Because I've got to tell you, I wish I'd thought of that myself. And I can't believe Dander's ahead of the pack.'

'Is there a prize?'

'Yeah, Ho will explain how he got a girlfriend. You can take notes.'

'I assume it involved cash,' Shirley said. 'Anyway, when Cartwright travelled, he didn't travel alone. On account of—'

'Being First Desk in all but name,' said Marcus.

'And thus requiring a body-watcher,' said Louisa.

'Yeah yeah yeah,' said Shirley. 'So you want to hear who it was, or not?'

Lamb said, 'It was Bad Sam, wasn't it?'

'Bad Sam Chapman,' Shirley said. 'That's exactly who it was.'

'So my name is Natasha, Natasha Reverde, and I grew up here, in this village. I moved away for a long time, but now I am back. This is something I have found, that as we get older, we need to return to our beginnings. This is not original, I think. But it is true.'

The house, like Victor's, was small, but there the resemblance ended. This was not only neat and clean; it was a loved space, and simply by being there, River was invited into Natasha's confidence. It felt a sudden promotion, from stranger to confidante, but he knew his resemblance to Bertrand was the trigger. It was as if he had become part of a family whose existence he hadn't been aware of. The fact of Bertrand's death he held to himself like a long-sworn promise or an imminent betrayal.

'So one evening, long ago, I met a man in a bar, and his name is Yevgeny, and one thing moves on to another. Yevgeny lives with his friends in a big house called Les Arbres, and when he takes me there I see that it is a very different way of life. They do not have jobs, but they are always very busy, very serious. Yevgeny is Russian, of course, but others are English and some German and Czech and a Frenchman too, he is called Jean. All Frenchmen are called Jean, but he really is.'

Her eyes grew darker.

'Yevgeny said they are all friends, all equal, but I think this is not so. One of them is not so equal, and he is the one they listen to. He gived, gave, not orders, but he makes suggestions, yes? And the suggestions he makes are the things that happen.'

'Were they all men?'

'Yes. Some of the men had girlfriends, local girls like me, but none of them are living there. And there is an older woman, a nursemaid, who calls in daily.'

'There were children?'

'Two small boys. Later, there were more.'

River waited, and again her eyes seemed to take on a deeper colour, as if the memories she was sinking into were staining her from the inside.

He said, 'Who was the man in charge?'

'His name was Frank. An American. Frank.'

'Did he have a surname?'

'I never hear it.' Natasha paused, listening to rain drumming on the windows. She had turned on two small lamps, whose glow didn't reach the corners, and the surrounding colours – the deep red of the throw upon the sofa; the cream and gold of the hanging on the wall – had grown richer in the half-light. River was reminded of Lamb, who also disliked overhead lighting, not for the unsubtle mood it threw upon a room's fixtures, but because he preferred the shadows.

'But he was American.'

'Yes. And he had an English woman, I remember. I saw her once, or more than once. Perhaps these occasions have melted into one.'

'Time plays tricks,' River said.

'She was very beautiful, and very cross, the time I saw her, and they have big argument, big row, and Frank tells everyone to leave. Yevgeny, he laughs, but we go for drive anyway. And when we come back, she is gone.'

'How long did you . . . know Yevgeny?'

'This was one summer only. Nineteen ninety.'

Which seemed a long time ago, to River.

'What happened?'

'Well, I fall pregnant. My parents are very angry with me, and with Yevgeny too. He was much older than me. In his thirties.'

'And how did he react?'

Her eyes became faraway again. 'He is happy. He say he will be good father, and we will live happily ever after. It is every young girl's dream, no?'

'Maybe not everyone's,' River said.

'No, this is true. Because if that happens, if I live happily ever after, it will mean being here for the rest of my life, in the next village along the river, and that is how far I will travel. And that is not what I want, you see? I want to go to Paris, to other cities, other countries. I want to see more of the world than the space between these two bridges.' She held her hands a few inches apart. 'For Yevgeny to take me away. Not keep me here.'

'Did you have the baby?'

'Yes. A boy, Patrice. And he does what babies do, which is cry a lot, and I was just eighteen.'

'I'm sorry, Natasha,' he said, without knowing why.

'So one night,' she said, as if he hadn't spoken, 'I leave the house with some money I have saved and I catch a train to Paris, which is how I get to see parts of the world which are not between these two bridges. And it is big and exciting and glamorous, and what happens to me there is what happens to lots of young girls who run away to the big city. I think you know what I mean.'

River, with Victor's words in mind, nodded briefly.

Natasha said, 'You are a young man, and you are English, and these things are great obstacles, but I will tell you this, that yes, I became a prostitute, and that is not something I feel shame for. There are things you do in life to be able to eat, yes?'

River said, 'We all do things to eat.'

'And this is one of them. I have worked in shops, also, and now I have a house-cleaning business, with three girls working for me, but once upon a time, a long way from here, I was

170

a whore, and to some people that is always what I am. To Victor, for instance. Who is nice enough person, but does not understand that people are not always the same.'

He decided he didn't want to know how Victor had discovered her previous profession. 'When did you come back here?'

'After some years. Ten, eleven? Things become bad in the city, and I decide it is better to return with what you call it, a tail between the legs, than stay there. But it is only because my father is dead that I am able to come back.'

River nodded. 'And Patrice?'

'All that time Yevgeny has him, at Les Arbres. My parents never see him, my father because he does not want to, and my mother because my father. But Yevgeny sends her photographs. I have these pictures still. I will show them to you.'

But she made no move to rise. Instead, she said:

'I went there, of course. To Les Arbres. But they do not let me in. Yevgeny, he comes out. He tells me I am not welcome, that I am no longer Patrice's mother. That he has a family, and does not need me.'

'I'm sorry,' River said.

'I too. Because I know he is right, I am not Patrice's mother. I give him birth, that is all. But still, I want to see him, I demand to see him, and then Frank comes, and Frank, he is very clear, very direct. He tells me that unless I leave, he will have police arrest me. He will tell them that not only am I a prostitute but a drug addict also, and other things like that. Threats.'

River knew better than to ask if she had been a drug addict.

For a while, Natasha sat gazing into her past, and then she rose and crossed the room, opened a drawer, retrieved something and returned. It was an envelope, unsealed. When she tilted it, several photographs slithered out; more than several.

They seemed to be in order already, the topmost one the earliest. It showed a man with dark Russian looks, holding an infant.

'Yevgeny,' Natasha said. 'With Patrice.'

More followed. The child grew older, learned to stand on his own feet; sometimes in the company of other children.

'Who are these?'

'The eldest two, they were at Les Arbres from the beginning. I do not remember their names. And here,' and she plucked a photo from the pile of her son at five or so, with another boy, slightly younger, 'this is Patrice with Bertrand. Bertrand is Frank's son.'

'Where did he come from?'

'I think the usual place,' Natasha said.

'I meant—'

'I am teasing. There are six or seven children in the end. All boys. The first two, and then Patrice and Bertrand and two or three more. All I know is what I hear, and what I see from photographs.'

'Yevgeny kept sending them, then.'

'While my mother lived. When she died, he stops. The last picture I have of my son is ten years old.'

This was said in a matter-of-fact tone.

'And the mothers, they were living there too?'

'Never for long. There were some Russian women, and a French girl, I think. An Englishwoman too, a different one. But they never stay long. Only the children stay.'

'Why do you think they left?'

'Once there was a rumour that bad things had happened, that the women were . . . killed or murdered or something, but the police, they make enquiries, and afterwards the rumours stop. The women, they move away because they are not happy there. They return to Moscow or London or wherever, and they leave their children behind, because this is how they like things to be. But I think it is how Frank likes things to be. Like with my own father, he says how he feels about things, and that is how the things become. They are the law. I think, at Les Arbres, Frank makes the law.'

River looked through the remaining photographs. Patrice grew older, Bertrand did the same, and in one shot the latter stood under a tree, the expression on his face familiar to River, though River couldn't think why. And again the thought struck him that this boy was dead now, and whatever future he might have had when this was taken was now an irretrievable mess on a bathroom floor. And even that presumably cleaned away by now; nothing more than a stain, an afterthought.

Another photo showed Patrice and another boy with two adult men.

'Who are they?' River asked, certain he already knew half the answer.

'That is Frank. The other, that is Jean. The Frenchman.'

Frank was tall, fairish, though not enough to be called blond; broad-shouldered and – here, at least – unshaven. He wore a short-sleeved shirt, and his arms looked strong and capable. He wasn't smiling. Rather, he seemed to be questioning the value of having his picture taken at all; as if he felt little need to have his presence confirmed by outside agency.

'Who's the other child here?'

Natasha said, 'That is Yves. He is called Yves.'

He looked younger than Patrice, and to River's eyes, an ordinary boy; his features a little blank; a canvas waiting to be scribbled on. Was he five years old? He might have been about that: River couldn't tell. But Natasha's tone had shifted, mentioning Yves's name. There was the same note of distaste as when she'd spoken of Frank. Distaste, unless it was fear.

But who would be frightened of a five-year-old, wondered River? And then remembered: five-year-olds grow up.

'You don't like this one,' he said.

'I do not know him.'

'But you know him enough not to like him.'

She was quiet for a while, then said, 'Sometimes you see him at the market, in the café. He looks at people like they are a different species.'

'In what way?'

'Like they are insects, or worse. Lower than insects.'

Growing up at Les Arbres, surrounded by men. River wondered what the boys had been taught.

He said, 'What did they live on, do you know?'

'Money?'

'Yes.'

'I do not know. Some of the villagers call them hippies at first, but even then it was late for hippies. And besides, they do not have guitars or take drugs, and there are not enough girls. So I think they have made their money somewhere and decide this is where they want to live, that is all. Somewhere remote, but not impossible. Somewhere . . . their own.'

'Did the children go to school?'

'No. Jean, he is a teacher, or he has qualifications. It is enough. They are educated at Les Arbres.'

'Which has now burned down.'

'Yes.' Natasha leaned forward. 'And that is why you are here, yes?'

'No. I didn't know that had happened. I didn't know about Les Arbres at all before today.'

And I don't know much more now, he thought. Or understand, anyway. But still, he had a grinding feeling in his stomach, as if he had ingested more knowledge than he was yet aware of, and it was trying to claw its way out.

Either that, or his hunger was becoming violent.

'Thank you,' he said at last. 'Thank you for speaking to me.'

'You don't know where they are,' she said.

'No.'

'But you are going to find out.'

'I'm going to try,' he said.

'If you find my son,' she said, 'you will tell me, yes? You will tell me where he is?'

River lied to her, as sincerely as he knew how.

Limping through the rain again, he made his way to the centre of the village and found a bank, with a cash-machine embedded in its wall. As he fed his credit card into its slot, he had the sensation of reappearing on the map; an awareness that he could now be tracked. His brief holiday among the dead was over. When emerging from the underworld, he vaguely recalled, it was best not to look over your shoulder; you could lose everything you thought you'd recovered. Even so, he took a moment to glance at the photograph he'd stolen from sad Natasha: her son, Patrice, and the other boy, Yves, their teacher, Jean, and the man Frank, who stared out from the celluloid as if already regretting the moment of contact it would produce, years later, here in the rain; the house that was the photo's backdrop a sodden ruin, and his own son a corpse in another country.

He had time to buy a bread roll, packed with cheese, before the bus arrived. And then he was on his way to Poitiers, thence to Paris, and from there, London: a journey he mostly slept through, though his dreams were of constant movement, and always with something swelling behind him; ready to pounce, ready to smother, ready to wash him away.

Back in the Park, on the hub, unfamiliarity had reimposed itself. Claude Whelan had been starting to feel he was settling in, but the conversation on the bus had thrust him back into the cold. He was the stranger again, the interloper, and no title he bore – First Desk, Chief Exec, God Albloodymighty – could bring him within the embrace of this chamber. And the glass wall of his office mocked the moment more.

Though it was always possible he was just feeling sorry for himself.

Diana had had coffee and sandwiches brought: a peace offering, Whelan thought, though again he might be over-dramatising. It was, after all, lunchtime. She had been running him through the logistics of the cold body protocol. How it had been mothballed once the wardrobe department was wound up, and how – like everything else to do with the Civil Service – this had not meant that the stalled product was consigned to the furnace; simply that it had been packaged, sealed, labelled, stored.

'We've had problems with storage space,' she said.

'So I heard.'

The problems in question had culminated in a shooting war in one of the Service's off-site facilities out beyond Paddington: 'putting the wild into the west', as a wit on the Limitations Committee had phrased it. Like many local unpleasantnesses – the deployment of Service resources to personal ends; the unseemly wrangling over parking-spaces; the decades-long cover-up of the sexual abuse of children by Members of Parliament – this had been quietly swept under the carpet, with the usual result: not so much a tidy floor as an unsightly bulge, which sooner or later someone was going to trip over, and break their career.

'But ID product has always been kept on-site, in one of the secure rooms.'

Diana broke off to unwrap a crayfish sandwich, bending its packaging into a nest so that wayward flecks of mayonnaise wouldn't soil her outfit. Then she removed the plastic lid from her coffee container and scraped the excess froth from it with a wooden paddle. Whelan watched, fascinated. The longer this went on, the less there'd be of the rest of his life, in which he had to cope with the dangerous stuff Diana was revealing.

But this wouldn't do. He was in charge – First Desk, Chief Exec, God Albloodymighty.

'So, then. How, precisely, do we determine who was responsible for stealing these—'

'Product,' she said.

'Product?'

'We can't keep calling them cold bodies, Claude. Apart from anything else, it might alert people to what we're talking about.' She raised her cup to her lips and breathed in coffee fumes rather than sipped. 'We are spies, remember?'

'Product, then. Do we have a list of suspects?'

'Well, there can't have been many people in a position to walk out of a secure room with several box-files' worth of high-clearance . . . product, but it was a long time ago. Whoever it was might have retired, moved on or dropped off the perch. Investigation would be a time-consuming business, and we don't have time, and it would inevitably attract attention, and we don't want any.'

'But apart from that,' he said.

'Apart from that,' she agreed, 'we would like to know who was responsible.'

'To what end?'

She said, 'I'm not sure I take your meaning, Claude.'

'I'm trying to determine what you regard as the best outcome,' he said. 'That we apprehend whoever's responsible in order to bring them to public justice. Or to make sure that nobody ever discovers the Service's involvement in the Westacres bombing.'

'Aren't you hungry?'

'I – what?'

'You haven't eaten your sandwich.'

He was still clutching it, in its wedge-shaped container. Something with chorizo. He didn't remember having been asked for a preference, or what he'd replied if he had been, but was pretty sure it wouldn't have been chorizo, if only because chorizo was one of those foodstuffs whose existence he only recalled when it was actually in his presence. Like yellow peppers. He was hungry, though, so tore the strip off the container, and carefully eased one sandwich out, though not carefully enough to prevent a globule of mustard dripping onto his lapel.

'Can I fetch you a—'

'I'm fine,' he snapped.

'The Service had no involvement in the Westacres bombing,' she said, as if the intervening pantomime had not occurred. 'Service product was misappropriated, and that's regrettable. But the Service itself had no involvement. Let's make sure we're on the same page on that one, Claude.'

Nothing in her tone suggested that this was a subordinate offering counsel to her boss. He glanced at Claire's photo, and it occurred to him that one of his first acts on taking up Dame Ingrid Tearney's mantle had been to neutralise – or at least, marginalise – a potential source of danger. He'd thought himself a pretty fine player of the game at the time. But it had been like trapping a mouse and releasing it miles away, then returning home to find a dragon in the kitchen.

A mouse can cause untold irritation, but there's nothing like the rain of fire a dragon can bring down.

Regaining an equable tone, he said, 'I think you can trust me to have the Service's best interests at heart, Diana.'

'Good.'

'Alongside those of the nation at large.'

'God, yes. The nation.'

He bit into his sandwich. The chorizo was spicy, and bit back. 'The missing product, though. You have the details?'

She was nodding before he'd finished; had the look, Whelan decided, of a satisfied teacher. He didn't care. Right this moment, he'd take anything he could get.

'If they're currently in use, we find them,' he said. 'We find them, and with their help, voluntary or otherwise, we discover who provided them with their identities in the first place. And then we draw a curtain over the whole dreadful episode.'

'Voluntary or otherwise,' she repeated. 'Perhaps you have the makings of a First Desk after all, Claude.'

'What are the names?'

'Robert Winters we already know. He's the only one to make a mark on the world so far.'

'And the others?'

'Paul Wayne,' she said. 'And Adam Lockhead.'

'Wayne and Lockhead,' he murmured. The names meant nothing to him, and he hoped they never would. Not in the way their brother-in-fiction Robert Winters did.

'I've fed them into the system,' Diana said. 'On a low priority.'

Whelan raised an eyebrow.

'Because the only high priority right now is Westacres,' she said. 'And we can't have anyone drawing a connection between those names and that event. Not until we've had a chance to . . . ensure the correct outcome.'

A safe pair of hands, he thought, nostalgically. That was supposed to be him. And almost without pause, his feet barely under First Desk, here he was: involved in what some – even Claire, he supposed – might consider a conspiracy. Almost unconsciously he reached out and adjusted his wife's photo. Little moments of contact, that was all he asked.

'Well then,' he said. 'Let's make sure that the correct outcome is what we achieve.'

Part Two

Nothing Like the Rain

10

B AD SAM CHAPMAN PUT no trust in itchy feelings.

Bad Sam, though, didn't have a lot of time for nick-
names either, and his own had followed him like a hopeful
puppy for years, its origins obscured by the passage of time,
but probably something to do with an occasional irritability.
He didn't himself think he was that bad. Everyone had their
moments.

Itchy feelings, though, were superstitious nonsense,
conjured into being by an overly greased diet, or too much
cheese. Nothing to do with a sixth sense – geese didn't walk
on your grave. You could step on all the cracks you wanted,
and your mother's back remained her own concern.

Which was why he had an irritable moment coming on,
because he had a bucketload of itchy feelings, every last one
of them screaming at him to avoid the cracks, to watch his
back.

This wasn't the first time he'd had them lately. He'd spent
the previous morning trawling amusement arcades in Brixton,
alert for one Chelsea Barker, the latest of the hundreds of
teenage runaways he'd searched for these past years, except
that Chelsea, God help us all, wasn't a teenager; Chelsea was
twelve years old. It was like looking for a goldfish in a piranha
tank – you had to be quick. So when the itchy feelings

overtook him, he'd thought they were on her account. Twelve years old, and she could be anywhere. She could be right behind him. So more than once he'd turned to check, as if that were the way things worked, and runaway kids came looking for him instead of the other way round, but there was never anyone there, except that there always was – there was always someone there, in London. And in the course of checking, he'd seen the same face twice.

Only twice, and just for an instant. A random stranger, one of the thousands on the streets every day.

But once upon a time Bad Sam had been a spook, which meant he could never rule out the possibility that one of those random strangers might be looking to tick his name off a list. So superstitious nonsense or not, he paid attention when the itchy feelings started.

Yesterday, this had involved a complicated ride to a Tube station three lines away, and a twenty-minute loiter on an unfamiliar platform, while he satisfied himself his tail was clean. The random stranger had been a young man with dark, serious eyebrows and two days' stubble, wearing a black leather jacket over a light-blue polo neck, jeans and trainers. Something European about him. Stone cold awake at three in the morning, Sam had run the face through his mental files, and hadn't found a match. There was a niggle, though – a loose thread at the hem of his memory. The stranger had been young, and Bad Sam had been out of the game for years. Maybe it was a family resemblance, but that made no sense. He'd been Secret Service, not mafia. Grudges weren't handed down father to son. At four he'd fallen asleep, but had dreamed of foreign travel, and its attendant irritations: the documents that were never in the right pocket; the steering wheel on the wrong side of the car.

This afternoon the itchy feelings were back, but the random stranger was nowhere to be seen.

It was another day of grey drizzle, London a cold wet misery, and Bad Sam was heading back to the office after his third morning of looking for, not finding, Chelsea Barker. His plan was to hit the phones again, and squeeze what leads he could from untapped contacts. London the cold wet misery was also a wolf-pack world, and twelve-year-olds who were the hardest articles their schools had ever seen snapped like peppermint sticks on its streets. Finding the child was the most important thing in Bad Sam's life right now, but still – those itchy feelings. Older, sterner creatures were snappable too. And who would go looking for Chelsea Barker then?

This junction here, Tube station, church and building site: you had to be careful crossing. You had to look all ways. Lurking in the shelter of the station, bracing himself to face the waiting weather, Bad Sam Chapman turned his collar up against grey London's worst.

Oh yes, grey London.

London was a class-A city, of course, constantly topping those lists which explained the world in bullet points. It had the best clubs, the best restaurants, the best hotels; it threw the best parties, and cobbled together the best Olympics ever. It had the best royal family, the best annual dog show and the best police force, and was basically brilliant except for the parts that weren't, which were like someone had taken all the worst bits of everywhere else and shored them up against each other. And the traffic was a fucking nightmare.

None of which was news to Patrice.

Who wasn't Patrice today, but that was hardly news either. His passport proclaimed him Paul Wayne, and this required no mental adjustment: Patrice had been Paul Wayne for as long as he could remember. And Paul Wayne was as much at home in London, even the bad parts, as anywhere in France; could order a drink either side of the river, and nobody would bat an eye. Because Paul Wayne didn't just speak English, he spoke *English* English, the same way he spoke French French. He'd have tied Henry Higgins in knots, and if that wasn't enough to piss Higgins off, Paul Wayne could have gone on to kill him with his bare hands in about fourteen different ways, because that, too, had been part of the training that had been taking place every moment of Patrice's life. Patrice's life was about being Paul Wayne. And today Paul Wayne was taking one Sam Chapman off the board.

Yesterday Chapman had spotted him and taken evasive action: ducking into the underground and adopting a sentry post at the end of a platform. Patrice hadn't enjoyed the two-second report he'd had to make – *Nobody at home. Will attempt redelivery* – but at least it had given him a clue as to the target. Sam Chapman looked like most other people tramping the streets in lousy weather: pissed off, down-at-heel, in need of a better raincoat. But Chapman was also a pro, or had been, and that stayed in your blood. Responses slowed, but they didn't disappear. When someone dropped a tray in a crowded restaurant, you looked every which way except towards the noise, hunting down the action it was meant to distract you from. And when you thought someone was tailing you you took evasive action, even if the thought was a second-hand murmur, a butterfly wing. If you felt a fool afterwards, at least you were alive to feel foolish. So Sam Chapman was that kind of target, which meant Patrice knew to prepare the ground this time; to check for escape routes and probable hideaways. A pro never went home with tingles running down his spine. A pro spooked on home territory took wing, and didn't look back.

So this was today's plan: spook him deliberately. Spook him, and watch him take flight.

Then bring him down.

Marcus had parked where he'd get a ticket.

'Put a note in the window,' Louisa suggested. 'Secret agent on call.'

He muttered something, a grumble about being designated driver. His fault for driving an urban tank, though; the only one with a car big enough to carry an unhappy passenger.

They were south of the river, half a mile from the Thames, near one of those busy junctions which rely on the self-preservation instincts of the drivers using it; either a shining example of new age civic theory, or an old-fashioned failure of town planning. On one of its corners sat a church; on another, earth-moving monsters re-enacted the Battle of the Bulge behind hoardings which shivered with each impact. A Tube station squatted on a third, its familiar brick-and-tile façade more than usually grubby in the drizzle. There was a lot of construction work nearby, buildings wrapped in plastic sheeting, some of it gaudily muralled with visions of a bright new future: the gleaming glass, the pristine paving, the straight white lines of premises yet-to-be. Meanwhile, the surviving shops were the usual array of bookmakers, convenience stores and coffee bars, many of them crouching behind scaffolding and some of them bookending alleyways which would be either dead ends where wheelie bins congregated or short cuts to the labyrinth of darker streets beyond. Once upon a time Charles Dickens wandered this area, doubtless taking notes. Nowadays the local citizenry's stories were recorded by closed-circuit TV, which had less time for sentimental endings.

Up one of those alleys was Elite Enquiries, the private

detective agency whose staff of three included Bad Sam Chapman, once of Regent's Park.

Chapman had been Head Dog, long before Louisa's time, and he'd left under a cloud whose rain had washed him up here: a third-rate agency specialising in evicting troublesome tenants, serving unwanted papers, and – Bad Sam's own forte – finding runaways. The image on the Web was of a shabby office resembling a minicab operation, but she supposed its low-rent appearance might play in its favour: if someone was lost among the rackety arcades, threadbare hostels and thrift-shop doorways of the city, this was the right sort of place to start looking. But anyway, they weren't here to evaluate Elite Enquiries' market position. They were here for Bad Sam.

'Okay,' Lamb had said. 'Let's bring him in.'

'On whose authority?' Louisa asked.

'I wasn't suggesting you stuff him in the back of a van,' Lamb said. 'Just ask him nicely.'

'And if he refuses?'

'Stuff him in the back of a van,' said Lamb.

'We haven't got a van,' Shirley pointed out.

Lamb looked at Marcus.

'What? It's not a van.'

But mere statement of fact wilted in the face of Lamb's indifference.

So here they were, round the side of the church in Marcus's suburban-warrior vehicle, the pair of them rendered feature-less by its smoked-glass windscreen. Marcus wore an earpiece, waiting for word from Slough House while they monitored the Tube station entrance, its irregular heartbeat skew-whiffed by the drizzle: dribs and drabs of passengers scurrying in; larger groups reluctantly leaving every three minutes or so.

The pattering on the car roof sounded like mice changing places.

'I hope Ho doesn't fuck up,' Marcus said at last.

'It's computer stuff. He knows what he's doing,' Louisa said.

'Maybe so, but he's a little prick. And I hate relying on a little prick to get the job done.'

'Yeah, tell me about it,' said Louisa.

They didn't know Chapman would be coming from the Tube. They knew he was out because they'd called his office, but that was the extent of their knowledge: that he wasn't in his office. It was, as neither had yet said out loud, a pretty half-arsed basis on which to start a surveillance, but it was all they had to go on until Ho came up with the goods. Meanwhile, Chapman might appear from the Tube station; he might swoosh past in a taxi; he might be wandering up the road from the other direction. But there were only two of them, and neither of them wanted to get wet, so here they were.

Marcus said, 'You're pissed off with him, aren't you?'

'With who?' Louisa said, though she knew who he meant.

'With Cartwright.'

'Why would I be?'

''Cause he didn't tell you he's alive.'

'I'm not his keeper. He wants to go haring off on a wild goose chase, that's his lookout.'

'You'd have had his back, though. If he'd asked.'

'We have a drink once in a while. We're not Batman and Robin. We're not even you and Shirley. You're more of a team than me and Cartwright.'

Marcus shrugged. 'Shirley's my bro. But she can be hard work.'

'I didn't want to be the one to say it,' Louisa said.

'River, though, he could have picked up a phone.'

'He's in joe country,' she said. 'Not on a city break.'

Marcus was about to reply, but his earpiece squawked in time to stop him.

★

Back in Slough House, Roderick Ho was sandwiched between monitors, a pair angled inwards so his face was washed in their glow. Some people – cowards – thought it was dangerous, getting too close to your screens. But they were the kind getting left behind by history, unless they were being abandoned by the future: Ho didn't care which, those fools were fucked either way.

On one of his screens was a satellite map of south London, on a scale that made it look like a circuitry diagram. On the other was a magnified portion of the same map, its focus an unremarkable alleyway half a mile south of the Thames. If Ho hovered his cursor over it, the legend Elite Enquiries would appear, along with its postcode and a link to 'further information'. The amount of data broadband delivered, half a spook's job was done for him, right there.

Course, if you wanted the rest sorted out, you looked to your Bonds, your Solos, your Hos.

Earlier, he'd jacked into the Park's tracking system and put the finger on Sam Chapman's mobile, 'putting the finger' being, he had decided, a cool way of describing tagging. Kim – his girlfriend – liked hearing about this stuff, how Roddy slipped in and out of systems like a cyber-ghost. The only problem was, Chapman's mobile wasn't showing up, which might mean he'd deliberately gone dark, and removed his phone's battery, or just that he was out of reach: in one of the capital's grey areas, where the signal fizzled to a damp wick.

'Tag him, find him, bring him in,' had been Lamb's instructions.

Sometimes, Ho wished he was like the rest of the Slough House crew. Dumb muscle got the easy jobs.

And if he said as much to Kim, she'd laugh, pointing out that the Rodster was a lot of things, but dumb wasn't ever going to be one of them. Except he couldn't say that to Kim, because he hadn't actually told her he was a spook – that was one of the first things they taught you, that it was the *secret* service. So he'd made it sound like he was private sector, working out of Canary Wharf, those huge glass canyons reeking of money and power: plenty of scope for a dude like the Rod-man, and really, was it such a bad idea? The crew here got called the slow horses, and Roddy Ho felt tainted by association. It'd break Lamb's heart if he upped sticks, obviously, but sometimes a man had to—

A red dot pulsed into life.

Behind him, Shirley said, 'What's that? Is that Bad Sam?'

Patrice spotted the target the moment he emerged on the pavement. The key to tailing someone was knowing where they'd end up: for two hours, he'd been sitting by a window in the public library, nursing an Americano from the coffee concession and blending with the computer users, the students, the people with nowhere to go. It was a handy spot, shielded by scaffolding, passing traffic and a general air of gloom, but all he had to do was step outside for Chapman to see him and take flight. To bring a pigeon down, first you set it on the wing. He'd learned to shoot in the fields round Les Arbres, and appreciated a moving target.

Thinking these thoughts he was already on his feet, skirting the coffee booth, trotting down the risers to the exit ramp—

'Watch where you're going!'

He tried to step past, but the newcomer, a burly man in a mobile fug of stale beer, caught his jacket.

'I said *watch* where you're *going*—'

Patrice put him on the floor relatively gently, and it only

took half a second, but he was in full view of the issue desk behind him.

'Hey! *Hey!* You can't do that!'

He could, and had, but he didn't want to hang around to discuss his abilities. Stepping over one nuisance, ignoring the other, he moved towards the doors, which obligingly parted, but not before someone had appeared between them, coming in from the street. He was wide and black and uniformed, and his face clouded suspiciously when he saw the man on the floor and heard the growing commotion.

There was, thought Patrice, always something.

Shirley said, 'Is that Bad Sam?'

'It's his mobile,' Ho said.

'So it's Bad Sam.'

'Unless someone else has his mobile.'

'So it's Bad Sam.'

Ho snorted, but yeah, it was Bad Sam. Who let somebody else have their mobile?

Shirley said into her own phone, 'He's heading down the High Street. If he's going to his office, he'll take the one, two, third on his left. It's an alleyway.'

'One, two, third?' Marcus said.

'I was counting. Can you see him?'

'Wait a sec.'

A muffled voice was Louisa, talking to Marcus.

Marcus said, 'Yeah, we have him. Over the road.'

'There, that was easy, wasn't it?' Shirley said. 'Pick him up and bring him in.'

'You're the boss all of a sudden?'

'You're gonna let him go just 'cos I said to pick him up?'

Marcus had a brilliant answer for that, but before he could deliver it Louisa was tapping his arm.

'He's turning off,' she told him, at the exact moment Roderick Ho said the same to Shirley.

Crossing the junction Bad Sam heard a crash, something heavy going through glass, and changed plans on the instant: there were always noises somewhere, and not all of them had to do with him, but he'd be an idiot to ignore the possibility, with those itchy feelings still scratching at his spine. So he slipped off the High Street before his turning, and headed down a narrow alley, where the ground was mushy with fag ends and the air smokily visible. Some of this was pumping from a vent set in the wall next to an open door, against which an olive-skinned man in a kitchen worker's smock was smoking a joint.

'Yo, Sam,' he said. 'Sammity Sam.'

He always said that, and it always wasn't funny. But Bad Sam always laughed, because you never knew when you might need a favour.

'Hey, Miguel,' he said. 'You didn't see me, and I wasn't here, right?'

'Never here,' Miguel agreed as Bad Sam slipped past him, and through the kitchen, and out of the café's front door onto another street entirely.

Here's a thing about men in uniform: they go through a window as easily as any other kind.

Turned out it was only a traffic warden, but that wasn't Patrice's fault. And it made no difference to the way the glass rained down around him, the fingernail-sized nuggets of it used in bus-stops and windscreens. Libraries, too, were prepared for sudden impact. Probably wise, given the cuts.

But there was no time to dwell on that, because people would have phones out soon, and then there'd be more uniforms coming, the serious kind. In the two-second grace that follows unexpected violence, Patrice turned his collar up and strode through the obliging doors to see, on the other side of the road, the target turning down an alleyway not his own.

Louisa was gone in a flash, sprinting for the road, hoping to get into that alleyway before Sam Chapman disappeared out the other end. Marcus was slower, pausing to click the car locked: it was his vehicle, damn it, and they were south of the river, and the family was already one set of wheels down. Dying at his desk would look the softer option if anything happened to this one. So by the time he reached the road Louisa was just barely leaping to safety on the other side, a bus-horn blaring her home. The surface was slick with rain, and hurling yourself out into traffic, assuming it would stop, worked fine in the movies, but Marcus had seen people hit by cars, and didn't fancy pissing sitting down for the rest of his life. Louisa was weaving in and out of people wielding umbrellas, and Marcus, running parallel with her, nearly crashed into a crowd gathered in a passage to his right: it was clustered round a large man lying in a puddle of glass and books. Noting the uniform, Marcus thought, *Well you won't be handing out tickets*, but his follow-up was more to the point: *Who put you through a window, mate?* Someone more aggravated than a ticketed driver; he must weigh eighteen stone. And nobody tossed eighteen stone through a window without practice, or a trebuchet.

He looked across the road. Louisa was gone. He grabbed the nearest onlooker. 'Who did this?'

'Are you police?'

'*Who?*'

The onlooker, scrawny, dandruffed, damp, said, 'He was just a bloke, know what I mean? Didn't look like he could throw a dart, let alone—'

A pro, thought Marcus. 'Where'd he go?'

'Didn't see, know what I mean?'

Marcus could just about work it out.

He scanned the area, but raining like this, most people hurrying, nobody stood out.

There was a gap in the traffic, though, so he took the chance and ran across the road.

When you flushed a bird, all you needed to know was which direction the sky was. Men were trickier, more devious.

But Patrice had studied maps, and knew that the alleyway the target had gone down led nowhere.

Which might mean the target was unlucky, and that was like finding money in the street. Hunting someone unlucky, you could just pick your spot and wait. But the target was a former spook, and while spooks made mistakes like everybody else, they didn't run down blind alleys two hundred metres from home. Patrice moved past the entrance without pausing; just another Londoner caught in the rain. A little further on he took the next left, and looked back to see a woman following the target's route.

There was hardly anyone on this street. The pavement was narrow, the kerbs flooded; parked cars lined the opposite side. To his left, a chain-link fence sealed off a space where a house had stood. From behind came the growing wail of a siren, but this didn't worry him. Add ten minutes for witness statements, and Patrice could be on the other side of London. Meanwhile, the target appeared from a doorway ahead and hurried up the road without looking round. Good tradecraft, thought Patrice, but in this case a mistake. He quickened his pace, and consulted the map in his head. Chapman would weave his way in and out of this tapestry of backstreets, trying to zigzag himself invisible, a common ambition when you knew you were prey. And in the attempt he'd pass through somewhere dark and lonely, maybe underneath one of the railway bridges which spanned the roads in this area. All Patrice would need was a second or two. He ran a hand through his hair. The rain was getting harder.

Ho watched the screen, lips moving. Behind him, Shirley said, 'What happened there? Is he going through a building? He's going through a building!'

She said into her phone, 'He's going through a building,' though Marcus had already gathered as much, twice.

Louisa emerged from the alleyway as he reached it. 'Dead end.'

'He's gone through a—'

'Building, yeah, I worked that out.'

'You got that map?' Marcus said, not to Louisa.

Into his earpiece, Shirley said, 'Left, then left again.'

Bad Sam knew he'd been flushed by the breaking glass; that he'd fallen for the automatic escape principle, the one that said *Fly. Now.* But knew, too, that he'd bought himself a tiny advantage, one he could keep hold of provided he didn't look behind.

He doesn't know you know he's there.

That in his mind, Bad Sam headed further into the maze of streets that looped round Corporation housing, dog-legged past schools, and threaded under bridges. In the rain he heard no following footsteps; just a steady patter on the pavements and, distantly, a police car's plaintive wail. *Don't look round.*

Louisa would have been off already, but Marcus caught her by the arm. Anyone else and she'd have broken his elbow – she was in the mood. But Marcus didn't break easily, and had a message to impart.

'There's someone else. After Chapman.'

'Who?'

'A pro.'

He released her.

And now she was away, faster than Marcus, who was getting a little heavy, frankly. A police car was coming; as she turned the corner it pulled up by the library, its blue light throwing ghosts on wet surfaces. This new street was narrower, and right-angled a few hundred metres on; a figure was disappearing round the corner. Could be Chapman. Back at Slough House Ho was tracking his movements, relaying them to Marcus, but Louisa was offline.

She glanced behind. Marcus was following, his features set in a grimace.

At the corner, she turned left. The road ahead forked, one tine winding under a railway bridge where a pair of youngsters were sheltering, hand in hand. A woman was approaching, dragging a basket on wheels; beyond her, heading away, a figure in a raincoat was hustling along. On the opposite pavement a younger man, leather jacket, shoulders hunched, was moving fast.

Marcus caught her, one finger holding his earpiece in place. 'He's ahead of us. Two hundred metres?'

'Wearing a raincoat,' she said. 'And there's the pro. Leather jacket.'

'He see you?'

She wasn't sure. She didn't think so.

Marcus said, 'Loop round at this next junction. If you're fast enough, you'll overtake him before he hits the main road.'

Making it sound like a challenge, which was probably deliberate.

She nodded and took off, breaking into a run once she'd rounded the corner.

Two of them, thought Patrice. The target was ahead, walking briskly, and there were two behind him: a suspicion confirmed by a reflection in a ground-floor window, cracked open to release a veil of blue smoke. If they knew what they were doing they would separate soon, though if they knew what they were doing, they wouldn't have let him spot them so easily.

They might come to regret that.

His hands were bunched inside his pockets. Rain slid down his neck. But the rain was his friend, keeping the backstreets clear, and people's attention elsewhere. The target had turned another corner, but that was fine. There were only so many corners left.

Have to lose some weight.

That wasn't so much Marcus's own mind forming thoughts as a small version of Cassie, his wife, making a guest appearance in his head.

Then Shirley's voice was in his ear, completing the duet: 'He's ahead of you. Why aren't you running?'

'. . . Sort of am,' he said through gritted teeth.

'Why aren't you running faster?'

He was tempted to toss the earpiece, but going dark was frowned upon, midway through an op.

The man in the leather jacket had turned the corner after Chapman, and any doubt he was following had now dispersed. True, there were only so many routes, and everyone looked furtive in the rain, but still: there was something about the way the man moved. He didn't break stride to avoid puddles, but didn't splash through them either. Handy gift to have. Marcus bet his feet were grateful.

Shirley said, 'Chapman's stopping.'

'Where?'

'Next left, then right. Taking shelter?'

'Taking guard, more like,' Marcus said, and felt something tighten in his chest; the same feeling he got playing blackjack, watching the dealer deal. Knowing, always, that he couldn't lose, whatever experience might suggest to the contrary.

The extra pound or two didn't fall away, but still: Marcus felt lighter as he picked up his pace, following the spook on Chapman's tail.

Another bridge over the road, this one with a train crossing. Its thunder filled the world for a moment, and then it was gone, and the rain was heavier, pounding the pavements ahead.

It seemed to Bad Sam Chapman that everything had grown darker.

His breathing was rough, and his thigh muscles aching: this without breaking into a trot. What age did to you, and late-night drinking. But age was inevitable, up to a point; as for late-night drinking, this was not easily avoided either. All political lives end in failure, someone once said. Spooks' lives, too, held more to regret than to cherish, a conclusion it was hard to ignore once the light drained from the day. You could stay up late brooding, or you could stay up late brooding drunk. There weren't many other options.

Bad Sam hoped like hell he'd find Chelsea Barker. He hated to leave things unfinished.

He crossed the road into a side street and passed a pair of wooden gates, chained closed, but loosely enough to allow for a gap. For the first time, he looked behind. His follower wasn't in sight; was leaving enough space between them to give Chapman the illusion of safety. Here it was, then. He took hold of one gate, pushed at the other, and ducked under the chain. He was in a garage forecourt: two black cabs parked against one wall; a workshop with its doors concertinaed open, a naked bulb glowing, but nobody in evidence. There'd be a hammer, a monkey wrench, something. Just give me a minute, Sam thought. Give me two. Time to catch my breath. He didn't even know why this was happening, but that hardly mattered: this, or something like it, had always been on the cards. He wasn't the only one who hated unfinished business. It went with the territory.

Patrice almost walked straight past, but there was that odd hint of movement; the suggestion that the gates were trembling in the rain. Chapman must be past the point of pretence – when you found yourself hiding in backyards, you were beyond caution and into the fear. Now was as good a time as any. His own pursuers had yet to show themselves; if he moved quickly, he and Chapman might finish their mission without interruption. Because it was a joint mission. Chapman had a significant role to play in its fulfilment. A murder is nothing without a victim.

Overhead, an aeroplane on the Heathrow approach was briefly visible below cloud, and then was gone.

Patrice slipped under the chain, one hand on the gate to prevent it wobbling. The yard seemed empty, though a light glimmered in the workshop. From his pocket he took a pair of thin leather gloves. When he snapped the poppers to tighten them at the wrist, the sound was the loudest thing on the planet.

When Louisa reached the junction the street was empty except for a fat woman, barrelling along like a boat in turbulent water. Louisa swore under her breath and did a quick 360-degree scan: there was nowhere for them to have gone. There hadn't been time. Which meant they'd left the street altogether: entered a building, a shop, something . . .

There were no shops. A wall this side of the railway bridge was so plastered in graffiti it looked camouflaged, ready to be dropped unnoticed into someone's acid trip; on the other side was a former gym, forfeiture notices pasted to its whitewashed windows. She glanced up at the bridge, but they'd have to be Spider-Man to have got up there. Spider-Men. And it wasn't like they'd be working in concert.

A pro, Marcus had said. The way Chapman had ducked for cover, he'd known there was someone on his tail. So he'd have gone to ground first chance he got . . .

Beyond the bridge, set back from the road, was a pair of wooden gates: a garage perhaps, closed at the moment, a loose chain dangling from slack brackets.

Through there.

She should wait for Marcus, who wouldn't be more than a minute – make that a minute and a half. But a minute and a half was a long time for a pro; long enough to do anything he wanted.

A sudden squall of wind chased a curtain of rain down the road. It had a bracing effect. She had a task in hand: take Bad Sam Chapman to Slough House. A taxi was approaching, slowing down for her, but Louisa was nobody's fare today. She trotted towards the gates, pushed them as wide as the chain would allow, and slipped into the yard in time to see a crowbar come hurtling at her head.

He moved like he could walk between raindrops. That was Bad Sam's uninvited thought, watching from behind one of the taxis while Patrice crossed the forecourt, heading for the workshop. In Sam's hand was a crowbar, plucked from a tool board nailed to the wall, and its heft in his hand triggered a slow-motion flashback: some things you don't forget. Like: don't swing a weapon that's more than a foot long. The motion leaves you open as a wardrobe. No: jab, hard, at the back of the skull. Then take as long as you like to line up your second shot; your man's not going anywhere. He's lying on the ground, his childhood memories leaking from a punctured head.

Which was the plan, and it didn't go wrong for some seconds. The man stood staring into the workshop as if waiting for Bad Sam to emerge with his hands up; Sam, meanwhile, rose and drifted across the forecourt behind him, the crowbar in a two-handed grip like a broom handle. And then it was gone, wrenched away so slickly, he could have sworn the man still had his back to him, but for half a moment he was staring straight into his face – yesterday's European stranger; no doubting that now – which wore no trace of emotion, and registered little effort, even as he jabbed with an elbow, hooked with a foot, and put Bad Sam into a puddle. On his back, he saw the crowbar raised high, ready to come slamming into his skull: night night. Instead, it whipped away through the air, and Chapman's eyes followed its flight to see it pound the wood inches from the head of a woman who'd just slipped between the gates.

I don't know who you are, he thought, but I hope you brought a gun.

Marcus arrived too late to see Louisa squeeze between the gates, but he heard her shriek; heard the clatter of heavy metal striking wood. In his ear Shirley was gabbling, and he pulled the earpiece out to focus on the here and now. A taxi had pulled up, engine running, and through its window the cabbie was asking where Stan was, he had a service booked, but Marcus was already running for the gates, which he hit shoulder first: some give, but no damage. Through the gap, he saw Louisa sprinting towards two figures in the middle of the yard: Sam Chapman prone, and leather-jacket man standing over him. His stillness, his readiness, put the fear on Marcus: not for himself, for Louisa. But there was no way he'd get through the gap in the gates: *Have to lose*

some weight, he thought again, this time with the hollow knowledge that even if he did so, it would be too late to help.

She wished she had a gun.

The crowbar carved its lunch from the gate just inches
from her head, then clattered to the ground: not a gun,
but it would do. She scooped it up. Chapman was down,
and the pro was standing over him but watching her;
measuring the distance between them, gauging her intent.
She lobbed the bar from one hand to the other, and his
stance adjusted minutely, but even as she changed hands
again, because there was no way she was using her left, he
was moving forward, stepping inside her swing so it was
only her forearm that struck him, and she dropped the
crowbar as the yard turned upside down.

When she hit the ground she rolled, but not far enough
to avoid his kick, which caught her left hip, and her leg went
numb.

Two of them, and both down. It had taken seconds.

There was no pride in the thought. He was simply moni-
toring the situation.

Patrice bent to collect the crowbar, the nearest tool for
finishing the job, and as he did so Chapman scrambled to
his feet. The old spook had been right to go for the jab, not
the swing, and if they were all sitting round a café table now
it wouldn't take either of them long to persuade the woman
of her mistake either. But rules were made to be broken,
provided you knew what you were doing; an excuse favoured
by assassins as much as poets. Patrice dropped to a crouch,
his back perfectly straight, and swung the tool into Chapman's
knee, making the old spook scream. Never outlive your
ability to survive a fight, Patrice thought.

He turned to the woman, but she was gone and something was flying towards him, a metal can, its contents spraying wide as it rotated in the air. It would have caught his face had he not been wielding the crowbar; as it was, he deflected it effortlessly, like a first-class batsman despatching the short ball. While he was doing that the woman was making a dash for the workshop, where any number of weapons might be waiting. So he threw the bar again: not javelin-fashion, but more like skimming a stone: it struck her ankles, and if she hadn't broken her fall with her hands, she'd have smeared her nose across her face. And this was as much comfort as the next twenty seconds had to offer her, he thought, because any chance he could leave her alive had disappeared when she came into the yard. Though she hadn't been alone, he remembered, a memory that took solid form the moment it occurred, as a black London cab slammed through the gates, sending blades of wood shivering into the rain; it screamed at Patrice sideways as the driver hit a handbrake turn, then tossed him over its shoulder as casually as a bull discarding an apprentice toreador.

Somewhere in the background, an angry cabbie was shouting.

11

'AND THEN HE GOT away,' said Shirley.
'Yeah, well—'
'Like a ghost. Or a ninja.'
'Or a ninja ghost,' said Ho.
'Fuck off,' Marcus told him. And to Shirley: 'Yeah, like a ninja. Or something.'

Because when you hit someone with a London cab, they generally stayed hit long enough for you to collect their ears, let alone their insurance details. But this guy was smoke: he must have gone over the cab's roof and hit the ground feet first. Which were already moving, like in cartoons: if not a ninja, at the very least Daffy Duck.

Though when Daffy Duck whacked folk with heavy weapons, they assumed odd shapes for a second or two, then shook their heads and walked away intact.

'How you feeling?' he asked Louisa.

'Same as last time you asked,' she said. 'That was ibuprofen, not horse tranquillisers.'

They were back at Slough House, in Marcus and Shirley's room, and Louisa's jeans, ripped in her fall, were rolled to the knee while her feet soaked in a plastic washing-up bowl nobody had known Slough House possessed – nobody except Catherine Standish, that is, who'd been there when they returned. It was a weird sort of reunion, with Louisa limping, and Bad Sam Chapman taking the stairs one at a time.

'You're back,' Marcus had told her, unnecessarily.

She'd touched him, briefly, on the elbow. Then said: 'Why'd you bring them here? They should be in A & E.'

'Slippery slope,' Lamb said. 'Once you start giving this lot the professional attention they require, there won't be enough of us left for a game of darts.'

'You can play darts on your own,' Roderick Ho said.

'Who was that guy?' Sam Chapman asked. 'Why was he following me? Why were *you* following me, come to that?'

'God, I hate catch-up scenes,' Lamb said. 'And a thank-you would be nice. I did just save your life.'

'Didn't see you there.'

'Yeah, well, I let others do the spade work.' He glanced at Marcus. 'Just a phrase. Let's not involve the thought police.'

'We'd need a SWAT team,' Marcus muttered.

While this was going on, Catherine had found the plastic bowl for Louisa to soak her ankles, and produced some ibuprofen. Louisa claimed through gritted teeth she was fine, but her ankles looked like she'd done service on a chain gang.

'The skin's not broken,' Catherine told her. 'That's something, anyway.'

It didn't feel like much to Louisa, but having Catherine say so was reassuring somehow. 'You back for good?' she asked.

'I hope not,' Catherine said, then followed Lamb and Chapman out of the room and up the stairs.

'She brought the O.B. with her,' Shirley told them.

'The O.B.'s here?'

'Upstairs with the Moira.'

Marcus shook his head. Chaos seemed the order of the day. That was certainly what Stan the Garage Man had thought, when he'd returned to find his forecourt a war zone: a black cab steaming in the rain, his gates in splinters. Marcus had shown him his ID, pointing to the line about Her Majesty's Service, and told him they were Duty men apprehending a VAT defaulter. Stan had cast an uneasy eye towards his work-shop, which was doubtless where he kept his books, and piped down. Though he did ask who'd pay for the gates.

'Send the invoice to your local tax office,' Marcus said. 'They'll see you all right.'

And now Marcus felt good, or better than in recent memory. It wasn't just smashing through the gates that had done the trick; nor sideswiping the bad guy in the process. It was more that he hadn't had to use his own car. This felt like a turning of the wheel – his luck shifting back to its proper position.

Except for the part about the bad guy getting away.

He said, 'I clipped him with the taxi, I know I did. Felt the impact.'

'And then he got away,' said Shirley.

'Shirl,' Marcus said. 'If you'd been there, you'd have decked him. We get that. But you weren't, and he's smoke. Okay?'

'Just saying.'

'Any word from River?' Louisa asked.

'Not even a postcard. Don't you hate it when colleagues go on holiday and—'

'When did Catherine get here?'

'I bet he won't even bring chocolates back. About half an hour ago.'

'What kind of state's the O.B. in?'

'He looked like a ghost. Confused and scared.'

'River was worried about him.'

'Yeah, well,' Shirley said. 'Running off to the Continent's a good way of showing it. Cool jeans, by the way.'

'Ripped jeans.'

'That's what I meant.'

'I pay good money for unripped jeans.'

'Kim wears ripped jeans,' Ho said. 'She's my girlfriend,' he explained.

'Really.'

'Ripped jackets too.'

'Are you still here?'

'Yes,' Ho said. They stared. 'No,' he said, and left. Before he'd crossed the landing, they heard Lamb bellowing down the stairs for him.

'Ripped jackets?' Marcus said. 'Is that a thing now?'

'No,' said Shirley. 'And asking if something's a thing now isn't a thing any more either.'

'You think Chapman has any idea what's going on?' Louisa asked.

'I hope somebody does,' said Marcus.

When Ho got to Lamb's office Lamb threw a handful of takeaway cartons at him. 'These things have been breeding. When you've chucked 'em out, go next door and fetch some new ones. Full.'

'. . . Full of what?'

'Chinese food, idiot,' Lamb said. 'Or "food", as you people call it.'

Ho brushed a lump of congealed rice from his jacket, then tried to rub the stain away. 'What kind, I meant?'

'Surprise me.'

Bad Sam eyed Ho with pity. 'It's Roderick, right?'

'. . . Yes.'

'Roderick, would you let me piss on you for a quid?' he asked.

'. . . No.'

'So why'd you let him do it for free?'

'Don't mind him,' Lamb explained. 'It's the pain talking.'

'When you open your mouth, that's a pain talking. What are you finding so funny?'

This to Catherine.

'You two,' she said. 'It's like watching dinosaurs having foreplay. Or *Top Gear*.'

'We've met, haven't we?' Bad Sam asked.

'One of my happiest memories.'

'You're very perky,' said Lamb. 'Happy to be back?'

Catherine told Ho, 'He doesn't need food, he's already eaten. But find me some ice, if you can.'

Ho slipped away, still rubbing at the mark on his new leather jacket.

She said, 'I've told you why I'm here. The Park are looking for the old man. I thought it best to bring him somewhere safe.'

'Which old man are we talking about?' Chapman asked.

'Your ex-boss,' Lamb said. 'David Cartwright.'

'Cartwright? He's still alive?'

'Yeah, but we're in injury time,' Lamb said. 'The guy who tried to whack you? There's a lot of that going round.'

'He tried to kill Cartwright?'

'Not personally. That particular gentleman ended up with a flip-top head. But I'm assuming the two events are not unconnected. Unless it's just open season on clapped-out spooks.'

'I'm pretty sure if that happened, you'd be top of most people's list,' Catherine said.

Chapman said, 'Well if the Park are looking for him, why's he here? He'd be safer with the professionals.'

'Well, that rather depends who signed off on the murder attempt.'

He stared. 'You think someone at the Park wants to kill David Cartwright? And me?'

'It's a theory.'

'They already gave me the sack,' Chapman said. 'It's a bit fucking cheeky having me murdered too. Besides, I'm old news. I don't even know who's running the place now. Tearney went, didn't she?'

'A victim of political correctness,' Lamb said sadly.

'Didn't she arrange several murders?'

'Well, that too. But the new boy, his name's Whelan, hasn't been there long enough to start throwing his weight around. No, if this thing's got its roots in the Park, it's like you. Old news. From back when Cartwright was one of the movers and shakers. You used to watch his back, didn't you?'

'Sometimes. It's not like he needed full-time supervision.'

'But he went walkabout occasionally.'

'What are you getting at, Jackson?'

'You went with him to France.'

'Oh Christ,' said Sam Chapman. 'This is about Les Arbres, is it?'

Moira Tregorian, too, was wondering at the turns the day had taken; from the secret thrill at the death of a colleague – well, it wasn't as if she knew him well – to its baffling reversal; from the lunch she'd expected to be an induction into the rituals of Slough House to the interrogation it had turned into instead. How well did she know Claude Whelan? What was the point of contact between her – Regent's Park's erstwhile office manager; wielder of the power of overtime; desk allocator to the Queens of the Database; timekeeper extraordinaire; marshal of the service contracts; fielder of stationery-related enquiries; occasional duty officer – and the brand-new, squeaky-clean First Desk? Did they belong to the same book club? Frequent the same church? Had they, perhaps – even spooks have their carnal moments –

indulged in an office indiscretion? And Lamb's blandly neutral choice of word here, barely more loaded than a water pistol, was utterly belied by his expression, which was a popish leer. She'd suspected Mr Lamb would be an awkward customer. She hadn't realised how much work 'awkward' could be made to do.

And then this: the arrival of her predecessor.

Whatever Moira Tregorian might have expected of Catherine Standish, this wasn't it. She had seen drunks before: who hadn't? They tended to vibrate slightly, as if tuned to a higher frequency than everyone else, and their skin was saggy and their hair poorly tended. They served, in other words, as a warning. But Catherine Standish seemed intact, a word Moira wasn't sure she'd used of a person before. She was intact: nothing obvious missing. It was disappointing, somehow, though she had managed to keep this reaction to herself, she hoped.

Meanwhile, she was still sorting through a hundredweight of memos from the Park, and now had an observer in the corner.

'He needs somewhere quiet to sit,' Miss Standish had said, barely glancing round her old office. 'He's had a long day.'

'Well, I don't know about . . .'

But already she was gone, and the old man – David Cartwright – was commandeering her chair, settling behind her desk as if this was his kingdom, and Moira the usurper.

So she had made him tea, and attempted conversation, until he slumped into a kind of vacancy, which Moira found mildly disturbing at first, then forgot about. It wasn't as if she didn't have work to do; a task which manifested itself, as her tasks tended to, in stacks of paper of varying heights, and which was soon accompanied by her usual repertoire of *'tchah's* and *'duh's*; of *well I never dids*, and *what on earths*; and, ultimately, a *bloomin' cuckoo is what this is.*

At which the old man snapped out of the realm he'd wandered into and said, 'Cuckoo?'

'Les Arbres was weird,' Bad Sam said. 'Like a commune, but more regimented. And without many women, though there were kids.'

Ho had returned with a bag of ice, which he'd solemnly delivered to Catherine, then left. Chapman was applying it to his knee as he spoke. The room was damp, and the radiator supplied little heat, merely banged and wheezed at intervals, as if clearing its throat. Lamb was slumped in his chair, fiddling with an unlit cigarette, and Catherine had retired to a dark corner, like a child hoping her parents won't notice she's still there, attending to adult conversation which had turned unsuitable.

'I was there to watch David's back, but it was a cushy gig. France was hardly hostile territory, the odd waiter aside. And you didn't have to worry about anyone flying the coop. Defection wasn't a big problem that year.'

'This was when?' Lamb's voice was uncharacteristically muted.

'First time? Summer after the Wall came down.'

'Tell me about Les Arbres.'

Bad Sam described the house, the grounds, the location. He'd counted eight male adults. 'I recognised one of them. Yevgeny, he was calling himself. First names only at Les Arbres. He was former KGB. He'd done a turn at the embassy in London, and back then we used to keep spotter's cards on the visiting talent. Molly Doran made them up. Remember?'

Lamb grunted.

'She'd tape their pictures onto playing cards, making a big thing of whether they were hearts or clubs or diamonds. Lover boys or rogues, she'd say. She was pretty good at telling who was which.'

'What jolly japes we all had,' Lamb said. 'Back when the world was teetering on the brink of nuclear catastrophe.'

'Oh, lighten up,' Bad Sam told him. 'We're all still here. Anyway, Yevgeny, he was a heart, I remember. Actual name, or embassy name, Ivor Fedchenko. But when I told Cartwright who he was, he brushed it off. Not important, he said.'

'And you let it go?'

'I hadn't been in the job long, but I knew my pay grade. I was a junior Dog, Jackson. He was David Cartwright.'

'What was he doing there?'

'Debriefing an ex-agent. Codename Henry. That's what the docket said, anyway.'

'And you stayed there?'

'Nope. Hotel in the nearby town. Angevin.'

'And you weren't present at these debriefings.'

'Like I said, junior Dog. Jackson, I was his driver, his minder, his bottle washer. I wasn't privy to classified discussions.'

'Debriefing a decommissioned spook doesn't sound like he was juggling the nuclear codes. You lay eyes on this Henry at all?'

'How would I know? Nobody was wearing their codename on a badge.'

'Who was in charge?' Catherine asked softly.

He said, 'There was an American, we weren't introduced. But he seemed to be Boss Cat. I think his name was Frank.'

'You think,' Lamb repeated.

'His name was Frank. What's this about, Jackson? It was years ago, it happened in peacetime, and nobody made a run at the old man. If you hadn't mentioned France, I wouldn't have remembered it.'

Lamb said, 'Cartwright was far too senior to be making house calls. I find that odd. How many visits did you make?'

'A couple. With me, anyway. The second was later that year.'

'And nothing unusual happened either time?'

Bad Sam said, 'You're sure this has something to do with what happened today?'

'I'm not even sure where Ho got that ice from. Right now, we're all in the dark.' The snap of a lighter disproved his point, and for a moment Lamb's face was visible. Catherine coughed. The lighter died, but Lamb's cigarette tip glowed red. 'There are bodies hitting the floor, though. That's usually a sign something's amiss.'

'The last night of our second trip, he was . . . distracted. Upset. Drank more than usual. And he was never too abstemious.'

'Warning to us all,' muttered Lamb, and was rewarded by a sigh in the darkness.

'There'd been a rumpus during the day. A woman turned up unexpectedly, Frank's girlfriend, and they had a fight. She could scream and shout for England, I gather, which she was, by the way. English. I guess the old man must have taken some of the collateral, because he seemed cowed. But it was over by the time I got there. She'd just driven away.'

'Where'd you been?' Catherine asked.

Bad Sam looked sheepish. 'Round back of the house, with a couple of the Russian guys. We were playing pétanque.'

'Sweet God in heaven,' said Lamb.

'So anyway, he started rambling on, telling war stories. I got the feeling he liked playing the old sage, you know? The grizzled warrior, telling fireside tales.' Chapman paused to adjust the bag of ice. 'So there was a fair bit of that. But towards the end, he was pretty far gone on the brandy, and making less sense, except there was one thing he repeated, said it twice. 'Wish I'd never heard of the damn thing,' he said. I asked what damn thing he meant. First time, he didn't reply. But the second time . . .'

Bad Sam paused again, moulding the icepack over his knee.

'For Christ's sake,' said Lamb. 'Stop milking it.'

'Project Cuckoo,' Sam said. 'He said he wished he'd never heard of Project Cuckoo.'

'Cuckoo?' the O.B. said. 'That what this is about? Project Cuckoo?'

Moira Tregorian said, 'I'm sorry, I don't . . .'

The old man shook his head. Last thing he'd been expecting. But there it was. Things came back to bite you. There was a saying, wasn't there, *as easy as closing a door*, meaning nothing simpler. Door shut, job done. He was sure there was a saying something like that. But what it didn't mention was making sure you were on the right side of the door when it closed.

He didn't know where he was. It seemed to him he'd climbed some stairs, but this wasn't like any part of the upstairs he was used to. There should be more light – all the best rooms in the Park had views – but this was one of the secretarial chambers, judging by its size. Bit of a cheek, stuffing him in this poky hole and expecting him to sing for his supper, but he supposed there was something to be said for it, telling stories in the dark. Hadn't he done this, time without number; telling stories to . . . Young lad. Keen as mustard. Found him in the garden, his scabby knees showing. Name would come back.

Cloudy as the present was, though, some things you didn't forget.

He said, 'Project Cuckoo. Right you are, then. You taking this down?'

And his voice sounded stronger now, because he knew which side of the door he needed to be on.

All he had to do was step through it, and close it behind him.

Cuckoo.

J. K. Coe said, 'There was a Soviet village, or there were rumours, anyway. It might have been a legend. There were a lot of them about.'

In the gloomy light of Lamb's room Coe might have been Marley's ghost, draped in invisible chains. There was nowhere to sit, so he leaned against the door. Hanging on a hook was a raincoat – it could only be Lamb's – from which ancient odours crept, released by Coe's pressure; a mummy's tomb of long-dead fragrances: cigarettes and whisky, and bus station waiting rooms, and damp desperate mornings, and death. Coe wondered if it was just him, or whether the others could smell it too: Lamb himself, and Catherine Standish, and the man called Chapman.

'Any time you feel like drifting off into dreamland,' Lamb suggested, 'feel free to use my arse as a pillow.'

'Give him a chance, Jackson,' said the woman in the dark.

'I say Soviet, but the point was, it was anything but. What they did was create an American town, picket fence, Main Street and all, way out in Georgia, or wherever. Just like there's an Afghan village on the Northumberland moors, in the military zone, except that's for strategic purposes. But this was for people to live in. Be born in and live in. Learning American English, and watching American TV. Spending American dollars. A sort of finishing school. That was Project Cuckoo, USSR-style. They'd have a different name for it. But it was a means of breeding a perfect simulacrum of the enemy, so you could learn the way he thought, the way he dreamed, the way . . . well, everything.'

Coe had been Psych Eval, in what felt like a different life.

One of the modules had been in Black Ops. That was a favourite with everyone, because you got to hear about the spooky shit. As in, this was the kind of shit spooks got up to once. But also as in, there was some seriously spooky shit out there.

'The theory was, if you wanted to plant a sleeper, that was the right kind of nursery to grow them in.'

Lamb growled, but it wasn't clear if this was an objection, an agreement, or a digestive necessity.

'And do you think it ever really happened?' Catherine asked.

'There was another story,' Coe said, 'that somewhere near the Red Sea, back in the sixties, there was a perfect replica of the White House. And the Sovs had someone living there for years, with a full staff, all English-speaking, and the point of him was, they'd initiate crises, and monitor his responses, and this would give them an insight into how the actual president might react to a given situation.'

'And do you think,' and it was Chapman this time, 'that *that* ever really happened?'

'No,' said Coe. 'You'd have to be insane to base strategic policy on how a puppet reacted to a fake crisis.'

'Yeah, that was the thing about the Cold War,' said Lamb. 'Everyone kept their heads.'

He seemed to lose his for a moment, but it turned out he was rustling about in a carrier bag under his desk. When he reappeared he was holding a bottle. There were two smeary glasses on his desk, the only items there which hadn't lately been used as an ashtray. He poured two fingers into one glass, four into the other, and pushed the former in Chapman's direction. To Catherine he said, 'If you want to nip straight from the bottle, be my guest.' To Coe, 'But you can buy your own.'

Coe didn't respond. He had spoken more in the past ten minutes than in the last six months. His head was pounding. There was a line of verse stuck in his mind, *a bright rain will wash your wounds*, and it kept circling round without going anywhere. He wanted his music back. If he had to be in Slough House, and he might as well be here as anywhere else, he'd rather be at his desk, earbuds planted, listening to Jarrett carving music out of the air: Nagoya, 12 November 1976. That would wash his wounds, he thought.

'Was there anything else?' he said.

'Are we keeping you up?'

'I just—'

'Yeah, well just don't.' Lamb half emptied his glass into his mouth and didn't seem worried about savouring the taste. 'So that was what the Reds got up to. Doubtless the Yanks had their own version. But what about us? Or wasn't that on the syllabus?'

Coe said, 'Not on the syllabus, no,' and Lamb's ears twitched.

'His name was Frank. Frank Harkness. American chap, ex-Agency, though I didn't find that out until later. That he was ex, I mean. Assumed at the time he was on the books. Well, you do, don't you? Assume the worst.'

Which was meant in jest but had a sour edge, spoken aloud. Never mind.

'Back then I was gunning for First Desk. Never admitted that before. But it's true, I took it for granted it was mine for the asking. Simply a matter of waiting out the incumbent, and keeping my copybook clean. Didn't seem too much to ask. Been doing it for years.'

Though there had been moments when his copybook hadn't been all that clean. When his conscience hadn't been spotless, come to that. But again: no time for nit-picking. The details. He had a daughter.

'Her name was Isobel.'

He wondered if he had skipped ahead here. But it didn't matter, the tape would be running. Spill it all out, let them join the dots for themselves.

'Lovely child.'

She had been, too. It was later that it had all gone wrong. But then, it was later that he was supposed to be talking about, wasn't it? Project Cuckoo.

'It wasn't Frank's idea, exactly,' he said. 'The notion had been around for a while. The Agency had tested it, and the Sovs had their version, of course. The Chinese. But not us. Nothing to do with morality or ethics – sheer pragmatism. There'd be big investment required, and the time we're talking about, well . . . Lines were being redrawn. Gorbachev was beating rugs in the Kremlin, throwing up dust clouds. Nobody knew what the world would look like once they cleared. So not much point in setting up a long-term project to confound our enemies when nobody knew who those enemies would be two Christmases down the line. We'd have ended up looking foolish. And the main objective of an intelligence service is not to look foolish if it can be avoided.'

The words were finding him now. He had always known they would, sooner or later. The Franks of this world were born damage-doers; in their one-eyed crusade to protect their innocent, they'd rain down fire on everyone in sight. And David Cartwright, God help him, had given this particular Frank a brand-new box of matches. So yes, he'd always known there'd be an accounting.

'But he had a different angle, did Frank. And you have to hand it to him, there were some things he saw more clearly than most. One thing had come to an end, so we had to be ready for the next. That's what he said.'

The old man's eyes crinkled with the effort of memory.

When this was done, he thought, he'd head back home to Rose. Cup of tea, or something stronger. Tell her about his day. Though maybe not this part, no. This story wasn't one he'd want her to judge him by.

His hands were trembling. Now there was a funny thing.

The woman said, 'Are you all right? Would you like another cup of tea?'

This was clever, he conceded. The art of a good debriefing: always allow for the possibility that you can have a rest, that it would soon be over.

You could never have a rest.

It wouldn't soon be over.

'Extremism, Frank said. That was what was taking hold in the Middle East. All very true, we told him, but it's not like they're exporting the stuff, is it? And if they want to chop the hands off thieves, well, it probably keeps shoplifting to manageable levels in downtown Baghdad. Because we'd just won a war, you see? We didn't want to hear about the next one, not yet.'

'I'm not sure you should be getting yourself into this state.'

'Frank, though, he thought we should be preparing ourselves. Because this wasn't going to be over in a hurry, he said. When you have an enemy with nuclear capability, it could all be over in seconds. When your enemy's armed with rocks and knives, they'll come at you slowly. Raise their children to hate you. They'll stare down through the generations, preparing for a war that lasts centuries.'

'I really don't think—'

'And he already had a network, you see. A network impossible to imagine even a year earlier. A couple of KGB agents, and others from the Soviet satellite states. Some Germans, a Frenchman. He called them his rainbow coalition. *Ha*.' The laugh was a bark. 'Combined experience, he said, these people knew more about counter-terrorism than any official service in the world, because they'd played both sides of the fence, do you see? Black ops. Give them the wherewithal, Frank said, and they'd establish a version of Cuckoo equipped to face the future. Fight fire with fire, that was the name of his game. You want to fight extremists, you have to raise extremists.'

He looked at the woman. She wasn't writing any of this down.

She said, 'And that's what you authorised him to do?'

'Well, no, of course we didn't,' David Cartwright said. 'He was a lunatic. We told him to sling his hook.'

Coe dry-swallowed; coughed. Ever Mr Empathy, Lamb poured himself another drink.

From the darkness, Catherine said, 'For God's sake, let him get some water.'

Lamb said, 'Oh, is he thirsty? Are you thirsty? You should have said.'

'Speaking out's not his forte,' Catherine said. 'That's rather the point.'

To his own surprise as much as anyone's, Coe said, 'I'm fine.'

'There you go,' said Lamb. 'He's fine.' He slumped even further into his chair. He already resembled a Dalí portrait. 'And as long as we keep the carving knives out of sight, he'll stay that way.'

The words put a buzz in the air. Coe could hear it, and knew that if he shut his eyes he'd feel it happen: the sharp edge slicing through his soft belly, then the slither and slap of all he contained falling wetly to the floor.

'You're not having a panic attack, are you?' Lamb asked kindly.

'No.'

'Does the thought of having one frighten you?'

'For Christ's sake, Jackson, leave him alone.'

Coe said, 'There were rumours. About Cuckoo.'

There were always rumours. Spooks love their stories: it's why they're spooks.

But Catherine said, 'Where did they come from? These rumours?'

'One of the course teachers,' Coe said, after a moment's thought. It felt strange, rummaging for memories from that part of his life when he was still whole. It was like poking round in somebody else's attic. 'It was a scenario one of the games teams was presented with, back when the Wall came down.'

'The pointy heads,' said Chapman.

Lamb said, 'Yeah. The ones who have consoles instead of ops. Tell me about this scenario.'

'The Park was approached by an American agent, a Company man, who wanted to tailor the Cuckoo idea. Instead of aiming it at specific national types, he wanted to see if it was possible to . . . to build an extremist. To raise a prototype fanatic. He was prescient, you'd have to give him that. He was thinking in terms of suicide bombers long before the West woke up to them.'

'And how,' said Chapman, 'did he plan to go about building a fanatic?'

'Indoctrination. You bring children up in the right environment, they'll be anything you want them to be. Catholic. Communist. Ballet dancer. Fanatic.'

Chapman looked at Lamb. 'An American. Frank?'

'Les Arbres was the middle of France, not a training camp in the desert,' said Lamb. 'They'd be more likely to raise a bunch of cheese-eating hippies than a suicide squad.'

From her shadows, Catherine said, 'But this was never done,

right? He was never given the go-ahead. Isn't that why it was all rumour and story? Never on the syllabus?'

'Like I said, it turned out he wasn't Company, he was ex,' Coe said. 'Former CIA. He'd been burned for unreliability. Once they found that out, he was shown the door. So no, his Project Cuckoo never happened. It just became one of those anecdotes that get swapped after lights-out.'

'So what was going on at Les Arbres?' Chapman said.

Lamb said, 'If he didn't get official backing from his own team, and didn't get it from the Park either, it looks like he went through the back door. And guess who was holding it open?'

'Cartwright?' Chapman said. 'Oh, come on – Cartwright?'

'And all these years later, they're trying to close it again,' Lamb said. 'So yes – Cartwright.'

'Oh lord,' said Catherine.

'What's up with you?'

'Why now?' she said. 'Why try to bury it now, after all this time?'

Lamb's eyes narrowed, and he squashed his cigarette into a coffee mug already half full of dead-ends.

'What?' said Bad Sam.

'Don't you see?' said Catherine. 'Project Cuckoo. Purpose-built fanatics . . .'

'Oh shit,' said J. K. Coe.

'Westacres,' said Lamb.

12

M ANY A TEAR HAS to fall, thought Claude Whelan
obscurely; a lyric from a forgotten song, a moment
from his past. Long-stemmed glasses on a starched tablecloth.
A dining room with a view of the sea; the windowpanes
spattered with rain. If he asked, Claire would know the precise
holiday, month and year, the name of the hotel. He was
hopeless with such details, his ability to memorise facts being
reserved for his working life. Outside of that, he simply had
the long view, like the one offered by those hotel windows,
and the generic details that might have come from anywhere:
the long-stemmed glasses, the pristine tablecloth.

He was in a stairwell, taking a moment away from the Hub.
A brief opportunity to ring Claire, let her know he'd be late.
She understood: of course she did. He was First Desk. The
country was shaking at the knees, the tremors from Westacres
still rocking the capital. She had fierce notions of loyalty. She
would have been shocked had he suggested he'd be leaving
soon.

'As long as it takes,' she'd said.

'Thank you, darling.'

'I'll make up the spare bed.'

And now he was watching raindrops coursing down the
windows, miles away from that holiday hotel, and brooding

on loyalty, and how it pulled you in different directions. His first COBRA session this morning, and his Second Desk had made a liar of him. Her reasons had been oddly persuasive, but treachery always had its convincing side. And there was a way out of this, of course: do his job, catch the bad people, and the problem would disappear. And this was what he intended to do anyway, so really, where was the difficulty?

But he knew that Claire, with her damn-the-torpedoes approach to ethics, would take a different view: she'd expect him to be on the phone to the PM by now, offering his resignation – the Service had dropped the ball; hell, the Service had polished the ball with an oily rag, pumped it up and handed it to the opposition. *Here you go. Do your worst.* All before his time, but no matter. You didn't have to be there when the ball was dropped. You just had to be standing in the wrong place when somebody noticed.

And Whelan knew that this was not only the honourable course, it was probably the safest, but . . . but damn it, *we'd be in lockdown, Claude. We'd have Special Branch going through every desk. It would make the Cambridge spies inquiry look like garden party chit-chat.*

So, not only the shortest-lived First Desk ever, but one whose microscopic tenure had seen the Service hobbled and chained; an onlooker at its own court martial.

He removed his glasses and polished them on the sleeve of his jacket. At moments of weakness, he liked to recall the codename he'd gone by over the river: Galahad. All the weasels – yes, that's what they were called – all the intelligence weasels were assigned codenames, largely so they'd reflect a little of the glamour of actual spooks. So: Galahad, and Claire had loved that. 'My knight in shining armour,' she'd said. Had there really been such knights, or were they just a bunch of talented ruffians? It didn't matter; remembering that he'd been

Galahad buoyed him. He'd been made to change it on his elevation: he was RP1 now; functional, yes, but boring. And now he was no longer alone; one last polish of his glasses, and back on they went.

Diana Taverner had found him. 'News,' she said.

He waited.

'Adam Lockhead. One of the . . .'

'Properties,' he said.

Cold bodies.

'He's turned up.'

A wave of relief flushed through Whelan. 'Where?'

'On the Eurostar. His passport lit up coming through border control. His train arrives in five minutes.'

'You'll have him arrested?'

'I've sent Flyte.' She paused. 'It would be best if there were no . . . official chain of custody. Just in case.'

Whelan looked towards the windows again: at them, rather than through them. The raindrops were choosing zig-zaggy routes to the sill, as if this were the safest way of navigating glass.

Catch the bad people, he thought, and the problem goes away.

'Well,' he said at last. 'Keep me in the picture.'

Coming through passport control before boarding the train, he'd had the sense of triggering a silent alarm. *Have a good journey, sir*, sure, thanks, but River read in the tightening of the chubbily pretty guard's eyebrows as she handed him 'his' passport that something had shown up on her screen. A red flag. But not so red they'd prevent him getting on the train.

Which might just mean they wanted him back in England with as little fuss as possible.

So on the train, while the grey winter landscape slipped

into darkness, before the train itself disappeared beneath the sea, he'd wondered how big a hole he'd dug himself into. Travelling on someone else's passport? Not great, though he could plausibly claim cover; he was a member of the Security Services, even if the claim would ring hollow to anyone who'd heard of Slough House. Travelling on someone else's passport, though, who was recently dead, shot twice in the face? That might take more confidence than he'd faked for the guard.

In the end, he'd fallen asleep, and only woke when the train was pulling into London: it was early evening, and the weather still foul. With no luggage to fuss with, River was first on the platform, joining the throng milling around St Pancras in the uncoordinated way of crowds everywhere. The Tube, he decided. He'd head for the Tube. That would be the best way of shaking them off.

That there was someone to shake off, he had no doubt. He might not be in joe country any more, but he was definitely back on Spook Street.

Emma Flyte spotted him stepping off the train. Youngish, fairish, reasonably athletic-looking, no luggage: there'd be other candidates, but she felt confident this was the one. She had her phone to her ear, which was as good as a disguise, most places. She said to Devon Welles, 'I think that's him.'

'Gotcha,' Welles said. He'd just arrived back in the city when Emma had called, and was now on a stool outside a sushi joint. 'Ready to play?'

'Soon as you like,' she suggested, slipping her phone into her pocket. Some jobs, you needed both hands free.

Sleep had left him spacey, off-kilter, and his unexpected trip to France felt distant already. More immediate were last night's events – the weight of the gun as he'd obliterated dead Adam

Lockhead's face. The red smears on the wall and the top of the staircase; traces his grandfather had left on his way down to the kitchen, where River had found him on arrival.

I knew he wasn't you.

But River was him now, or was using his passport. Adam Lockhead; also Bertrand, son of Frank. A French–American hybrid using an English cover. He wondered what had happened at Les Arbres, and how much his grandfather knew about it; wondered, too, whether the blood on his grandfather's hands went deeper than smears left on the furnishings. River had always known the O.B. was a spook, but some parts of the picture he'd purposefully left vague. His grandfather must have been responsible for many deaths: by omission, by sacrifice, by deliberate targeting. But he wondered how many times the O.B. had actually pulled a trigger. It would be ironic – though he wasn't sure 'ironic' was the word – if the only death David Cartwright had brought about with his own stained hands had been committed while no longer in his own right mind.

He was out of St Pancras now, heading for the underground platforms it shared with King's Cross. River could never be here without remembering the morning he'd crashed this place: a fucked-up training exercise during rush hour, a misidentified 'terrorist' – *blue shirt, white T-shirt* – and a projected hundred and twenty people killed or maimed; £2.5 billion in tourist revenue lost . . . He didn't know how these figures had been reached, but it didn't matter, because whichever way you added them up, the bottom line came out the same: River was now a slow horse, King's Cross the hurdle he'd fallen at. Being here was like having a toothpick jammed under a fingernail. If it was up to him he'd blow the damn place up, but that was what had got him into trouble in the first place.

Then there was someone too close behind him, and before he could turn, a rock-like hand had taken a grip on his upper arm.

'Adam Lockhead?'

It was a man who'd taken hold but a woman who was speaking; a strikingly attractive blonde.

'I think you've mistaken me for someone else,' he said.

'Well, we'll soon find out, won't we?'

In her hand she somehow had his passport – there were posters on every surface warning you to watch out for pickpockets, but none of them suggested that professional dips would get quite so in-your-face about it.

'No, that's you,' she said, opening it. 'Adam Lockhead. Or did you mishear?'

River found himself being steered out to the street, the three of them walking abreast like colleagues heading to a meeting. 'I'm a member of the Security Services,' he said as they stepped into the grey evening.

'Excellent,' she said. 'Because that gives me so much jurisdiction you wouldn't believe it.'

Few things gave an honest copper as much satisfaction as making an arrest: it was only afterwards, once you got solicitors, the CPS, the whole judicial machinery involved that things siphoned off into paperwork and loopholes. She wasn't a copper any more, and this wasn't precisely an arrest, but Emma Flyte wasn't above feeling a quiet hum of pleasure as she climbed into the back seat alongside the prisoner. Devon, too, was feeling the moment: she could read this by the set of his shoulders, and the way he carelessly tossed the parking ticket they'd received into the footwell.

But this was police too: the tickle in her memory, looking at 'Adam Lockhead'.

It was rush hour's last grumble, and as Devon pulled away into the slow-moving traffic up Pentonville Road, Lockhead looked round. 'This isn't the way to the Park.'

This was true. They were heading for another safe house – if the Service ever diversified into private rentals, they wouldn't have to worry about the cuts. On the other hand, they'd have nowhere to stow problems like Adam Lockhead while they worked out what to do with him.

'Keep him isolated. Don't interrogate him. Restrain him if necessary.' Diana Taverner's instructions: Emma was starting to feel more like Lady Di's personal gopher than head of internal security.

'Who is he?' she'd asked; a not unreasonable question, she felt. But Taverner's response had nearly melted her mobile: a twenty-second blast of controlled fury, following which she'd repeated her instructions. Keep him isolated. Don't interrogate him. Restrain him if necessary.

If not for that, Emma certainly wouldn't have said what she said to Lockhead now, which was: 'Have we met?'

He stared, his expression utterly serious. 'I think I'd remember.'

It was the mole on his upper lip. Not that she recognised it, precisely, but it nudged something, a tantalising knowledge on the edge of recollection. She opened his passport again, glanced at the photograph. Not the same man. Similar, but there was no mole, and the words *You're gonna need a pair of tweezers and a sieve* made their way to the surface. She'd almost landed the memory – was about to reel it in, drop it on the deck of her conscious mind – when something punched the car's side panels, and her teeth crunched together as Lockhead slammed into her and the whole world blinked.

He hadn't been able to achieve the speed he'd have liked – it was central London: walking pace the usual ceiling – but he hit the target hard in the circumstances: swerving out into the opposite lane when the oncoming traffic hit a lull, then a violent full-on smash to the driver's side. He was out of his own recently stolen vehicle inside seconds, limping slightly from the morning's events, but otherwise unscathed. The target car's driver was a hefty-looking black man whose reactions had been distinctly below par, and had mostly consisted of being swallowed by his airbag.

All around them, cars were screeching to a halt and pedestrians pointing. It was still raining, of course; the ideal setting for an accident.

His second of the day.

After being sideswiped by the taxi on the garage forecourt, an impact he'd barely had time to brace for – instinct had taken over; his body ignoring his mind, leaping for the roof, pulling himself over the cab even before it had screamed to a standstill – Patrice had lost himself in the same side streets Sam Chapman had tried to vanish into, with more success, because nobody came looking. They were all too busy picking themselves up off the ground. The rain had continued to hammer down, and the skies growled occasionally, as if hating to give the impression they were already doing their worst. By the time he'd re-emerged on a main road the pavements were largely empty, and the gutters were swirling with oil-flecked water, puddles swamping the intersections.

Nothing like the rain for clearing the streets.

He'd rung home, the part of him that hated to do this standing no chance against the part that insisted he follow protocol.

'Package still undelivered.'

This was greeted with a silence that whistled down the line all the way from Europe, he wasn't sure exactly where. That, too, was protocol.

Eventually, Frank had spoken. 'Are you compromised?'

Meaning injured or taken.

Patrice said, 'I'm gold,' because any other metal would have meant the opposite. The injuries he'd collected rolling over the taxi weren't worth enumerating. Injuries only mattered if they slowed you down: if they didn't, you were gold. 'I'm gold.'

'Bertrand lit up.'

So did Patrice, hearing that. It was unprofessional, but it couldn't be helped; if Bertrand was alive, things might yet be all right. Yves was gone, of course, blasted to pieces in lunatic martyrdom, but that didn't mean everything was over. They simply had to clean up the mess he'd left, by laying a thick cold blanket over anyone who knew who they were. That had been Yves's real legacy. He had wanted to fulfil what he'd come to believe his destiny, but all he'd achieved had been to make it necessary to destroy all traces of his past.

Which existed only in fragments. Like Patrice, like Bertrand, like all of them, Yves had had his childhood removed even while it was happening, and replaced by qualities Frank favoured: obedience to him, and reliance on no other. Attachments were encouraged only because without them, there was nothing to purge. Patrice remembered how, for Yves's seventh birthday, Frank had given the boy a photograph of his mother, the first Yves had ever seen. Frank allowed him to look at it for five full minutes before handing him a box of matches. Yves had not hesitated for a second. There had been glee in his eyes as he had trampled the resulting oily mess beneath his feet.

Always, he had gone further than any of them. Patrice had been frightened of Yves, a little. He sometimes wondered if Frank had been too.

Bertrand, though, had been the attachment Patrice had

never purged himself of. If Bertrand was alive they could complete this mission together and get the fuck off this godforsaken island.

But 'Where?' was all he said.

'St Pancras. The Lockhead passport.'

You never asked where Frank got his information. You simply knew he had a network, the ghostly remnant of his CIA connections. Someone, somewhere, had picked up a phone when Bertrand's passport was flagged at border control. But this in turn meant the Lockhead identity was blown . . .

These thoughts winking into place in the time it took him to say, 'I'm there.'

He ended the call. No point waiting for instructions. Life at Les Arbres had taught him to grasp what needed doing, which here meant reaching St Pancras before the action moved on. If Bertrand's passport was flagged, there'd be security waiting. And of all the things that couldn't be allowed to happen, Bertrand falling into the hands of MI5 ranked way up high.

What he'd been doing on the Eurostar – where he'd been and why – could stay on the burner for now. What Patrice needed was a car.

Luckily, there were a number of these in the immediate area.

River banged his head on the roof when the car struck, then again on the blonde's head when she crashed into him. Their own car – not his, but he was identifying with it in the circumstances – had been shunted sideways into a set of railings, and the attacking vehicle had bounced back some yards and was stationary in the middle of the road, blocking traffic. He couldn't smell smoke, but the air had turned thick with damaged-car smells: petrol and scraped metal.

The view in front of him was bendy and improbable. It took a moment to understand that the airbag had deployed.

He raised a hand in front of his eyes, and the gesture took forever. Not concussed, but inside a bubble of time that wouldn't allow free movement. His hand looked like nothing he recognised. For a moment he was remembering a rabbit dead on a counter, but there was no clear reason for recalling this, and the next instant he wasn't. His hand was just his hand. His head hurt, but he wasn't concussed.

The driver gave a groan, muffled by the airbag. The woman, meanwhile, pulled herself upright and shook her head. Her perfect face was going to have one hell of a bruise, supposing they lived through the next few minutes.

Someone was getting out of the enemy car.

The blonde's jacket had fallen open, and River could see her sidearm holster, her Heckler & Koch: he had a hand to its grip before her own locked round his wrist and she snarled, not words but angry sounds. River pulled back, and tried to open his door, but it was jammed shut by the railings. The blonde was easing her gun free in a clumsy, mechanical way. 'Devon,' she said. Concussed. Or geographically challenged. And his door still wasn't opening.

But the door on the blonde's side was. A young man peered in, dark-featured, his leather jacket streaky with rain, and River knew him – had seen his photograph – and maybe the young man knew him too, because for a second his face creased into a series of shapes: recognition, puzzlement, disappointment. Then it became a cipher again, right at the moment the blonde woman released her gun at last and pointed it at him.

'Step back,' she said. 'Then get on the ground.'

Her voice was impressively firm.

The young man wasn't paying attention, though. He was staring at River.

The blonde released her seat belt and leaned towards the open door, her gun inches from the man's face. 'Now!'

He stepped back, hands raised, but no higher than his shoulders.

The woman climbed out of the car.

Guns didn't worry Patrice much, or not ones he could see, anyway. Ones he could see were there for effect; they were for pointing while people shouted, and they always shouted the same thing: *hands up, on the ground, assume the position.* But there was no fall-back. The people who wanted you to lie on the ground weren't going to shoot you if you didn't, because if they were the type to shoot you, they wouldn't be telling you to lie on the ground. They'd be shooting you.

So the woman wasn't a bother, but the man was. Because he wasn't Bertrand, but in that first moment, Patrice thought he was: they had the same features, almost; the same hair. Eyes. Something was going on; crawling under the skin, like a worm inside an apple.

The sky growled, and rain kept raining.

From somewhere not far away, a siren wailed.

The woman was out of the car now; had her feet planted firmly the correct distance apart, arms outstretched, her left hand steadying her right wrist. Which might mean she'd used guns before, or just that she'd seen some movies.

'I told you to get on the ground.'

'What's going on here?'

Patrice didn't need to turn to know this was a civilian.

Without taking her eyes off Patrice, the woman said, 'Sir, I need you to get back in your car. Everything's under control.'

'Are you sure about that?' Patrice asked.

'Shut up. And get on the ground.' Then, to the interfering stranger, she repeated, 'Sir, get back in your car!'

'I'm going to call the police.'

'Fine. Do that. From your car.'

Patrice said, 'This is getting complicated. You've got civilians butting in. The rain makes things worse. And the police are going to have trouble getting through all this traffic.'

'I told you to get on the ground.'

'It's wet. And I need to talk to your prisoner. He is your prisoner, right?'

Whether he was or not, he was emerging from the car too, one hand on the roof to steady himself: it was surprising, Patrice thought, how shook-up the human body could be by something as trivial as a car wreck. But it all depended on whether you were expecting it or not.

'On. The. Ground.'

The woman again, trying for the air of someone who didn't intend repeating herself, though, as Patrice could have pointed out, she'd already done so several times, and hadn't shot him yet.

He took a step nearer, hands still at shoulder height. From behind him a voice, the same one as before, shouted something about the police, though most of his words were washed away by the noise of rain on car roofs. There was a pleasant hissing sound, too, from the engine of the car Patrice had stolen, which now required medical attention. On the pavements umbrellas huddled together in protective formation. It looked like a musical was about to break out.

The woman said, 'I'm not going to—'

And at the same moment, the man said, 'Patrice.'

'—tell you again.'

'Patrice.'

This from behind her, the man she knew as Adam Lockhead, and a puzzle-piece slotted into place: they knew each other;

this was a rescue. She moved to one side so she could cover both. Devon was still in the car. Emma hoped he wasn't hurt, because she could really use back-up.

That spark fizzed in her brain again, *you're gonna need a pair of tweezers and a sieve*, and it was Jackson Lamb, the grubby spook who smelled like booze and fags and a million sins. And who'd misidentified a body as River Cartwright, because this was him here now, a mole on his lip.

And still the car-crash man wasn't lying down; had in fact moved closer. If he thought she wouldn't shoot, he was dead wrong, and might any moment just be dead, because this was three scant days since the Westacres bomb had killed all those kids, and if it wasn't precisely open season on wrongdoers, the tabloids wouldn't be making a fuss.

'Patrice? I'm just back from Les Arbres.'

'Shut up,' she said, her eyes on Patrice. 'And get back in the car.'

'It burned down, Patrice. There's nothing there any more.'

'I know,' said Patrice, and Emma opened her mouth to tell him one last time to get on the ground before she shot him, and never mind this was probably being uploaded to YouTube as she spoke – except she didn't speak, because Patrice wasn't a metre away, he was touching distance, and her outstretched arms were pointing skywards. The gun fired, and there was mayhem.

On the pavements, umbrellas scattered. On the roads, cars moved again, despite having nowhere to go.

The gun was no longer hers. Patrice had it, and was pointing it at her face.

If Patrice said anything, River thought – if he threw her words back at her, *get on the ground* – it would feel safer, somehow; as if control had shifted, but was still an issue.

237

As it was, he thought Patrice was about to shoot the woman dead.

Partly it was the gunshot, still echoing overhead. A loose bullet rips a hole in normality, through which more violence might slip.

He said, 'Patrice?' again, making it a question. 'Patrice? You don't want to do anything foolish now.'

Given that Patrice's most recent exploit had involved engineering a car-smash on a busy London road, this didn't carry as much weight as River might have hoped. So he stepped forward and stretched an arm out in front of the woman. Speaking of foolish things: this would stop a bullet like the butter stops a knife.

He said, 'It's not what Yevgeny would want.'

'. . . Who are you?'

'Tell him to put the gun down. The nasty squad'll be here any second.' This was the blonde, sounding preternaturally calm. Rain had plastered her hair to her skull: River knew women for whom that alone would cause hysterics, forget the car crash and the gun.

But her intervention wasn't helping.

'Shut up,' he told her. Then, to Patrice, 'She's right, though. You've got less than a minute.'

'Twenty seconds,' she said. 'Max.'

Which, thought River, wasn't as comforting as she appeared to think – once the police arrived, the last place you wanted to be was next to anyone holding a gun. For a force that prided itself on being unarmed, the Met had racked up an impressive number of civilian casualties lately. True, you had to include all the unshot suspects to get a fair picture, but that was best done on the sidelines, not in open range.

And he really wanted to hear Patrice's story before the pair of them were cut down in the street.

'Who are you?' Patrice repeated.

'Adam Lockhead,' River said.

The name cut a groove through Patrice's expression. 'No. Where's Bertrand? And why . . .'

Sirens. Though it was the ones you didn't hear you had to worry about: they'd be flattening themselves behind car cover; sighting on the three of them from somewhere overhead.

The same thought must have struck Patrice. He lowered the gun. 'Okay. We're leaving.'

'We?' the blonde woman said, and at the same moment Patrice – his motion so fluid he might have been an eel passing through water – jabbed her in the throat with his free hand. She dropped without making a sound. That would come later.

River swung a punch, which for some reason hit Patrice not on the side of the head, which was where he'd been aiming, but in his open palm, which closed round River's fist and squeezed so hard he felt it in his toes.

Patrice spoke so calmly he might have been choosing fruit. 'We. You and me. Or I'll kill you here.'

Which sounded like he was reserving the option to do this elsewhere later, but River didn't see he had a choice.

'There,' Patrice said, pointing through the blocked traffic towards a narrow street where a crowd still loitered – though they scattered when Patrice fired a shot over their heads.

Then he found himself running, Patrice on his heels, and behind them the noise grew muted: the keening of sirens, pulsing through the rain; the blaring of the traffic, still trying to work out what had happened; and the gasping of a blonde woman on her knees in the road, learning the hard way how to breathe again.

13

S OME WHILE AGO, SHIRLEY had constructed a wall chart
based on those signs you see on entrances to building sites:
WE HAVE GONE __ DAYS WITHOUT AN ACCIDENT. Hers read:
WE HAVE GONE __ DAYS WITHOUT HO BEING A DICK, and
she'd made a number-card to slot into the empty space. One
side of it read 0. So did the other. It amused her to swap it round
occasionally. It was the little things made office life bearable.

She did this now before slumping into her chair. It was
past home-time – and the slow horses didn't so much keep
office hours as nurture and cherish them – but today wasn't
ordinary, and no one was ready to leave. There was a reason
she had joined the Service, and if much of the original impulse
had been smothered under Jackson Lamb's tutelage, it could
yet be sparked into life by the feeling that something big was
happening; something that promised action, and excluded her.

Like this, for instance: the Google alerts popping into her
inbox.

'Are you seeing this?' she asked.

She was talking to Marcus. Louisa was still there – her feet
in a washing-up bowl, like a character in a seventies sitcom
– but her eyes were closed and she didn't respond. Nor did
Marcus, immediately. He was intent on his monitor, and Shirley
could tell by his scowl was either regretting a poor judgement

call at an online casino or looking at his bank account. Lately, Marcus had been having money troubles – that was putting it mildly. Lately, Marcus and money had been undergoing a trial separation. And things didn't look good for them. Before long, Shirley guessed, money was going to be heading out the door for good; was going to walk out on Marcus, and leave him all alone in the world, except for his wife and kids.

And he persisted in thinking she was the one with problems.

'Seeing what?' he said, without looking up.

Her alerts included 'armed terrorist London'.

'YouTube,' she said. 'Holy fuck! Is that River?'

She clicked and played it again. It was a grainy image, made grainier by rainfall: someone's phone had captured it at a junction on Pentonville Road, and it showed the aftermath of a collision. One car had shunted another into a set of railings and sat sideways, steam pumping from its bonnet. A man was leaning into the impact vehicle: checking they were okay, you'd have thought, except he suddenly raised his hands and backed up as a gun came into view.

'When did this appear?'

Louisa was behind her now, barefoot, watching her screen.

'Couple of minutes.'

The gun was attached to a blonde woman, who emerged from the car still pointing it, followed by—

'There, see? Is that River?'

—a man who didn't appear to be armed. But it wasn't clear whose side he was on, because the woman seemed keen to keep him within the ambit of her weapon.

'It might be,' said Marcus, who'd come to join them. 'He's obviously pissed her off.'

But it was too fuzzy to be sure. The characters kept fading in and out of focus, in tune to the excitement of whoever'd been wielding the phone.

And then something happened so quickly, none of them could tell what it was: the first man made a move, and the gun went off. There was a communal scream from an invisible audience, and the image turned first skywards, and then became a collage of pavement and moving feet, while background voices swore, and asked each other what they'd just seen.

The clip ended.

'Play it again,' said Louisa. 'Freeze it on River.'

They watched the first twenty seconds again, leaning closer when Shirley hit Pause.

The frozen rain blurred the three figures to dark outlines.

Louisa said, 'Yes. Yes, I think it is.'

Shirley clicked on Play, and there was movement again, and a gunshot, street-lit rain, and pavements, and stampeding feet.

'When did this happen?' Louisa said.

'Not long ago,' Shirley said. 'Fifteen minutes?'

'Any text?'

Shirley scrolled down to the helpful caption: 'Holy fucking shit!' it read, followed by a screed of expert online thought:

fella with a gun innit

terrorists cant drive strait lol

OMG what is hapening to London!!!

'That was Pentonville Road?' Louisa asked, hobbling to her chair and stooping for her socks.

'You seriously heading out there?'

'I'm bruised, not crippled,' she snapped, but winced as she padded her feet dry with a tissue.

Marcus shrugged. 'Suit yourself. But it's still pouring.'

Shirley was watching the film again. 'So he buggered off to France for the day, and soon as he's back he's in the middle of this shit? How come he gets all the fun?'

Marcus said, 'Can you get this picture any clearer?'

'No. But I'm pretty sure it's River.'

'It's the other one I'm looking at.' Marcus tapped a finger against the screen. 'I think he's the joker from this afternoon.'

They both looked up, but Louisa had already left.

'Shall we go with?' Shirley said.

'She'll be fine. Place'll be crawling with cops.'

Shirley hadn't been so much worried about Louisa's welfare as anxious not to miss anything. But if there were cops, it meant the action was already elsewhere. General rule of thumb was, the police turned up afterwards.

She said, 'Coe was just with Lamb, wasn't he?'

'I think I heard him coming back down.'

'I'm gonna have a word,' she said. 'I wanna know what they were talking about.'

Sam Chapman said, 'So now what?'

'Another drink?'

'That's your answer?'

'Do you have a better one?'

Bad Sam sighed and pushed his glass across the desktop.

J. K. Coe had left the room at a nod from Lamb. Rain still beat on the windows, its percussive onslaught muffling thought. Elsewhere in the city, in the slowly filling pubs, the weather had become the main topic of conversation, the Westacres bombing fading into the background like a persistent hangover; something that had to be lived with, but didn't need constant discussion. London always overcame attempts to cow its spirit. Not even 7/7 had brought the city to a standstill. Though, as Lamb liked to point out, the anniversary two-minute silences did slow it down a bit.

Watching him refill Chapman's glass, Catherine said, 'Very bonding, I'm sure, but not helpful. Do we really think a project David Cartwright set up more than twenty years ago was responsible for Westacres?'

'Put like that,' said Lamb, 'it does sound like something only an alcoholic, a has-been and a post-traumatic headcase could come up with.'

'I've worked out which one I am,' she said. 'I'm having trouble with you.'

'I left myself out. I'm just facilitating blue-sky thinking.'

'Either way,' Chapman said, 'shouldn't we be passing this on? Is Diana Taverner still Ops?'

'Oh yes,' said Lamb.

'I take it you're not the best of friends.'

'We speak on the phone, we sometimes meet up. Every now and then she tries to have me killed.' He shifted a buttock. 'I can't remember if I've ever been married, but it sounds like that's what it's like.'

Chapman said to Catherine, 'He's not kidding, is he?'

'No.'

'What about the new guy, then. Whelan?'

Lamb tortured his chair further by leaning back: if a living thing had made the resulting noise, you'd have called a vet. Or the police. 'I can just picture how that'll go,' he said. 'Hi, Claude. You know this bomb? Well, it turns out your Service built it, wound it up and let it go. Do you want to call a press conference, or should I?'

'Nobody's saying they'll be happy to hear it,' said Chapman. 'But they've got to be told.'

'Maybe they already have been,' Lamb said. 'Whoever came after the old man came from France, fine, but what about this afternoon's joker? Was he from the same place? Or are the Park in on the act and cleaning up the mess? Because that would be standard practice for the old guard, and all I know about the new guy is, he sent us Grendel's mother through there. So he hasn't made my Christmas list yet.'

'And this is how you make operational decisions?'

'When I don't have a coin handy.'

'This place is as messed up as it looks, isn't it?'

'You know me,' said Lamb. 'I always demand the highest professional standards.'

He farted, though whether as illustration or punctuation wasn't clear.

Bad Sam wafted a hand and said, 'Jesus, Lamb, did something die inside of you?'

'I used to wonder that myself,' Catherine said quietly. 'But I'm pretty sure he's always been like this.'

'Thanks for your support,' Lamb said. 'Now why not make yourself useful and go fetch the old bastard?'

From his lips, River's term of affection soured into abuse. Catherine said, 'Seriously? You're going to interrogate him?'

'You make it sound so brutal,' Lamb said. 'I'm not going to hurt him.' He paused. 'I'm probably not going to hurt him.'

'You're not going to lay a finger on him.'

He said to Bad Sam, 'She has this thing about older men. Her last boss blew his brains out, but that's probably a coincidence.'

'You were Charles Partner's Girl Friday,' Sam Chapman said. 'I knew I recognised you.'

'"Girl Friday"?'

'We had a chat after he died, didn't we?'

'It's nice that you think it was a chat,' Catherine said.

It had lasted for hours, was her memory. In the paranoia that had followed Partner's death, everyone was suspected of knowing more than they should have. Catherine, who had known significantly less, had borne the brunt of the Dogs' investigation, and, newly sober, had become instantly nostalgic for those alcoholic blackouts that had been a feature of her recent past.

There were those who would have assured her that they

had only been doing their job. Chapman, wisely, wasn't one of them.

Lamb said, 'Either he knows more than he's pretending or less than he should. Either way, let's probe those gaps in his history, shall we?' He shifted his bulk, and the chair complained again. 'If you don't fetch him, I will.'

She shook her head, but only for her own benefit, and that was as far as her resistance went. Because it was true, they had to know what David Cartwright knew, so she rose and left the gloomy office to collect him.

River's room – or River and Coe's room, as Shirley supposed she ought to be calling it – was in semi-darkness, the only light Coe's anglepoise, spilling a thick yellow cone over his desk. For once he wasn't plugged in to his iPod, and while his hands were splayed on the desktop, he didn't seem to be indulging in his fake piano bullshit either. For a moment, Shirley considered turning away; leaving him to his thoughts, which were probably dark enough that you wouldn't want to spill them on anything delicate. All men were dickheads until proven otherwise, that was a given. But what Coe had said to Marcus, *You gonna tie me to a chair and shave my toes off with a carving knife?*, was way too specific to be voiced at random. So yeah, dark thoughts. But on the other hand, there was a time for quiet brooding, and that time wasn't when Shirley was in need of information. So, 'You were summoned,' she said.

He watched as she came into the room, halting by his desk.

'Hello? Your secret's out, Mr Piano Man. We all know you can talk.'

His eyes shone like wet dark stones from the recess of his hood.

'You were summoned by Lamb. Whatever you had to tell

him, you need to tell Marcus and me. Because more shit is going down by the minute, which means that anything we can use as a shovel, we want to know about.'

She was quite proud of that remark, but it didn't get her anywhere. Which was annoying, and would annoy anyone, right? His absence of reaction.

'Someone tried to whack Chapman,' she said. 'And River's just been caught on camera staging a gunfight for the tourists. And all of this, whatever it is, involves Slough House, which means it involves me. So start talking, buddy boy, or I'll make you. Are you clear on what that'll be like?'

He had to be – everyone knew Shirley had collected a bagful of scalps out near Hayes last year. But whatever Mr Piano Man thought, he was keeping to himself. And just to underline the point, he reached into his hoodie's pouch and retrieved his iPod.

You are not gunna do this, she thought.

He did, though. He set it on the desk in front of him, and slotted the earbuds in place.

So she did the only reasonable thing in the circumstances, which was rip them from his head.

What happened next was weird. Her plan, if you could call it that – her *expectation* – had been to give him a slap. Open-palmed, nothing serious: even HR would agree he deserved that much. But before her hand had made contact, something sharp was under her chin, pushing upwards: he was on his feet, and the dark wet stones of his eyes were black with anger. Shirley found herself on tiptoe, clutching the desk for balance. He leaned close, the blade at her chin forcing her upwards.

'You don't touch me,' he said.

She blinked.

'Ever,' he said.

There were ways and means, she thought. Push his hand

aside, then a blow to the jaw or the stomach, or just reach out and detach his testicles with one rough twist: any or all of these were no more than a heartbeat away.

On the other hand, his knife would be inside her head before she'd completed any of them.

'Are *you* clear on that?'

From the doorway, Marcus said, 'Oh, for fuck's sake.'

Neither turned to look at him.

Marcus said, 'You. Coe. Put the knife down, okay?'

Coe said nothing.

'If I have to come over there and take it off you, I'm gonna ram it where the sun don't shine, I'm warning you.'

Coe said, 'I'll put it down.'

'. . . Good.'

'But she has to say it first.'

'Has to say what? Uncle?'

'She knows.'

Something trickled down Shirley's jaw; might be sweat; might be blood. There was no way to confirm which. If she looked down, she'd impale herself on his blade.

'Shirley?' Marcus said. 'You know what he's on about?' He paused. 'Probably best not to nod.'

She licked her lips.

Any normal person, she thought, would at least have glanced Marcus's way. But Coe's eyes had never left hers through this whole conversation.

All she'd wanted was to give him a little tap. Teach him some manners.

She swallowed.

Marcus said, 'Shirl?'

She said – whispered – 'I'm clear.'

Coe nodded, and just like that the knife was gone. He tucked it into the pouch of his hoodie and sat down.

Shirley put her hand to her chin, then looked at her fingers. Sweat.

Marcus shook his head.

'They've been watching me for weeks,' the O.B. said. 'Thought I hadn't noticed. Streetlights blinking on and off. Woman at the post office asking questions. It was obvious what was happening. You're not writing this down.'

'We have invisible pixies to do that,' Lamb assured him.

'You think that's helping?' Catherine asked.

By way of answer, he poured himself another drink, or tried to. The bottle didn't hold much more than a double.

The O.B. sat in the centre of the room. Catherine had placed a chair there, and rearranged Lamb's lamps so much of the light fell around, rather than directly onto him. It wasn't an interrogation. That's what she told herself, though it could easily have been mistaken for one by the casual passer-by.

And what most alarmed her about all this, she thought now, was how she seemed to have slid back into her former role: Slough House's chatelaine; Lamb's doorkeeper. Was this what her future held? Another season orbiting Jackson Lamb's dark star? She was going to see today through – make sure the old man was safe – and then kick the house's dust from her heels and launder Lamb's smoke from her clothes.

For now, though, here she was, and the old man seemed happy to hold forth, and if it was true that his answers bore little direct relevance to the questions, they circled the subject at hand, as if closing in on a slippery truth.

'And you,' he said, addressing Chapman. 'They let you indoors now, do they? I thought your job was to wait by the car.'

'Times change,' Bad Sam said softly. 'Tell us about the other night.'

'What other night?'

'Somebody came knocking on your door,' Lamb said. 'And for some reason, you shot him in the head.'

A cunning light switched on in the O.B.'s eyes. 'How do you know about that?'

'Assume we were working the streetlights,' Lamb said. 'He was pretending to be your grandson, wasn't he?'

Cartwright said, 'There he was, bold as brass, asking about the heating, wanting me to tell him about my day. All part of the act, you see? Yes, I was supposed to think he was . . . who you said. My grandson. The one with the name.'

Lamb opened his mouth, and Catherine said, 'Don't.'

'Said he'd run me a bath. As if I couldn't run a bath for myself, if I wanted one.'

And he closed his mouth firmly, as if he'd said enough on that subject.

He hadn't gathered himself together, Catherine thought; not really. Or if he had, he'd done so somewhere else, and was just poking his head round the door.

Chapman said, 'He was an enemy.'

The O.B. stared.

'And you defended yourself.'

'Didn't know I had a gun, did he? Think twice about playing that trick again.'

Chapman was about to continue, but Lamb cut across him. 'We think he came from Les Arbres. That make sense to you?'

'. . . France,' the O.B. said.

'Yeah, France. Hence the funny name. Les Arbres's where you used to visit your old friend Henry, remember? Way back in the nineties, when you had a working head. But Henry wasn't really called Henry, was he? And—'

'You're frightening him, Jackson,' Catherine said.

'And what he was doing was running Project Cuckoo.

Remember? Cuckoo, like you're becoming, or pretending to. Cuckoo, which was all about raising children to be something they're not. Back in the day, we'd have wanted to grow little Soviet generals, so we'd have a clue what the real ones were thinking. Except we didn't, in the end, because even by Cold War standards, it was a barking mad idea. But you—'

'Jackson . . .'

'—didn't let that stop you, did you? You went ahead and did it anyway.'

His voice had grown louder until it filled the whole room, and when he stopped the air shivered, as if settling back into place. The old man had a frozen expression now, halfway between fear and confusion. Catherine thought: she should bring this to an end. Escort the old man out. He'd be better off taking his chances in the rain, or at Regent's Park, than sitting here listening to Lamb exorcise whatever demon had seized him.

And maybe that's what she'd have done, she told herself later, except that Cartwright started to speak again.

Halfway to Pentonville Road, Louisa nearly missed her turn: not missed as in forgot to take it, but missed as in didn't bother, and kept on in a straight line north; past the shops and churches, the mosques and synagogues, that were fast becoming familiar landmarks; the supermarket she used on her way home; the park that signalled the easing of urban tension. Wipers wiping fit to bust, she could be pulling into the residents' parking area behind her block in twenty minutes, and running a bath not long later; a glass of wine poured, quiet music playing; the patter of the rain upon the windows promising sleep. But duty got the better of her and she made the turn, and headed towards the crime scene down Pentonville Road.

It was like a circus would be if circuses involved fewer clowns. Cop cars had arrived in droves, and cops were occupying every corner, some talking to huddled groups of civilians, others clustered round a car she knew from the YouTube film was the attack vehicle, itself looking like a mechanised assault victim – its front end folded in, and glasswork from its headlights scattered like frozen tears. The impact car, meanwhile, had been slammed sideways into a set of railings. Always, collision scenes had an air of inevitability about them, as if the resulting damage had been written into the vehicles' design specs. The police might have been there to confirm that everything had happened as required, and nothing been left undone.

She was feeling battered herself: torn jeans, hurt legs. But adrenalin was a powerful painkiller. 'I think he's the joker from this afternoon,' she'd heard Marcus saying as she'd hop-skipped down the stairs in Slough House. If she'd needed another trigger, that was it.

Having parked as near as she was able, Louisa showed her Service card to a reasonably experienced-looking cop, by which she meant one who'd found somewhere sheltered to stand. He seemed suitably impressed. One day, she thought, someone at Regent's Park would notice that the slow horses' official ID made them seem, to the uninitiated, like genuine Service personnel, and then they'd take them away and replace them with cardboard badges cut from a cereal packet. But until that happened, Louisa was able to get answers to a series of questions:

Yes, a gun had been fired.

No, nobody had been hurt.

There was nobody in custody.

The area was being searched.

Couple of your people in the car that was struck . . .

'My people?'

'Funny buggers,' said the policeman.

She looked up and down the road. Streetlights were on, and shop windows spilt yellow and gold squares onto the pavements, but visibility was poor, rain blurring pedestrians into fuzzy cartoon shapes. She'd been wondering how two men could have vanished so easily in the middle of the city, but the question answered itself. It was dark, and the rain washed away colour and difference, turning everyone into somebody else. There were witnesses, but most would contradict each other in that special way witnesses had, repainting the same event a dozen different shades of grey, and there'd be CCTV too, but she knew the work involved in tracking a quarry by camera, and it produced the kind of evidence useful in court, months after the event. For on-the-spot discovery, you'd be better off sticking notices to lampposts.

Now she was here, it was clear she'd made the wrong call at that junction. She should have gone straight home. Damn River; all it would have taken was a swift phone call, and he'd have saved her untold grief . . . Untold grief was what had happened when Min died; untold because she'd had nobody to talk to. Thinking the same thing had happened to River had threatened to shatter the recovery she'd made: the new home, the new life, the evenings watching trees swaying in the darkness. So damn him for all that, but where was he, and what was happening?

One of the group clustered round the attack vehicle peeled away and approached. She was a wet blonde woman, her suit looking like it was halfway through a rinse cycle; one side of her face turning overripe from a recent collision. She'd been in the impact car, thought Louisa; had been holding the gun. The gun the trickster had snatched with a movement so smooth it might have come from a dance routine.

Funny bugger, definitely.

A judgement confirmed by the first word out of her mouth: 'Service?'

Louisa showed her card again.

'You're one of Lamb's crew. The slow horses.'

'We get called that,' Louisa said.

'And Cartwright's another.'

'It was him with you? In the car?'

'Do you all act dumb all the time? Or is it not an act?'

'We take it in turns,' said Louisa. 'It was him in the car, wasn't it?'

'Until his buddy came to rescue him.'

Louisa laughed.

'What?'

'River having buddies. Never mind. You don't know who it was, then?'

'I know he's called Patrice. Like I say, a buddy.'

'Yeah, well. Either way, he left you in the dust.' Louisa was remembering something she'd heard about the Dogs, about who was in charge now. She said, 'You're Emma Flyte, aren't you? You're new to this.'

'So I keep being told.'

'Your fifteen seconds of fame is up on YouTube, they tell you that? This Patrice, he's quite . . . disarming.'

'Are we trying to be funny, Agent Guy?'

'A real charmer, is all I meant. He do that to your face?' Louisa indicated her own feet. 'He took a crowbar to my ankles earlier. I'm betting River didn't go with him voluntarily.'

'Exactly what,' Emma Flyte said slowly, 'is going on here?'

'Wish I knew,' Louisa said. 'But I'll tell you this much. Patrice – you're sure about that?'

'Patrice,' Flyte said.

'Patrice tried to kill a former spook today. So whatever

you're doing to find him, do it faster. Before he kills Cartwright too.'

Flyte turned away, looking back towards King's Cross, where a lot of angry traffic was building up. 'Uh-huh,' she said. 'It didn't look to me like that was his plan.'

'Where are we going?' River asked.

Patrice looked at him, his face expressionless.

'Okay. Just thought it was worth asking.'

It was thirty minutes since they'd left the scene on Pentonville Road, and they'd crossed half the city since: had doubled back to King's Cross and caught a taxi to Great Portland Street.

'Been a bit of bother back there,' the driver informed them, pulling away. 'Some lemon going mental with a shooter. Roads'll be closed any minute.'

'I wondered what the police cars were doing,' Patrice had answered, texting as he spoke.

Another shot past; unmarked, its blue light looping through its back window as it bullied through a queue of traffic.

'The weather brings them out,' the cabbie said, with the air of one delivering a universal truth: that whenever it rained, there was gunfire in the city.

When the taxi dropped them, they walked to Baker Street. Patrice still had the gun, though where he'd secreted it, River couldn't tell. If down the back of his waistband, as River suspected, he must have spent hours practising how to walk, sit, move, without looking like his haemorrhoids were flaring.

And if I make a break for it, he wondered, will he shoot me in the back?

It didn't matter. Well, it mattered, but it wasn't an issue. Last thing he was doing was leaving Patrice's side; not until he'd had a chance to question him about Les Arbres, about the commune, and about why Patrice's comrade-in-arms had come to kill the O.B. Though, ideally, he'd remove the gun from Patrice's possession before the discussion turned to precisely what had happened to Bertrand.

Not quite a prisoner, then, though hardly an accomplice, he stayed by Patrice's side as they headed into Baker Street station and descended into the Tube once again.

A manhunt would have kicked off by now. There'd be footage from Pentonville Road; someone would have been aiming a phone as Patrice waved the gun around. The Tube was a good place to be, then. With no Wi-Fi, at least no one was down-loading their images while they bucketed from one station to the next. Patrice stayed close; one hand on River's shoulder, as if for balance. So yes, River thought, they were in it together. Whatever 'it' was. And however it turned out.

As they approached Embankment, Patrice's hand squeezed. Okay, okay, I get it. River led the way off the train, up the escalator; turned towards the river entrance. Still raining, of course. He'd no sooner dried off from today's French rain before being drenched in the English variety. Still, it was nice to be home.

They stood at the top of the steps, looking at wet traffic, a wet bridge; the wet South Bank across the wet Thames.

'Do you have a plan?' River asked.

'There is always a plan,' Patrice said.

'That's good. Is that Sartre?' Not expecting a reply, he didn't wait for one. 'Who were you texting in the taxi?'

'You like to talk,' Patrice said. 'Maybe you should talk about Bertrand. What happened to him. And why you have his passport.'

'That was Bertrand's? Because it didn't have his name on it. And, you know, a passport, you kind of expect—'

'You know I have a gun.' He turned and looked River in

the eyes. 'And the only reason you're still alive is that I need answers from you.'

'Yeah, see, that's not a great interrogative technique. Because it implies that once I've *given* you your answers—'

Patrice hit him so quickly that nobody saw: not the passers-by, hurrying through the rain; not the fellow travellers still sheltering from the downpour. Certainly not River. First he knew about it was, Patrice was lowering him into a sitting position, murmuring calm words.

'He's okay.' This for the benefit of those near by. 'He gets claustrophobic, that's all.'

To River: 'Maybe put your head between your knees?'

Somebody said, 'Are you sure he's all right? Should we get help?'

'He'll be fine. I'm always telling him, we should take taxis. But no, he insists on the underground, and here we are again.'

'My boyfriend's just the same.'

Any other time River might have protested the emphasis on 'my', but at the moment he was coping with a lot of frazzled nerve ends, as if Patrice had laid into him with a cattle prod rather than his little finger, or whatever it was he'd used to do whatever it was he'd done.

Someone else said, 'Anyone got any water?' and everybody laughed.

Don't mind me. You all enjoy yourselves.

Patrice maintained the fiction established for them by sitting next to River and putting his arm round his shoulders. He leaned close, as if whispering sweet consolation, and reminded River: 'That required no effort on my part.'

River said, 'Last time someone hurt me like that . . .'

He paused for breath.

'Yes?'

'I knocked half his brains out with a length of lead pipe.'

Patrice made a show of looking here, there, in front, behind. 'Don't see any lead pipe.'

'You won't.'

Patrice's phone chirruped. 'Do you mind? I really ought to take this.'

He stood and walked a few paces off. River looked around for a length of lead pipe, but his heart wasn't in it.

The other travellers had moved on, braving the rain, because there seemed little alternative. He wondered if, later, they'd watch the news and say to each other *Do they look like . . .?* and *Nah, surely not.*

Patrice finished his call. River watched him while he stared for a moment at the Thames, as if suddenly struck by its night-time beauty; the lights along the Embankment smeary in the rain. Then he looked at River.

'So,' he said. 'What's the dazzle ship, and where do we find it?'

'His name was Frank,' the O.B. said.

He stopped.

Catherine braced for another Lamb onslaught, but none came. Because he had done all he needed, she thought; he'd thrown the switch, and now all the old man's memories would come tumbling forth.

She should have hustled him out while the thought was fresh in her mind.

'Came to the Park with his ridiculous plan. Cuckoo by name, cuckoo by nature. Even the Yanks hadn't gone for it. Well, not a second time. Had tried it back in the sixties, of course, and came a cropper. Hushed up the details. Not that hushing things up ever worked. First law of Spook Street. Secrets don't stay secret.'

He paused. Catherine could have sworn something shone

in his eyes: unshed tears or bottled-up secrets. Something waiting to spill.

'So we told him to pack his wares and move his pitch.'

Again, the pause. This morning, Catherine remembered, he had seemed a man adrift; unmoored by encroaching dementia, and pushed further out to sea by last night's events. And now he'd washed up somewhere, but it wasn't quite here and wasn't quite now, and if his sentences recaptured the brim and snap of his younger self, they were messages from a bottle launched long ago, and she doubted he knew who he was talking to. Memory was doing all the work, blowing through the old man like he was a seashell, and when it was done he would be smooth and empty.

Chapman said, 'But you didn't quite cast him away, did you?'

He spoke gently, to Catherine's surprise. Her experience of his interrogation technique had been a little different.

David Cartwright blinked, then blinked again. He mumbled something, and she had to replay the sound in her head a few times before she thought she'd caught it: a repetition of what he'd said earlier, *First law of Spook Street.*

'He came to my house. Weeks later. Living in the city then. Bayswater. It was the fag end of summer, and he was . . . different. He suggested a drink. I suggested he disappear, if he didn't want to find himself in pokey.'

She remembered River telling her of evenings spent like this, the young man listening to the old one, spinning spook yarns, brandy in hand, and wondered if that was where David Cartwright had retreated in his mind.

He needed River, she thought. But River was out slaying dragons, or looking for dragons to slay.

'Knew what he wanted, of course. Saw it in his eyes when he showed up at the Park. Because he was one of the believers.

His Project Cuckoo, it wasn't just a strategy he favoured. No, he thought it was our only possible direction, that we'd be doomed without it. That was his faith, you see? Why the Agency got shot of him. Nothing more dangerous than a believer.'

Because believers were always on a quest, for one Holy Grail or another. And quests were fuelled by the blood of anyone who happened to get in the way.

'So I thought he was there to make one last plea. If I got on board, he knew I'd carry the Park. More power behind the throne than there ever is sitting on it.' He grew cunning, like a man with a magic ring in his pocket, about to show what it can do. 'You'll have to turn the tape off now.'

Bad Sam said, 'There's no tape. You can speak freely.'

The old man tapped the side of his nose. 'Do I look like this is my first time?'

Sighing theatrically, Lamb opened his desk drawer and reached inside it. Something made a clunky noise. It might have been a hole punch. 'There,' he said. 'Now, your American crusader. What did he want?' He was revolving his glass in his hand, and by the lamp's yellow glow Catherine could see its sticky surface, its film of smudged fingerprints. 'Well, we know what he wanted. But how did he get it? Why did you give it to him?'

'I never . . .'

'The Park turned him down. We've established that. And the Yanks had kicked him out. But the following year there he is, middle of France, running his little colony, raising his children as prototype terrorists. And there you were, checking on his progress. But not officially. Because as far as the records go, you were paying welfare visits on an old spook. So whatever happened, you did it under the bridge. Why?'

She shouldn't be party to this, she thought again, but it

was too late; everything was too late. Jackson Lamb would ebb and flow, and the old man would crumble. Whether there'd be anything left of him once it was over was anybody's guess. And she had promised River she'd look after his grandfather, but God help her, she wanted to know too. Whatever had happened back then, it had sown the seeds of the Westacres bombing, and she wanted to know what it had been. Because she'd been kidding herself if she'd thought she'd escaped Slough House. It didn't matter where she was, she was as much a spook as Lamb, and every bit as hungry to learn these secrets.

'He had something on you,' Lamb said. 'He turned the screw. What did he know?'

'He's had enough,' Bad Sam said. 'Let's leave it for now, shall we?'

'He's had enough when I say he's had enough. What did Frank have on you, Cartwright? What did he know that you wanted kept hidden?'

'Jackson—'

'You said it yourself. Secrets don't stay secret, not on Spook Street.'

'Stop now, or I'll make you stop,' Bad Sam said. 'I mean it.'

'Frank had something. What was it?'

'Leave him, Jackson,' Catherine said.

And the old man said, 'Isobel,' and started to cry.

14

'WELL,' LOUISA SAID. 'I wasn't expecting this.'

Her companion said, 'I've been up for eighteen hours. I've spent most of them in my car, and the rest looking at bodies, being lied to, locking up innocent people, and letting a French whackjob steal my gun. Oh, and having what feels like my cheekbone broken by the very hard head of that colleague of yours. Who, when my day started, was dead. I deserve a drink or seven after that.'

'No argument,' Louisa said, who hadn't been fazed by being in a bar; just by Flyte's invitation. She was drinking fizzy water: her car was down the road. But Emma Flyte was putting away tequila shots, one either side of a Mexican beer, and nothing about the way she was doing this suggested amateur status.

'Met your boss this morning,' Emma said.

Ah, Louisa thought. It was rare you got the chance to hear first impressions of Lamb. 'And how did you get along?'

'He gave me about a dozen good reasons for bringing disciplinary charges against him.'

Louisa nodded seriously. 'If you decide to do that, I very much want to be there when it happens.'

'I'm not going to,' Emma said. Her beer bottle had a piece of fruit lodged on its rim for some reason, and she pushed it inside with her thumb. It fizzed. 'I mean, he's a pig. And he lied about whose body he was looking at, which might come back and bite him yet. But I'd sooner have him telling me lies than Diana Taverner. When that lady plays hide-the-soap, she does it for keeps.'

Louisa let that image sparkle and die before saying, 'Maybe you and Lamb have more in common than you think.'

Emma's phone buzzed, and she glanced at it. 'The Park.'

'Uh-huh.'

'They probably want to know what happened out there,' Emma said, nodding towards the door, the outside world, Pentonville Road. 'And how come Adam Lockhead has, ah, evaded custody.'

'I thought you said his name was Patrice.'

'It's Cartwright I'm talking about.' Despite the booze, her voice was steady. 'That's the passport he was using. Adam Lockhead. News to you?'

'I'm about three laps behind everyone at the moment,' Louisa said. 'All I know is, this Patrice? He's a pro. And as we've established, armed. In fact, his becoming armed is doubt-less clocking up views on YouTube as we chat. So all in all, it might be an idea to be out there looking for him instead of in here self-medicating.'

'When we find him, it won't be because I'm outside getting wet,' Emma said. 'It'll be phoned in by some beat-cop who listened to his radio chatter.'

'D'you think that'll be before or after he kills Cartwright?' Louisa said. 'I realise you're not that bothered either way.'

'He didn't look to me like he wanted to kill Cartwright. He looked startled, I thought. Startled to see him.'

'River can be a pain in the neck,' Louisa agreed. 'But he's not actually alarming. Not at first glance.'

'Where'd he been?'

'I gather he's spent the day in France.'

'Why?'

'When I see him, I'll ask. You used to be with the Met, right?'

'Yes.'

Louisa grinned. 'Missing it yet?'

The phone buzzed again, angrier this time, the way phones get. Emma sighed, and moved a few steps away. 'Flyte.'

'Tell me that's not you I'm watching. Along with half the population of the Western world.'

'I doubt it's that many,' Emma said. 'Most of them'll be viewing it twice. You have to factor that in.'

Diana Taverner said, 'Are you drunk?'

'Not yet.'

'How did this happen? How did any of it happen?'

'It happened because I wasn't given enough information,' Emma said. 'So when we were sideswiped by a professional hitman, we weren't expecting it. In the circumstances, we got off lightly. Unwelcome publicity notwithstanding.'

'You call that lightly? What would heavy look like?'

'It would involve my body lying in the street. Who was Adam Lockhead supposed to be?'

'That's way outside your need-to-know.'

'Fine. So do you want me to forget who he really is? Because another couple of tequilas might do the trick.'

Taverner said, 'What are you talking about?'

'The man you sent me to collect, the one whose passport said Adam Lockhead, he's River Cartwright. Who for a while last night we thought was dead. Stop me if I start making sense. It would be a good note to end my day on.'

In the pause that followed, the usual bar clatter seemed to increase, as if anxious to fill any void in its jurisdiction. Emma wondered if Taverner was running the video again, to check what she'd just said.

Maybe so, because when she next spoke she said, 'It does look like Cartwright. Did he say anything?'

'He knew the hitman.'

'Why do you keep calling him that?'

'He hit us with a car. It's the shortest version of that I can think of.' Emma was missing her drink, so she wandered back to the table. The way things had come undone, it didn't seem to matter who heard what. 'Cartwright called him by name. Patrice.'

'Where are they now?'

'Do you know, that's a really good question,' Emma said, reaching for her shot. 'Not sure. London?'

'Are you anxious to lose your job?'

'I figure that's out of my hands.' There was a short interval, during which she saw off her tequila. 'The Met's on the case now anyway. Can't keep this one quiet. He was firing a gun in the street.'

'Your gun.'

'I hadn't forgotten. You haven't asked about Devon yet.'

'. . . What the hell has Devon got to do with anything?'

'Devon Welles. He was driving the car.'

'Oh. Right. He's not dead or anything?'

'Couple of cracked ribs. I packed him off to A & E. You want me to have Giti Rahman released?'

'Why would I want that?'

'Because there doesn't seem much point hanging on to her. Whatever it is you're so desperate to keep under wraps is leaking worse than a broken sieve. I'm not sure which'll happen first, a Freedom of Information request or an offer for the film rights.'

'Ms Flyte, all that's been broadcast to an easily amused world so far is your own inability to carry out a straightforward arrest. And if you want your career to survive that hiccup, I suggest you keep a low profile from now on.' She paused. 'You're a disappointment. Go back to the safe house. Sit with Ms Rahman. And if I ever relieve you from that not particularly onerous duty, you'll know hell just installed air conditioning.'

Emma put her glass down. She thought: another round exactly like that, and the varying degrees of pain, humiliation, embarrassment and anger she was feeling would subside into a molten mass from which she needn't emerge until morning. It might even have stopped raining by then.

She said, 'Lady Di? I wish I could say the same about you. About being a disappointment, I mean. But no, you more than live up to everything everyone says.'

She disconnected.

Louisa said, 'Wow. Was that your career I just saw leaving?'

'Tell me you don't know what that feels like.'

'You want another drink?'

'What I want is a cup of coffee. Can you organise that? Because I need the bathroom.'

Louisa, watching Emma retreat to the back of the bar, decided to hang on a while; join her in that coffee. Her flat with all its quiet comforts would still be there later. And sticking with Flyte might give her the inside track when River and Patrice broke surface.

Pissed off as she was with him, she had to admit that all the exciting stuff happened round River.

Somewhere not far away – or not as the pigeon flies, though few cared to do so in the cold wet dark: even London's pigeons have their limit – River was adding this to his list of unexpected beauties: a dazzle ship in the rain, its perspective-bewildering doodles becoming extra smeary, its black-and-white pipe-and-funnel finish ballooning into ever more cartoony shapes. It seemed to shimmer in the downpour, as if the lights trained on it were all that anchored it in place.

Patrice said, 'That's something.'

River, as if explaining an object of national pride to a tourist, said, 'They were painted like that to confuse submarines. It made it harder to sink them, to pinpoint them as targets.'

'And that worked?'

'Well, this one's still here.'

Though its patterning was not the First World War design, but a recent *hommage*, jauntier than the original.

HMS *President* was moored on the Embankment, on the approach to Blackfriars Bridge. In the background, cars and buses crossed the Thames, their tyres a swooshing soundtrack. This riverside road was quieter; one lane closed to traffic. Someone was always trying to improve the capital's roads, and if they ever finished the job, they might turn out to have succeeded. Meanwhile, canvas-shrouded fencing was pitched along a stretch of kerb, reaching from the ship's purpose-built jetty up to the bridge itself, lanterns fixed to it at regular intervals. These too wobbled in the wind, bouncing dizzy halos off the sturdy buildings on the other side of the road: banks and publishers and other dubious institutions.

River and Patrice had walked, because they were already so wet it made no difference, and it didn't seem like something a pair of fugitives would do: stroll along in the pouring rain, pointing at the sights along the way.

Though their apparent camaraderie didn't stop River wondering whether Patrice would kill him before the night was done.

He could run for it, of course. But running from trouble had never been a core skill; running towards it was more his thing. And running wouldn't give him the answers he was after.

A figure waited near the dazzle ship, on its walkway's sheltered platform. Before they reached him, River said, 'There's something I should tell you.'

Patrice showed little curiosity, but so far, apart from that moment he'd first laid eyes on River, he hadn't shown much of anything. Had simply transmitted a dull grey pulse, performing each action as it was required; as if he were a wind-up construct, its movements oiled to perfection.

'I met your mother today,' he said. 'Natasha.'

Patrice said nothing.

'She misses you.'

Patrice shook his head, but still said nothing.

'She wants to know you're all right. It worried her, when Les Arbres burned down. Any mother would worry.'

'I have no mother.'

'She didn't abandon you, you know. Or at least, she came back. She wanted to see you, to be with you. They wouldn't let her.'

'I have no mother,' Patrice repeated.

'She was there for years. Never far away. In case you needed her.'

Patrice looked at him and said, 'Those things never happened. Stop talking.'

'I will if you want. But I don't think you do.'

As casually as if he were swatting a fly, Patrice reached out to slap River's cheek, but River had been expecting this, or something like it, and blocked the blow. But not the second, which was aimed at his throat. Patrice pulled it at the last second, or River would have been laid out on the pavement.

Patrice said, 'Stop now. Or I'll make you.'

Maybe he had a point.

The figure under the shelter watched them approach. He wore a raincoat, its collar up, but there was something familiar about him, about the way he stood. Because this was Frank, of course. His hair thinning; his cheekbones more pronounced; but still tall, fairish, broad-shouldered. Strong and capable. His way of growing older had been to grow more like himself.

As they reached him, he opened his arms. Patrice stepped dutifully into them, and Frank kissed him on one cheek, then on the other. There seemed little affection in the gesture. It was more, River thought, like a general greeting a soldier back from the front.

'I didn't know you were in England,' Patrice said.

'You didn't need to know I was in England,' Frank said. He turned to River. 'You're River Cartwright.'

'And you're Frank. I didn't get your surname.'

'Harkness. Frank Harkness.'

The accent was American, but with its corners sanded away by European exile.

River said, 'Great to have this opportunity to chat. You sent someone to kill my grandfather.'

There were noises from the boat, whose features included a bar; overlapping voices and the tinselly ringing of glasses, mostly muffled by the rain. There was nobody in sight. River could have shouted without risk of being overheard.

To his surprise, Frank laughed.

River said, 'You do know what happened, right? To your boy, Bertrand.'

Patrice took a step nearer, like a dog reacting to danger.

'You want to call him off?' River said.

Frank said, 'It's okay, Patrice. He's got things he needs to say.'

'Why did he have Bertrand's passport? And he said he was at Les Arbres.'

269

'There's nothing to see there,' Frank said. 'Not any more.'

'But why—'

'Excuse us,' Frank told River. 'This won't take long.'

It took River a moment to realise he was being asked to give them some privacy.

Well, he couldn't get any wetter.

From the laughably inadequate shelter of a nearby tree, he watched Frank put an arm round Patrice's shoulder and lean in close. Whatever instruction or advice he was offering demanded intimacy . . . Water snaked down River's back, throwing an uncontrollable shiver into him; a full-body spasm. How long had today gone on for? It had already been old when he'd arrived at his grandfather's to find the body in the bathroom. How much longer, and what would happen yet?

Then Frank kissed Patrice again, and stepped back.

When Patrice approached River, he tensed, wondering if he'd just witnessed a Godfather moment; the older man explaining to the younger why he, River, had to die. But instead Patrice paused, then leaned forward, hands in pockets, and kissed River on the cheek. One cheek only.

He said, 'We will speak again soon.'

Then he walked back the way they'd come; just a man hurrying through the rain, eager for the next place of shelter.

'Sorry about that,' Frank said. 'Patrice, he's a little confused right now.' He produced a pack of cigarettes, and offered them to River, who shook his head. Frank used a lighter, and the space filled with blue French smoke. 'On account of your grandfather killing his best friend.'

'And your son.'

'Uh-huh.' He might have been acknowledging a vaguer relationship. Someone he shared a lift with once, perhaps. 'I can't believe he let that old bastard get the better of him. It's like, lesson one. Don't let your guard down just because the target appears harmless.'

River said, 'The *target* was my grandfather.'

'I hadn't forgotten.'

River wanted to punch the cigarette clean out of his mouth. Break his nose, black his eyes, watch him crumple in the rain. But instead of using his fists he said, 'I shot your son's corpse in the face. To mess up the forensics. I thought it might buy us twenty minutes.'

'His name was Bertrand.'

'I don't care.'

'You should,' said Frank. 'He was your brother. It's good to see you, son. How've you been?'

Taverner disconnected and said: 'I swear to God, I sometimes think I'm the only thing standing between this place and total chaos.'

Claude Whelan looked up from his laptop. Four viewings of the YouTube video now, and any further information it held wasn't going to reveal itself on a fifth. The young man who'd brought it to Diana's office had assured them it was being assessed by experts, its every pixel weighed and measured. Whether any knowledge thus acquired would help save Claude's bacon, or ensure it was served extra crispy, would no doubt become clear in its own sweet time.

Diana said, 'The other man in the car – the one who was using the Lockhead property – Flyte says it was River Cartwright.'

For a moment, Whelan's mind didn't bother taking this in. Then he said, 'River Cartwright? He was supposed to be dead. What's he doing with a cold body passport?'

'Let me think.'

He was happy to. As long as she was doing that, she wasn't

binding him more tightly inside this mad conspiracy which had just looped back on itself. The Cartwright mess – that's what she'd called it this morning, back when he'd thought he was in charge round here – the Cartwright mess had nothing to do with Westacres. Cartwright was a Service legend who'd subsided into dementia, shot his grandson, and gone walkabout in Kent. Though apparently it hadn't been his grandson after all . . .

The fact that it was Taverner doing the thinking didn't prevent Claude from having ideas too.

He said, 'David Cartwright?'

'Yes,' she said, already working the same seam.

'He was around at the right time. Twenty years ago.'

'He could have taken the properties. Nobody would have questioned anything he did. He was Charles Partner's right hand.'

'But why?'

'Why anything? Money, power, sex – it doesn't matter. If one of the cold bodies came to his door and ended up dead, you know what that means?'

'They're cleaning house,' said Whelan.

Once, late at night in New York City, he'd sat with Claire in the back of a yellow cab as it tore down Broadway, and watched each set of traffic lights turn green at their approach. Sometimes, problems solved themselves: each question finding its own answer before you'd arrived at it.

He said, 'Cartwright supplied the cold bodies to someone long ago. And now they've gone operational, they're covering their tracks. With Cartwright dead, they're secure.'

'Except,' Diana said. 'You know what's wrong with this picture? It's hung backwards. If you're a terror group planning a Westacres, you tie up your loose ends first. They should have come for Cartwright before the bombing.'

'But they didn't. So maybe—'

'They didn't know the bombing was going to happen,' Diana said.

Out on the hub, the work of the Service continued. There was a muted flatscreen on the wall whose rolling news channel remained fixated on Westacres. Relatives of the dead were fair game now, the three-day interval deemed long enough for mourning, and the transforming power of involvement in world-events had rendered several of them experts in counter-terrorism. One such was performing now, his head bobbing angrily as he explained the failings of the intelligence services, their laxity, their incompetence. Whelan could see him through the office's glass wall. It must be of comfort, he thought, to pretend you had an understanding of how the world operated. Especially when it went wrong, and the result was carnage: broken bodies, torn flesh, and lives forever damaged.

He said, 'I'm not sure which is worse. That someone planned this, or that it's all some colossal fuck-up.'

'Welcome to Regent's Park.'

'Let's back up. Young Cartwright had Adam Lockhead's passport. There was a body at Cartwright's house. Ergo—'

'It was Adam Lockhead's body,' Diana said.

'So young Cartwright turned up in time to foil the assassin, then went haring off across the Channel on the killer's passport. He was walking back the cat. Trying to find out who wanted to kill his grandfather.'

'Well, if nothing else, it shows the old man really does have dementia,' Diana Taverner said. 'Otherwise he could have just asked him. Saved himself a journey.' Briefly she raised her fingers to her lips, and he understood that she was a smoker, unconsciously miming a nicotine hit. 'So the question is, what did young Cartwright find out? How much does he know?'

'And who came after him?' Whelan said. He reached out

273

and tapped the pad on his sleeping laptop, making the Pentonville Road video come to jerky life once more.

Taverner said, 'The only thing that makes sense is, he's the other cold body. Paul Wayne.'

'And he's not rescuing Cartwright, he's abducting him,' said Whelan. 'So he can find out where the old man is now.'

His eyes flicked from the small screen in front of him to the larger one out on the hub. As if it were part of an installation, the recurrence of violent action in urban iconography, the YouTube film was playing on that one too now: more fodder for the debate on how the effort to keep the streets safe had fallen short. First Westacres, now this. Already, there'd be those straining to join the dots between the two. If anyone managed it, you'd hear the howls of outrage even while the screen remained mute.

Diana Taverner said, 'You realise, the more complicated the situation gets, the simpler the solution becomes.'

'I'm not going to want to hear this.'

'I don't care. As long as you're First Desk, there are decisions you'll have to make. Not for your own good, not for mine, not even for your wife's—'

'Leave Claire out of this.'

'Of course. But I'm simply stating facts. Your choices are no longer about your own moral comfort. They're about the greater good.'

'And the greater good, as you see it—'

'Is the survival of this Service.' She pointed towards the hub. 'Westacres happened. There's nothing we can do about that. But we've stopped similar things happening in the past, and we'll do so again in the future. Provided we're allowed to. Provided we maintain what trust is still out there.'

'There's not an awful lot of that about,' Whelan said, indicating the television.

'There'll always be those pointing fingers. But the vast majority? They trust us to keep them safe. Because if they didn't, they wouldn't be doing what they do – getting on trains, walking down streets, visiting shops. They'd be holed up in their bedrooms, living off canned food and bottled water. That's the measure of our success, Claude. That the country still leads a normal life, even while we bury the dead.'

'I'm not sure Marketing'll approve that as a slogan.' He closed the laptop. It was good to have these visible punctuation marks: without them, conversations might go on forever. 'What are you suggesting we do?'

'The obvious. We have an armed terrorist on the streets, accompanied by a rogue agent. They present a clear and present danger to the populace.'

'You want me to issue a shoot-to-kill order.'

'Well there's no point shooting to wound. People would only get hurt.'

'Diana—'

'It's what I'd be suggesting even if it weren't for the . . . additional aspects of the situation.'

'But it would certainly suit our interests if this pair were dead, and unavailable for interrogation,' he said. 'Except young Cartwright's not exactly rogue, is he? I mean—'

'His actions have been unwarranted, unauthorised, and he's been involved in a violent death. We can argue semantics if you like, but nothing he's done today has improved his CV. Which was already less than exemplary.'

'Still—'

'And we have reason to believe his grandfather made possible one of the worst ever terrorist outrages on British soil.'

'Hardly the grandson's fault.'

'So why has he been hiding him?'

'We're not likely to find out if we have him gunned down in the street.'

'And if he's allowed to talk, then the media coverage we've seen so far is going to look like a PR script. This is a turning point, Claude. It's not just your career that'll be over. And mine. It's the Service as we know it. Which is imperfect, sure, and sometimes slow to respond, but we can make those things better – you and I. But not if this fiasco becomes public. If that happens, we'll have nothing to build on. Because there'll be no trust and no public belief. It'll all be buried under the Westacres rubble.'

If Taverner hadn't been here, he'd have reached for his wife's photo. Would have found strength in that contact, even though she would never agree to what was being offered him: a swift way out of a situation not of his making. But then, he had been here before, hadn't he? He had found his way out of corners in ways that Claire wouldn't have approved of. Corners she hadn't known he'd been in.

'What about David Cartwright?' he said at last.

'He'll turn up eventually. But it's not like he's going to be making any sense. No, this is our chance to make everything go away. And it's not even a push, Claude. It's a nudge. The Met will be going in heavy-mannered whatever recommendations you make.'

'I can't give instructions to the police force.'

'But you can make a call to the PM.'

He could feel it sliding out of his reach, any sense that he had a choice in what was about to happen.

'Young Cartwright is not an enemy of the state.'

'If he's discovered what his grandfather did, then he very likely is. Because that would mean he has information that can do serious – irreparable – damage to the Service. And if that doesn't make him an enemy of the state, I don't know what would.'

It had been hours, he thought, since she had referred to the sword she'd left dangling over his head; the false information he'd fed COBRA. Instead, she wanted him to find his own way to the decision she'd placed in front of him.

If he did what she wanted, he'd be bound forever in her coils.

If he didn't, she'd throw him to the wolves.

With a wash of nostalgia, he remembered life across the river, where the worst he had to contend with was the passive-aggressive needling of his fellow weasels.

He said, 'This isn't right.'

'Maybe not the right thing to do. But it's the right decision to make.'

Nothing in her demeanour, he thought, indicated that she'd ever had a moment's self-doubt in her life.

Keeping his face as expressionless as possible, Claude Whelan reached for the phone.

A police car flashed past, or didn't; the sky growled dramatically, or held its breath. Mermaids might have risen from the Thames, and the dazzle ship taken to the air. Probably all that happened, though, was the rain. If asked to reconstruct the moment later, that's all River would have been able to swear to.

'. . . What did you say?'

'You heard me, River. I'm your father.'

'My *father*?'

'You want to hear it in a Darth Vader voice?'

River didn't want to hear it at all.

He blinked several times, but nothing altered. They were under a shelter on the bank of the Thames, whose night-time reflections were rendered impressionist by steady rain. From the dazzle ship's bar drifted a murmur of voices, and an unidentifiable tune. And here was Frank Harkness, who'd run some

277

mysterious commune in the heart of France; who'd raised boys like Patrice, like Bertrand, and sent them out to be killers.

And he had an English woman, I remember. I saw her once, or more than once. Perhaps these occasions have melted into one.

Natasha's words, floating back to him the way those reflections floated on the water.

She was very beautiful, and very cross, the time I saw her, and they have big argument, big row, and Frank tells everyone to leave . . . And when we come back, she is gone.

His mother had never stayed with anyone long. Even her eventual marriage, which had elevated her into comfortable respectability, hadn't gone the distance, her husband having succumbed to a dicky heart within three years of their union.

The distance she'd come, the respectability she'd assumed: all of that was summed up in her use of the phrase *dicky heart*.

'How can you *possibly* . . .'

He could almost see his words, so effortfully did they struggle into the air. And then crash to the ground, unable to reach the end of their sentence.

'We should go inside,' Frank said. With a tilt of the head, he indicated the bar behind them; the comfort room on the dazzle ship. 'You look like you could use a drink.'

'. . . How can you possibly be my father?'

'Seriously? We need to have this conversation?' Frank shook his head. 'I gathered you were a late starter, but—'

River grabbed him by the lapels and shook him, but it was clear that Frank was allowing himself to be shook. To be shaken. There was a solidity to his frame, something like a tree trunk – you could push on it all day and night, but there was no way you were toppling it without serious tools.

'That's better,' Frank said. 'For a moment there, I thought you were going to pass out. But this is better. You're strong. You'll do.'

278

'You're lying.'

'You know I'm not. If you thought I was, it's the first thing you'd have said.'

River let him go. 'That's just mind games. That's bullshit. You can't *possibly* . . .'

But already it felt like knowledge he'd been deliberately resisting till now. Already it felt like he was the last to know.

'We met, we fell in love, she became pregnant. Your grandfather didn't approve, do I need to tell you that?'

The O.B. and his mother, and the rift that had driven them apart. For years he'd watched on the sidelines, with neither party giving anything away. *He had missed the original Cold War by years. This one would do until the next came along.*

'He drove a wedge between us. What did she tell you about me?'

'Nothing. She told me nothing. She never speaks of you.'

'Well, you have to hand it to the old man. When he drives a wedge, it stays driven.'

This time a police car did flash past, though flash was not the word. It slowed, rather, while its occupants gave them the once over, before negotiating the chicane the roadworks had assembled. There was other traffic too, none of it important.

'Why did he do that?'

'Drive us apart?'

'Yes. Why would he do that, especially if – if me. If she was pregnant. Why would he do that?'

'Maybe he didn't like the thought of having a Yank for a son-in-law. Or he was worried I'd take his precious daughter way over the big blue sea.'

'No.'

'No he didn't find her precious, or—'

'No, you're lying. None of that's anywhere near the truth.'

He was thinking of all those years, all those conversations.

All the times his grandfather had asked 'whether he'd heard from his mother': never using 'Isobel', as if this would presume on a deeper acquaintance . . . River had missed her terribly for all of his life, without ever admitting it out loud. And the reasons he was being offered here were nowhere near enough to account for that.

Frank said, 'Okay, there was a little more to it. Your grandfather – he was a great one for making deals.'

'Tell me what happened.'

'There were certain things I needed. A project I had to get off the ground. If I kept away from Isobel, your grandfather would . . . smooth the way. Allow certain things to become possible.'

'Les Arbres,' River said.

'How much do you know about that?'

It might have been an enquiry at a dinner party.

'You ran some kind of commune there,' River said. 'And burned it to the ground the same day you sent your boy out to kill my grandfather.' He ran a hand through his hair, and it came away sopping wet. 'Which smells like cover-up to me. This project of yours went badly wrong, didn't it?'

'There've been mistakes,' Frank said. 'I'd be the first to admit that. But nothing we can't get right next time.'

'And you tried to bury it by killing my *grandfather*!'

'And I'm sorry. That was the wrong approach. I get that now.'

'The wrong *approach*? What the hell are you, a fucking self-help guru? You sent your own son – who *died*, by the way. Your son *died*.'

Frank said, 'He knew the risks.'

'And that's all you've got to say? That he knew the risks?'

'You think I'm not screaming inside? I'm hurting, River. Believe me, I am. But Bertrand was . . . there was a mission, and it's still going on, and when you're out in the field you lock the hurt inside. There'll be time for that later.' He paused. 'For both of us.'

Not going there, thought River. Not going there. But part of him went there anyway, joining dots and filling in corners. His half-brother . . . More than a passing resemblance. No wonder he thought he'd get away with turning up at the O.B.'s house, pretending to be River. No wonder River had been able to use his passport.

And River had obliterated that face, in the name of operational expediency.

But not going there.

'What's the mission?' he said.

Frank smiled a crooked smile. 'Right now?' he said. 'Right now, River, the mission is you.'

The gunplay on Pentonville Road had sent further tremors through the city, making the old and the vulnerable nervous, but adding a sweet edge to the nightlife of the young. This Wild-West frisson had its upside. Just like in frontier towns, the risk of sudden death was greater, but your chances of getting laid were similarly enhanced.

Patrice recognised this in scenes glimpsed through windows as he made his way through the heart of London. Social interaction had been tightened a notch. People were smiling more brightly, their laughter strung a note higher, everything more brittle. Which was useful. A group was emerging from a bar, armed with umbrellas and busy with laughter. He fell in among them, his expression breaking easily into companionship. 'I couldn't hitch shelter as far as the next Tube, could I? I have got so wet today!'

'Course you can, darlin'.'

'Hey, a little less of the darlin's, you!'

'Take no notice of him.'

An umbrella shifted on its axis, and he was offered its protection.

'That's great,' said Patrice. 'Thanks.'

'It's not just the rain you've gotta watch out for,' somebody slurred. 'Mad people out there waving guns about.'

They moved in tortoise formation, past the pair of policemen on the corner who were peeled and alert for suspicious pairings.

'Evening, officers.'

'Keep the streets safe!'

Patrice smiled and nodded with the rest of them, and slipped free at the next corner. Two of the girls invited him to stay with the party – there was always a party – but he had a gun in his pocket and a destination. And an instruction from Frank, who had been giving him instructions since he was a toddler, and who had ensured, way back then, that there was no question of Patrice not carrying them out.

'An address,' Frank had said, out of earshot of the young spook who'd been pretending to be Adam Lockhead. He'd recited it slowly. Aldersgate Street.

Patrice knew not to ask why. Frank let him know anyway.

'It's where he's stationed,' he'd said, indicating the young spook. 'And that department doesn't run to safe houses.'

'So Chapman might be there,' Patrice guessed.

'And the old man too. You know what to do.'

Patrice did, but Frank told him anyway.

'Kill them all. Call me when you're done.'

Patrice nodded.

He was heading past Smithfield Market now, all shuttered up against the evening.

Aldersgate Street was minutes away.

15

Back in Slough House, Shirley was reliving her near-death experience.

'He's a fucking psycho,' she said happily.

'And this is fun because . . .?'

'Keeps life interesting. Hey, what if we get him annoyed at Ho? Roddy'd shit himself if the Mad Monk pulled that knife trick on him.'

'Yeah, well, it wasn't so much a knife trick,' Marcus pointed out, 'as just a knife.'

They were in their office, the overhead bulbs growing starker as the darkness outside solidified, and the more Shirley replayed the YouTube videos – and there were two now, another Citizen Journalist having uploaded footage – the surer she became that it was River caught on camera. Which was cool. The last time the slow horses had found themselves on a war footing had been the most fun she'd had since being kicked out of yoga class for starting a fight. If this turned out to be Slough House business, she might get to punch some heads. At the very least, this would give her something to talk about at her next anger management session.

Besides, there was nobody waiting at home. Not that she wanted to run through that sorry scenario again, even in the privacy of her own head.

She said, 'I'm going to make a cup of tea. Want one?'

But Marcus only grunted.

Ho was in his diving bell, gazing at the world at the bottom of the sea.

That's what it felt like, anyway.

After fetching the ice for Chapman's knee – and Jeez, it was painful the way old folks crumbled: Ho was broad-minded, it was one of the things Kim, his girlfriend, most admired about him, but seriously, old people made him feel ill – he'd returned to his machines. He planned to stay late; there was stuff he preferred to do from a Service computer. It was kind of a dare – a task he'd been set. A quest, even. A quest, and the prize was his lady's hand. Though after four dates, and the amount of money he'd shelled out, her hand was the least he was owed.

It wasn't that she wasn't into him. Roddy Ho didn't fool easy, and Mama Internet had taught him well. When a chick was really into you, there were ways you could tell, and one of the ways you could tell was when she said 'I'm really into you,' saying it low and breathy into his ear, friendly as a kitten, her leg brushing across the front of his trousers.

So yeah, she was into him. It was just that so far, at evening's end, she'd had an important reason for getting home alone, a sick flatmate or a need to be up very very early next day, 'but *soon*, Roddy, soon,' which was a phrase he'd hugged to himself like a hot-water bottle once he'd got home alone himself. *Soon*. He liked the sound of that. And if completing a quest made soon come sooner, then he was up for it. That was definitely the right phrase.

So anyway: his task. What had happened, the evening before, Kim, his girlfriend, had been asking him how he did what he did; how he hacked in and out of other people's networks, big and small. He'd had to laugh. 'Hacking,' he'd explained, implied slicing and chopping, like using a machete to move through a jungle. But when he did it – 'When Roddy Ho does it, babes' – ghosting was the word you were after, because he left no tracks, and nobody knew he'd been there.

'So you can't, like, change anything? You leave everything the way it was?'

Again: ha! She was so cute and so sexy, but she really didn't get the things the Rodster could do with a keyboard.

'Kim,' he'd said. 'Babes.' She loved it when he called her that. 'I can change anything I want. I just make it look like it's always been that way, you dig?'

And she dug, of course she did, because she laughed too in that sexy way she had, and gazed at him with liquid eyes.

'That's great, you're so wonderful, because . . .'

Because it turned out she had a friend with a problem.

Long story short, the friend had been ripped off by the company she worked for, well, *used* to work for, only they'd fired her for some made-up shit when the real reason was she was too good at her job, and they couldn't afford to pay the commission they owed her – 'Thousands of pounds, Roddy' – and now *she* couldn't afford a lawyer to sue them, so if there was any way he could 'ghost' into this company's system and adjust their accounts so the money they owed her ended up on her credit card or something, that would be beyond wonderful. Because she was such a sweet friend, and pretty too, and she'd be so grateful to Roddy, and Kim would be grateful too, and wouldn't that be nice, Roddy having two pretty girls feeling grateful and friendly towards him at the same time?

And Roddy had gulped and adjusted himself, and said, 'Sure, babes,' but it had come out squeaky.

So anyway. As luck would have it, Kim had had the

company's details jotted down on a piece of card, which was in front of Roddy now. So it was just a matter of getting into submarine mode, diving into the Dark Web, and it didn't matter that the others were still floating round Slough House, because not one of them would realise what he was up to if they were watching over his shoulder.

Because he worked better at low temperatures, he opened the nearest window, let cold, damp air refresh him, then settled to his quest.

At the junction where the road from Smithfield ran under the Barbican complex, Patrice took shelter outside a gym which was disgorging toned, sweaty City workers, bags in one hand, smartphones in the other, already catching up on what they'd missed while on the treadmill. The massive structure overhead kept the rain off, but the air was damp, and the pavements lumpy with some kind of deposit from the concrete overhangs. It felt like the entrance to an underground garage.

For one brief moment, he remembered the cellar.

Each of the boys, on their twelfth birthday, had been locked in a cellar at Les Arbres, with no natural light and just one candle. Every morning, a single bread roll and a beaker of water was delivered. And every morning, they were told they would be released as soon as they asked for their freedom. Bertrand, Patrice remembered, had lasted just seventeen days before asking to be released. Patrice remembered Frank's look of disdain at his son's reappearance, as if it were an act of cowardice, or betrayal. Patrice himself had lasted a full month: at the time, a new record.

Yves had lasted two.

Frank should have known, he thought now. Frank should have known that there would come a time when Yves's desire to prove he could go further than any of them would see him step over each and every line there was. He had grown too used to the darkness. It was a wonder he had survived so long in the light.

But this thought, that Frank should have known, demanded punishment, and Patrice submitted to the moment, lashing out at the pebble-dashed wall, then licking the resulting blood from his knuckles. He had deserved that. Nobody could have known where Yves's demons would take him. It was this place that was breeding such ideas: rainy London, its blues and greys seeping into his soul. Well, Patrice wouldn't be here much longer. This last task done, he and Frank could vanish back to the mainland: Les Arbres was smoke and ashes, but they'd find somewhere. And the others would return – except for Bertrand, of course; except for Yves – and life would start again.

But before that could happen, the old man David Cartwright, who had been there at the birth of Les Arbres, had to go. So did Sam Chapman, his driver, his muscle. That they had survived the first attempts to remove them could be assigned to their own blind luck, or to his and Bertrand's incompetence; or perhaps, he thought now, it had been because of the weather; this never-ending blanket of rain: slowing the joints, dulling reactions. Well, that was about to come to an end. The young spook had worked in that building over the road, the one Frank had called Slough House, and there was a reasonable chance, a working possibility, that that was where the two targets currently were. It was also possible that by now they had shared their knowledge of Les Arbres with the young spook's colleagues, which rendered the target pool larger. It was important, then, that this time there be no mistakes.

Pulling his collar up, he crossed the road.

Lamb paused in the yard to light a cigarette, sucking in

smoke and holding it so long there was barely anything to exhale. Rain on his hat filled his head with the beating of drums.

The door behind him opened, and Catherine was there. She stood in the hallway, framed by light, and said, 'He's in some distress.'

'Boo hoo.'

'I've left him with Moira. She'll make him a cup of tea.'

'Why stop there? Tell her to tuck him in. Read him a story.'

'He's an old man, Jackson.'

'He's an old man with blood on his hands. Let's not pretend he's a victim here.'

'He couldn't know what would happen. He thought he was protecting his family.'

'Protecting himself, more like.' He turned to her. 'Last thing he wanted was his daughter shacking up with an ex-Agency oddball. Because that might scupper his chances of getting to be First Desk, right? These days they appear on *Newsnight*, reviewing Bond films. But back then, the whole secrecy thing was more of an issue, and nobody wanted Service gossip headlining in the tabloids.'

'He never wanted to be First Desk.'

'Uh-huh. And Buzz Lightyear never wanted to be first man on the Moon.'

'I don't think you mean Lightyear. And besides, getting Frank what he wanted didn't work out, did it? He still never got to be First Desk.'

Lamb said, 'By the time he'd finished kitting Frank out, running the money through whatever back-channel he dug, the old man probably thought he'd better keep his head down. Putting your hand in the till, that's one thing. Shovelling the proceeds the way of a paramilitary organisation, that's border-line treason. He might have rescued his daughter from the clutches of a lunatic American, but he screwed his own career in the process. I suppose that's a kind of justice.'

'She never forgave him.'

'For rescuing her?'

'I don't suppose she saw it as a rescue,' Catherine said. 'Besides, it wasn't just her he was rescuing, was it?'

'You're going to tug my heartstrings now? Remind me there was a foetus involved?'

'If he hadn't bought Frank off, he'd have been delivering his unborn grandson into Frank's hands. And Frank would have got what he wanted eventually, because Franks always do. Which means he'd have found some other way to fund his Cuckoo project, and—'

'And River would have been part of it. Yes, I get that.'

'So why are you so sure his hands are dirty?'

Lamb didn't reply.

'I'll bet you've done things—'

'Some of them on his orders.' Lamb tossed his cigarette against the wall, and a brief firework bloomed in the dark. Then he reached into his raincoat pocket and pulled out what appeared to be a sock. After gazing at it for a moment, he put it back.

Catherine said, 'Where are you going, anyway?'

'I'm out of drink.'

'And you're fetching your own these days?'

'Yeah, well. Sometimes I get my hands dirty too.'

He slunk out into the alleyway that led to Aldersgate Street.

Catherine watched him go, then shut the door, and headed back upstairs.

Moira Tregorian had her hands full again: when was it ever any different? Make him a cup of tea, if you please. This was Her Ladyship, of course; *Ms* Catherine Standish, dishing out orders as if neither of them knew her discharge papers were sitting on the desk in broad daylight, not that there was much of that to be seen. Daylight.

'Here you go, then.'

She put it in front of him, and if she did so a little abruptly, causing it to slop over the rim, well, it wasn't as if he was about to complain, was he?

'It's already sugared,' she added.

And then, because he stared at it uncomprehending, she felt ashamed, and said, more gently, 'You want to drink it before it gets cold. You need a warm drink inside you.'

Whether he did or didn't seemed beside the point, somehow. There was precious little else she could do for him.

There was work to do, because there always was. Nobody had ever accused Moira Tregorian of not pulling her weight, not that her weight was anything anyone ought to be making comments about. There were still files and folders here from last September, and she had a good mind to call Ms Standish in, ask if she wouldn't mind lending a hand as a good part of this confusion had happened on her watch? But she could imagine the frosty answer she'd get from that one. Queening it over the whole department as if she were the Lady of Shallots or someone. No, that wasn't who she meant. The other one.

'Lady Guinevere,' she said out loud.

That was who she meant.

There was an unseemly slurping from the old man as he revived himself with a healthy gulp of tea. When he set the cup down, he said, 'King Arthur.'

Oh Lord help us, she thought. He thinks we're playing Snap.

But she was still feeling guilty about her rough treatment of him. And it was nice to have someone to talk to, even if it was childish nonsense.

She said, 'Sir Lancelot.'

'Sir Percival.'

She wasn't even sure Sir Percival was a real one, to be honest, but she didn't want to spoil the old man's game. 'Sir Gawain,' she said, conscious that if this went on much longer, she was going to run out of names.

'Sir Galahad.'

Galahad, she thought. Now that was funny – that rang a bell.

Where had she come across Galahad recently?

But the answer wouldn't come.

It was clear that nobody used the front entrance – you only had to look at the door, its peeling black paint, to know it hadn't been opened in years – which meant there must be another round the back. So he passed the Chinese restaurant, on whose grubby windowpane was fixed a yellowing menu, and reached an alleyway lit only by window-leakage from the neighbouring office block. It was one of those lost areas every city knows; an unconsidered gap between postcodes. To his left was a wall with wooden doors set into it at intervals, and when he tried the second one, it opened. Now he was in a small, mildewed yard, looking up at a dismal building which must be Slough House. For a department of the Secret Service, it didn't seem too secure. That said much about the value placed on its inhabitants.

Patrice took the gun from his pocket. The woman who'd owned it had been Service too, and it struck him briefly how difficult it would be for her, knowing her own weapon had been used to erase her colleagues. But this was no more than a blur on his mental horizon; an awareness of the weather elsewhere.

He tried the door, which jammed a little. He had to lean

on it, pushing upwards on the handle to ease it open without making a noise. But that took only a moment. And then he was inside, and on the stairs, the gun dangling by his side, as if it were of no more weight or importance than a pint of milk.

Marcus could hear Catherine talking to Shirley in the kitchen. There was a kind of comfort in having her back in Slough House – they were two of a kind, after all. A gambler and a drinker; funny they'd never discussed their respective addictions. Except it was anything but funny, this situation they were in. His family life was more than fraying at the edges; it was perforated right down the middle, and one quick tug would leave him floating wide and loose. As for Catherine – well, she seemed serene. But what kind of life was she living, really; what demons had smuggled themselves into her private corners? So no, of course they'd never spoken of such things. Besides, he'd never admitted it out loud before, had he? Had rarely said as much to himself.

'I have a gambling problem,' he said, very quietly. The words barely bothered the air. His lips moved, but that was about it.

He shook his head. If Shirley had been around for that, he'd never hear the end of it.

And because she wasn't, he pulled open his desk drawer and stared down into it again. The one thing he could sell, get serious money for – a couple of ton at least – without Carrie knowing. He'd brought it in that morning, carried it through the rush-hour crush in his raincoat pocket; had half expected Lamb to have found it by now – creepy, the way that man knew what was going on around him without appearing to open his eyes. And this evening, when he left, he'd take it with him, though he wouldn't be heading straight home. There was a place round by St Paul's, a stationer's shop, except it wasn't. It had a back office where a man who looked like a hobbit kept court: Dancer, his name was, and Dancer bought guns, and sold them on again to people whose motives it was best not to enquire into.

Putting a gun on the street – can I really do that? Marcus wondered.

But I need the money.

He needed the money and he'd always need the money, the same way Catherine would always need a drink. Except Catherine needed a drink without taking one. Marcus looked down at the gun in his drawer and thought of all the uses it could be put to once it was out of his possession. Uses he'd never know about, though he'd never stop wondering. But meanwhile, he'd have a couple of hundred and could pay some bills; pay more than a few, if he did the clever thing and used the money to stake himself a bigger win . . .

Or I could go upstairs right now and talk to Catherine. She'd listen. Help.

Yeah, he thought. I should do that . . . Except no, not really. Because he didn't have a problem. What he had was a run of bad luck, and the thing about runs was, they came to an end.

A couple of hundred in hand. All he'd need was one glimmer of light and he could turn his whole situation round. Then buy the gun back off Dancer before any harm was done. He smiled to himself at the thought of this happening, soon.

Then he wondered who that was, out on the staircase.

Bad Sam's knee still hurt, for all the anaesthetising effects of Lamb's bottle, but he had to stand anyway, and leave the office. Volkswagen had nothing on Lamb when it came to unfiltered emissions . . . Letting the icepack slump to the floor, he tried a little weight on his leg and found it more or less bearable.

Half hopping down to the next level, where the kitchen

was, he found Catherine Standish and another woman – Shirley? Shirley – the former busying herself with the kettle while the latter watched. Shirley was short with suede-cut dark hair; broad at the shoulders, but not without a certain appeal, provided you were a lot younger than Bad Sam, and didn't mind things getting edgy. That was a lot to read into a brief acquaintance, but she had a legible face. She said nothing when Bad Sam arrived, but watched him closely.

Well, he thought. It was a good thing someone round here was reasonably alert.

He said to Catherine, 'I'm sorry.'

A lesser woman would have raised an eyebrow. She simply looked at him.

'For after Partner died. The interrogation.'

She nodded.

'But it had to be done.'

She nodded again.

Shirley was looking from one to the other, like a cat at a tennis match.

Catherine said, 'He's gone for some more alcohol. But I'm making tea.'

'That would be great.'

Sam felt released from something; he wasn't sure what. Like he'd said, the interrogation had to be done; if it hadn't been him, it would have been someone else. And he hadn't given it a moment's thought in years. But still, in this woman's company, he couldn't help feeling he'd done her a wrong, and was glad to be forgiven. If that's what this was. And he—

A gunshot cut the thought off.

Two gunshots, rather; one following the other so swiftly, they might have been two halves of a single sound.

★

Sam said, 'Is there a—'

'Lamb's desk.'

'Get it.'

She vanished up the stairs while Shirley rattled open a drawer, finding only a corkscrew she gripped in her right fist, its twirly point becoming a wicked extra finger.

'Upstairs,' he told her.

'And then what?'

J. K. Coe appeared in his doorway, his hood puddled around his shoulders, his blade in hand. He looked at Shirley. 'What was that?'

The light on the lower landing went out.

Bad Sam said, 'Get behind that door. Barricade it.' He was reaching for the kettle as he spoke; it was still grumbling to itself, steam gusting ceilingwards. 'Now.'

He pushed past them, bad knee forgotten, and leant over the banister. As a dark figure appeared on the next flight down, Sam dropped the kettle on its head.

Catherine knelt by Lamb's desk, tugged at the bottom drawer, found it locked. There'd be a key somewhere, but she didn't have time: there was a metal ruler on the desktop, acquired to break him of the habit of shattering plastic ones, and she slid this into the gap and pulled upwards until the drawer gave. From it, she pulled a shoebox and – because the mind won't stay in its kennel – found herself thinking *When did Jackson last buy a pair of shoes?*, a thought that burst like a bubble. The lid of the shoebox was taped in place, which cost her another second. And then Lamb's gun was in her hand, surprisingly small, though heavy enough. There was nothing else in the box – no bullets – so she hoped it was loaded: time would tell. As she left the room, the door to her old office opened, and an irritated Moira Tregorian appeared.

'What in the blessed name of—'

'Stay in there!' The gun in her hand would have done the trick anyway. Moira changed colour and faded back inside, closing the door behind her.

Catherine was on the stairs when she heard the third shot, and almost felt it on her cheek – the displaced air the bullet pushed aside on its upward journey.

The kettle missed Patrice's head by half an inch, though it struck him on the shoulder, spouting scalding water onto his face. He leaned back against the wall to rub his eyes. The kettle bounced down the staircase, its contents arcing across the walls, and overhead a door slammed. Vision still blurry he raised his gun, and when he heard someone on the stairs, fired blind. The bullet whistled up the stairwell and buried itself in the roof.

Deliberately, he banged his head against the wall, twice. Clarity of a kind returned.

Ignoring his scalded cheek, Patrice took the stairs two at a time, swivelling on the half-flight to aim at the figure on the landing above.

Coe grabbed Shirley and pulled her into his room, where she swiped at him with her corkscrewed fist and tried to get back onto the landing. He tripped her, and when she hit the floor he threw his knife aside to grab her by the collar and the seat of her jeans, and haul her back.

'*Fuck you*—'

'Yeah, you too.'

He was reaching for the door when Catherine appeared from upstairs, looking wild – her hair had come loose and floated wide behind her, and in her eyes was something savage; in her hand was Lamb's gun.

'*Move!*' Sam Chapman screamed – he was emerging from Louisa's office, where he'd flung himself after hurling the kettle downstairs. Now he was brandishing a chair, and moving like someone who'd forgotten his knee didn't work.

Coe grabbed Catherine, pulled her through the open door, and slammed it shut.

Bad Sam Chapman hurled the chair at Patrice just as Patrice raised the gun and fired again.

Frank had been right, or half right at least: it was Sam Chapman on the landing; Chapman, whom he'd hunted yesterday, and earlier today. *Package undelivered.* Not any more, thought Patrice, and fired just as a chair came hurtling towards him; one of its slats splintering in flight as the bullet ricocheted off it; the chair itself, a wooden thing, caught him mid-chest. He barely blinked. This was what they fought with, kettles and furniture? A door slammed, then another; they were hiding in their rooms. There was a fairy tale about the houses little pigs built. They were about to find out how it ended.

Patrice kicked the chair aside, and arrived at the kitchen landing.

There was a lock, a bolt like you'd find on a toilet door; something to let outsiders know it was occupied, but not hefty enough to deter assault. Coe used it anyway, then got behind River's desk and pushed it towards the doorway.

Shirley stepped round him and drew the bolt back.

'What the *hell* are you—'

'Marcus,' she said.

'He's either okay or not, but you can't—'

'Don't tell me what I—'

There was a crash from the landing. A splintering noise.

'Shirley?' Catherine said. 'Lock the door. Or I'll shoot you.'

'Or,' said Shirley, 'you could give me the gun, and I'll go shoot him.'

Bad Sam didn't know how this had happened so suddenly, so completely, but it had, and when things went to the wire, you did what you could. This wouldn't be much. Sonny Jim out there had a gun, and Sam had none; and Sonny Jim, judging by the afternoon's events, barely needed a weapon. He could take Sam apart with his bare hands if he wanted. And then he'd do the same to the others, including – especially – the old man upstairs, who had been under Sam's protection once, and was again now, not that this would help him. Sam ought to push something against the door, to slow events down, but there didn't seem any point, and when he put his hand to his side, he understood why he felt this way. That last shot, as Sam had thrown the chair – well, bullets had to go somewhere. That was a law of physics, or nature; a law, anyway, that Bad Sam Chapman had just found himself on the wrong side of.

He wished he'd had a chance to find Chelsea Barker. He hoped someone else would go looking.

And then the door burst off its hinges, and Sam's hopes shut down.

The old man said, 'Sir Bedivere.'

Moira Tregorian closed her eyes.

'Sir Kay.'

There was more gunfire from downstairs.

When Patrice kicked the door it almost came apart, the wood was so rotten. He stepped over it, shot Sam Chapman in the head, then checked the room, but it was otherwise unoccupied. The kitchen, too – a galley space no bigger than a barge's – was empty, though the other office door was closed. There would be targets behind it. He braced and kicked, the flat of his right foot hitting the door squarely.

This one held against his first assault, but wouldn't withstand a second.

The door tried to pound its way into the room, and only just changed its mind. He'd kick once more, they knew, and be inside.

'Bullets?' Shirley said.

Catherine shook her head miserably.

J. K. Coe had blade in hand again, but it looked small and brittle; the wrong weapon for the occasion. He said, 'Spread out. He might not get all of us.'

Catherine grabbed the first thing to hand, the keyboard from River's desk, and yanked it from its cable. She wielded it two-handed, unsure whether she was preparing to hurl it or use it as a racquet, swat back the bullet he'd fire her way—

She thought: *I could really do with a drink right now.*

The door splintered open.

'Sir Tristan,' the O.B. said. 'Sir Bors, Sir Gareth.'

'Shut up!' Moira screamed. 'Shut up shut up shut up!'

'They all died, you know,' the old man told her, unperturbed. 'They started with such promise, but they all went the same way in the end.'

There was another crash from downstairs as another door bit the dust, and then there was more gunfire – two shots? Three? Enough of them, anyway, to silence the old man.

He looked her way, visions of long-ago knights put to rest.

A short while later, they heard someone climbing the last flight of stairs.

When the door fell Patrice planted himself in the doorway

and levelled the gun. There were three targets: a man, two women. Choosing the order in which to drop them took no time – the shorter woman, who held a gun, was the threat; the man, who had a knife, would be next; the older woman, who appeared to be wielding a piece of office equipment, last. David Cartwright was not among their number, but Patrice knew from the earlier commotion that there were more people upstairs. He sensed that the woman's gun was empty, because there was fear in her eyes, and she did not look like someone who would be scared holding a loaded gun. Microseconds, these thoughts took. Less. It was part of what he'd learned at Les Arbres, in its woods and in its cellars; that you measured a situation in the moment you became part of it, and that what you did next was less action than response – you became part of the inevitable: that was what he had been taught. What would happen next was fixed from the moment he'd kicked the door down. All that remained was for the bodies to hit the floor. He aimed at the young woman and pulled the trigger, and in his mind was already turning to fire at the man, was already aware that the other woman had thrown a keyboard at him, and that he would turn and shoot her too before it reached him; and all of this was inevitable up to the moment that the whisky bottle flung by Jackson Lamb from the stair-well smashed into his temple, throwing his aim off – he fired three times, but his bullets bit air, bit glass, bit plaster. He landed on top of the broken door, and for a moment, all was quiet.

She took each set of stairs in a single leap; would have broken an ankle, a leg, a neck, if she'd noticed what she was doing. But there was no plan driving her, simply an imperative; an impulse that carried her to the doorway of her office, where it failed her. She had to reach out to its frame for support, and take several breaths before taking her next step.

The room was much as Shirley had left it. Her PC, never the quietest of beasts, was humming to itself, awaiting instructions. The steamed-up windows were weeping; the carpet was rucked. Marcus, though. Marcus was different. Marcus sat behind his desk, but had been thrown back against the wall, his chair balanced on two legs like an animal performing a party trick. His eyes were open. There was a hole in his forehead. There was a mess on the wall behind him.

On the floor, next to him, a gun. He'd got one shot off, but had only killed his desk.

Shirley waited for this scene to change, but it didn't. When there was a noise at her back she knew it was Ho, emerging from a hiding place.

'You're alive,' she said, without turning round.

'Uh-huh.'

His voice didn't sound familiar, but then neither did hers.

He said, 'I hung out the window. I nearly fell.'

She didn't reply.

After a while he said, 'What about Marcus?'

'Marcus didn't make it,' she said, and turned and went back upstairs.

16

THE RAIN WAS NEVER going to stop. It had found a loophole in the weather laws and henceforth would fall without interruption, soaking the guilty and the innocent alike, though mostly the former, a statistical inevitability. From the dazzle ship's sheltered platform, River could see the neon blur it was making of the South Bank, drawing a grey curtain across the monolithic pile that was Sea Containers House, and dampening the Coca-Cola colouring of the Eye to a dotted outline.

He said to Frank, 'Mission? Me? What are you talking about?'

'You're wasted where you are.'

'What would you know about it?'

'I've made it my business to know. You went into the family business. You know how proud that makes me? I was CIA, back in the day. And still fighting the good fight.'

'No,' said River. 'Whatever fight you're fighting, it's dirty.'

'You don't know the full story. What we were trying to do at Les Arbres, it benefits everyone. Everyone.' He waved a hand, taking in the Thames, which meant the whole of London. 'Look around. When you went into the Service, it was to protect all this, wasn't it? You wanted to serve, to defend. And what have you ended up doing? Slough House is a cul-de-sac.

A joke. Everything you might have been, all the promise you showed, and you're spending your days finding different ways of stapling bits of paper together.'

'Are you about to offer me a job? Because sending someone to kill my grandfather's a hell of a recruitment strategy. Or did you get your definitions of headhunting confused?'

'Okay, that was an error. I've admitted that. But it's brought us here. You, me. And you now have the opportunity to decide what you want the rest of your life to be. Because if you stay in the Service, River, you'll be in Slough House forever. And if you leave, what will you do? Get an ordinary job in an ordinary office?'

'I haven't much thought beyond seeing you charged with conspiracy to murder.'

'Seriously, son, that's not going to happen.'

Son. River shook his head. He was foggy with disbelief still: his father? His *father*? It was like the punchline to a failed joke he could already see himself repeating in bars. *And then guess what he said? No, go on, guess!*

'I get that you're mad,' he told Frank. 'And for all I know, you drag that I'm-your-daddy line out every time you meet someone new. But what I want to hear is what triggered this whole thing. What made you burn your house down and send your son to kill my grandad? You'll be coughing all this up at the Park soon. Might as well give me the preview. Think of it as making up for all those missed birthdays.'

'Son—'

'And stop calling me that.'

'Why? It's who you are.'

River became aware, though they'd been there all the time, of high red lights glowing way up in the dark, marking the tips and joints of the ubiquitous cranes.

Frank had a red tip too: the end of his Gauloise. From

behind its brief curtain, he said, 'I know it sounds insane, after this past couple of days. But think about it, River. You can carry on at Slough House, which you just know is designed to kill your spirit. Or you can come join me and do some serious good. I promise you. What we're doing, what we started at Les Arbres − it's about protecting all those things you hold dear. About making a difference.'

River said, 'What do you mean, this past couple of days? For me, this all started last night. What happened before then?'

And as the tip of Frank's cigarette glowed bright again, he realised he already knew.

'I turn my back for five minutes,' said Lamb.

Catherine had found some plastic ties in a drawer, the kind that tightened on themselves and had to be cut loose. With them, Coe had secured Patrice to the radiator, which − if she hadn't prevailed on Shirley to turn it off − would have scorched his flesh by now, adding burnt meat to the other smells crowding Slough House: the gunpowdery whiff of a discharged firearm and the leakage from two fatal head wounds. Only Lamb's voice was a normal sound. Everything else was stunned and reduced, like a recording of its own echo. Even the heating, running down to zero, failed to summon its usual clamour: the bangs and ticks from the ancient pipework were a half-hearted symphony, a weary requiem.

'I said—'

'We heard. Now is not the time.'

Lamb gave her a savage smile. 'When's good for you? If I hadn't come back, there'd be eight corpses, not two. You're supposed to be Secret Service, not sitting ducks.'

He was holding the bottle he'd brought Patrice down with, his fingers curled around its neck. The way he was caressing it, you might think it was his favourite survivor.

But Catherine shook her head. No. We're all his joes, and he's just lost two.

She said, 'We need to call the Park.'

'We'll call the Park when I say so.'

'We've got two fatalities, Jackson, and we can't just—'

'Like I said. When I say so.' He kicked Patrice's foot. 'Show me this video.'

Ho fiddled with his phone, then passed it over. Lamb watched the YouTube moment, sneered, then tossed the phone back. Ho caught it, nearly, then went scrabbling about on the floor.

Lamb kicked Patrice again. 'You kill Cartwright too?'

Patrice was conscious, but hadn't spoken yet. Maybe he couldn't. Once he'd gone down Lamb had stamped on his face, just to be sure, and he currently had fewer teeth than he'd started the day with. His jaw was a purple mess, his jacket and shirt blood-soaked. Lamb's shoe hadn't got off scot-free, come to that, but he wasn't avidly image-conscious, so didn't mind.

'You listening?'

'I can make him talk,' Shirley said quietly.

'I don't doubt it.'

She'd do it the way Marcus had shown her: with a cloth over the face, and a jugful of water.

'Seriously, I can—'

'No.' But Lamb too spoke quietly.

Shirley had Patrice's gun. It still reeked; something that didn't get mentioned much in the movies, in the books. Her hands would be stained with its residue. Anyone would think she'd pulled a trigger.

The room seemed curiously empty, given there were five of them. Six if you counted Patrice. But no Marcus. Nobody was going to be counting Marcus again.

Lamb looked at Catherine. 'The old man okay?'

She nodded. It was the first thing she'd checked. Moira Tregorian had fainted when Catherine opened the door. She was still upstairs, descent being beyond her yet. Catherine had rescued the bottle of whisky from her drawer – its long-term purpose being to lure Jackson back from a clifftop, or encourage him over one; whichever situation cropped up first – and had poured both David and Moira a hefty slug. As for herself, she'd wavered. For half a second, maybe less, she'd spent a small eternity balanced on the rim of a glass.

Ho had recovered his phone and was leaning against River's desk. He looked smaller – diminished – they all did. They really needed to call the Park. The police, even. This was Lamb's kingdom, but kingship had its limits.

Lamb said, 'If he killed River, I doubt he bothered to bury him after. Someone check the news, see if there are bodies on the streets.'

Nobody moved.

'Did I die too, and not notice? Because if I'm a ghost, I'll tell you this. I go *whoo*, you fucking jump.'

'I'll do it,' said Ho.

Catherine thought he sounded about twelve.

On River's desk were the contents of Patrice's pockets: a passport in the name of Paul Wayne, a mobile phone, a wallet containing euros and sterling. A ticket for the Chunnel train. Did it still get called the Chunnel? She hadn't heard that in years. On his way past the desk, she noticed, Ho lifted the mobile. She didn't doubt Lamb saw this too, but he said nothing.

J. K. Coe was against the wall. His head was uncovered, and his hands jammed into his hoodie's pouch. Catherine could read nothing in his eyes, which were fixed on Patrice, who despite the damage Lamb had wrought was not only conscious but alert, as if the blood and associated liquids pooling from his jaw were a mask, beneath which he was planning his escape.

She shuddered. When he'd kicked through the door, gun in hand, she was sure she was on her last breath.

I could really use a drink, she thought; unsure whether it was a memory from that moment, or the same need reaching the surface again.

Lamb dropped to his haunches suddenly; did so without a sound, though there were times he'd audibly creak and groan if he had to do anything strenuous, like reach into a pocket. His face inches from Patrice's he said, 'Are you the last of them? Or is your bossman, Frank, is he around too?'

Patrice's eyes betrayed no emotion. His lips didn't move. Catherine didn't think his lips moved. It was hard to tell, though, messed up as his face was.

She said, 'It's not going to work, Jackson. He's not going to talk.'

Lamb looked up at her, and for a moment there was something in his eyes she'd never seen before, and then it was gone. She wasn't sure what it had been.

Roderick Ho appeared. He was holding Patrice's phone.

'There's only one number been called from this,' he said.

'Uh-huh.'

'And if I piggyback on the Service program—'

'You can trace it,' said Lamb. 'So what are you hanging about for?'

Louisa had finished her coffee and was having a pee when her phone rang, of course. She'd have ignored it, except it was Lamb.

Knowing him, he'd register the acoustic, and that was all she'd hear about for weeks.

'Yeah,' she said, trying to keep her voice low, so it wouldn't bounce off the porcelain.

'Where are you?'

'A bar off Pentonville. What's up?'

Because he didn't sound normal.

'How soon can you get to the Embankment?'

'What's happened, Lamb? Who got hurt?'

She didn't want to say 'killed', but that's what she meant. Last time she'd heard Lamb sound like this—

'I ask how fast you can get somewhere, I don't expect you to waste time asking questions. Call me on the way.'

He disconnected.

She finished up, washed her hands, collected Emma on her way out the door.

'Where are we going?'

'Embankment.' Her car was boxed in, but with a little nudge to the vehicle in front, she got loose.

Best to think about stuff like that, and about how it was still raining, and the best route to the Embankment, rather than anything more serious.

Like: who just got hurt, or worse.

Given Lamb's failure to make any loo-based jokes, it was probably worse.

River said, 'Westacres. Oh, you crazy fucker. Westacres is what happened. That's what started this off.'

'Son—'

River punched him. It felt so good, for so many reasons, that he did it again: on the nose, then on the right cheek. Frank fell back against the railings and rainwater poured onto him. He shook his head, spraying water, then touched his nose, which was bleeding. He found a handkerchief, dabbed at the blood, and said, 'Seriously, two free shots, and that's the best you can do? Maybe Slough House is what you deserve.'

He put the handkerchief back in his pocket.

Three cars went past in succession, heading north, towards where the earlier action had been.

Frank said, 'It wasn't meant to happen. It was an exercise, an exercise in what's possible. What can happen when the state doesn't protect its people, when—'

'You fucking madman, you sent one of your boys—'

'No. Not sent. Not to do what he did. He was – he went over the edge. Maybe I should have seen it coming. Maybe nobody could have. I don't know. But it happened, and it's a damn tragedy, but you know what? Some good might yet come of it. And wouldn't you want to be part of that?'

River couldn't reply. Didn't have the language.

Frank's nose was still bleeding, and he pinched it with his fingers. Then shook his head. 'We're running out of time, son. I need to know what you plan to do.'

'You seriously think I might join you?'

'I hoped so. Or maybe I knew you wouldn't. Maybe I just wanted to see you, talk to you. We could have been something, you know that? It gives me a kick, you going into the Service. A chip off the old block, and you didn't even know it.'

'My grandfather raised me,' River said. 'Everything I am's because of him. You're just a fucking lunatic. If you are my father, that's an accident of birth. But you were the accident, not me.' He did something he didn't remember ever doing before, and spat at Frank's feet. 'And you're right, you're running out of time. You've seen me, talked to me. Now I'm taking you in.'

'Oh hell,' said Frank. 'I really didn't want to hear that. Because I don't want to hurt you, son, but I really don't need the Security Services on my heels just yet.'

309

'Too bad,' said River.

'And I'm guessing you don't have a phone with you, or you'd have used it by now. So tell you what. Give me ten minutes, okay? All I'll need. Ten minutes. Then raise all the alarms you want.' He reached out suddenly, grabbed River by the elbow, and pulled him into an embrace. Into his ear he said, 'Your place is with me, son. Not with that pack of losers. Think about it. We'll talk again.'

River tried to pull away, but the older man's grip was iron. 'I'm not giving you ten minutes,' he said. 'I'm not giving you one.'

'That's my boy. But you don't have a choice.' He kissed River hard, on the lips; a brief and violent contact.

And then lifted him off the ground and threw him over the low wall into the Thames.

The gun in Shirley's hand grew heavier.

It was odd, but all she wanted to do was sleep. Earlier that day, she'd been pissed off at missing the action – even seeing Louisa's chain-gang bruises hadn't mollified her: she'd have liked to have been there in that Southwark garage, see if she'd have fared better. But now Patrice was tied to a radiator, wearing half a pint of blood on his jaw, and Marcus . . . Marcus was still downstairs. And she felt so damn tired, so very very tired. She wanted to put the gun down, crawl under the nearest duvet and sleep for a week. Wouldn't need medication. Just let her head hit a pillow, and please don't let her dream.

Especially not about Marcus, and the mess on the wall behind his head.

J. K. Coe was looking at her with his usual absence of expression.

'What?' she snarled.

Funny how she could still do that, go from nought to sixty

on the pissed-off-ometer in the time it took Coe to blink.

And then it returned, crashed in like a wave: a weary tsunami threatening to lift her up and toss her away like a broken puppet.

Lamb was talking to Louisa again. 'No, I don't know what he looks like. He's an American, that any help? And maybe he's got Cartwright with him.'

There was that tinny susurration you get when the other part of the conversation's happening somewhere else.

'Why? What possible use is talking to her gonna be?'

There was another squawk of static from his mobile, following which he handed it to Catherine.

'For some reason she wants to talk to you.'

Catherine took the phone and left the room. Shirley could hear her talking to Louisa, quietly, as she made her way up the stairs. And then a door closed, and her soothing murmur was cut off.

Lamb looked around at what was left of the company: Shirley Dander, Coe and Roderick Ho. 'So she's telling Guy we've lost two. You think that's a good idea? Think that'll put her at her operational best?'

Nobody had an answer. Nobody knew anything.

For once, Lamb didn't press the point. Instead, he made a cigarette appear out of nowhere, and lit it. He looked grey. He always looked grey, more or less, but was now a shade greyer. He dragged in smoke, blew a cloud at the ceiling, and said to Shirley, 'Made your mind up yet?'

Shirley stared.

He said, 'Not to put too fine a point on it, but your partner's head looks like someone took a shovel to a watermelon. If you're happy to let the wheels of justice take their course, that's up to you. But if you want to discuss matters with the Terminator here, you go ahead. I'm going for a smoke.' He flapped the hand holding his cigarette. 'You're not allowed to do that indoors any more.'

Ho watched as Lamb left the room, then looked at Shirley nervously.

'What?' she said.

'Nothing.'

'Then fuck off.'

So he did; following Lamb part way down the stairs, then peeling off into his own office, closing the door behind him.

J. K. Coe stayed where he was.

Shirley said, 'You too.'

'Me too what?'

'Fuck off.'

He shook his head.

'I'm not going to ask twice.'

'You didn't ask once yet. You just told me to fuck off.'

'So why haven't you?'

'Because it's my office. Where'm I supposed to fuck off to?'

'That's more words than I've heard you say before,' she said. 'Put together.'

'Yeah, well. Big day.'

Patrice coughed; a thick, phlegmy noise.

It startled Shirley. She'd more or less forgotten he was there; as if he'd ceased to have human significance, and been reduced to one factor in an equation, the others being Shirley herself, the gun in her hand, and the half-second it would take to act.

The gun, which still felt so very very heavy.

J. K. Coe said to her, 'You don't want to do this, do you?'

But she really did.

'Fuck it!' said Louisa. 'Fuck it fuck it *fuck* it!'

'What?' Emma said. 'What happened? That was Lamb?'

Louisa shook her head. The lights of London blurred. She was driving through heavy rain, and had just been told Marcus was dead, Bad Sam Chapman too . . .

Marcus, dead.

Marcus had saved her life once, on London's tallest rooftop. He'd shot a man who'd been about to kill her, and Louisa's only regret was that she hadn't been able to kill the bastard herself. And this afternoon too, bursting through those wooden gates in a commandeered taxi: if he hadn't done that – shit, she'd be dead all over again. Dead twice over if not for Marcus.

She'd never met his family, never been to his home – Christ, they were a dysfunctional bunch, the slow horses; in each other's pockets half their lives, but never taking the time to share the other moments.

And now they'd be diminished, smaller, less of a unit. Marcus, apart from anything else, had probably been the only thing keeping Shirley Dander from going postal on a daily basis.

'You okay?' Emma asked.

Louisa nodded, and blinked her vision clear.

'This is Patrice we're hunting?'

'One of his team.'

'Good enough.' Emma unbuttoned her coat and checked her weapon.

'I thought you'd lost that.'

'I took Devon's. He's not going to need it in A & E.' She thought about that. 'He's probably not going to need it in A & E. How much further?'

'Just after Blackfriars Bridge,' Louisa said.

Emma squinted through the windscreen. 'There's some kind of commotion up ahead. That'll be our stop, right?'

There were roadworks, metal fencing dividing the road in two. On the river side, there was no road surface and plastic bollards blocked the way. Temporary traffic lights herded traffic into single file, shepherding them left. Louisa pulled right instead, ploughed through a row of bollards, and hit the brakes so hard the back of the vehicle was briefly airborne.

'Jesus!' Emma shouted.

A cluster of people at the end of the dazzle-ship's jetty were examining the water below in a manner suggesting emergency. Despite being winded, Emma was out of the car first. Something about her – the bruise on her face? – must have conveyed authority, because the crowd parted for her, offering overlapping commentary:

'We can't see him!'

'He's gone under!'

'There were two of them—'

'The other one legged it.'

'What happened?' she said, and was echoed immediately by Louisa:

'Who's in the water?'

A man in a blue coat said, 'There were two of them out here, acting odd. An older bloke and a young man, fairish hair—'

'Who's in the water?' Louisa repeated.

'The old one tipped the young guy over the side. I saw him from the bar window.'

The water below was black and rained-on and furious.

'Oh, fucking hell,' said Louisa.

An orange lifebelt bobbed lonely on the surface. There was no sign of anyone reaching for it.

Louisa pulled her coat off.

'What?' said Emma.

'Go after him – the old guy. Find him. Stop him. Now.' Then she said 'Fucking hell' again, and peeled her shoes off.

Emma said, 'Which direction did he go?'

The man in the blue coat pointed, and Emma ran.

Louisa climbed onto the wall and scanned the water. There was no sign of River. The rain was pummelling down, and she was already as wet as she'd ever been – she waited one second for someone to tell her not to be stupid, but the group had fallen unaccountably silent. There was a police car approaching, and police cars were famously loaded with heroes, and would soon deliver someone more professional, more trained, and more prepared to jump into the Thames. But the longer she hung here, the longer River spent underwater. Fucking hell, she thought again. But before the second syllable had formed, she was airborne, and then she wasn't.

When he'd hit the water, his lights had gone out. Not far to fall, perhaps, but a little too far to be thrown: any surface was going to welcome him the way gravity welcomes the apple – it rattled him to the core; stole his breath, then swallowed his body, wrapping him in a bone-numbing cold that somehow held the promise of warmth later. And he didn't know which way was up. He kicked, and seemed to move, but his lungs were bursting – he tried to turn, but everything felt heavy, his shoes, his coat, his limbs. Every action pushed him further into darkness. He couldn't tell if his eyes were open. Soon his lungs would give up, and he would be forced to inhale. After that, the darkness would be complete.

His hand brushed something, he didn't know what. He reached for it, but it was gone. And then he felt his body slowing down. Why fight it? He was in the river. It had been bound to end this way. He was drifting face down, and there was a light somewhere but it couldn't reach him. He'd gone too deep. Slowly, slowly, River gave up. He breathed deep, and filled himself with water. After that, there were only two possible directions he could go. It was with some relief that he noticed he seemed to be heading upwards.

Most times of day, Thames Path was kerb-to-wall joggers only slightly less cavalier than cyclists with regards to legitimate pavement users, but Emma was on her own as she hared under Blackfriars Bridge, its ice-cream colouring lost to the night and the weather. Everything was shades of grey, barring the odd blur in her peripheral vision – she was regretting those tequilas, regretting the beer they sandwiched, but was propelled onwards by the thought of having someone in her sights – a way to reclaim the day. Success would mean the sack of woe she'd laid out to Louisa in the bar could be knotted and dumped in the river.

Thoughts of Diana Taverner being dumped in that same sack, maybe with a couple of angry weasels for company, were a comfort . . .

Her breath was heavy, blood hammering in her ears, but there was a figure ahead of her so she ratcheted it up a notch, her footsteps echoing against the underside of the bridge. He must have heard her, but didn't turn; he stepped, instead, into a halo of streetlight which transformed the rain into a torrent of gemstones, then disappeared up the flight of steps leading roadwards.

Emma slipped, crashed into the wall, just managed to keep her balance – *Christ*, she could have ended up in the water too. She shouted after the vanishing man, and didn't realise until she'd heard herself that the word she shouted was *Police*. She was so winded it sounded more like a bark. Reaching the stairs she took them three at a time, her legs rubbery. Round the dog-leg corner, more steps, and she was on the bridge itself, where everything was louder, noisier – a bus passed; a big red box of curious shapes behind steamed-up windows, but the pavement was bare as a singleton's cupboard: no vanishing man. She turned, checked the other direction: the same. He'd come up the stairs, but hadn't reached the top.

Think.

A blue light was spinning on the other side of the road, a police car turning onto the bridge from the Embankment. A black van, too. The nasty squad. They'd be alert for mischief after Pentonville Road, and she had a gun in her pocket. Entirely legitimate, but accidents happened. She turned and went back down the steps. Level with the landing, upright in the Thames, sat a temporary structure bearing a winch or crane of some sort, alongside a workman's hut and assorted junk impossible to make out in the dark. Whatever it was for, bridge maintenance or riverbed dredging, it was the only place the vanishing man could be. He must have jumped, and given how close behind him she was, must have done so without hesitation. Reached the landing, saw the platform, climbed onto the wall and jumped. Some nerve.

She peered across. There was one light, set into the deck, illuminating the bridge. Everything else was in shadow, and there was no movement that couldn't be explained by the rain and the rocking of the river. Here, leaning out over the water, the rain sounded different. It hit the river with a constant hiss, as if large machinery were operating nearby.

The gap between the thigh-high wall enclosing the staircase and the edge of the platform was a couple of metres at most.

Which wasn't much. A distance she'd not think twice about jumping most days of the week; but most days of the week it wasn't raining, she wasn't pissed, there wasn't a cold deep river down below. But he couldn't have gone anywhere else. He had to be on that platform, behind that hut, crouched in the shadow of that crane or winch – stop overthinking it; make the bloody jump. She stepped up onto the wall, made the beginner's error of looking down, and it might have all been over in that same second if some survival instinct hadn't kicked in, the kind that decided she might as well jump as step back to the nice safe stairs. Maybe not a survival instinct, then. Maybe her internal idiot. Either way, she jumped, and for half a moment was a statistic waiting to happen, and then landed on the platform, its wooden decking solid as a road, but twice as slippery. She went down on her hands and knees, and had to grab one of the crane's metal joists to haul herself up. Some of the shapes took solid form: crates and buckets and a toolbox, some metal poles and an industrial-sized bobbin wrapped with cable. And then there was movement from behind the toilet-sized cabin; it might have been a shadow flung from the far bank of the river, except shadows didn't assemble themselves into solid human shapes. The vanishing man stepped out of the dark and unvanished.

'You're under arrest,' she told him.

He punched her in the face.

Or would have done; she leaned sideways and his fist missed her by a whisker, but she slipped and went down again anyway. Her coat, she thought – her coat was going to be such a mess. Partly because she'd just landed on her back in an oily puddle. But mostly because her hand had just found her Service weapon – Devon's Service weapon – and as she pulled it from her shoulder holster it snagged on her coat's lining, so the shot she fired tore a nasty hole parallel to its middle button. She didn't hit him – hadn't intended to – but she stopped him in his tracks.

'I should have fucking mentioned,' she said. 'Stop or I shoot.'

And suddenly there were bees everywhere, a swarm of bright red bees dancing around her; around the vanishing man too, who looked down at her with quite a charming grin. He raised his hands above his head, though kept his eyes on

Emma rather than raise them to the bridge where the nasty squad had gathered, their laser-sighted guns trained on the pair of them. A metallic voice was suggesting she drop her weapon *now*. She dropped her weapon. And still they danced, the flight of red bees, humming over her upper body as if awaiting the order to dive and sting. It could easily happen. She'd be the last to know. But even that couldn't stop Emma doing what she did next, which was roll sideways and vomit two tequila shots, a beer and two black coffees.

Some of which went on her coat.

Shirley said, 'Like fuck I don't. Right now, it's all I want to do.'

She was still holding the gun; Patrice was still chained to the radiator. J. K. Coe was leaning against the wall, which seemed to be his preferred location. Because, it occurred to her, standing like that, nobody could come up behind him.

But someone could come up behind her, and did.

Catherine said, 'Shirley, Marcus is dead. Nothing can change that. And if you kill this man now, it will haunt you forever.'

'I've killed men before.'

'While they were chained to a radiator?'

She didn't reply.

'This is different,' Catherine explained.

Shirley thought: I can handle different. What she couldn't handle was the thought of this man walking around a world he'd ejected Marcus from.

She raised the gun and levelled it at Patrice, who watched her without changing expression.

But the gun felt heavy in her hand.

Catherine said, 'Shirley. Please. If you kill him like this, you might never sleep again.'

'Sleep's overrated.'

'Take it from me, it's really not. Sometimes it's the only thing that can get you out of bed in the morning. The knowledge that you can get back into it come night.'

'He was my friend.'

'He was mine too. He was a good man. And he wouldn't want you to do this.'

'You think?'

'I know.'

J. K. Coe said, 'She's right.'

'What?'

'Marcus wouldn't want you to kill him.'

'How would you know?'

'Psych Eval. Remember?'

The gun felt so very very heavy.

'Marcus thought you were a prick,' she told him.

'He was your friend, not mine.'

Catherine said, 'Shirley. This isn't an op. It would be an execution.'

'I don't care.'

'You will.'

It felt like the heaviest thing she'd ever held in her hand.

'I don't want him to be alive when Marcus isn't,' she said.

'I know.'

'He should die.'

'But you shouldn't kill him.'

Silently, Coe offered his hand. She looked at it, then at the gun in her own. Then at Patrice, who was still on his back, cuffed to the radiator. A short time ago, he'd been indestructible; storming Slough House, killing Marcus, killing Sam.

Shirley really wanted him dead.

But she didn't want to kill him. Not like this.

And she felt so very very tired.

She heard Catherine sigh softly as she lowered the gun into Coe's waiting hand.

Anger fucking management. Marcus would be proud.

Then Coe shot Patrice three times in the chest.

'There you go,' he said, and handed the gun back to Shirley.

River rolled and threw up Thames water, then opened his eyes. He was staring at wet pavement. He rolled again and a blurry face, inches from his own, took shape, slipped out of focus, then slipped back in again.

'Louisa,' he said, or tried to. It came out 'Larghay.'

'In future,' she told him, 'pick up a fucking phone, yeah?'

Then she pulled away and all he could see was the rain, still steadily falling.

In the glow from the streetlights, the drops looked like diamonds.

17

T HE RAIN HAD STOPPED, which was such a longed-for, such an unexpected outcome, that all around the city people were saying it twice: the rain has stopped. The rain has stopped. Slough House was all but empty that night, twenty-four hours after the attack. There was still a stain on the wall behind what had been Marcus's desk; another on the carpet in Louisa's room, where Bad Sam had fallen; and a third in Coe and Cartwright's office, beneath the radiator. But the bodies had been removed, and someone, probably Catherine, had cleared away the smashed chair and assorted debris. The broken doors were propped against walls, waiting for the paperwork to go through enough channels that some-body, somewhere, would give up and sign a chitty allowing them to be replaced. Until then, Slough House would be largely open-plan.

Jackson Lamb's door was undamaged, but stood ajar, allowing a little grey light to spill onto the landing. The room opposite, once Catherine Standish's, was in darkness, though its door too was open. And on the stairs was a noise, a series of noises, made by someone on their way up; someone unused to the creaking staircase, the damp walls, the various odours of neglect in the stairwell, which it would take industrial solvents or environmental catastrophe to shift.

When Claude Whelan reached the uppermost landing he paused, as if unsure the ascent had been worth it.

'In here,' something growled.

Suppressing a shudder, he went in.

Lamb was behind his desk. His shoeless feet rested on top of it, his right heel showing through a hole in one sock, and most of his toes through a hole in the other. There was a bottle in front of him, and a glass in his hand, whose emptiness was presumably a temporary anomaly. The room's only light source was to his right, a lamp set on a thigh-level ziggurat of dusty books: telephone directories, Whelan thought. An analogue man in a digital world. Whether that was obsolescence or survival trait, time would tell.

He said, 'Legend doesn't do this place justice.'

Lamb seemed to consider several responses before settling for a fart.

'Or you,' Whelan added.

'Maybe leave the door as it is,' Lamb suggested.

There was a visitor's chair, so Whelan took it.

Not much of Lamb's office could be seen in the gloom. A blind was drawn over the only window; a cork noticeboard hung on one wall. And there was a clock somewhere, which Whelan couldn't see; instead of ticking, it made a steady tap-tap noise, a dull repetition which seemed to underline how appalling the passage of time could be.

Lamb refilled his glass, then reluctantly waved the bottle in Whelan's direction. When Whelan shook his head, he set it down again, unstoppered. 'Can't remember the last time we had First Desk here,' he said. 'No, hang on, yes I can. Never.'

'We don't usually make house calls,' said Whelan. 'But in the circumstances . . .'

'What, dead agents? Yeah, that's always a photo op.' Lamb

rested his glass on his chest, his meaty fingers embracing it. 'Did you tie a teddy to a lamp post?'

Whelan said, 'You wanted a meeting. We could have done this at the Park.'

'Yeah. But that would have involved me making the effort instead of you. Frank coughing his guts up?'

If the sudden switch fazed Whelan, he hid it well. 'He's been . . . cooperative.'

'I'll bet.'

'We've not had to adopt unorthodox measures to make him talk, if that's what you're thinking.'

Lamb said, 'I was thinking you'd have to get seriously innovative to shut him up. I mean, he told Cartwright his life story. It's not like he's shy.' He raised the glass to his mouth without taking his eyes off Whelan. He resembled a hippo enjoying a wallow. 'But what surprises me is you took him alive. I'd have thought Lady Di would have had the trigger pulled as soon as he broke cover.'

'That was her stated preference, yes.'

Lamb looked interested. 'You overruled her?'

'We'd reached a point where I either agreed to do her bidding evermore, or drew a line in the sand. And there'd been quite enough blood shed in London's streets for one week.'

'Not only its streets,' said Lamb. 'So what's he had to say for himself?'

Whelan shifted in his chair. He was finding it difficult not to stare at Lamb's feet. It was like catching sight of a joint of meat hanging in a butcher's window and wondering what the hell that had been when it was still attached to its body. He said, 'Lamb, your team's been at the sharp end, I appreciate that. And you've suffered a loss. But that doesn't make you privy to classified intelligence. What Frank's had to say is being analysed as we speak. And in due course there'll be a report. But it'll be eyes-only, and your eyes won't be on the list, I'm afraid.'

Or anywhere near it.

Lamb nodded thoughtfully. 'Good point. I mean, a lot of this has gotta be pretty sensitive, right?'

'Precisely.'

'Like how Frank's whole operation was originally funded and resourced by the Service. I presume that'll be bullet point one when the report's finished.'

The *tap-tap-tapping*, Whelan belatedly realised, wasn't time hammering away but water dripping, off a loose section of guttering perhaps. Leaks can happen anywhere.

He said, 'I'm not entirely sure it would be in everyone's interests for that . . . supposition to be made official.'

'So Lady Di's influence hasn't left you entirely unsoiled.'

'I wasn't wholly naive to start with, you know.'

'We'll get to that later,' Lamb said. 'You sure you don't want a drink?'

'I don't want to deprive you. Your bottle's nearly half empty.'

'I know where I can lay my hands on a fresh one.' He indicated a second glass, hiding behind the phone on his desk. To Whelan's surprise, it looked more or less clean.

He'd never acquired a taste for whisky. More of a brandy man. But he was developing the sense that he wasn't going to get through this conversation unaided, so this time accepted the offer.

While Lamb poured, he said, 'There, that makes this just a nice friendly chat, doesn't it? Colleagues winding down after a hard week. Nothing official about it.'

'If you'd come to the Park,' Whelan said, 'there'd be a recording.'

'Now you're getting it.' Lamb leaned back. 'Bad Sam

Chapman put in some hard years for the Park, and he was a good soldier. Leastways apart from losing all that money he was. And Longridge had his moments when he wasn't pissing his salary away on the slot machines. And if nothing else, I reckon I'm owed something for the mess they've made of my carpets. So let's hear the edited highlights of Frank's post-Agency career, shall we? All unofficial, like.'

A good operative, Whelan had heard, knew how to make a threat sound like a digression.

He took a sip of whisky. He had spent all day at the Park; had arrived there before dawn, leaving Claire asleep – he'd looked in, but hadn't wakened her – and for most of the hours since had been watching, rewatching, footage of Frank Harkness. Lamb was right: getting him to talk hadn't been a problem. It rarely was, with unhinged narcissists.

'You know about Les Arbres,' he said.

'A nursery for terrorists,' Lamb said. 'Yeah, I'd grasped that much. What was he doing, training them in black ops before they'd done their A–B–Cs?'

'Pretty much. And there was a KGB hood too, who specialised in what Harkness called mental calibration.' Whelan sighed, and let his head rest on the back of his chair. What he could see of the ceiling was a scarred, cobwebby expanse of distempered plaster. 'You know what Harkness identified as the biggest threat to our way of life? Here in the West?'

'Radio One?'

'That we encourage our kids to think for themselves. While those who'd bring our towers down teach their children to sacrifice their lives without a moment's thought. No, more than that. Teach them that death, their own and ours, is their victory, their apotheosis. And we're trying to fight them with kids who've grown up thinking their smartphones are a human right.'

'And Frank thought this paranoid bullshit made him a visionary?' said Lamb. 'He should have written a blog. Saved us all a lot of grief.'

'He's not entirely without a point.'

'And the West isn't entirely without weapons of mass destruction. Let's not pretend we're babes in the wood.'

'Either way,' Whelan said, 'what Harkness wanted was that same dedication, the same energies, only – as he put it – on our side.'

'Jesus wept,' said Lamb. 'And that's what he got.'

'And that's what he got. Eventually. A troupe of young men trained in all the black arts at Frank's disposal. Which, seeing as his crew was made up of a bunch of former Cold War warriors, was pretty much all of them.'

Lamb was empty again. He remedied this situation, making sure that it wouldn't reoccur in the foreseeable future by filling his glass to the brim. 'Then what?' he said.

Whelan said, 'There have been several . . . events, over recent years.'

'"Events". There's an administrator's word.'

'Frank's team ran terror operations in cities throughout Europe. Düsseldorf, Copenhagen, Barcelona, others. Some quite small towns too. Pisa. That struck me as odd, I don't know why. But lots of tourists, I suppose.'

'I assume these were fairly *quiet* terror jobs,' Lamb said. 'On account of I don't remember hearing about them.'

'They were dry runs. Unarmed, though fully functional, bombs left in strategic places. Water sources "poisoned" with harmless but visible pollutants. Food distribution outlets, travel networks, energy suppliers, hotels – all compromised in specific, targeted operations.'

'He was playing games.'

'He claims that after each operation, security was tightened not only at the target site but throughout the city, and even nationally. Loopholes were plugged. Weak links dispensed with.'

'Did it not occur to him to write the odd letter?'

Whelan said, 'We both know that wouldn't have had the slightest effect.'

'You sound like you approve of what he's been up to.'

'Each operation he undertook, he attempted to duplicate within the year. In all but one case, he was unable to do so.'

'Well, rah-de-fucking-rah for him.'

'His point, he says, is we're sleepwalking into catastrophe. If IS, or whoever comes next, gets serious – his words – they could level whole towns with little more effort and coordination than it's taken them so far to become the global bogeyman. Paris is attacked and the whole world trembles, but how many people died? One hundred and thirty? Harkness estimates the theoretical body count his team have racked up to be into the thousands, and he counts those as lives saved. Because they couldn't happen again.'

'Until Westacres put a dent in his average.'

Whelan looked up at the ceiling again. 'As you say.'

Lamb put his glass down for the first time since Whelan had entered his office. From his pocket he produced a grey rag which turned out to be a handkerchief. He blew his nose, examined the results, raised his eyebrows, and tucked the handkerchief back out of sight. Then reached for his glass again. 'Let me guess. One of his mentally recalibrated robots blew its wiring.'

'That's the risk he was always running,' said Whelan. 'But it didn't seem to have occurred to him. He thought he'd raised a troupe of perfect soldiers. They had firearm skills, explosives skills, they knew how to live under the radar. But the whole point of the Cuckoo programme was, the subjects have to believe they're who they've been trained to be. He wanted terrorists, and that's what he got. At least in one instance. He was called Yves, by the way. If it matters.'

'And not Robert Winters,' said Lamb.

'No. Well. False IDs were part of the process.'

'Pretty professional ones too, I imagine.' Lamb produced a cigarette from somewhere and plugged it into the side of his mouth. 'That would have been part of the set-up package, wouldn't it? Along with the explosives he used for his suicide overcoat. I mean, I can't imagine him waltzing through the Tunnel with that little lot in his hand luggage. That would really be putting the lax into relaxed.'

'No,' said Whelan after a pause. 'They were already here. Frank had a cache from a raid on an armoury back in the early nineties. It was thought at the time to be an IRA operation, but . . .'

'But it was Frank acting on information received. And we all know where the information came from.' Lamb lit his cigarette, and was momentarily wreathed in blue fumes. When it cleared, his eyes seemed yellow. 'The same place as the funds used to set up Les Arbres in the first place.'

'You'll understand we're not particularly anxious to have that feature in the report,' Whelan said.

'Oh, I can see it might not play well down the corridor,' Lamb said. 'I mean, we're supposed to be protecting the citizenry. Not providing the wherewithal for lunatics to massacre it.' He breathed smoke. 'So one of his Mini-Mes blows a gasket and performs a wet run instead of a dry one. Which is why Frank has to scorch the earth. David Cartwright being top of his list.'

'We're still not clear on Sam Chapman's role,' Whelan said.

'He carried Cartwright's bags back in the day. Including to Les Arbres.'

'Ah.' He waved a hand to dispel Lamb's smoke. 'That's one of the areas Harkness wasn't so forthcoming about.'

'Alongside how he got Cartwright on board by putting his daughter up the duff? There's an angle they don't teach you at spook school. But shall I tell you what's more interesting right now?' Lamb inhaled deeply, and when he spoke his voice was pinched. 'Your use of the past tense. *Wasn't* so forthcoming. Had an accident, has he?'

'Not . . . exactly.'

Lamb stared, and it seemed to Whelan his yellow eyes became tinged with red. 'You're not fucking telling me you've let him go.'

'As we've established,' said Whelan, 'the full story is not one we want becoming public knowledge. And he still has comrades out there, don't forget. If we . . . wrap a black ribbon round his file—'

'Or put a bullet in his head.'

'—we can be sure it'll come back to haunt us.'

'And having him alive means it won't?'

'We do what we can,' Whelan said. 'But we're at the mercy of events. This is one huge mess we're dealing with. It's not possible to clean it up. The best we can hope for is to . . . minimise the repercussions.'

'So he creates fucking havoc trying to keep his story secret, and we end up doing his job for him? He'll be wanting a sponsorship deal next time. Where is he now?'

'He slipped the leash about ten minutes after hitting the street.'

'There's absolutely no part of this in which we come out looking good, is there?'

'Not really, no.'

'Plus ça bloody change. I swear to God I'd defect, if there was anywhere worth defecting to these days.' He emptied his glass.

Whelan took another sip from his own, then set it down,

still mostly full, on Lamb's desk. 'Other business,' he said. 'I've set the wheels in motion for Longridge's death-in-service payment. Five years of salary, tax free. It should come through by the end of the week. Beginning of next at the latest. You might want to let his wife know.'

'Five years,' said Lamb.

'Standard terms.'

'Except Longridge was operational.'

'He was what?'

'What I just said. Operational. As in, on an op.'

Whelan said, 'As I understand it, Slough House is deskbound.'

'But I have managerial discretion. Says so somewhere, I can't be arsed to find the paperwork. Anyway, I sent Longridge and Guy out on the streets yesterday afternoon, and until such time as I sign off on his field report, his status remains operational. Doesn't look like he's going to be doing any typing anytime soon. Therefore . . .'

'Seriously?'

'He qualifies for the active agent increment. Ten years, not five. Or his family does. Money won't work where he's gone.'

Whelan shook his head. 'That'll never get through Legal. I barely accept it as English myself.'

'Doesn't matter. It's not going through Legal. Sign off on it in the morning, and pass it on to Finance. Lady Di's still letting you sign things, right?'

'Lamb, I have every sympathy. You lost an agent. But the active increment only applies to joes in the field, and with the best will in the world—'

'See, the thing is, shut the fuck up. Let me explain why. Moira Tregorian – remember her? She's the superannuated dinner lady you sent over here, day one of your reign – she spent a lot of time with old man Cartwright yesterday, and gave me what I assure you was a very thorough debriefing. I've got pissed in less time than it takes her to finish a sentence. Anyway, one of the details she shared was his recitation of the names of the Knights of the Round Table, which he launched himself upon on account of having lost his marbles, and this got her worrying about where she'd heard the name Galahad lately.' Lamb leaned back. 'Ever heard Moira Tregorian trying to remember where she first heard something? It's like, you can fuck off and read *Lord of the Rings*, and when you come back she's still talking. Anyway. Long and short of it is, she still can't remember. But I've got a fair idea. Want me to go on?'

Whelan found that he was holding his whisky tumbler once more; had frozen in the act of delivering it to his mouth. He said something which didn't work, so cleared his throat and said it again. 'There's no need.'

'Ah, what the hell. We're both men of the world. You were Galahad when you were over the river, right? She didn't know that, but it took me thirty seconds to find out. And took my boy Ho not much longer to trawl through the duty books for the nights Tregorian was duty officer. And guess what? There you are. Galahad, calling in a Collect request.'

'I've heard enough, Lamb.'

'Word is, you're a happily married man. Making a Hollywood musical of the fact, let alone a song and dance. So how come you needed rescuing from the clutches of the Met, Claude? After they'd picked you up for kerb-crawling way out in London Fields? Quite the regular, apparently, trawling for tarts every night. Watching but not buying – always worries the working girls, that. Thought they might have a headcase on their hands.' Lamb leered. 'So. Things not so rosy in the bedroom? Lovely wife a little icy where it matters?'

Whelan said, 'Claire – she – it's been some years since –

look, none of this is your business, none of it. We have a very special marriage.'

'Just not a particularly active one.'

'Shut up! How dare you! What could you *possibly* know about . . . Just, just shut up. That's all.'

Lamb said, 'None of my business. That's right. Or wasn't, up until the moment you learned of your elevation to First Desk, and started worrying Tregorian might do some nasty maths – you know, putting two and two together. Not hard to square whichever Dog came round to prise you from the Met's grasp – nothing like a promotion to ensure loyalty – but you can't bribe a gossip, can you? Or you can, but it does no fucking good. Best thing is, get her out the way before any pennies start to drop. Bit unfair, some might call it, but that's life in the big leagues, eh, Claude?'

'You've made your point.'

'Good. So anyway, Tregorian's retiring: medical grounds. Post-traumatic bed-wetting, or whatever the PC term is. Seems all those bodies round the place have put her off coming back. So you can add sorting her pension out to your to-do list.' Lamb smiled a crocodile smile, every bit as fake as its tears. 'Then she's off both our backs.'

Whelan stared at him for what felt like a long time, though it didn't discomfit Lamb. At last he said, 'And what about you?'

'What about me?'

'What will it take to get you off my back?' He glanced around the office. 'A desk at the Park?'

Lamb said, 'Well, I'm glad we've had this little chat.' He dropped his cigarette into a mug of ancient tea, where it briefly disappeared, then bobbed to the surface, alongside several others. 'I'll expect to hear from Finance in the morning. Leave the door open, would you? I like a through draught.'

Whelan didn't move.

'Oh, I'm sorry,' said Lamb. 'That last bit meant fuck off. Didn't they teach you subtle over the river?'

'They taught me lots of things,' Claude Whelan said at last. 'I'm sure we'll meet again soon.'

He drained what was left in his tumbler and placed it on Lamb's desk. Then he left. This time, he took the stairs swiftly.

When the door downstairs slammed shut Catherine Standish appeared from the room opposite Lamb's, and crossed the landing in her usual quiet manner.

'Do you reckon that last bit was a threat?' Lamb said.

'He certainly hoped you'd think so.'

'Huh.' He leaned across to pour the last of the whisky into the glass Whelan had been using, then pushed it nearer Catherine.

She sat.

He said, 'If he survives another month of Diana Taverner, I'll maybe start to take him seriously. Until then, he's just a mouth in a suit. I've had bowel movements that worry me more.' He reflected a moment. 'Quite recently, come to think of it.'

'A topic for another day,' said Catherine. 'That was a good thing you did. For Cassie, I mean.'

'Who's Cassie?'

'Marcus's wife.'

Lamb said, 'I just like fucking with Finance, you know that.'

'He didn't say anything about Patrice.'

'No, well, they're probably still cutting him up. Wouldn't want to jump to conclusions about cause of death just because he's got a few holes in him.'

Catherine picked up the tumbler and held it in front of her, using both hands, as if it were a chalice. Lamb's eyes narrowed, but he didn't say anything.

She said, 'You stopped Shirley from making him talk.'

'Uh-huh. Missing fingernails or water-filled lungs might have made "self-defence" tricky to pull off.'

'You're aware there'll be abrasions where we cuffed him?'

'That would account for him being so cross and dangerous when he got loose. Necessitating extreme measures.'

'Lamb—'

'For fuck's sake. He killed an agent, not to mention an ex. You think anyone's going to care he got his ticket punched? When they've finished with his body they'll burn it and dump the ashes. Nobody's going to be issuing warrants.'

'And what about Coe?'

Lamb said, 'Yeah, Coe, you know, I think he might work out.'

'He shot an unarmed man, Jackson! Who was tied to a radiator!'

'Okay, so whoever coloured him in went over the lines. But he was doing a job. You think I was going to watch that French punk taken away in a Black Maria? When I've got a joe plastered over a wall downstairs?'

'So you were letting him do your dirty work? That doesn't sound like you.'

'A good boss provides opportunities for personal growth and development. I think we were all winners, on the day.'

'Lamb, this isn't a laughing matter. Coe needs arresting or he needs help. One or the other.'

'I don't care. I'm losing staff at a rate of knots here.'

She said, 'You once told me it didn't matter about staff leaving. That there'd always be other fuck-ups to take their place.'

'I like it when you talk dirty. Are you going to drink that?'

'Isn't that why you gave it to me?'

'Force of habit.'

Catherine said, 'Yes, I'm aware of how habits work, thank you.'

To prove she wasn't the only one who knew that, Lamb lit another cigarette. He inhaled, removed it from his mouth, and addressed his next question to it, rather than to Catherine. 'So. Are you coming back?'

'Are you asking?'

'I just did.'

'No, you asked whether I was or not. That's different from asking if I will.'

Lamb said, 'It's a good job you're on the wagon. I hate to think what crap you'd come up with drunk.'

Catherine raised the glass to her lips and breathed in. She smiled a little, though to herself rather than at Lamb. Then she put it back on the desk.

Lamb retrieved it, and poured its contents into his own.

She said, 'Shirley's a mess. So is Roddy. God knows what state River's in. And Coe . . . Well, we've covered Coe. He's either PTSD or a psychopath. It would serve you right if I left you to it.'

'I'd lock 'em in a room and let 'em fight for the gun.'

'There's always Louisa, of course. She's pretty reliable.'

'Well, it's a sliding scale, isn't it?' said Lamb. 'Least fucked-up employee of the week. We should have a plaque.'

'I'll make a note,' said Catherine. Then she rose and crossed the landing to her own office, from which she emerged a moment later wearing her coat.

She made little noise on the staircase, well used to its repertoire of squeaks and groans. Even the back door behaved for once, and she exited Slough House with little effort and less noise.

A few moments later, the heating went off.

And a chill descends on Slough House, as chills are wont to do; a chill accompanied by a series of gurgles and bangs as the ancient boiler begins its nightly ordeal of sucking warmth from the air. From the top floor, this process sounds like the rattling of old tin bones, and nowhere are bones rattled more fussily than in Jackson Lamb's office. He listens to his radiator die its death, and smokes a last cigarette, and drains a final glass. And then he rises, leaving his lamp to cast its weary glow on an empty room; he wrestles himself into his raincoat, and trudges down to the next landing, his heavy tread coaxing maximum complaint from each stair.

Outside the kitchen, he pauses. The offices here are door-less now, and he can see into Louisa Guy's room, with its recently scrubbed and disinfected patch of carpet the approx-imate size and shape of Dead Sam Chapman. He does not know, but would not be surprised to learn, that Louisa is asleep already, early as it is; he suspects she has achieved some semblance of peace these past few months, and in those circumstances, sleep would be his own drug of choice. To the other side lies River Cartwright's room; now J. K. Coe's room too. Sleep is probably not on Cartwright's immediate agenda, but then, thinks Lamb, Cartwright has some fairly radical new information to absorb; that, for instance, he owes his birth, his very existence, to the messianic schemes of one mad spook, just as he owes his lifetime since to the handed-down dreams of another. For Lamb has no doubt that David Cartwright has slipped past the point of no return; has embarked on an irrevocable descent into mental twilight, haunted by the real-isation that what he helped sow across the Channel years ago has bloomed in carnage colours on his own doorstep. How the younger Cartwright will come to terms with this – if he ever does – is, as Catherine Standish recently observed, a topic for another day; whether the older Cartwright will be brought to book for his ancient sins, Lamb wastes little time contem-plating. He has been a joe most of his working life; is still a joe whenever the lights go out. And one thing joes learn quickly is that those who write the rules rarely suffer their weight.

As for Coe, Lamb meant what he said earlier to Standish: that J. K. Coe might work out – though, for Lamb, 'working out' might not indicate as positive an outcome as that phrase usually conveys. Might be useful to Lamb would be another way of putting it, not always an unmitigated delight to those so designated. But whatever his future holds, at this precise moment J. K. Coe, too, is casting his eyes around an empty room; in his case, the sitting room he has spent little time in this past year or more, ever since the evening he spent here naked and petrified, at the mercy of a dangerous man. There hasn't been a night between that one and this that Coe hasn't stared wide-eyed at the dark, wondering what torment it holds, but for some reason he feels he might sleep dreamlessly tonight. And gazing round, he decides that come the weekend he will rearrange the furniture, or perhaps heave it down to the pavement for locals to pillage, and replace it all. And he spreads his hands in front of him, splays them wide, and sees very little trembling. The music in his head is not quite silent, but his fingers at least are resting.

Another flight of stairs. There are stains on these walls which are highly mysterious even to Lamb; stains that seem to arrive of their own accord, and yet own the appearance of having been there always. He is aware that his slow horses occasionally harbour similar thoughts about himself.

On the next landing, he pauses again. One of the rooms here is Roderick Ho's, and Ho's whereabouts, activities, hopes, dreams and desires have only ever concerned Lamb when Lamb is busy thwarting one or other of them. So it doesn't matter to him that Ho is currently explaining to Kim – his girlfriend – that he was unable to carry out the favour she wanted because of something that came up at work; or that, when she petulantly suggests that he has misrepresented his talents to her – that he is, in short, little more than an unreliable fantasist – Ho's response, babes, is to close his eyes and replay in his mind what never happened: his sudden emergence from his hiding place, his overpowering of the lone gunman, his bringing Marcus back to life . . . Little light finds its way through his closed lids, though some small part of a tear squeezes out. But no matter.

The other room is Marcus and Shirley's, now Shirley's alone. It smells fresh, because a painter has been, but the painter has plied his trade very much in the ethos of Slough House, which is to say, with little enthusiasm and less care. It is true that the wall behind what was Marcus's desk is now whiter than it has been in years, but only the middle section has been repainted, leaving even the most casual onlooker to wonder what has been painted over, and even to imagine that this freshness hides an undercoat of dubious quality. Something not quite eradicable, of a morbidly stuccoed texture, and lingering effect.

But Lamb won't spend his days staring at this wall. That will fall to Shirley Dander, who is out clubbing now; has hit the dance floor unfashionably early, and to everyone watching appears to be celebrating something marvellous; flailing her limbs in an uncoordinated mess of ecstasy, just violent enough to prevent anyone getting close, and piercing her fraudulent joy. She is a dervish tonight, a priestess in her own brand-new religion, and the object of her adoration is fury. For Shirley is not managing her anger; she is allowing it to take root, and will nurture it within, and when the time is ripe, will cut it loose.

Lamb knows none of this, of course. But he can guess. He can guess.

A final dog-legged set of stairs. Now he is at the back door, which sticks – it always sticks – as if reluctant to see him leave, but leave he does, with a grunt and a roll of the shoulder. Locking it behind him, he stands in the mildewed yard, looking up for the few brave stars London has to offer. But none are shining on Slough House. Instead, a feeble light stains the window of his own office, some storeys above; a light kept mostly in check by the ever-drawn blinds, but managing still to press itself against the grimy glass. For a moment, Lamb is transfixed by what his room – his lair – his life – looks like from the outside, but this passes. Then, with his collar turned up, he leaves the yard, and no one sees him go.

ACKNOWLEDGEMENTS

M Y THANKS, AS EVER, to all at Soho Press in New York, especially Bronwen Hruska.

Here in the UK, my editor Mark Richards pointed me in the direction of the dazzle ship – literally; we were standing on a rooftop at the time – and I'm grateful to him for that and much else. Thanks too to the whole of the John Murray team, particularly Nick Davies, Ross Fraser and Becky Walsh. Yassine Belkacemi is a star.

Juliet Burton has been my literary minder for longer than either of us care to dwell on, and when not scrutinising small print has kept me up to speed with *The Archers*, shared the pain and glory of being an English cricket lover, and just generally been there when needed. Thank you, dear.

And thank you for various reasons to Alan Judd, Chris Edwards, Daphne Wright, Helen Giltrow, Jamie Laurenson, MSJ, Nick Smith, Sarah Hilary, Will Smith, my mum, my siblings, their partners and their offspring.

Those hoping to find HMS *President* on the Victoria Embankment will be disappointed, as it disappeared from its berth a day or so after I finished *Spook Street*. I have form in this area: setting scenes of novels in locations that are rapidly demolished, redeveloped or removed. Any suggestions as to how I might monetise this talent will be gratefully received.

MH
Oxford,
July 2016

For the further misadventures of Jackson Lamb
and his crew of no-hopers,
pick up a copy of

LONDON RULES